Murder Most Charming

An Eliza Darcy Mystery

JESSICA BERG

Murder Most Charming
An Eliza Darcy Mystery™: Book 3
Red Adept Publishing, LLC
104 Bugenfield Court
Garner, NC 27529
https://RedAdeptPublishing.com/
Copyright © 2026 by Jessica Berg. All rights reserved.

---

1.   http://StreetlightGraphics.com

For my husband, who believes in and supports my wild dreams!

Chapter One

Champagne, Canapés ... and Catastrophe?

I have received notice from Betty that Berryhill Manor, the neighboring estate, has been let at last. I had begun to worry that the lovely manor house would soon go to ruins. Betty has gleaned from village gossip that a Mr. Henry Crawford is to take the house, and his sister is to keep house for him. I do hope they make for lovely neighbors.

Lizzy Bennet Darcy

Pemberley 1815

Champagne still flowing? Check. Immaculately dressed waitstaff still offering canapés and tiny hors d'oeuvres on silver trays? Check. New Year's Eve ball guests still laughing and twirling about the room? Check. Impromptu karaoke session still assaulting everyone's eardrums? Sadly, check.

Despite the warbling of an inebriated guest, Eliza Darcy sighed with relief, sipped her sparkling beverage, and surveyed Pemberley's ballroom. Eliza's staff had outdone themselves bringing to life Eliza's envisioned white-and-gold party theme: white poinsettias with gold accents, gold and white balloon arches, tulle-wrapped columns, and flocked trees sparkling with gold decorations. The night had gone so well, or "absolutely brilliant" as her British cousin, Joy Bingley, put it, that Eliza was positive fate had smiled upon her. The grandfather clock ticking away in the corner showed two hours left before she and her guests rang in the New Year. Eliza saluted it with her glass, hoping drinks would hold out and guests would keep enjoying themselves.

"Right, then. How long will you keep those Christmas decorations up?" Joy swayed as she gestured with her brandy glass toward the lighted twelve-foot flocked Christmas tree in the corner, which was resplendent in white poinsettias and gold ornaments. "I get Chrisssstmas spirit and all, but that bloody behemoth will gather dust soon enough, won't it?"

Eliza cupped her ear. "I can't hear you over what's become the worst karaoke session in history." Not that karaoke went back too far in history, but Pemberley's guests had held the microphone for what felt like millennia. She'd never hear "Man, I Feel Like a Woman" or "Don't Stop Believing" the same way again.

Joy made an X with her fingers at the tree. "Tree. No longer Christmas. Kill it."

Instead of answering her inebriated cousin, Eliza glanced at her best friend, Belle Knightley, who had arrived at Pemberley two days earlier. "Ask Belle. She knows how long I keep my Christmas decorations up."

Belle, wrapped in enough silver fabric to resemble a disco ball, grinned. "Joy, how do you feel about redecorating the tree for Valentine's Day?"

Joy shook her head, making her diamond chandelier earrings sway. "You're mugging me off, aren't you?"

Belle flicked her newly dyed red hair. "At least Eliza'll have a reason to decorate it with hearts and chubby little cherubs. Right, Eliza?" She jerked her chin toward the tall, dark-haired, blue-eyed Heath Tilney sporting a blue cashmere sweater and khakis, butchering the Bee Gees hit "Stayin' Alive."

Joy shuddered. "I had no idea a person could make disco worse. You know what ended Heath's and my romance? Hearing him sing in the shower. Proper dreadful."

While her cousin had a point, Heath had other qualities that made up for his terrible singing and complete lack of rhythm. Eliza's tummy warmed more from Heath's other talents than the champagne. "Be nice. It's the start of a new year."

Joy winked. "Oh, this is me being nice. Speaking of New Year's, I've sorted my resolution." She motioned for Belle and Eliza to lean in and whispered, "I'm going to make Jack Willoughby marry me."

Eliza held her breath, expecting more tears. Joy had sobbed earlier when Jack Willoughby, family friend of the Darcys and longtime schoolmate and flirt buddy of Joy's, had turned up with his plus-one: a black-haired siren in a ruby-red dress that hugged her generous curves. Ever since Eliza had arrived in England the previous June, Willoughby was all she'd heard about. Joy claimed he was hers and would one day make it official, though he had no clue that was supposedly his mission in life.

Belle tilted up on the tips of her stilettos to see over the crowd. "Which one's Jack Willoughby?"

Joy pointed toward a man with wavy chestnut hair, a Grecian nose, and sharp cheekbones. "He's the pillock with that... that..."

"Woman in the red dress," Eliza offered, attempting political correctness.

Joy ignored her. "With that dreadful bit of skirt who, besides looking like a ghastly wrapped Christmas present, is cross-eyed."

"She's stunning." Belle grinned. "What's a pillock, and why is Willoughby one?"

"A pillock is a fool—an idiot. A stupid person. He's one because he won't marry Joy," Eliza explained.

"Why? What happened? Did you two break up?" Belle asked.

Joy focused on the tip of Belle's nose. "No."

When Joy didn't elaborate, Eliza sighed. "Jack Willoughby doesn't know he's supposed to marry her."

"Why not?"

"Because Joy has failed to tell him he's supposed to," Eliza said.

Belle studied Joy's crestfallen face. "You're serious?"

Joy's eyes glimmered with tears, and a tear trailed down her cheek.

Eliza pulled Joy into a side hug. "Chin up, Joy. You know Willoughby. He's fickle. That woman—"

"Tart," Joy snapped.

"That *woman* will be history once you step in." Eliza attempted an encouraging smile.

"But I've been part of his picture for ages." Another tear spilled down Joy's cheek and landed on her green velvet dress.

The pair often flirted with such outrageous audacity that Eliza wished to outlaw all forms of public displays of affection at Pemberley, except where she and Heath were concerned, naturally. Willoughby liked Joy well enough, and perhaps all he needed was the go-ahead from her. "I have a strange feeling that once he knows you're in love with him, he'll abandon all others. Then you can propose to him."

"I told you he has to propose first. A man should know when a woman wants him, quit faffing about, and get on with it."

"You're giving men far too much credit, or you're spending too much time with those fictional men in all those romances you write," Eliza said.

"They, at least, have the good sense to do whatever the bloody hell I want them to." Joy pouted.

"A woman can propose too. If I hadn't caught Greg cheating, I might've asked him to marry me." Eliza shivered, adjusting her slipping silver strap. "No, my resolution is the opposite of Joy's. No more men. For three hundred sixty-five days, I'm abstaining from them."

Joy raised her glass. "Hear! Hear! Sod the lot of them. Who needs them?"

"Didn't you say you'd make Willoughby marry you?" Eliza guided Joy toward the door.

Joy narrowed her eyes at her. "I say, you do have a frightfully good memory. How annoying."

Eliza pressed her lips together. "Come on, Joy. Let's find your bed, okay?"

"No, let's find Willoughby."

Since he was busy with his date, Eliza steered Joy away. "He's staying the night, remember? Propose in the morning."

Joy's unfocused gaze swept across Eliza's face. "You're right, I am."

Eliza shot Belle a sideways glance and gave Joy a thumbs-up. "That's the spirit. But off to bed first, or you'll be in no condition to propose anything to anybody."

Belle jerked her head toward the refreshment table. "While you tuck her in, I'll mingle with the fancy Brits." With a tiny finger wave, she weaved through the crowd and vanished.

Heath hit the last notes of the Bee Gees classic, and Eliza considered congratulating him on reaching an impossibly high note before taking Joy to her room. But then Great-Aunt Iris appeared, resplendent in a shimmering gold velour tracksuit, minus her usual briefcase-size purse, squeaking her way over to them in white sneakers.

Eliza kissed her great-aunt's proffered cheek, which was gilded in rouge. "I thought you and Great-Uncle William went to bed hours ago, something about not bothering ringing in another unspectacular New Year."

Great-Aunt Iris fluffed her white cloud of hair. "William is already tucked up in bed with a book and his favorite whiskey. Claimed his dancing days are behind him. Though I could have convinced him otherwise if I'd tried." A mischievous smile played on her lips, and she winked. "I, however, am as young at heart as I was at your age—how old are you again, dear?"

"Twenty-six." Almost twenty-seven, but a March birthday was hardly worth celebrating anyway.

"Yes, well, when I was your age..." Her eyes twinkled, and her already-rouged pink cheeks reddened. "Anyway, I slipped out when your great-uncle nodded off, and here I am, ready to welcome the New Year." She rubbed her hands. "Do you think this year will bring a new adventure? I miss the excitement of our sleuthing days."

"You talk like it's been decades instead of a few months since our last brush with murder and mayhem."

"It feels like decades, and at my age, you don't have decades to wait." Great-Aunt Iris scanned the room with eagle-eyed intensity.

"What or whom are you looking for?" Eliza asked.

"Our next adventure. From the looks of some of those here, you've invited some dodgy sorts, and I'm convinced one of them will either wind up dead or be the killer." She pointed near the Christmas tree with a gnarled finger. "Like Basil Huxley, for instance. He's a proper scoundrel, that one."

Eliza squinted at a potbellied seventy-something-year-old man sporting a tweed jacket. Between the monocle nestled in his left eye socket, his shiny bald head, and a mustache to make Hercule Poirot jealous, Basil Huxley fit his name to perfection. "Did he steal your spot at bingo night?" Eliza mimed twirling a villain's mustache.

Great-Aunt Iris eyed Eliza like she'd grown extra ears. "Good heavens, no, my girl. Bingo isn't my game. Poker's more my style."

"What's he done that makes him such a degenerate?"

"It's only gossip, naturally, but enough people can't stand the sight of him that I do wonder why he doesn't hire personal bodyguards."

"Then why was he on the guest list Uncle Fitzwilliam gave me?"

"He's headmaster of a posh school in the area. Lambton Prep. Fitzwilliam likes to keep the local 'dignitaries' feeling pleased with themselves. Makes them easier to manage if they think they have Lord Darcy's blessing." Suddenly, her gaze narrowed, and she drew in a sharp breath. "Whatever possessed you to invite him?"

"Who?" Eliza scanned the room, curious who had drained the pink from her great-aunt's cheeks.

"Hunter Crawford."

"Who?" Eliza asked again, frowning.

"*Who* brought the owl?" Joy giggled.

Eliza patted her great-aunt's hand. "You'll have to be more specific. I invited nearly a hundred guests—friends from Lambton, acquaintances of yours and Uncle Fitzwilliam's, and neighbors."

Great-Aunt Iris pulled Eliza and Joy closer to the refreshment table, pointing at an attractive man of medium height with chestnut hair. He was chatting up Belle. "Hunter Crawford is the wastrel son of Hubert and Henrietta Crawford." She shifted her finger to the right. "There. They're wearing matching plaid." Her waspish tone suggested she'd rather see them donning fig leaves to cover their business districts than watch the fifty-something couple parade around in fancy plaid outfits. "As mad as hatters, the whole lot of them. They own Berryhill Manor, which borders Pemberley to the north. Dreadful family. Always have been. Always will be."

Eliza scrunched her nose. "That name sounds familiar. I think Elizabeth wrote about them in her diary." She made a mental note to check when she had the chance.

Joy let out a few gusty *H* sounds. "The Crawfords are keen on the letter *H*."

Great-Aunt Iris eyed Joy. "Well, I shouldn't know about that, but Hunter has a thing for the ladies, or so I'm told. You'd do well to give him a wide berth. He's as untrustworthy as they come." Her wrinkled cheeks flushed.

Joy leaned precariously close to Great-Aunt Iris and whispered, "He's got nothing on Willoughby, though."

Eliza steadied Joy. "Speaking of Willoughby, let's get you to bed so you can properly propose in the morning."

"Who's proposing in the morning?" Heath joined them, looped an arm around Eliza's waist, and pulled her back against solid muscle.

"Me." Joy beamed a crooked smile.

"Who's the lucky chap?" Heath asked, a grin tugging at the corners of his lips.

"Well, it's certainly not you, old boy," Joy said.

"Thank heavens for small mercies." Heath kissed the top of Eliza's head. "Eliza here would pine for me for the rest of her days if you snatched me up again, wouldn't you, love?"

Eliza playfully jabbed him in the ribs. "You'd get a solid week. Probably more but no less. Either way, you're off the hook from proposals in general, since Joy is planning to ask Willoughby to be her happily-ever-after in the morning when she can see straight."

Heath craned his neck to look over the crowd and grinned when he spotted the soon-to-be-affianced man. "He looks utterly clueless, poor blighter." A whoosh of air left his lungs as Joy's elbow connected with his ribs.

Eliza whispered an apology to a bent-over and red-faced Heath and ushered Joy away as her great-aunt scolded Heath, telling him to "stop faffing about and rescue Belle from that dreadful Hunter."

After ensuring Joy was safely tucked up for the night, Eliza closed the door and tripped over Caesar. She caught herself, *tsk*ed at the orange Maine coon, and ruffled his fur. "Your New Year's resolution must be to kill me and find a new owner. Maybe Mrs. B, who'll feed you anything at any time without questions."

Caesar meowed at the mention of Mrs. Bankcroft, the cook, and butted his head against her hand.

"Yes, yes, my demise would be a travesty indeed, and after gaining twenty pounds and having to slither across the floor, you'd finally be sorry."

Caesar sat, lifted his leg, and licked himself.

"That's what I thought." Eliza chuckled, gave him a final scratch, plucked an orange hairball from her ruffled sapphire skirt, and headed down the hall to the grand staircase.

While she would much rather find Heath and escape the prying eyes of guests, especially Great-Aunt Iris, who had an uncanny way of tracking them down no matter where they hid on the estate, Pemberley's New Year's Eve party was still in full swing. As mistress of Pemberley, she was duty bound to attend. More than ever, that role settled on her like a well-worn robe. While she still hosted fancy weekends for corporations, politicians, and celebrities, Pemberley felt more like her home than an estate she needed to save. Not that Pemberley was in as dire danger as before. Thanks to Uncle Fitzwilliam's Midas touch and teamwork, Pemberley's coffers were nearly restored. Nearly.

Eliza paused over the initials *E* and *F* engraved in the black-and-white marble flooring of the foyer, representing her sixth great-grandparents, Elizabeth and Fitzwilliam Darcy. The legacy they'd started hundreds of years ago was still going strong. While plenty of people had tried to destroy what they'd built, no one could demolish it. If Pemberley could survive murder, mayhem, and secreted wanted men, it could survive anything.

Hope bloomed in her chest. The upcoming year brimmed with promise. Pemberley had weathered its fair share of destructive forces. Surely the universe wouldn't bring more disaster.

Eliza rapped her knuckles against an oak table in the foyer. A knock on wood couldn't hurt to appease superstition.

M usic from the ballroom reminded Eliza of her duties, and she marched along the marble flooring toward the ballroom, her silver heels clicking out a sharp staccato beat.

Before Eliza could step through the door, Belle sailed out of it, bringing the scent of warm vanilla bean and champagne with her. Her right hand clutched a glass of the sparkling liquid while the other held tight to the handsome Hunter.

He was even better looking up close, and though Eliza, in her four-inch stilettos, was taller than him, he somehow loomed larger than life before her. Confidence and charm oozed from his pores, lending credence to his ladies'-man reputation.

Belle tugged Hunter closer to her side. "Eliza, this is Hunter Crawford. Hunter, this is my best friend, Eliza Darcy."

He flashed a brilliant smile. "Miss Darcy," he said with a respectful dip of his head, "I've heard a lot about you, and it's my absolute pleasure to finally meet you properly." He extended his hand in greeting. "I do apologize for gate-crashing your party, but my parents didn't fancy me moping about at home all on my own on New Year's Eve."

Eliza shook his hand and smiled back. "Thank you. In my experience, it's far easier to ask for forgiveness than permission. I hope you're enjoying yourself?"

"It'd be difficult not to." He threaded his fingers through his curly chestnut-brown hair. "Your friend here has been charming and thoroughly entertaining."

Eliza glanced at her flushed-faced friend. "She certainly is, isn't she?"

"Without question, and I've been trying to convince her to dig up her American roots and plant them here permanently, but sadly, she's chosen flowers over me."

"My flower shop won't allow me more than the two weeks I've already taken. I'm terrified of what I'll go back to already. But I refuse to start the New Year with worry. I'm going to live it up and deal with the aftermath later."

"Care to start your I'll-deal-with-it-later resolution with a stroll through the gardens?" Hunter held his hand out to Belle. "We shouldn't let the heaters and fairy lights go unappreciated. It's like a winter wonderland out there."

Belle gave Eliza a tiny finger wave and sashayed down the hall, her laugh echoing behind her.

Eliza grunted. So much for her best friend's three-hundred-sixty-five-day fast from men. Something about Hunter bothered her. Despite his smile, good looks, and charm, something didn't sit right. He was far too smooth for his own good... and for the good of the women he met. Unease settled in her gut, and she hoped her previous knocking on wood covered best friends and good-for-nothing men.

Eliza contemplated grabbing Belle and locking her in a closet to protect her from herself, but that would go over as smoothly as giving Caesar a bath. She'd learned the hard way that unlike normal cats of his breed, water was not his jam.

"Penny for your thoughts?" Heath's voice soothed her frayed nerves, and she melted into his welcoming embrace at the double-door entrance to the ballroom.

The open doors framed Eliza's view of the New Year's Eve party. Some guests whirled on the dance floor to bad karaoke, proving that some people would dance to anything. Others chatted in small groups, while a steady line visited the refreshment tables. Waitstaff moved quietly, offering hors d'oeuvres and flutes of champagne to hungry and thirsty guests. Judging from the smiles, laughs, and party vibes pouring from the room, the guests were enjoying themselves.

Her gut twisted, and she stiffened at the sense of impending doom. She squirmed under Heath's touch when the sensation in her stomach turned to stone-cold granite.

"Eliza?" Heath tilted her head up and gazed down at her. Concern flickered in his cornflower-blue eyes as he smoothed his hand against the bare skin on her back where the sapphire velvet cloth dipped low on her waistline. "What's the matter?"

"Nothing."

"Rubbish."

She rested her forehead against his heart. "I can't shake the feeling that something's about to go very wrong."

He kissed the top of her head and pulled her close. "Fancy telling me about it?"

"Wish I could. It's just a feeling—hard to put into words." She traced a figure eight over his chest. "Do you know Hunter Crawford well?"

"Not really. Only by reputation from Oxford. He's a few years older than me, and according to legend, he's a financial whiz and something of a playboy. Lots of broken hearts in his wake, if you believe the gossip." His brow furrowed. "Why do you ask? Do you know him?"

"I accidentally invited him to the party when I invited his parents. Great-Aunt Iris already gave me an earful, and now Belle's gone off with him."

Heath laced his fingers through Eliza's. "Hunter might have a dodgy reputation, but his parents are here, and there's a room full of guests. Besides, he'd have to be a complete idiot to try anything under your uncle's roof."

"True, but Uncle Fitzwilliam's been MIA ever since he opened the billiard room. Probably losing his shirt in a game of pool."

"He's fleecing every one of their shirts, including mine, in a brutal game of poker." Heath plucked at his blue V-neck cashmere sweater and pulled out the inner linings of his khaki pockets. "I'm completely skint. You don't love me for my money, do you? Because if so, you'll have to find something else to fancy about me."

He cupped the back of her neck and ran his thumb over her skin. Under Heath's warm gaze, Eliza's worries melted away, and all that mattered was him. "Looks like my New Year's resolution has changed from working out more to finding a different man." She sighed so dramatically that her high school drama teacher would have been proud.

A wicked grin spread across his lips, and he grabbed her hand and hauled her up the grand staircase to her bedroom. "In that case, it's only fair that you allow me one more chance to convince you of my other qualities." He pressed her against the doorjamb and kissed her.

When something bumped against Eliza's leg, she broke from Heath's embrace and glared down at Caesar. "If it's not Great-Aunt Iris, it's the darn cat." She scratched between Caesar's ears. "Not tonight, buddy. I have another roommate." She pressed a finger to her lips and whispered to the blinking feline. "Don't tell."

After another gentle scratch between Caesar's ears, Eliza pushed Heath into her bedroom and shut the door firmly in the cat's face. Let Pemberley's guests ring in the New Year with champagne and the midnight fireworks show. She planned to usher in the New Year with a different kind of fireworks display.

Chapter Two
Death Comes to Pemberley ... Again.

The Crawfords called this morning to introduce themselves as our new neighbors. What charming company Darcy and I found in Mr. Henry Crawford. I am uncertain about his sister, Miss Mary Crawford, however. She reminds me of Caroline Bingley. I'm sure she will improve upon further acquaintance. Mr. Crawford played with Adelaide Rose, spinning her about until she squealed with laughter. Not many gentlemen give attention to three-year-olds, so he has already won my favor.

Come to think of it, Miss Crawford admired little Fitz with all the proper exclamations a baby is due. Perhaps she's not like Caroline after all.

Lizzy Bennet Darcy
Pemberley 1815

"I say, Eliza, you sure know how to throw a proper do." Jack Willoughby sauntered into the breakfast room as the grandfather clock chimed nine o'clock, wrapped in a maroon robe that looked suspiciously like Uncle Fitzwilliam's and tied with what appeared to be the gold rope used to hold back the drawing room tapestries. Despite the telltale purple smudges under his eyes, the greenish hue to his skin, and the fact that he wasn't properly dressed, he appeared ready to conquer the world—or at least breakfast.

Even in a bathrobe and tapestry rope, Willoughby remained every inch the suave gentleman Eliza had met upon first arriving at Pemberley. She'd been spared his romantic schemes and having to partner with him at croquet, however, thanks to Heath's timely entrance. While Willoughby had sulked for a few hours afterward, he'd recovered quickly and become a dear if annoying friend. From the way he looked at Joy, though, Eliza was certain there wasn't another woman for him, even if he hadn't realized it yet.

Willoughby wandered along the buffet, lifting lids only to set them back down, ignored every food item, and ended by pouring himself a generous cup of black coffee.

He dropped into the chair next to Joy, gave her elbow a cheeky nudge, and winked. "Where'd you scarper off to last night? I was hoping to have a dance with you. Because of you, I got lumbered with Melissa the *entire* evening. Did you know she's cross-eyed?" He took a fortifying gulp of the black brew. "Never would have guessed."

"Of me? You're the one who brought that... that..." Joy squinted at him, slammed her teacup back onto its saucer, and angled herself away from him.

Willoughby raised his eyebrow at the rest of the table, but neither Heath nor Uncle Fitzwilliam nor Great-Aunt Iris had anything more to offer than mystified shrugs. Eliza didn't have the heart to tell him that as long as he considered Joy nothing more than a flirt buddy and a second-choice emergency date, Joy's heart would break every time he brought another woman into his life.

The breakfast room door opened again, and Great-Uncle William shuffled in, leaning heavily on his cane. His shock of disheveled white hair was a contrast to his ironed and crisp khaki slacks, striped red-and-green dress shirt, and green wool sweater. Despite the cane and slight hump in his back, he looked like a tall country gentleman ready to putter in the garden or tend to small livestock.

Great-Aunt Iris immediately stood, but he waved her off with a gnarled hand.

"Sit, sit, my dear. I'm not an invalid. Yet." He lowered himself into the chair next to his wife with a soft grunt.

"William, you should be resting," Great-Aunt Iris fussed, though her eyes twinkled with happiness.

"Nonsense." He accepted a cup of tea from Tash with a grateful nod. "It's New Year's Day, and I wanted to breakfast with the family."

Eliza smiled at her great-uncle. He looked better than he had in months. Color bloomed in his cheeks, and a sparkle lit his rheumy blue eyes.

"Happy New Year," Eliza said.

"And to you, my girl." He squeezed his wife's hand. "Though any year with this one is a happy one."

Great-Aunt Iris rolled her eyes, but her blush gave her away. "Such nonsense."

"Speaking the truth," he murmured, bringing her hand to his lips for a gentle kiss.

Eliza's heart hummed with happiness, and she turned her attention back to Willoughby, gesturing to his outfit with her fork. "Is this the beginning of your New Year's resolution to start a new fashion?"

"Rather not. But when a chap can't locate his trousers—"

Joy snorted then coughed, her already-red cheeks burning crimson.

Willoughby patted her on the back. "I say, old thing, are you all right?"

Joy angled herself even farther from him, stuck her chin out, and stared out the window.

After a puzzled look at her, Willoughby cleared his throat. "Right, then. When a fellow can't locate his trousers, one must resort to desperate measures." Willoughby raised his coffee cup toward Uncle Fitzwilliam. "Frightfully sorry about borrowing your dressing gown."

Uncle Fitzwilliam looked heavenward as if seeking divine intervention. "And might one enquire why you're using part of the tapestries as a belt?"

"Hardly my fault if you've misplaced your dressing gown belt. Desperate circumstances, I'm afraid. And when one wakes up with—"

Joy shot up from her chair so quickly that it crashed to the floor. "Jack Willoughby, you are an absolute tosser, and no one—least of all anyone in this room—gives a fig how you lost your trousers, where you mislaid them, or their present whereabouts. Perhaps you ought to check with that cross-eyed trollop you brought round last night."

"Ah, so I wasn't the only one who noticed she was cross-eyed. Splendid. Thought my eyesight was going dodgy."

With a growl, Joy stomped out of the room.

"What's got her knickers in a twist?" Willoughby's gaze followed her retreating form. "Never thought I'd see the day Joy Bingley was rendered speechless."

Great-Aunt Iris, who had been silently watching the theatrics from her spot at the end of the table, *tsk*ed. "You two remind me of William and me when we first met. We were always at loggerheads, but I'll tell you all that tension led to—"

"Eliza, where's Belle?" Uncle Fitzwilliam's face turned beet red, and from his widened eyes, he was clearly grasping for any change in subject.

For a second or two, Eliza considered egging Iris on to share the juicy details, if only to escape the cat-that-got-the-cream looks her great-aunt had been shooting her all morning. She finally took pity on Heath and her uncle, who shared the same pinched expression. Willoughby continued to sip his coffee like it contained elixir from Mt. Olympus.

"I'm sure she's still sleeping," Eliza said. "She's in full vacation mode and deserves to start the new year with a lazy morning. I'll have breakfast taken up to her on a tray in a bit."

Great-Aunt Iris tutted. "With how she was carrying on with that frightful specimen of a man, it's little wonder she needs her rest."

"And who might this frightful specimen be?" Uncle Fitzwilliam asked, a grin tugging at his lips.

"Hunter Crawford."

"I wasn't aware he was on the guest list." He raised an eyebrow at Eliza.

"He wasn't, but his parents were. He tagged along as their plus-one, I guess."

Uncle Fitzwilliam's forehead wrinkled. "Those Crawfords are an odd bunch, and I wish I hadn't put them on the guest list at all. A few months back, they dusted off some centuries-old land dispute, claiming that the Pemberley estate encroached on their property. Complete codswallop, that."

Eliza grinned. Not often did her uncle use slang. But when his frown deepened, her grin disappeared. "Why'd you put them on the list, then?"

"Burying the hatchet and all that, I suppose. I was trying to be decent about it. Be the bigger person. Show I wasn't put out or rattled by their ridiculous accusations."

"Is there any validity to their claims?" Heath asked.

"Of course not." Great-Aunt Iris's cheeks flushed. "The Crawfords have always been grasping and will snatch up anything they can lay their hands on. Dreadful vultures, the lot of them."

"I reread parts of Elizabeth's journals this morning to see if my memory served me correctly, and I hit paydirt. Looks like the issue with the Crawfords and Berryhill Manor drama started in 1815. A Henry and his sister..." Eliza snapped her fingers, trying to conjure the woman's name. "Mary. That's it. From the sounds of it, the Crawfords' charming veneer didn't last long."

"Sounds familiar now that you say that. I remember chuckling to myself, reading the entries about Elizabeth and Darcy's 'lovely' neighbors." Uncle Fitzwilliam sighed and ran a hand over his muttonchops. "I suspect this same tiresome dispute has been dusted off at least once a generation since a Crawford took control of Berry-hill."

"Well, if it's been shot down for hundreds of years, I wouldn't worry about it," Eliza said.

The wrinkles in her uncle's forehead deepened. "That's the difficulty. They claim to have unearthed fresh evidence proving the Darcys have been in the wrong for centuries, and they're threatening legal action."

"And you still invited them, Fitzwilliam, knowing all this?" Great-Aunt Iris's voice trembled with indignation.

"Yes, Aunt." Uncle Fitzwilliam straightened in his chair and squared his shoulders. "As I mentioned, I was attempting to extend an olive branch. If I hadn't invited them, they would have likely interpreted that as an admission of guilt. I did what I thought best under the circumstances." His shoulders relaxed. "Besides, no harm came of last evening, and they both departed looking pleased. The evening went rather well. Perhaps this marks the beginning of a proper reconciliation."

Eliza bit her tongue against reminding her uncle that he had misread his ex-wife, Nancy, for years and of the damage that had caused him, his family, and the estate. "You're right. Let's hope the Crawfords will realize that a good relationship with Pemberley serves them better than a contentious one." She pushed back her chair. "I'll see about having breakfast delivered to Belle."

Tash, the Darcy's beloved butler, entered the breakfast room, his normally dour face sagging even further. "Lord Darcy, Detective Chief Inspector Wentworth to see you, sir."

Wentworth, looking as stoic as ever in his crisp suit, strode through the door, quickly closing the distance between the entrance and the table. White stubble he apparently hadn't had time to shave that morning caught the light against his russet-brown skin, his dark-amber eyes flashed with anger, and his lips pursed as if he'd been sucking on a lemon. "Darcy, might I have a word?"

"Happy New Year to you as well, Wentworth. Do join us for breakfast, won't you?" Uncle Fitzwilliam gestured to an empty chair.

Wentworth's gaze swept the room, pausing when he made eye contact with Eliza. A flicker of pity crossed his features. "I'm afraid it's not a happy New Year for everyone. An anonymous tip came into the constabulary last night. Hunter Crawford is dead. Murdered. And his body was found on your property."

I *should have knocked harder on wood.* Eliza clutched Heath's hand as they approached Belle's room. Wentworth had demanded the guest list and ordered everyone currently under Pemberley's roof to assemble in the drawing room.

Despite Eliza's oversized knit sweater, she shivered. Just when she'd thought a new year would bring reprieve from death and mayhem, it had dropped like the New Year's Eve ball in Times Square right on her doorstep—again.

Heath stopped and squeezed her hand. "I shouldn't worry if I were you. Early days yet, innit? And if Hunter's body was found on the edge of Pemberley, chances are he was killed elsewhere and dumped at the first opportunity. Pemberley's got massive woodlands. It's the perfect spot for someone trying to hide a body."

Pemberley's woodland stretched for miles, and Eliza had yet to explore all of it. "You're right. I want nothing to do with this murder or this case." Even though the mysterious location and odd anonymous report had her sleuthing instincts tingling.

Heath pressed the back of his hand against her forehead. "You all right, love?"

She swatted his hand away. "You're incorrigible."

"And that's why you love me, yeah?"

Eliza rolled her eyes. "Sure is." She took the last few steps to Belle's door and knocked. "Wake up, Sleeping Beauty."

When no response came through the oak door, Eliza knocked again. "Belle?"

More silence followed. Eliza opened the door and stepped into the dark room. "Belle?"

Nothing.

Eliza flicked on the light to reveal an empty bedroom drowning in purple hyacinths. From the bedspread to the wallpaper to the rugs on the floor, hyacinths bloomed from every surface. But Belle was nowhere to be found, and nothing suggested she'd spent the night there.

Worry crawled up Eliza's spine. With Heath at her heels, she raced to the drawing room, burst through the door breathless, and slammed straight into Wentworth's back.

Wentworth's growl died in his chest. "What is it?"

"It's Belle. She's not in her room, and there's no sign she slept there." Eliza gripped Wentworth's forearm.

"Who's Belle?" Wentworth asked.

"My friend. She flew in a few days ago for a visit." Eliza steadied her breathing. "Do you think something happened to her? Do you think she's..." Bile rose in her throat, and she couldn't finish the question. Belle had last been seen with Hunter, the murder victim, the night before. The worst possibilities tumbled through Eliza's mind, making her stomach churn.

Joy wrapped Eliza in a hug. "I'm certain everything's fine. Pemberley's an enormous estate, and it's easy to get lost. Remember your first few days here? You couldn't find your room, and we almost let you make a trail of breadcrumbs. Though that wouldn't have worked a jot, since Caesar would've eaten them anyway."

"I agree with Joy," Uncle Fitzwilliam said. "She's most likely risen early, made her bed, and gone for a walk." He offered a reassuring smile, but a flicker of concern flashed in his eyes.

"Belle doesn't get up early unless her alarm forces her to, and even then, she does it grudgingly. I'm not sure she's made her bed since she was old enough to argue that she'd mess it up again, so what was the point," Eliza said.

"Perhaps the staff have tidied her room," Heath suggested.

"No. The staff haven't reached the guest rooms yet. I saw them still cleaning the ballroom, so I know they didn't make the bed this morning."

"Well, let's not sit here like bumps on a log." Great-Aunt Iris hauled all five feet, one inch of herself to her white-sneaker-clad feet and settled her briefcase-size purse on her hip. "I'll check the ground-floor rooms in the west wing."

Uncle Fitzwilliam offered to look belowstairs and in the tunnel in case Belle had found her way in and wandered off on an adventure.

Wentworth gathered some officers and led a search of the grounds.

Joy and Willoughby volunteered to check the east-wing rooms, leaving Heath and Eliza to search the first-floor rooms and the attic in case Belle had wandered into the less desirable parts of the rambling building. The attic had turned up empty, and with every empty room on the first floor, Eliza's heart pinched. She rubbed the spot on her chest, hoping to ease the growing ache.

Heath wrapped her clammy hand in his warm one. "Don't worry, love. I'm certain Belle will turn up with one heck of a story to tell."

Eliza couldn't speak past the lump in her throat. They'd reached the last room on the first floor. If Belle wasn't there, they'd have to report defeat to the search crew.

The door creaked open, revealing another flower-patterned room but no Belle.

Eliza swallowed down the panic threatening to suffocate her. "Let's go see how the others are doing."

Her cell phone buzzed, so she pulled it from her leggings pocket and tapped the unread text from Joy.

Found her. Small drawing room at the far end of the east wing.

"What on earth is Belle doing in that room? I didn't even know it existed until months after I'd been here." Eliza clutched her phone and sprinted down the hallway, Heath on her heels. "The one time Joy's not overly detailed," she huffed as she hooked a right at the bottom of the main staircase and ran down the mansion's main artery.

She skidded to a stop outside the unused drawing room's door and drew a deep breath. No sense causing Belle undue panic with her own anxiety. Grabbing Heath's hand, she dragged him into the room.

Belle sat hunched over, her hands folded tightly in her lap. Her silver dress from the night before looked a little worse for wear, and her hair, littered with leaves and twigs, hung in tangled rivulets over her shoulders. Tiny scratches marred her face, and one of her exposed ankles was swollen. A greenish tint discolored her normally peach-colored skin, a telltale sign that Belle was about to lose the contents of her stomach.

She was hungover.

Which probably means she had two drinks instead of one, Eliza thought as she dropped to her knees in front of her friend and reached for her hand.

"Don't." Wentworth's sharp command echoed through the room, making everyone except Belle flinch.

Eliza's shoulders tensed. "Why not?"

Instead of answering her, Wentworth evaded eye contact and spoke into his police radio and requested an ambulance.

"Belle, are you—"

Belle waved a hand dismissively then seemed to regret it as she cradled her stomach and turned even greener. "A few scratches here and there, a sprained ankle, and such. This detective"—Belle tilted her head in Wentworth's direction—"wants to take me in for a *full* examination."

The emphasis on "full" caught Eliza's attention as she took in the state of her best friend's dress. "What? What happened? Did Hunter touch you? Because I swear if he did, I'll ... I'll..." Eliza hung her head and stared at the faded Oriental carpeting. She could do nothing because the man was dead. "I don't understand," Eliza said, hating that her voice sounded weak.

"I don't remember anything from last night, and from the state of things..." Belle gestured from her head to her toes then stuck out her right hand, revealing fingernails encrusted with a dried brown substance. "And the fact that I can't account for my whereabouts or the events leading up to Hunter's death, I'm being taken into custody." She slid Wentworth a look. "Covering all the bases, or so I hear."

Eliza whirled around. "Why on earth are you taking Belle into custody?"

"Because I have reason to believe your friend here is involved in Hunter's murder."

E liza sputtered. "Have you lost your mind, Wentworth?"

"Eliza, my dear..." Uncle Fitzwilliam tried to guide her toward a chair.

She shook him off and squared up with Wentworth. "Why would you even say something like that? What makes you think she's—"

Wentworth nodded toward Belle. "That's what she wore last night at your New Year's Eve ball?"

"Yes, but what does that have to do with—"

"And when did you last see her?" Wentworth asked, flipping open his notebook.

"You do know that I'm right here, right?" Belle asked, some of her usual fire back.

Wentworth sighed. "Eliza, I thought you'd trust me enough to know I'm not railroading anyone here." When Eliza raised her chin higher, Wentworth shook his head and sank into a nearby leather wingback chair. He glanced around the room, his gaze lingering on Great-Aunt Iris, who sat in the matching chair, calmly knitting as if nothing had happened.

Wentworth turned to Willoughby. "And you, sir, are?"

"Willoughby. Jack Willoughby. Family friend and Joy's old school chum."

"I'll ask you to leave, Mr. Willoughby. The constable stationed outside this room will take down your statement, and you can wait for Miss Bingley elsewhere."

Joy protested. "But you can trust him. He's been friends with the family for years."

"You can tell me all about it later, but now, Miss Bingley, I have a murder to solve. I haven't got time to share details with every Tom, Dick, and Harry in Derbyshire. Do I make myself clear?"

"Perfectly," Joy mumbled.

After giving Eliza's hand a reassuring squeeze, Willoughby left the room, closing the door behind him.

"Wentworth, there was no need to exclude him." Uncle Fitzwilliam paced the tiny room, his hands clasped behind his back.

"I don't come to Pemberley trying to tell you how to manage this posh place, do I? So don't try to tell me how to do my job. The only reason I'm letting the rest of you stay is because I know I can trust you." He shot a side glance at the little lady still knitting as if a murder hadn't occurred. "One of these days, it'll be the death of me or my career, but until you give me reason to think otherwise, I'll keep you in the loop."

Belle groaned. "I don't feel good. I'm going to be sick."

Eliza whirled around, grabbed an empty urn, and thrust it into Belle's hands in time.

Unable to comfort her friend, Eliza turned her attention back to Wentworth. "Well?"

Wentworth's shoulders sagged, and his brow furrowed, creating deep lines in his russet-brown skin. "Material that matches her dress exactly was found at the crime scene, clutched in Hunter's fists. Because of the state of her dress and the fabric found at the scene, there's precious little doubt she was there moments before he died."

Eliza's face heated, and she swallowed the angry words she wanted to fling at Wentworth. "Little doubt? Oh, I have more than a few little doubts. Haven't you considered that she was the victim and fled an attack from Crawford?"

Eliza sat on the edge of the couch next to Belle, crossed her arms, and tilted her chin, awaiting Wentworth's rebuttal.

Belle grunted. "No, I think your friend here seems to think I bludgeoned Hunter over the head, he grasped my dress in the attack, and I fled the scene."

"Now, don't go putting words in my mouth," Wentworth said. "I have to follow the evidence and track every lead until it either pays off or hits a dead end."

"What was the method of murder?" Eliza asked.

"Preliminary reports show blunt-force trauma to the head." Wentworth double-checked his notes. "Not sure of the weapon yet, but there are plenty of rocks and tree limbs that could have done the job."

"Do you remember anything from last night?" Eliza asked her friend.

Belle's face scrunched, and after several moments of silence, she faintly shook her head. "I'm sorry. No. I remember teasing you about the Christmas tree still being up, dancing with Hunter, and walking through the—" Belle's voice caught, and a sob ripped from her throat. "Garden. But nothing after that. I'm so sorry."

"You mean you were deliberately outside last night? It was two degrees Celsius." Wentworth arched an eyebrow.

"I had heat lamps and hanging lanterns scattered throughout. It was a winter wonderland despite the cold night," Eliza said.

A knock at the door preceded two paramedics. Wentworth took them to the corner of the room and spoke quietly. Eliza tried catching a sliver of the conversation but failed. It didn't take her long to figure out the gist when one of the paramedics started putting paper bags on Belle's hands.

Before Eliza could react, Joy jumped to her feet. "Right. What's all this, then? What are you doing that for?"

Wentworth glanced at her from where he knelt beside Belle, taking notes. "Feel free to join your *friend* if you'd like, Miss Bingley. We already have far too many cooks in the kitchen."

Joy planted her hand on her jutted hip. "Well, I never—"

"I'm in no mood for your theatrics. You have a choice. Behave and stay or clear off."

Eliza feared Joy would choose the wrong option, but her cousin finally retook her seat.

"Do you remember how you got to this room, Miss Knightley?"

Belle shook her head. "I'm sorry. I don't remember anything after the garden." She groaned again, made a face, and grasped the urn, the paper bags encasing her hands crinkling as she gripped the pottery's neck.

Wentworth, looking a little green about the gills, backed away and beckoned for Eliza. Lowering his voice, he said, "Look, Eliza, I have no choice but to take your friend in for questioning—" He held up a hand, cutting off her retort, and placed it on her shoulder. "Look at me." After Eliza complied, Wentworth squeezed her shoulder. "I'll keep you in the loop as much as I can. But you also need to understand that I have a job to do and won't allow any personal connections to get in the way."

Eliza sighed. "I understand. I don't like it, but I understand."

"I didn't ask you to like it. I'm asking you to stay out of this and let me do my job."

"I'm coming with." She made herself as tall as her five-foot-ten-inch frame would allow. "And don't try to stop me. I'd sneak in anyway and make everyone's lives a living hell."

Apparently resigned, Wentworth shook his head. "The day you listen to me the first time is the day I fall over from a heart attack from the shock of it."

"I wouldn't give me any ideas," Eliza said before taking her place again beside Belle.

Chapter Three
A Charmer's Just Deserts

The Crawfords dined with us this evening. Miss Crawford spent most of the evening regaling us with her planned improvements to Berryhill Manor. Darcy kept silent for most of the evening, which is not like him when among friends. When I pressed him, he chuckled and said, "I wonder how Miss Crawford will feel about her grand plans when the future Mrs. Crawford replaces her." I now wonder that, too, as Mr. Crawford is a charming single man of some fortune and, whether he wants a wife or no, surely will not remain single for long.

Lizzy Bennet Darcy
Pemberley 1815

Four hours later, Eliza collapsed into an oversize leather chair in her uncle's study. Exhaustion seeped into her bones, and she was sure that if she tried to stand, her legs would buckle beneath her. As much as she loved her cousin and great-aunt, it was better to look weak in front of a smaller audience. Joy and Willoughby were off questioning the staff that hadn't already left for the holiday to see if anyone had witnessed anything, while Great-Aunt Iris had holed herself up in her private sitting area, poring over paperwork and files accumulated over generations of Pemberley's masters since the first Crawford took ownership.

"How's Belle?" Heath asked as he settled beside her.

Eliza laced her fingers through his. "After performing all the required tests and taking samples from her hair and fingernails, plus treating her scratches and sprained ankle, the doctor released her back to Wentworth. He's detaining her on suspicion of murder." Eliza's voice hitched, and she breathed deeply to stem the flood of tears threatening to consume her.

"He can only hold her for twenty-four hours—ninety-six in some cases—without officially charging her. Did the solicitor I arranged show up?" Uncle Fitzwilliam handed her a glass of water.

Eliza drained the contents in a few gulps before placing it on the nearby coffee table. "Yes. Thank you so much." She smiled appreciatively at her uncle. "Knowing there's someone in her corner makes me feel better. I argued and begged and pleaded to stay with her, but Wentworth ordered me to go home and threatened to throw me into a cell if I didn't listen."

"Good thing you did. You can't help your friend from inside a jail cell." Uncle Fitzwilliam tapped the guest list spread across his large mahogany desk. "Wentworth asked me to go through this lot."

Eliza eyed the sheets of paper. "This is going to take you forever."

"Care to join me?" Uncle Fitzwilliam asked, a look of hope glinting in his eyes.

"As riveting as this looks, I think this is a task I'll leave for you." Eliza chuckled at her uncle's deflated expression. "Besides, we need to find out all we can about Hunter. The better we can understand the motive behind his murder, the faster we can get Wentworth off Belle's scent. And I can't do that from here."

"I'll have a word with a few of my Oxford mates." Heath rose to his feet. "Hunter was quite the character, and from what I recall, he was legendary on campus." Heath walked from the room, his cell phone already pressed to his ear, his deep voice greeting an old friend.

"I'll hunt down Joy for a trip into Lambton. Between the two of us, I'm sure we can sniff out some dirt on Hunter." Eliza tapped out a text to Joy to meet her in the foyer.

Uncle Fitzwilliam stared at the guest list in front of him and massaged the back of his neck. "And I'll finish up here then check in with Aunt Iris and see what she's managed to uncover about Pemberley's past dealings with Berryhill Manor." He placed his hand on Eliza's and squeezed gently. "Do be careful on this one, my dear. I'm afraid the Crawfords are not to be trusted, and the sheer brutality of this crime suggests a murderer who won't take kindly to someone poking about, asking awkward questions." He turned his attention back to the guest list and started scrawling the guests' names into three different categories.

Eliza wanted to dismiss her uncle's warning, to say this wasn't her first rodeo and that she had everything under control. But the truth was she didn't. Not only had someone viciously attacked her best friend, but that same someone had probably killed Hunter and framed Belle. Her uncle was right. The viciousness of the murder promised a long and dangerous hunt for answers.

Basking in the old comfort of her uncle's study and breathing in the familiar scent of leather and pipe tobacco wasn't an option. And while she wished she could snuggle into one of the large leather chairs and reread her great-great-great-great-great-great-grandmother Elizabeth Bennet Darcy's words, she couldn't. She had work to do.

Eliza's phone pinged, and she smiled at Joy's response to her earlier text: *Now look who's waiting for whom. I'm taking a screenshot for posterity's sake.*

Eliza chuckled and tapped out a reply: *Hold your horses. I'll be there in a jiffy.*

Joy: *Blimey, tell me you're Midwestern without telling me you're Midwestern.*

Eliza: *And tell me you're not British without telling me you're not British.*

She ran upstairs to grab her purse and coat then dashed back down to find Joy tapping her foot at the bottom of the steps. "What are you waiting for?" Eliza grinned at Joy's scowl.

"No worries." Joy jingled her Range Rover's keys as they headed toward the main entrance. "We'll make up for lost time in transit, won't we?"

"That's what I'm most worried about," Eliza mumbled, following Joy to the garage.

Eliza glared through the passenger window at the Trusty Teapot's Closed sign. "We'll get nothing done. No place is going to be open on New Year's Day."

Rain pelted the glass and streamed down in rivulets. Fog had rolled in, and despite the SUV's heater blasting hot air in her face, Eliza shivered. "I was hoping to talk to Monica. She always knows the ins and outs of this village. That's the perk of waitressing at the hot spot for gossiping ladies."

"Text her. Ask if she can meet us at the pub. It'll be open." Joy pulled away from the curb and drove down the nearly empty cobblestone roads toward the Foxed Hound.

"I knew there was a reason I dragged you along," Eliza said.

Joy pulled up outside the pub, the Range Rover's tires scraping against the curb. "Besides my quick wit and ability to charm information out of anyone with a Y chromosome?"

Eliza rolled her eyes. "Besides that."

After tapping out a text to Monica, Eliza laid her head against the seat's headrest. The pub's sign swayed back and forth in the gusty wind. Through the fog, she could barely make out the tipsy fox with a pint in its paw saluting incoming patrons.

With the first lull in action since Wentworth's horrible news about Hunter's death and Belle's arrest on suspicion of Hunter's murder, the enormity of it all crashed down on her. Eliza hadn't had time to process the fact that her best friend was sitting in custody for a crime she couldn't have committed—ever.

"It all feels like a dream," Eliza whispered.

"I am sorry about Belle. I've been meaning to chat with you about the whole business, but after all the pandemonium broke loose, I didn't get a chance." Joy squeezed Eliza's hand. "How are you holding up?"

Eliza's shoulders sagged. "I can't wrap my head around it. Everything feels surreal, like a nightmare I'll eventually wake up from."

"Remember, you've got your dream sleuthing team behind you. Honestly, what can't you sort with me, Heath, and Great-Aunt Iris at your side?"

Eliza gave Joy a weak smile. "You make a solid point."

Her phone pinged. "Oh, it's Monica. She can meet us in about fifteen minutes."

"Right, then. That gives us time to hash out some things and grab a drink." Joy grinned and hopped from the Range Rover's driver's seat. "Last one in buys the first round."

Eliza shook her head. After the amount her cousin had put away at the party, she didn't know how Joy could stomach another round.

Eliza followed her cousin into the pub and blinked in the dim atmosphere. The overcast and foggy weather outside gave the pub a closing-time vibe rather than its normal midafternoon social hour. She hadn't set foot in the pub since the Wentworth debacle the previous September. Memories of how her friend had nearly gotten railroaded by an old nemesis with a grudge came flooding back with startling clarity.

Joy snagged a table in the back corner, and Eliza settled into the chair beside her, pulling a notebook and pen from her purse.

Eliza clicked the pen open. "What did you and Willoughby manage to get from the staff?"

Joy huffed. "That muppet? Might as well have paired me up with the village idiot."

"Joy, he's not that bad. If he were, you wouldn't want to marry him, right? Look, Willoughby is probably stuck in a 'just friends' rut with you because he doesn't have the courage to change things. I see how he looks at you in those unguarded moments. You're more than just a friend to him."

"But he should—"

"And if he doesn't? Are you going to just sit back and pout whenever a new woman is in his life? You conjure up all sorts of romances in your novels. Why can't you do it for yourself in real life?"

"I don't know," Joy said, fiddling with the cutlery in front of her. "I suppose I'm scared. What if he truly only wants to be friends? It would break my heart, and I don't think I could handle it. It's safer not knowing."

Eliza reached over and squeezed Joy's hand. "But is the current state of things something you want to continue on for months? Years?"

Joy smiled sadly. "It's easy for you to talk. You and Heath seem to be made for each other. Heck, you met on a plane, then fate brought you together at Pemberley, and it's been sunshine and roses for you ever since."

"Give what I said some thought, okay? If you and Willougby can't sort yourselves out, I'll need to get Aunt Iris involved. From the way she's been studying you two, I'm afraid she's got some wicked plans up her sleeve."

Joy shuddered. "Fair point."

"Good," Eliza said then grinned up at the waitress who had sidled over to their table.

After the tired-looking woman took their orders of two diet sodas and fish and chips, Joy grinned. "I bet she enjoyed the New Year's festivities a bit too much."

"Like someone else I know." Eliza gave her a pointed look.

Joy raised her water glass in a mock salute. "You only ring in the New Year once a year, don't you?" She took a sip. "Anyway, back to the job at hand. Willoughby and I got a bit from Willow before she left to visit her family."

"I knew Willow would become essential to Pemberley." The new staff member had played a crucial role in hiding Wentworth from his enemies in Pemberley's secret passages. Since then, the young woman had consistently impressed Eliza with her dedication to the Darcy family and her work ethic. "What did she tell you?"

Joy lowered her voice. "Turns out one of Willow's mates, Paisley Foster, was left heartbroken and skint by our charming Mr. Crawford. Got her pregnant four years ago then refused to help with the baby."

"You're kidding. I thought this guy was supposed to be sooo charming." Nausea churned in Eliza's stomach at the thought of Hunter alone with Belle. Not for the first time did she wish Belle could remember the events of that evening. Even just the thought of Hunter trying to take advantage of Belle had a burning anger replacing the queasy sensation in her gut. Eliza clenched her fists.

"That's this bloke's specialty," Joy said, glancing at Eliza's white knuckles.

"Does anyone else know about this?"

"No. Even Willow was short on details. Apparently, Hunter didn't want it advertised that he'd 'spawned a little brat' with Paisley, and for some reason, she went along with it. Kept her lips sealed."

"Did Willow know why?"

"Not that she told me." Joy shook her head and sighed. "Paisley had to drop out of uni, and she's now a single mum barely scraping by. Willow claims the trauma of it all has essentially turned her mate into a shell of her former self."

"Poor girl." Eliza jotted down the information in her notebook.

"Hiya, Eliza and Joy." Monica's cheery voice rang out across the pub, and she waved as if she hadn't seen them for months instead of a few days ago.

Eliza returned her wave and smiled when the young woman settled into a chair between her and Joy. "Happy New Year, Monica."

"Cheers. Same to you both." Monica's brown eyes sparkled with a youth and vivacity Eliza only wished she possessed. At twenty-six, she was only seven years older than Monica but undoubtedly older by decades in spirit.

"Right, then." Joy planted her forearms on the table and leaned forward. "What can you tell us about Hunter?"

Monica's cheeks flushed as Eliza opened her notebook and clicked her pen. "He's exactly the sort of bloke every girl fancies but knows she shouldn't because he'll break her heart into a million pieces."

From Monica's pink cheeks to her fidgeting fingers, Eliza suspected Monica had learned the hard way that some men, no matter their good looks, were rotten to the core. "Not from personal experience, I hope."

"Let's say I learned my lesson without getting too badly burnt." Monica stared into her lap for several seconds before forcing a smile and shaking herself as if sloughing off his memory. "But we're not here to chat about me. How can I help?"

After the waitress dropped off the fish and chips and diet sodas and took Monica's order of tea, Eliza filled Monica in on the case so far, including the impending murder charges against Belle. "What else can you tell us?" she asked.

Monica's forehead scrunched. "That's difficult to say. He's a charming bloke—everyone says so—but oddly enough, they don't say that for long. Yet people keep—kept—getting caught in his web."

She sighed. "I know that doesn't help much, but I don't know how else to put it. He was a proper snake oil salesman who hoodwinked everyone and never got his comeuppance."

Joy snorted. "I've come across a few of his sort before. Always able to talk themselves out of sticky situations and leave their victims feeling like it was their fault all along, not his."

Monica snapped her fingers. "That's it! That's precisely how he was."

Eliza nibbled on a fry and jotted down the apt description of Hunter. "He oozed confidence when I met him last night. Too bad for him I have a pretty good radar for disingenuous people. If only I'd stopped Belle from going with him."

"She's a grown woman, and you're not her mum," Joy said.

"I know, but hindsight's always twenty-twenty. Knowing what I know now, I would have risked her wrath and locked her in one of Pemberley's hundreds of closets." Eliza took a deep breath, calming her racing thoughts. "What can you tell us about Paisley Foster?"

"Nothing much. She and I weren't close. She's a few years older than me. About your age, I think. All I know is that after Hunter got his claws into her, she was never the same again."

The waitress delivered Monica's tea, and after taking a bracing sip of the steaming liquid, Monica sighed. "I'm terribly sorry your friend got trapped in his web and that she's hurt because of it. I'm sure Wentworth will realize he's got the wrong woman when he sees that many others had far greater motives to kill Crawford. People who would have gladly sent him on to meet his maker."

"I hope so, too, but the evidence puts her at the scene of the crime." Eliza stared at her uneaten fish. "I know she didn't do it. She couldn't have. But when Wentworth gets a thought into his head, he's like a darn bulldog and won't let go."

Joy plopped a fry into her mouth. "Then we'll be the ones to unclench his jaws and make him see sense."

"You know Wentworth as well as I do. Might as well ask us to trek Mt. Everest. It'd be far easier," Eliza said. "The only way we'll convince him is with cold, hard facts."

"You two are far too much alike. Both as stubborn as mules, both born with bulldog tenacity." Joy grinned.

Eliza wanted to argue but knew Joy was right. "Anyway, where do we go from here? As much as I don't want to dig up old heartache, we need to talk to Paisley."

Monica shook her head. "Good luck with that one. She'd sooner slam the door in your face than talk to you. She's had enough of village busybodies and certainly won't tolerate you asking questions." Monica stirred her tea, the clinking of the spoon the only sound for several seconds. "You could start with Hunter's mate from uni, Lucinda Fairchild. She's an estate agent in town."

"Wait a minute. That name sounds familiar." Eliza tapped her chin then snapped her fingers. "Yes, she was on the guest list for the New Year's Eve ball. I don't remember whether she RSVP'd. She'd talk to us about Hunter, though?"

"Lucinda's a good egg. I'm certain she'll help however she can to see justice done for an old friend." Monica took a sip of her tea and set it down with a clink. "Sorry I wasn't much help."

"You were a great help." Eliza reached for Monica's bill.

"I can sort my own tea," Monica protested.

"Consider it a thank-you for coming out in this awful weather. Besides, you need to save every penny for university, right?"

Monica grinned. "Too right. Got a letter the other day. I was accepted into the University of Derby."

"Congratulations! That's fantastic," Eliza said. "What's the Trusty Teapot going to do without you?"

"They don't need to worry about that for ages yet. I won't start until autumn anyway." Monica checked her phone. "I'd best be off.

Told Mum I'd be back in time to help her prep for a big family supper. Cheers."

After Monica left, Eliza pushed her uneaten food around her plate with her fork. "I have a strange feeling this case is going to get messy."

"That's what happens when the victim spent his life hurting and taking advantage of people. I'm afraid sorting out the people who didn't fancy killing him will be our trickiest job." Joy stood. "Well, we can't crack this case sitting here."

Eliza drained the last of her drink and, after leaving cash with a generous tip for their waitress, followed Joy out of the pub, into the drizzling rain and thick fog. "At least the weather matches how I feel inside," she muttered, hauling herself into the Range Rover's passenger seat with a heavy sigh.

Chapter Four
Love of Money Is the Root of All Evil

Miss Crawford came for tea today, and while I have striven to give her the benefit of the doubt, my jaw aches from clenching my teeth in her presence. A particular gentleman of Darcy's and my acquaintance came up in conversation with other ladies present, and Miss Crawford made a most uncomfortable comment:

"Ten thousand a year covers a multitude of sins." What sins she was referencing, I have no idea. If she was merely referencing Mr. Stafford's occasional stammer and shyness, then I worry Miss Crawford's matrimonial pursuits will only lead her to heartache and loneliness.

Lizzy Bennet Darcy
Pemberley 1815

After getting Lucinda's contact information from her uncle, Eliza tapped out a text, asking if she'd mind meeting with them. Within minutes, Lucinda replied, inviting them to her house on the edge of Lambton.

Soon, Joy pulled up in front of Lucinda's home. From its cream-colored stone walls and thick wood trim to the thatched roof and red ivy climbing its walls, the cottage was something from a fairy tale. Smoke puffed from the brick chimney, completing the picture of the most English-looking home Eliza had ever seen.

Joy whistled. "Blimey, bet this place cost a pretty penny."

"How much?"

"Chocolate-box cottages like this fetch over six hundred thousand pounds. Trust me. I had a go at buying one before you arrived last year. I tried buying *this* one, actually." Joy pulled down the visor and checked her makeup in the tiny mirror. "It'd been shut up for ages with no one living in it, but it never went on the market. Whatever the reason, I was never able to get in contact with the owners. It's rather brilliant that you let me mooch off the Pemberley estate. Otherwise, I'd probably be holed up in some seedy flat or something."

"No, it's a good thing Uncle Fitzwilliam doesn't mind you pilfering from his brandy stash." Eliza chuckled, hopped out of the SUV, and hurried up the cobblestone walkway to knock on the green wooden door. "Well, here goes nothing."

Within seconds, the door opened, releasing the scent of cinnamon rolls and a blast of warm air. A petite woman in her thirties with red-rimmed eyes smiled at them. A stab of guilt pierced Eliza's conscience. There she and Joy were, bothering the woman while she was mourning her friend's death. *What kind of heartless person have I become?* Perhaps dealing with death too many times had numbed her to its reality.

"I'm so sorry. We shouldn't have come today of all days." Eliza turned to go.

"No, no, please. Come on in out of the wet and cold." She ushered them inside, took their coats, and hung them on a coat tree in the corner of the small entry. Turning to face them, she held out her hand in greeting. "I'm Lucinda Fairchild. Last night's party was such a crush that I didn't get a proper chance to introduce myself. Would you care for some tea? I've made cinnamon rolls. Would you like one?"

"No, thank you. I feel bad enough that we're even here." A waft of cinnamon teased Eliza's nose. Her earlier lack of appetite vanished, and her stomach growled. "We're sorry, and we can visit another time."

Lucinda waved away Eliza's second round of apologies. "Your stomach has other plans. Besides, we all deal with grief differently.

Mine is to bake and bury myself in the company of others. So, tea and cinnamon rolls?"

After exchanging glances with Joy, Eliza nodded. "That would be wonderful. Thank you."

Lucinda guided them down the short entryway, through an oak-framed doorway, and into the sitting room. White plaster walls gleamed in the well-lit space. A fire crackled and popped in the fireplace, casting dancing light onto the dark beams crossing the ceiling. Two oversize upholstered chairs faced the fireplace, and a mahogany coffee table overflowed with magazines and newspapers.

"You have a beautiful home," Eliza said as she settled into one of the chairs.

"Thank you. There was a lot to do to the house after I moved in, but it's all come together brilliantly. Do make yourselves comfortable. I'll be back with tea and treats."

"Must originally be from Cornwall," Joy said as she wandered about the room after Lucinda left.

"What makes you think that?" Eliza asked.

"I wasn't certain until she dropped the *h* on *house*. I've got several mates from Cornwall who, no matter how long they've been away from their home county or how much their accent has blended with another, give their West Country roots away somehow." Joy tucked her hands behind her back, examining the antique treasures scattered about. "This place has some real history. That's for certain."

Eliza stretched her socked feet toward the fire, willing the heat to seep into her chilled toes. "This is the coziest place I've ever been. Sometimes Pemberley's grandness makes it hard to feel at home. That's why I love Uncle's study so much."

Joy finished her tour of the room and settled into the matching chair. "I could curl up right here with a good book and read for hours."

The gentle tinkling of teacups accompanied Lucinda's soft laughter. "I've dreamed of doing exactly that on many occasions."

Eliza nudged a pile of magazines aside on the coffee table, clearing space for the silver platter of treats.

"Thank you. Please excuse the mess. I keep meaning to sort through this pile, but I spend more time at work than at home. By the time I get back, I haven't the energy for tidying." Lucinda offered a rueful grin. "I tell my clients who are busy getting their homes show ready to do as I say, not as I do." She poured the tea and gestured toward the tray. "Please, help yourselves."

Eliza selected a roll and took a bite. "Oh, this is amazing."

"Thank you. It's my nan's recipe." Lucinda pulled a wooden rocking chair from the corner by the fireplace closer to the coffee table and eased into it. "Every time I bake, I relive the most wonderful memories of her. I bake for that reason alone." She twirled a strand of dark-brown hair around her index finger and gazed into the fire.

Eliza brushed crumbs from her cream cable-knit sweater. "I'm sorry for what happened to your friend. It's truly terrible."

Lucinda ducked her head and studied the red roses painted on the teacup in her hands. "There's no need to apologize. Company's good to keep my mind off things." She smiled at Eliza. "Your text mentioned that you wanted to speak to me about Hunter. What exactly do you want to know? I'll admit he and I had lost touch several years ago, and despite living in the same area, we rarely saw each other except at special occasions like your ball last night."

Eliza filled Lucinda in on the day's events and Belle's arrest. "So, I'm trying to help my best friend, and to do that, I need to understand the victim."

"Because knowing the victim gives you a clearer picture of his killer?" Lucinda asked, scooting toward the edge of her chair.

"Yeah, that's the long and short of it," Joy said, reaching for a second roll.

"I'm so sorry your friend got caught up in all this. How dreadful." Lucinda shook her head. "I'll be happy to help you, but as I mentioned, he and I hadn't spoken much in recent years. I do know people who might be willing to talk to you. I could give you a list of their names and contact details. Would that help?"

"That would help more than you know." Eliza pulled her notebook from her pocket and handed it to Lucinda. "If you could jot down their names and numbers, that'd be wonderful."

Lucinda smiled. "I can do one better than that. I'll ring them first to let them know you'll be getting in touch. Some of these people are private, and they'll be more receptive if they know you're connected with someone they know and trust."

"I can't thank you enough for your help," Eliza said.

"Think nothing of it." Lucinda wrote a list of names in the notebook. "Your friend deserves her freedom, and Hunter ..." Her eyes filmed over with tears, and she fanned her face. "Sorry. It's still hard to talk about." She raised a hand when Eliza opened her mouth. "No, there's no need to apologize. Everyone deserves justice, yeah? And if I can help even in the smallest of ways, I'm all for it."

For the first time since Wentworth had broken the news that morning and settled Belle into the back of a police cruiser, a flicker of hope spurted to life.

B ack in the Range Rover, Eliza studied the list of names and numbers Lucinda had jotted down. Rain pelted the windows, and fog hung thickly in the air. For the second time that day, adrenaline drained from her system, leaving her exhausted and deflated. If the people on the list were anything like her, they'd resent being disturbed at home on such a dreary day and on a holiday, no less.

"I vote we leave these people alone until tomorrow. I'm sure Mr. Harry Foster, who I assume is Paisley's father, would rather we bother him tomorrow at his place of business than interrupt his holiday." An image of Belle sitting in a jail cell on New Year's Day flashed through Eliza's mind. "I wish I could visit Belle." She crossed her fingers that Wentworth would see reason in the next twenty-four hours.

"I know. If only we had Great-Aunt Iris with us. I'm sure she could create enough of a distraction to buy you a few precious moments." Joy backed out of the driveway and headed toward Pemberley.

Eliza snorted. "Knowing Wentworth, I'm sure he's already warned his constables about innocent-looking white-haired ladies and told them not to trust anyone. Besides, we can't help clear Belle's name if we're locked in a cell right next to her."

Fifteen minutes later, Joy and Eliza joined Uncle Fitzwilliam, Great-Aunt Iris, Heath, and Willoughby in the study. The familiar scent of leather and old books soothed Eliza's frayed nerves. After ordering tea, she collapsed onto a leather couch, rested her head on Heath's shoulder, and filled everyone in on her and Joy's conversation with Lucinda.

"Her name sounds familiar," Willoughby said. "I think I danced with her when I couldn't find Joy to rescue me from Melissa." He winked at Joy then looked about in confusion when she tilted her chin up and glared at him.

"Did she happen to mention she knew Hunter?" Eliza asked.

"No. We made small talk. The weather. The food. Her dress." He grimaced. "I wasn't aware that two people could talk about a single dress for so long."

Heath chuckled. "Sounds riveting."

"Oh, if you only knew the trials and tribulations of not usually liking maroon but not being able to resist the cut and buying it anyway for the party." Willoughby smirked and studied his cuticles. "But that's what separates the posh from the philistines."

Great-Aunt Iris studied them for a moment and harrumphed. "Looks like we've all come up against a wall. Fitzwilliam and I found nothing in those old documents except proof that Berryhill Manor and Pemberley have feuded since the 1800s. The original Berryhill Manor owner, Henry Crawford, sued the first Fitzwilliam Darcy for encroaching on Berryhill land, and it's been a sore spot between our families ever since. Whatever new evidence the Crawfords claim to have is as ridiculous as their dress sense."

Uncle Fitzwilliam drummed his fingers on his mahogany desk. "Be that as it may, I doubt the land dispute plays any role in Hunter's murder."

"I agree," Eliza said. "We need to concentrate on who Hunter was. From what Monica told us at the pub, Hunter was a toxic charmer who got what he wanted, left his victims blaming themselves and too embarrassed to speak up, and escaped any repercussions for his actions."

"Sounds like a right bloody arse if you ask me," Willoughby said then blushed when Great-Aunt Iris pinned him with a regal glare. "Sorry, Mrs. Darcy."

Great-Aunt Iris *tsk*ed. "Don't apologize to me, young man. In a case as serious as this, you should have used stronger language. That man was rotten to the core." She harrumphed and returned to her knitting with renewed vigor.

Eliza tilted her head and studied her great-aunt. From her reaction to Hunter's presence at the ball to the red blotches staining her cheeks as she knitted viciously, Eliza sensed there was something her great-aunt was keeping close to her chest. "You're not wrong. If half of what Monica said is true, there's a long list of people out there who, if they go to his funeral, will be there only to make sure he's dead."

"Good riddance to bad rubbish, I say." Great-Aunt Iris looked around the room, blushed more deeply, and dipped her head.

Heath gave a low whistle. "That's not the picture I got from my uni mates. His legacy at Oxford is still that he was a charming but elusive bloke. Some even joked he was the British Great Gatsby. Always had wads of cash and threw the wildest parties, but no one knew how or where he got his money. Rumor has it that after he became an investment banker, his wealth only exploded."

"Did you go to university at the same time as him?" Eliza asked.

"He's older than me by a few years. I'm twenty-nine, so he was in his early thirties."

"Thirty-four to be precise," Uncle Fitzwilliam said.

"Did anyone have a grudge against him?" Eliza asked.

"Not the ones I spoke to," Heath said. "All they could remember was the mystery that surrounded him. I have a few more people on my list, but I couldn't reach them today."

"So we have a mysterious Great Gatsby character with a talent for charming people to their destruction then leaving them guilty and alone while he gallivants off to work on his next victim?" Joy asked.

Willoughby cleared his throat. "I... uh... know I'm new to whatever it is you all are doing, but shouldn't we focus on where he got his money? Not many students have boatloads of cash to throw massive parties that make them campus legends. Unless they're from money, of course."

"Willoughby has a point." Eliza smiled at him. "What are some ways a college student could get their hands on that type of money?"

Great-Aunt Iris's knitting needles, which had been clicking and clacking so forcefully that Eliza feared they'd snap in two, stopped. The room fell silent. Her knuckles whitened around the needles. "He swindled innocent people out of their life savings."

Uncle Fitzwilliam's brow furrowed. "How do you know this?"

"Because... Because he fleeced me out of thousands a few years back with an investment opportunity that I should have known was too good to be true."

Uncle Fitzwilliam sat beside her on the chaise longue and gently took her hand. "Oh, I'm terribly sorry, Aunt Iris. Why didn't you say anything? I might have been able to help you."

Great-Aunt Iris studied the tips of her white sneakers. "And admit I was a daft old woman taken in by a smooth-talking charmer like him?" She shook her head. "No, I was too embarrassed by my own foolishness to tell anyone, including your uncle William. He still doesn't know."

For the first time in her life, Eliza finally understood what it meant to see red. Anger spread through her like wildfire, sweat beading on her skin. "How much did he steal from you?" she asked, her voice as gentle as her clogged throat would allow.

"Twenty thousand pounds."

Eliza's gasp disappeared among the others' cries of horror. Only Great-Aunt Iris remained silent, sitting stoically upright.

Uncle Fitzwilliam unleashed words Eliza hadn't thought him capable of, while the younger generation peppered the air with colorful adjectives about Hunter.

Eventually, they all ran out of steam. Several seconds of silence filled the study.

"There's no fool like an old fool." The defeat in Great-Aunt Iris's voice broke Eliza's heart.

"You are not a fool." Eliza held her hands. "You are not, and no one in this room will let you believe that about yourself. You're one of the wisest people I know. Hunter victimized you. That's not your fault."

"He didn't force me to give it to him, my dear. I was taken in by his good looks, his charm, and his lies about how our business venture would finally bring the two families together and end generations of silent war. I fell for it." Her eyes filled with tears. "I invested that money for you, you know. Long before I met you and without ever thinking I would, I planned to gift you the proceeds after my death." A tear dripped down her wrinkled cheek and plopped onto the back of Eliza's hand. "He stole your inheritance."

Eliza embraced her. "I'm so sorry, but the money doesn't matter to me. If I had to choose between getting an inheritance from you and finally meeting you, spending my days with you, I'd choose you every time."

Great-Aunt Iris sniffled and gently pulled back from Eliza's embrace. "There, there. Enough of this nonsense." She patted Eliza's cheek and offered a quivering smile. "Don't you worry about an old bird like me. You've got a murder to solve and a friend to save."

The door to Uncle Fitzwilliam's study opened, and Tash entered, pushing a tea trolley laden with petit fours, finger sandwiches, and steaming tea.

"Tash, what are you doing here? I thought I gave everyone the day off."

"I didn't think it right to leave, miss. Not with everything that's going on. Mrs. Bankcroft stayed on as well."

Eliza's heart swelled, and she jumped to her feet, giving the stoic butler a hug. "Thank you, Tash. But... your families. Surely you both had plans."

Tash's face flushed crimson, and he awkwardly patted her back before untangling himself from her embrace. "I will take my holiday after you've solved this case, Miss Eliza." He surveyed everyone's faces, and his craggy features tightened with worry. "Is everything all right, Miss Eliza? Have you received word about your friend Miss Knightley?"

"No news yet, but we're hopeful that Wentworth comes to his senses soon." When Tash's gaze swept across the assembled company, Eliza sighed. "We were discussing the unlikeable character of Hunter."

Joy muttered, "Bloody tosser."

"I'm afraid Miss Bingley is right." Tash's craggy face turned stonelike.

"Did you know him?" Uncle Fitzwilliam asked.

"Yes, sir." Tash's normally stoic voice had an edge.

"I take it the acquaintance wasn't a friendly one?" Eliza asked gently. "Do you mind telling us how you knew him? It might help our investigation."

Tash drew himself up to his full height and squared his shoulders. "I don't mind at all, Miss Eliza. He bilked my mother out of her life savings, leaving her penniless. I believe the stress and shame proved too much for her already-fragile health, and she passed away soon after."

"I'm so sorry, Tash. How awful," Eliza said softly. "Did she contact the police?"

"No, miss. By the time she realized what had happened, it was too late. Even when I urged her to report it, she was too ashamed to admit she'd been taken in by such a bounder. She couldn't bear the thought of anyone knowing."

"That seems to be his MO," Heath said. "Charm them and leave them high and dry. I wonder how many people he swindled. Lambton is a tight-knit community, and people do talk."

"But not about their deepest shame," Great-Aunt Iris said. "Those people, particularly ones of the old guard like me, tend to bury such humiliations deep."

Willoughby rose and poured himself and Joy each a cup of tea. "So, what we have here is a victim everyone had reason to kill."

"And I have a strange suspicion our list is going to grow longer the more we dig into Hunter's dealings." Eliza piled a plate with tiny desserts and sandwiches and sat next to Heath, offering him some. "Tomorrow, Joy and I will visit Harry, since he's first on the list that Lucinda gave us."

"If you don't mind my saying so, Miss Eliza, Harry is a decent chap," Tash said.

"Do you know him well?" Uncle Fitzwilliam asked.

"Yes, sir. He moved into the area several years ago from up north. Yorkshire, I believe. We connected through our church. He's as solid as they come, sir."

"Did he ever speak to you about Hunter?" Eliza asked hopefully.

"I'm afraid not, Miss Eliza."

Eliza bit into a dainty cucumber sandwich and chewed thoughtfully. "His daughter is Paisley Foster?"

"Yes, miss." He frowned. "Dreadful business about his girl. She had such a bright future before some bounder got his claws into her."

"Did Harry give any indication who the man was?" Eliza asked.

"No, I'm afraid Harry kept that close to his chest." Tash tipped his head. "If there's nothing else, sir?"

Uncle Fitzwilliam smiled appreciatively. "No, that will be all, Tash. Thank you for your insight."

After Tash left, Willoughby was the first to break the silence. "That's another name added to our who-wanted-Hunter-dead list."

"It'd be easier at this point to figure out who *didn't* want him dead," Heath said.

"What a life he led." Uncle Fitzwilliam settled in his leather chair behind his desk. "Imagine, instead of people queuing up to sing your praises, people have to work out who despised you least and had the smallest motive to do you in."

"His friend Lucinda was genuinely bothered," Eliza said.

Joy snorted. "I imagine the only ones truly cut up by his death are his parents."

The study door opened, and Tash reentered, his face drawn. "Lord Darcy, Mr. and Mrs. Crawford are here to see you. I've put them in the drawing room."

After the door shut, Uncle Fitzwilliam massaged his temples. "Speak of the devil."

Worry crept into Eliza's thoughts. "Are they here to accuse you of wrongdoing in Hunter's death?"

"I've no clue." Uncle Fitzwilliam walked toward the door.

Another thought struck Eliza like a blow. *What if they're here to make a fuss about Belle, accusing her of killing their son?*

Eliza jumped to her feet. "Can I come with you?"

"Of course, but why?"

"Because I'd like to get a read on them. Besides, if they start throwing accusations around about family and friends, I want to be there to defend them."

Uncle Fitzwilliam gestured for her to go ahead, and Eliza straightened her shoulders, raised her chin, and prepared to meet the parents of a charming con man everyone had reason to murder.

Chapter Five
Kooky Crawfords and a Gossiping Cook

I no longer know what to think of our new neighbors. At an assembly in Lambton last evening, I spoke with Lady Dennison, who informed me that Miss Crawford has made several pointed inquiries among our acquaintance about Darcy's connections and Pemberley's income. Lady Dennison, not one to speak out of turn, mentioned as well that Mr. Crawford has been paying particular attention to her daughter. She's a sweet girl with thirty thousand pounds, but I fear that it is not Honoria's personality that draws the charming Mr. Crawford.
Lizzy Bennet Darcy
Pemberley 1815

As Eliza and Uncle Fitzwilliam walked down the main hallway toward the drawing room, Eliza checked her watch and stifled a yawn. It wasn't quite six o'clock, but New Year's Day had felt like an entire year.

Uncle Fitzwilliam rested a hand on her shoulder. "Why don't you get some rest? I can handle the Crawfords."

From the glint in his eyes to his steely jaw, Eliza knew he could handle the pair, but she needed to meet them herself. She couldn't imagine being a parent to such a despicable person, and as someone who believed in nurture over nature, Eliza suspected the Crawfords had raised a spoiled brat who took whatever he wanted from people he considered weaker than him.

"No, meeting them will give me deeper insight into Hunter, and I'll need all the help I can get with this case."

"I'm afraid you're right." Uncle Fitzwilliam paused at the drawing room door, pulled his shoulders back, and pushed it open, wearing an appropriately somber expression. "Mr. and Mrs. Crawford, please accept my deepest condolences on the tragic loss of your son."

"Most kind of you, Lord Darcy. The news has left my wife and me shattered, I'm afraid," Hubert Crawford said, looking every inch the country gentleman in gray trousers, a white dress shirt, a tie, and a blue velvet coat that suspiciously resembled a man's smoking jacket. He stood and offered his hand to Uncle Fitzwilliam.

"Please do call me Fitzwilliam. We've been neighbors far too long to stand on such tedious ceremony, wouldn't you say?" He gestured for Hubert to sit and settled into the chaise longue across from the Crawfords.

Eliza sat beside her uncle, and while he continued expressing his sympathies, she studied the married couple. She'd only glimpsed them across a busy ballroom the night before in their New Year's finery of fancy matching flannel outfits. Before entering the drawing room, Eliza had expected them to look tired and worn out, their eyes red rimmed and their noses scarlet from grieving. Instead of looking like bereft parents, however, they sat stoically across from her and Uncle Fitzwilliam as if they were discussing nothing more than the weather.

Hunter's mother, Henrietta, especially looked unfazed by her son's death, a far cry from what Eliza thought a mother would look like after losing a child. Her eyes showed no hint of tears, and her cheeks and nose remained peach colored and unblemished. The woman looked positively ageless and untouched by grief.

No white or silver streaked her dark-auburn hair, and whether the color was natural or not, the woman's forehead remained smooth. Eliza rubbed her index finger over her own forehead, noticing a few wrinkles, most notably her what-in-the-heck wrinkle that formed from her confusion at others' stupidity. Henrietta Crawford had clearly had work done, and from her tight expressions, Eliza figured Botox was a large contributor to the fifty-something-year-old woman's inability to show emotion.

Hubert, on the other hand, looked his age. His silver hair was cut with military precision, and wrinkles etched the man's face. But like his wife, he showed no signs of grieving.

Eliza's heart sank. While Hunter had been a wastrel in life who deserved jail time for destroying people's lives, the fact that his parents seemed unfazed by his passing tugged at her heartstrings.

"Isn't that so, Eliza?"

Eliza blinked and stared at her uncle. "I'm sorry?"

"I was telling the Crawfords that we're willing to help out as much as we can during their time of grieving."

"Yes, right, of course." Eliza smiled apologetically. "I'm sorry. Last night's tragic events are so awful. I keep getting caught up in my thoughts, trying to process it all."

Henrietta dabbed her dry eyes with an equally dry handkerchief. "Yes, poor Hubert and I have been beside ourselves."

Eliza's eyebrow twitched. "Yes, I'm sure. I can't imagine what you're going through. My great-aunt Iris always says that a little spot of tea goes a long way to soothe frayed nerves. Would you like some?" Eliza walked to the bell pull and tugged it once.

"Oh, you are a dear," Henrietta said. "Tea sounds lovely. You're most fortunate in your cook, Miss Darcy—"

"Eliza, please."

"Then you must call me Henrietta." The offer sounded as artificial as her claims of woe.

"Well, then, Henrietta, I couldn't agree more about Mrs. Bankcroft. She's Pemberley's secret weapon. That's for sure." Noting the greedy glint in Henrietta's eyes and suspecting the woman might try poaching Pemberley's cook for herself, Eliza leaned forward and whispered conspiratorially, "She's often told me she's gotten offers from other estates, but she's firmly sent them on their ear, as she puts it."

Henrietta sighed, the largest scene of emotion she'd displayed yet. "Yes, good and loyal staff is so hard to come by these days. Isn't that so, dear?" She placed a hand on her husband's thigh.

Hubert nearly jumped from his seat, stared questioningly at her hand, and sputtered, "Quite so, my dear. Quite so. Veritable revolving door of staff."

"Sadly, they leave as quickly as they arrive, and I'm not sure why." Henrietta sniffled delicately.

Eliza exchanged meaningful looks with her uncle. It hadn't taken her long since arriving at Pemberley to understand what earned staff loyalty. Trust between both parties was essential. She still dealt daily with her surly housekeeper, Mrs. Underhill, whom Eliza suspected of being Nancy's spy. Only her uncle's unwillingness to dismiss someone without proof kept the woman employed.

"An exodus I hope will soon end," Hubert said, an edge to his voice.

"Whatever do you mean, my dear?" Henrietta asked.

Hubert's laugh rang empty and hollow. "Do you not know? How can you be so blind?"

"You can't mean to suggest that our Hunter had anything to do with—"

"Hunter was a bad egg, and his carrying on with the female servants left Berryhill Manor without proper staff for months." He glared at his wife with such disgust that Eliza cringed.

Uncomfortable silence filled the room. Eliza breathed a sigh of relief when Tash entered, pushing a tea trolley.

After serving tea and ensuring everyone had at least one biscuit, Eliza sat and looked expectantly at her uncle.

He took the cue. "Hubert, while I've enjoyed our conversation, I'm still puzzled about what brought you here so soon after... such a recent tragedy."

Hubert dabbed the corners of his mouth with his napkin. "Ah, yes. I thought you should know that I'm dropping the lawsuit against you for property rights infringement. No need to disturb old dirt, is there? Let bygones be bygones, eh?" He raised his teacup in a toast to Uncle Fitzwilliam.

Uncle Fitzwilliam quirked an eyebrow at Eliza and raised his teacup to the Crawfords. "Indeed, let bygones be bygones."

What was that about?" Eliza asked Uncle Fitzwilliam as they walked back to his study.

"I haven't a clue. That was one of the most peculiar meetings I've had in ages, and I can't fathom why they came here today—of all days—to announce they're dropping the lawsuit. One that he was more than willing to threaten me with not long ago."

"Maybe inviting them to the ball worked," Eliza said.

Uncle Fitzwilliam clasped his hands behind his back. "As much as I'd like to believe that, Eliza, I suspect there's more to all this than meets the eye."

"You're right. It's strange that hours after their son's death, they come to us—dry-eyed, I might add—showing more emotion over losing staff than losing their son. They could have waited days, even weeks, to tell you they'd changed their minds about the lawsuit."

"Not if they have an attorney on retainer. Those bills add up quickly. It's not a coincidence that they dropped the lawsuit hours after Hunter died."

"Hunter seems to be at the center of everything." The weight of the case settled in Eliza's chest like a brick. She paused as they neared the study door. "I can't believe Belle was out in those woods at night with him. She's as stubborn as the day is long, but she's not stupid. What could she possibly have been doing? Was Hunter going to attack her? Did the killer plan on killing her, too, but she escaped fast enough? And what happens if I can't solve this before Wentworth charges Belle with murder? I can't fail my friend. I can't."

Uncle Fitzwilliam rested his hands on her shoulders. "In the short time I've known you, you've struck me as a young woman who doesn't give up until the job is done. I'm not saying the journey will be easy. Quite the opposite—"

"Can we skip to the part where you say I won't fail and that I'll get Belle and me to our destination unscathed and without blood, sweat, or tears?"

"I'm afraid I can't promise that, but I'll do everything I can to help. Don't forget your sleuthing team either. Your assortment of oddballs works well together." He massaged the back of his neck and mumbled, "Somehow."

Great-Aunt Iris's grand scolding leaked through the oak study door. At Willoughby's hurried apologies, Eliza shared knowing looks with her uncle.

Uncle Fitzwilliam smiled. "Besides, with Aunt Iris as your secret weapon, what more could you possibly need?"

Eliza pushed open the door and paused.

Willoughby cowered in the corner of a leather couch while Great-Aunt Iris stood over him, her knitting needles quivering with indignation. Joy stood nearby, her face crimson with suppressed laughter and her hand clamped firmly over her mouth. Heath sat on the other side of the couch, shaking his head at the spectacle.

Uncle Fitzwilliam and Eliza burst into laughter, and all four of them turned toward the door. Great-Aunt Iris lowered her knitting needles and attempted a contrite look that crumpled the moment her Cheshire cat grin reappeared.

"What in the world is going on?" Eliza asked.

Joy gestured toward Willoughby. "I'm afraid that the village idiot—"

"Hey!" Willoughby slid to the front of the couch but slunk back when Great-Aunt Iris shot him a withering glare.

Joy's grin widened. "Anyway, *Willoughby* had the cheek to claim that Agatha Christie was by no means the queen of mystery and that Her Majesty could have bestowed the title of dame upon a more deserving author."

"Rookie mistake," Heath muttered.

"I beg your pardon, young man? What was that?" Great-Aunt Iris cocked her head like a bird of prey.

"I said Willoughby's an idiot, ma'am." He flashed a winning smile at her.

Great-Aunt Iris preened. "Quite right. Just so we're all clear on this matter." She pointed a knitting needle at Willoughby like a sword. "Now then. What have you to say for yourself, young man?"

"Dame Agatha Christie is indeed brilliant, as you've pointed"—he eyed the tip of her knitting needle warily—"out thoroughly, Mrs. Darcy."

"There. You're forgiven, Mr. Willoughby. I'm beginning to see what Joy finds appealing about you." She tottered back to her chair, settled into it with a heavy sigh, and resumed her knitting.

Jack Willoughby's lips moved silently, as if he were struggling to work out what the octogenarian had said. Joy's face went pale, and blotchy patches of color mottled her cheeks. Heath leaned over, clapped Willoughby on the shoulder, and muttered something Eliza couldn't make out.

Eliza leaned toward her uncle. "This is the dream team you were talking about earlier?"

"The very one, I'm afraid," he said, laughter dancing in his voice.

Eliza sat on the arm of the couch next to Heath. "At least you weren't the victim of knitting needles this time."

"New year, new us." He gestured toward the white-haired lady placidly knitting in her chair.

"More likely Willoughby is still new to the ropes. After he leaves tomorrow, your ribs will be reacquainted with her needles," Eliza said.

"I'm afraid you're right." Heath narrowed his gaze at Great-Aunt Iris. "She looks so sweet and innocent, doesn't she? You'd hardly think her capable—"

"Of death by knitting needle." Willoughby plunked his head against the back of the couch.

Joy rolled her eyes. "Oh, quit your whinging, Willoughby. You look perfectly intact to me."

"As if you'd care." Willoughby pouted. "You bloody well stood by while she threatened to skewer me with the same instrument she's currently using to knit a baby blanket. If that's not cold-blooded, I don't know what is."

"Just wait until she starts going on about all the enemies she took out during the war." Eliza grinned.

January 2 dawned bright and cold. Eliza shivered and pulled the covers over her chilled nose. *If Pemberley's rooms can still be cold enough to nip at my nose, what must it have been like for the poor souls who lived here before central heating?*

Groaning, she rolled over and scowled at the frost coating her window. The only thing that could truly warm her was Heath's embrace, but since he'd left the night before to prepare for a long day at the office, she had only Mrs. Bankcroft's coffee to look forward to. Even Caesar had abandoned her that night, choosing Great-Aunt Iris over her.

Eliza threw back the covers, ran to the bathroom en suite, plugged in the heater, and stood directly in front of it. Despite the warm air blowing on her, she shivered as she readied herself for the day. After sweeping her long black hair into a messy bun, she pulled on a pair of insulated leggings and an oversize wool sweater and slid her feet into slippers. A glance in the mirror confirmed she'd been up half the night tossing and turning. She made a face and mumbled, "Good enough for who it's for," then left her room in search of coffee and breakfast.

Bypassing the breakfast room for the moment, Eliza traipsed into the kitchen and plunked down on the barstool next to Mrs. Bankcroft's working station.

"Morning, lass." Mrs. Bankcroft lifted the mass of dough, thunked it on the countertop, and with her plump hands continued to knead the mass. "Looks like you didn't get a wink of sleep last night, did you?"

"It's that obvious?" While sleep had evaded her, visions of her best friend sitting alone in a jail cell hadn't. Add to that the real nightmare that Wentworth could arrest Belle for Hunter's murder, and Eliza hadn't slept at all.

Mrs. Bankcroft jerked her chin toward the coffeepot. "Help yourself to some coffee, my dear. There's tea if you want it, but coffee's what you need."

Eliza grunted as she slid off the stool and shuffled to the coffeepot. She poured the steaming beverage into a rose-embossed china cup and settled back on the stool. After taking a bracing sip, she sighed. "Have you ever lived a nightmare, Mrs. B.?"

Mrs. Bankcroft thumped the dough with extra energy. "I lived with Mr. Bankcroft for the better part of twenty years, lass."

When no explanation came, Eliza swallowed another sip and studied the woman before her. She opened her mouth to ask for clarification but took in how Mrs. Bankcroft was punching the dough ball and thought better of it. "What can you tell me about the Crawfords?"

Eliza had dreamt of them the previous night as well—the parents who seemed glad their son was dead and the quick and strange dropping of a property rights case they'd threatened her uncle with weeks before the New Year's Eve ball. Staff of large estates knew more about the estate and neighboring properties than the owners, and if anyone had their finger on the pulse of Pemberley and Berryhill Manor, Mrs. Bankcroft did. Since Eliza hadn't been the one to talk to the staff the other day, she wanted to hear it directly from the cook.

Mrs. Bankcroft paused in her kneading of the dough ball. "They're a bunch of nutters, or so I hear tell."

"In what way?"

"I don't hold with idle chatter."

"It's not idle chatter, Mrs. B. It's part of my investigation."

Mrs. B.'s left eyebrow shot to her hairline, and she snorted. "So that's what you young people are calling it nowadays." At Eliza's huff, she waved her flour-covered hand in surrender. "Berryhill Manor's cook, Mrs. Carmichael, and I go way back to school days, and according to her, the Crawfords can't keep hold of staff for love or money. Something to do with the wandering hands of their son." Mrs. Bankcroft began rolling out the dough. "The lad even tried it on with Mrs. Carmichael, who put a flea in his ear, I can tell you."

"Why, she's old enough to be his—" At Mrs. Bankcroft's scowl, Eliza smiled. "His mother, at least."

Eliza wasn't sure about Mrs. Bankcroft's age, but from the lines on her face and the stoop in her shoulders, she had clearly seen plenty of what life had to offer. If Eliza had to guess, which she did, since she wasn't about to ask for clarification on Mrs. B.'s age, she'd place the woman in her mid-sixties.

"No, there's something not right about that boy. God rest his soul. Always has been, according to the staff. They eventually had to switch to an all-male staff, barring Mrs. Carmichael, of course, but that soon went to pot since most men don't fancy doing women's work."

What Tash had said about his mother and what Great-Aunt Iris had said about Hunter and her money kept nagging at her. "Have you heard about anyone losing money to Hunter?"

Mrs. Bankcroft set down the rolling pin and leaned across the counter. "You didn't hear this from me, lass, but Mrs. Carmichael whispered about... oh, a few years back now... that the Crawfords were in a right state financially and had to let most of their staff go—the ones they'd managed not to lose to the roaming hands of their son. Word was they'd lost it all in a dodgy investment."

"Was Hunter behind it?"

"That, I don't know, but from what I do know of that poor excuse for a man—God rest his soul—he took what he wanted, how he wanted, and when he wanted, no matter the cost." Mrs. Bankcroft returned to rolling out the dough. "Makes me appreciate and love you Darcys more and more every time I hear tales from other estates. You and your uncle and his father before him always knew how to treat your staff properly."

Eliza squeezed Mrs. Bankcroft's hand. "You're the absolute best. Thank you for the coffee."

Mrs. Bankcroft blushed. "Get along with you, lass. I'll have breakfast up presently and can't finish with you nattering on and peppering me with questions."

Eliza squished the cook in a quick hug, grabbed her coffee, and hustled from the kitchen before Mrs. Bankcroft could react to her show of affection.

As Eliza walked to the breakfast room, she turned over in her mind the news Mrs. Bankcroft had shared. Hunter's wandering hands had driven a wedge between the family members, and if the Crawfords had lost money in a bad deal because of their son's poor advice or deliberate misdirection, that could give the parents reason not to mourn his death.

Eliza paused at the breakfast room's entrance. Perhaps that was what the land dispute was about. It could have been Hunter's idea to dig up the old claim. Uncle Fitzwilliam had mentioned that the Crawfords claimed they had new evidence. *What if it was a forged document to strengthen their case?* If it had worked and they'd won the suit, Uncle Fitzwilliam would have paid a substantial sum.

Eliza's heart pounded. Perhaps the Crawfords were guilty of more than being unfeeling parents. With their son's bad behavior and role in their financial ruin, they could be guilty of his murder.

Chapter Six

Great-Aunt Iris and the Rather Dishy Butcher

Adelaide Rose caused commotion this morning when she escaped her nursemaid and tore into the garden with wild abandon when the Crawfords were calling. While both siblings were all smiles and complimented her spirited nature, I noticed Miss Crawford's expression when she thought no one was looking. I sincerely doubt Miss Crawford's outward show of warmth. Perhaps she will not improve upon acquaintance.

Lizzy Bennet Darcy
Pemberley 1815

Eliza entered the breakfast room and gaped at Belle, who sat slumped in a chair, slowly stirring the steaming beverage before her. Wentworth sat beside her, and the look he sent Eliza suggested all was not well. Uncle Fitzwilliam sat at his usual spot at the head of the table, his face drawn and pale.

"Belle." Eliza settled herself next to her and brought her into a side hug. Her heart twisted at Belle's haggard looks.

Belle rested her head on Eliza's shoulder, and tears trickled down her cheeks.

Eliza skewered Wentworth with a look. "You promised you'd take good care of her."

"I did. She got the proper medical attention, and I even arranged for her to have one of the best of my cells. Sadly for your friend here, jail cells aren't designed for comfort, and one rarely enjoys a decent night's sleep under such circumstances."

Eliza was about to remind Wentworth that she'd saved him from learning that firsthand several months ago, but at her uncle's quick head shake, she bit her tongue. "So, I take it you aren't going to arrest Belle for Hunter's murder?"

A sob wracked Belle's body. Normally strong and athletic, Belle looked as fragile as a newborn calf.

"Let me get her to bed, then we can talk." Eliza didn't wait for Wentworth's reply. She eased Belle to her feet and helped her out of the room and up the stairs. "Oh, Belle, I can't believe this is happening to you. I'm so sorry."

Belle's laugh came out harsh and bitter. "Don't apologize. You didn't do anything wrong. I did. I failed myself. I failed my common sense. I should have known something was off about him. Whatever possessed me to go out alone with him, I'll never know."

Eliza paused as they reached Belle's bedroom door. "Don't say that. This wasn't your fault." When Belle refused to meet her gaze, Eliza gently lifted Belle's chin until their eyes met. "This. Wasn't. Your. Fault. Hunter took you out to those woods, and even if you don't remember what happened, I can guarantee he didn't have respectable plans. You got caught in his web, one he used to trap many women, I'm sad to say."

Belle bit her bottom lip. "I feel so stupid."

Eliza opened Belle's bedroom door and pulled down the bedsheets. "You are one of the smartest people I know. Now, let's get you to bed. After some rest, maybe you can remember pieces of New Year's Eve, okay?"

She tucked Belle in then left the room and closed the door behind her. Leaning against the doorframe, she closed her eyes. Eliza had never seen her friend in such a broken state, and it shattered her heart. She pushed away the feeling of dread settling over her. She would not—could not—fail her friend.

With renewed purpose, Eliza returned to the breakfast room and settled across from Wentworth, watching him wrap up his conversation with Uncle Fitzwilliam. She'd worked with Wentworth long enough to know his bark was worse than his bite, and he wasn't a fool. While he bristled at her interference, he never let pride get in the way of seeing reason, even when her theories sounded absurd. If she had to trust anyone with her friend's future, she was glad it was Wentworth.

He turned to face her, clasped his hands, and placed them on the table. "How's she faring?"

The genuine concern in his voice made Eliza's throat tighten. "She's had better days, but a few hours of sleep should help her feel better and remember what happened the other night." She rubbed her forehead. "Belle didn't say anything, did she?"

"No. She can't remember a thing. I'm still waiting on the tox report, and the lab is backed up donkey's years." Wentworth sighed. "I know you don't think highly of me right now, Eliza, but my intention is to find Hunter's killer, not punish a possible victim, and the more I think about it, the more I believe your friend was a potential victim of his rather than the killer." He gestured for her to sit when she shot to her feet. "That doesn't mean everything's sorted, mind you. Don't get your hopes up. She remains a viable suspect, and while I can't legally charge her now, as I have no evidence directly tying her to the case, she's still on my watch list."

"You said you don't think she did it."

"I *don't* think she did, but all the circumstantial evidence points to her. The lab and DNA results won't come back for weeks, and I have nothing concrete to hold her on, let alone charge her with."

"But she flies back to the States in two weeks."

"We'll cross that bridge when we come to it. For now, I'm releasing Belle into your hands, sans passport, trusting that you'll take proper care of her while I dig further into this case." He pointed at her. "And you keep your nose out of police business."

"You know I can't do that. Not with Belle involved. Besides, what would have happened if I hadn't stuck my nose in your business back in October, huh?"

Wentworth shot a glance at Uncle Fitzwilliam, and when he found no support there, he turned his attention back on Eliza. "Just don't get in my way."

"Likewise." Eliza crossed her arms.

Uncle Fitzwilliam's lips twitched. "Come now, you two. You're the finest team of crime solvers this side of the Atlantic. If anyone can bring a hasty conclusion to this dreadful business quickly, it's you two."

"And us, Fitzwilliam." Great-Aunt Iris shuffled into the room, wearing a marmalade-colored tracksuit, Caesar nipping at a piece of yarn trailing from her purse and Joy at her side. "You can't forget the real stars of this group."

"What about Heath?" Joy asked.

"We won't tell him he's the weakest link, but every group has one. Luckily for him, he's handsome enough to earn his keep." Great-Aunt Iris settled into her chair and dropped her large purse at her feet. Caesar pounced on the string and, within seconds, had tangled himself in baby-blue yarn.

Eliza rolled her eyes and helped the mewling feline out of his mess. After he was freed, he looked at Eliza as it were her fault and lay at Great-Aunt Iris's feet, his back to his owner.

Tash and the other staff members brought in breakfast, arranging everything on the buffet.

Once everyone had loaded their plates with scrambled eggs, sausages, the American- style biscuits Mrs. Bankcroft made specially for Eliza, and fruit and settled back into their seats, Eliza asked Wentworth to share any new information.

"How about quid pro quo?" Wentworth stabbed a piece of sausage and chewed thoughtfully.

Eliza told him everything they'd learned about Hunter, from his wandering hands to his shady financial dealings, including the money he'd taken from his own parents. When Uncle Fitzwilliam's brow furrowed, she filled everyone in on her conversation with Mrs. Bankcroft.

"That's odd," Joy said. "She didn't mention any of that when Willoughby and I questioned the staff yesterday."

"I had to convince her I wasn't fishing for gossip and that I was conducting a real investigation."

Joy popped a grape into her mouth. "Right, then. Note to self: channel my inner English teacher and play the semantics game for proper results."

Eliza wanted to believe Joy's jest, but she was ninety-nine point nine percent sure semantics wouldn't help her solve a crime that had killed one man and put an innocent woman under the scowling gaze of Detective Chief Inspector Finn Wentworth.

An hour later, Eliza checked on Belle and found her softly snoring. She eased out of the room and nearly knocked Great-Aunt Iris over.

Eliza grabbed her shoulders to keep her from toppling. "Sorry about that! You're like a ninja, though. Didn't even hear you coming."

Great-Aunt Iris's grin nearly reached her ears. "You're not the first to say that in the past two days." Her smile turned cheeky. "That's what I've been telling you since you arrived at Pemberley, my girl. Nobody notices me. They think anyone with white hair and wrinkles is a daft old biddy who's lost the plot. Little do they know my brain's as sharp as a tack."

While Eliza's great-aunt looked like the average eighty-something-year-old lady, she knew there was more to her than a cloud of fluffy hair, a penchant for believing everything she watched on the telly, a wardrobe full of colorful velour tracksuits and purses that could pass for suitcases, a passion for knitting that bordered on addiction, and a disturbing active romantic life with her husband. No, her great-aunt was her secret weapon, and it was time to deploy her.

"Any plans for the rest of your morning?" Eliza clasped her arms behind her back and fell into step with her great-aunt as they headed down the corridor toward the stairs.

"Are we going sleuthing?"

"Can't get anything past you, can I?"

"You figured this out far quicker than Fitzwilliam and Andrew ever did. Unfortunately for them, they still haven't caught on."

Eliza smiled at the mention of her father. "When we've solved this mess of a case and freed Belle from Wentworth's suspicion, you need to tell me more stories about my dad and Uncle Fitzwilliam. I'm sure those two got into a world of trouble."

"I'm not saying I'm getting on, dear girl, but I might pop my clogs before I finish telling all their misguided adventures."

"That many?" Eliza grinned.

Great-Aunt Iris *tsk*ed and gripped the banister as they descended the stairs. Once they reached the foyer, she brushed at a few white smudges that looked suspiciously like powdered donut remnants on the front of her marmalade-colored tracksuit. "They might look like proper gentlemen now, but they were once known as the Pemberley Pains in the Arse."

Eliza choked on her spit and waved away Great-Aunt Iris's attempts to clap her on the back. "I'm all right."

"You sure? That's how one of my distant cousins died." Great-Aunt Iris pursed her lips. "No, wait. Cousin Honoria died from mistaken identity. It was Clarence who choked on air."

"How does someone die from mistaken identity or choking on air?" Eliza asked, though she wasn't sure she wanted the answer.

"Oh, it was a dreadful business. Poor Honoria went in for a routine procedure to help with her 'women's troubles,' but doctors' surgeries and operating theaters weren't as organized back then. The nurses muddled her up with another patient who looked exactly like her and sent her for the wrong surgery. Doctors took off her leg."

"That's horrible."

"Poor thing died from sepsis a few days later. She was only thirty."

Eliza had heard operating room horror stories before, but knowing she was related to one through distant bloodlines sent shivers up her spine. After hearing Honoria's tragic tale, Eliza hesitated to ask about Clarence, but her curiosity won. "What about Clarence and his choking on air?"

"Simple. His wife loathed him and did him in." Great-Aunt Iris ambled toward the drawing room.

"Wait." Eliza caught up with her. "That's it?"

"Oh, heavens no, but there was never proof his wife, Ivy, had murdered him. I always suspected she'd put ground peanuts in his food, knowing full well it would kill him. He died of asphyxiation."

"There's an unsolved murder in our family?"

"Which has always intrigued me." Great-Aunt Iris settled into a brocade settee. "And with your penchant for sleuthing, I get to relive my Sherlock days." Her forehead furrowed. "Not that those got me anywhere or brought any justice to poor Clarence. Now, then. What's our plan?"

Eliza shook her head at the abrupt shift in topic. "Yes, right. We need Joy. We're off to Lambton to visit Harry."

Eliza tapped out a text to Joy, and within fifteen minutes, they reached the outskirts of the village. A far cry from the empty streets on New Year's Day, traffic, car and pedestrian, flooded the streets, causing Joy to pepper the air in the Range Rover with British swear words, which had Great-Aunt Iris harrumphing with regal disapproval.

Eliza grinned at the dynamic duo and turned her attention out the window. When she'd first arrived in Lambton nearly half a year ago, the quaint loveliness of the village had struck her immediately. Businesses of all types dotted the streets, and whether the structures were timber-framed with smooth white walls topped with thatch roofs or built from brownstone and crowned with wood or clay tiles, they all captured the essence of an idyllic British village. Unlike in spring, summer, and fall, no flowers spilled from the countless window boxes.

Instead, business owners and homeowners had decorated those boxes with evergreen, holly, and ivy. The recent rain had washed away the flocking of snow on the greenery, but the village still radiated festiveness. Not long ago, Eliza had sung carols outside some of the homes and businesses, the joy of the holidays warming her as much as the spiced wine and Heath's hand in hers. Now, however, she struggled to capture even a glimmer of the hope that the Christmas season had sparked. *Poor Belle.* And while she disapproved of Hunter's dastardly deeds, he hadn't deserved death. Justice, yes. Death, no.

Joy pulled up in front of a storefront with a bottom half made of tan stone and an upper half of smooth white walls crossed by dark, heavy beams scrawling across it in a W-shape. Harry Foster, Purveyor of Fine Meats and Cheeses, was written in bold white lettering on a green wooden sign that spanned the length of the business. Unlike its neighbors, the storefront had no wintry or holiday greenery and no window boxes to fill, even if the decorative bug had bitten Mr. Foster.

"It's doolally to sit here and gawk," Great-Aunt Iris piped up from the back seat, looking as excited as a puppy promised a walk. "Besides, Mr. Foster is renowned throughout the area for his delicious sausages. Perhaps if you're nice to him, Eliza, he might give us some for Mrs. Bankcroft to prepare for breakfast tomorrow."

Eliza shared glances with Joy and grinned at her great-aunt. "How about I ask questions about Hunter, and you can charm your way to his sausages."

Great-Aunt Iris's cheeks pinked. Instead of rewarding Eliza's statement with a royal sniff and a harrumph, she fluffed her hair and adjusted her fur-lined hood. "I do hope, Joy, that you haven't got bags of useless clothes from recent shopping trips in the boot of your car, as we'll need room for sausages." She opened her door and, without help, stepped down from the SUV, landed gracefully on her feet, and sashayed up to the entrance.

Eliza hopped out of the car and shut both her door and the one Great-Aunt Iris had left wide open.

Great-Aunt Iris opened the green business door and, with hips swaying, walked on through.

Joy joined Eliza on the sidewalk and nudged her shoulder. "Let me guess. Back in her day..."

Eliza snorted. With Joy at her side, she entered Harry Foster's shop to the tune of her great-aunt's trilling laughter and Harry's booming response.

We might go home with sausages yet.

A rich blend of allspice, garlic, onions, mace, fennel, and coriander made Eliza's mouth water. Tubes of salami hung from a rack in front of the door that she assumed led to the curing room. She didn't know much about salami making, but she'd eaten enough of Harry's Genoa salami to know that after the curing process, he'd have another winner on his hands.

While she'd savored the famous meats and cheeses at parties and at Pemberley, she'd never met the man. His solid build towered over them, and though he was in his fifties, his thick black hair showed only the faintest traces of silver at the temples. He had a neat, well-trimmed beard and the kind of weathered hands that came from a lifetime of honest work. While he wasn't her cup of tea, Eliza wouldn't doubt that plenty of women found excuses to pop by and inquire about Harry's sausages.

His laugh boomed from his chest at something Great-Aunt Iris had said, and Eliza marveled at the odd pairing they made. At five-foot-one, Great-Aunt Iris barely came to the man's belly button, but that didn't stop her from batting her eyelashes at the giant.

Joy leaned close to Eliza and whispered, "Probably how she wooed Great-Uncle William."

"She always told us she was a firecracker back in her day, and I can't help but be impressed. Maybe you could learn a few tricks from her."

Joy sniffed and crossed her arms, but when Great-Aunt Iris laid a delicate, wrinkled hand on Harry's muscular forearm and the man's cheeks flamed bright red, Joy's arms dropped to her sides. "Bloody hell! She's a right pro."

"I hope you like sausages," Eliza whispered before stepping closer to the unlikely pair and extending her hand in greeting.

Harry's calloused hand engulfed hers in a firm grip. "Miss Darcy, it's a pleasure to meet you."

"Mr. Foster, it's so good to finally meet the creator of some of the best meats and cheeses I've ever had."

"Mrs. Darcy here was telling me how much you Pemberley lot enjoyed the last purchase," Harry said in a Yorkshire accent that added warmth to his words. "She's well on her way to making me throw in a few bangers on the house." He winked at Great-Aunt Iris.

Her cheeks turned so red Eliza worried the action might be too much for her. Death by a good-looking beefcake like Harry was probably how her great-aunt wanted to go out, but it'd be hard to explain to Great-Uncle William. She'd have to invent something for the poor man, who was still besotted with his wife.

"She has that effect on a lot of people." Eliza gently clasped her great-aunt's arm and drew her closer in case the woman did faint. "I hope you don't mind us bothering you at work, but Lucinda Fairchild said you'd be willing to discuss Hunter Crawford with me."

At the mention of Hunter's name, Harry's genial face hardened. A vein in his temple turned dark purple, and his hands clenched into white-knuckled fists. "Don't know why you'd want to ask questions about that man. Some people were meant to die, and I, for one, am not sorry that good-for-nothing tosser is dead. I'd like to shake the killer's hand, I would."

Eliza took a step back, bringing her great-aunt with her. "I'm sorry. Um... perhaps today isn't a good day for you. We can come back later." She turned but stopped at Harry's deep sigh.

"No, it's me who needs to apologize, miss. Lucinda told me you'd be coming by, asking questions about Hunter. Something about your friend?"

Eliza eyed him cautiously, worried that something she might say would set him off again. "My friend Belle is under suspicion for his death, and I know she didn't do it. Learning more about Hunter might help me figure out who wanted him dead. If you'd rather not talk about him right now, I can come back at a better time."

"Now's as good a time as any. Why don't you three come into the back room? I'd hate for some village busybody to overhear and go blabbing my story to all of Lambton. Not that they don't know too much already."

They followed him into the back room and sat at a small table covered in old newspapers with enough coffee stains on them that they could have passed for unearthed documents from the 1700s.

He swept the collection aside and gestured to three rickety chairs. "Sorry I can't do better, ladies. Haven't had many visitors back here since my poor wife passed nearly ten years ago. Poor Bertie, she'd have given me a right telling off for my shoddy housekeeping."

"I'm sorry about your wife," Eliza said as she settled gingerly in a wooden chair that she doubted could support a toddler. Judging by her companions' faces, they were thinking the same thing.

"Ta, lass. It's enough to know she's pain free now and shaking her head in disbelief as she watches me muddle through life. Especially with our daughter." Harry tinkered with an old stove. The gas ticked for a few seconds before a burst of blue flame erupted from the old burner. "Don't know about you lovely ladies, but I'm gasping for a cuppa."

After the water boiled, he poured it into a teapot, grabbed a sturdy stool from under a bushel of onions in the corner, and settled onto it. "Right, then. What did you want to know about that dreadful excuse for a human being?"

Chapter Seven
Mr. Foster's Sausages and Even More Scandal

I had the most enlightening conversation with Lady Dennison today when she called. Since Mr. Crawford has shown her daughter, Clara, particular attention, Lady Dennison has taken it upon herself to discover all she can about him. And she is not happy with what she has found. It seems that the Crawfords left an estate named Mansfield Park in Northamptonshire in a rush.
Lizzy Bennet Darcy
Pemberley 1815

Eliza dipped her head as hatred blazed in Harry's eyes, transforming his warm hazel gaze into something poisonous and green.

He must have sensed her unease, because he shook his head and sighed. "I do apologize again, love. That bloke's name alone brings out a side of me I never knew I had until he went after my lass and…" He dragged his fingers through his thick black hair.

"Willow, Paisley's mate and one of Pemberley's staff, told me what he did to your daughter. I understand why you hate him," Joy said.

"Hate? I'm not sure there's a bloody word in the Queen's English that describes how much I loathe that pillock." Harry ground his fists into his thighs.

"I couldn't agree more. I feel the same about two dreadful individuals who interfered with and nearly destroyed my dear nephews' lives," Great-Aunt Iris said, her voice trembling.

"I'm sorry to hear that. I really am. Folk can mess about with me all they like, but the moment they go for one of mine, that's when I proper lose it."

"What can you tell us about Hunter?" Eliza asked.

"Besides the fact that 'e's a right tosser?" He shot an apologetic glance at Great-Aunt Iris. "Beggin' your pardon, Mrs. Darcy, for the language."

She waved his apology away with a dismissive flick of her wrist and gestured toward Joy. "With Joy around, I've grown accustomed to colorful language, I'm afraid."

Joy pressed a hand to her heart and gasped. "Me?"

Harry poured tea into four chipped coffee cups and handed them around. "Much as I can't stand the man, Hunter were a charmer, he was. The sort of bloke who could get what he wanted when he wanted it and left nothing but disaster and destruction in his wake. Just like he did to our poor Paisley."

"Do you mind telling us what happened?" Eliza asked gently.

Harry took a bracing sip of tea, and for a few seconds, Eliza worried he had clammed up. He set his cup on the table with a sharp clink, and tea sloshed across the surface. "Our Paisley fell for his charm, and I hate to admit it, but I took a right shine to him from the start. Thought of him as a son, I did, and when our Paisley started talking marriage, I were that excited to bring Hunter into the family fold." His eyes shimmered with unshed tears.

"But then he got her pregnant and left her destitute," Eliza prompted gently.

"That man didn't just abandon our lass. He left her a shadow of herself. I try to help where and when I can, especially with my granddaughter, Hazel, but times are hard, and no matter what I do, it never seems enough to bring our Paisley back to how she was."

"Do people know Hunter's the father?" Eliza asked.

Harry's jaw clenched. "No."

Joy raised an eyebrow. "How in the bloody hell did that juicy tidbit of gossip stay a secret?"

"Oh, people suspect. Always have done. Nothing you can do about old biddies, but for three years now, the whispers and questioning looks only get worse, especially as little Hazel grows up and looks more and more like her father." His voice hitched. "Paisley's threatening to leave the village, to move as far away as possible. But she's skint, and that's the only thing stopping her from leaving, taking Hazel with her."

Eliza toyed with the teacup handle. "Why didn't Paisley name Hunter as the father? Surely he'd have coughed up something."

Harry's gaze darted about the tiny room, and a blush stained his cheekbones. "Misplaced pride, I guess." He folded his arms across his massive chest.

Sensing the lie and that Harry was done talking, Eliza rose to her feet. "Thank you for your time, Mr. Foster. I appreciate you talking with us." She wondered if Harry had lost money to Hunter like everyone they'd spoken to, but judging by the hardened look on his face, she kept her question to herself—for the moment.

He ushered them from the back room. "I do hope you can help your friend, Miss Darcy."

"Thank you." Eliza gently clasped her great-aunt's arm to keep her from perusing the glass cases stocked with all sorts of meats and cheeses, and her stomach rumbled. "Let's leave Mr. Foster to his work."

"You go ahead, my dear. I need a word with Mr. Foster." Great-Aunt Iris raised a regal penciled-on eyebrow. "Alone."

When her great-aunt showed no sign of budging, Eliza thanked him again, and with Joy at her heels, she stepped outside. Eliza shivered as she hurried to the Range Rover. From the passenger seat, she peered through the shop's large picture window. She couldn't make out what Harry and her great-aunt were discussing, but their serious expressions and somber head shakes quickly transformed into animated hand gestures and broad smiles.

"Looks like Aunt Iris has found herself a new friend." Joy laughed as he pulled out a large wooden box and filled it with not only sausages but also other meat and cheese delicacies. "We're going to eat well tonight."

Eliza studied the pair suspiciously. "I'm not sure what she's up to now, but I have a strange feeling she got more out of him than free food."

The shop door opened, and Eliza hopped out of the Range Rover, popped the back open, and after thanking Harry once more for his help and kindness, helped her great-aunt into the SUV.

As Joy pulled away from the curb, Eliza grinned at Great-Aunt Iris. "Looks like you managed to charm your way to some sausages after all. Joy wants to know your secrets."

"Pish posh. You girls nowadays haven't the foggiest idea how to get what you want from a gentleman. Take Joy here." A gnarled finger poked the back of Joy's headrest. "With that absolute wastrel of a young man, Jack Willoughby. She could have him wrapped around her finger in seconds if she'd only show a bit of pluck."

Eliza wanted to argue, but in Joy and Willoughby's case, her great-aunt was spot on.

Joy pouted. "Why are men so bloody stupid?"

"They always have been, and they always will be, my dear." Great-Aunt Iris pulled her fur-edged hood from her head and fluffed her hair. "Which is why we women must prove ourselves the cleverer sex and take the initiative. If not, the human race would have died out millennia ago. Now, I have some exciting news to share, and Mr. Foster's sausages made me frightfully peckish. Take me to the Trusty Teapot, girls."

"Yes, ma'am," Joy said.

Eliza chuckled. Something had gotten into her great-aunt, and since she was a sucker for punishment, Eliza couldn't wait to see what else the octogenarian had up her sleeve.

T he Trusty Teapot hummed with noise and buzzed like a beehive with the newest village gossip, which was rife with recounts of New Year's Eve tales.

Great-Aunt Iris raised an eyebrow at a group of youngsters sitting at the Pemberley squad's usual table by the large picture window, tutted disapprovingly, and proceeded to walk, queenlike, toward the back. If her great-aunt had worn a robe, Eliza imagined her shifting it ceremoniously to the side before sitting. With no robe, however, Great-Aunt Iris's enormous turquoise purse did the trick, banging against the chair before toppling to the floor. Yarn, knitting needles, and other odds and ends spilled from the purse's depths.

Eliza knelt, scooped up the scattered contents, and chuckled at the pair of large fabric scissors in her hand. "What on earth do you plan to do with these things?"

Great-Aunt Iris sniffed. "For one, I needed something to snip the yarn, and I've gone and mislaid my small pair. For another, you never know when the village's ruffians will have a go at one's person. Don't you remember that dreadful Oliver Wright?"

Eliza shuddered at the memory of the man and his part in the hubbub the previous fall surrounding the false accusations concerning DCI Wentworth. "Yes, and if I remember correctly, it was *you* who attacked his person."

"A good memory is hardly a virtue, my dear." Great-Aunt Iris snatched her purse from Eliza and tucked it safely under the table. "Besides, the contents of a lady's handbag are private and not something to wave about in public."

"What *do* you have in there that would cause a village scandal?" Joy asked, her lips twitching with amusement.

"Never you mind, girl. Back in my day, a girl's handbag was her lifeline. One never knew what one might need until the moment arose. How you girls manage to venture out into the world with nothing but your mobiles and that goo you slather on your lips is beyond me." Great-Aunt Iris smiled over Eliza's shoulder. "Ah, Monica, wouldn't you agree?"

Eliza struggled to her feet and dropped into her chair with relief.

From the twinkle in her eye, Monica had clearly heard every word. "Absolutely, Mrs. Darcy, which is why I never leave home without my bum bag."

"I beg your pardon?" Great-Aunt Iris's eyes bulged.

"You see, Mrs. Darcy, it's a small bag with a pouch that sits right about here." Monica gestured around her waist with both hands.

Eliza fought the urge to offer the American name for the accessory inexplicably making a comeback from the eighties and nineties. She knew the word *fanny* meant something different and naughty to Brits and didn't fancy giving her great-aunt heart palpitations.

"That's clever." A telltale gleam in her great-aunt's eyes warned Eliza they'd soon be visiting Lambton's shops for fanny packs.

"I suppose so, but Mum says some things from the nineties should have stayed in the nineties." Monica wrinkled her nose. "What can I get you ladies?"

After they'd ordered, Eliza leaned back and smiled at her great-aunt. "So, what did you and Harry discuss? And what's this news of yours?"

Great-Aunt Iris leaned forward conspiratorially and motioned for Joy and Eliza to do the same. "Mr. Foster," she whispered, "informed me that Hunter also stole thousands of pounds from him through some dodgy investment scheme." Her cheeks flushed. "The same nonsense he pulled on me."

"How did you get him to tell you that?" Eliza asked.

Great-Aunt Iris fluffed her hair. "A lady has her ways."

Joy looped her arm across the back of her chair and studied the octogenarian with newfound respect. "You're absolutely brilliant."

"You know what this means, don't you?" Eliza sighed at their blank stares. "Harry has motive and plenty of it to kill Hunter. He's a large, muscular man who could easily inflict deadly force, which gives him means. But he couldn't have known Hunter would be at the party. So we have plenty of motive, could have means, but no opportunity."

"Could he have found out somehow?" Joy asked. "Someone could have tipped him off that Hunter was at Pemberley. Harry could have lured him to that spot and—"

"Then why take Belle?" Eliza asked. "Seems if Hunter was meeting up with a man he knew hated him, he wouldn't take an audience."

"Maybe he's cowardly enough that he would have. Insurance of sorts," Joy said.

"Mr. Foster doesn't look like a killer," Great-Aunt Iris protested. "Besides, he makes the most excellent sausages."

Monica arrived with their order. After setting down their drinks and a three-tiered platter of dainty desserts and sandwiches, she crouched down and rested her elbows on the table. "So, have you gotten any further with you-know-who?" She glanced over her shoulder. "This place is crawling with the village's worst busybodies, so watch what you say."

"What do you know about Harry Foster?" Eliza asked, keeping her voice low.

"He's a decent bloke, from what I hear. Mum always said his wife's death changed him, and everything with Paisley..." Monica shrugged. "Trauma changes a person, I suppose."

"What was his relationship with Hunter like?" Eliza asked.

"According to local gossip, it soured overnight. People have their theories, but the real reason for their sudden falling-out has never come from Mr. Foster himself." Monica frowned. "I suspect it has something to do with Paisley."

Not wanting to break Harry's trust, Eliza kept the real reason to herself. "Thanks for your help, Monica. If you hear anything else, could you let me know?"

Monica stood, tapped her finger against her nose, and grinned. "At your service. Enjoy your tea."

After Monica left, Eliza took a sip of her Ethiopian spiced tea. While Harry seemed to have all the ingredients for a proper murderer, Eliza wasn't convinced. Still, not willing to scratch anyone from her list of suspects so early in the game, she put him at the bottom.

"What's going on in that mind of yours?" Joy asked.

Eliza blinked several times. "Sorry about that. What good would it have done for him to kill Hunter years after he broke Paisley's heart and ran away with Harry's money?"

"I'm afraid many people endure their pain, even think they've moved past it, when something triggers them into madness. Saw it plenty in the aftereffects of the war." Great-Aunt Iris's hands shook as she brought her teacup to her lips.

Not wanting to unpack her great-aunt's pain in the middle of a crowded tearoom, Eliza patted her spotted and wrinkled hand. "You're right. As much as I like the man, I'm afraid he's still on our list."

"If we must." Great-Aunt Iris tutted. "Although how a chap who makes such brilliant sausages could be a killer is beyond me."

Eliza chuckled, relieved to hear her great-aunt back in working order. "One never knows the inner workings of a person's mind."

"Speaking of a gentleman's sausages, I must dash back to Pemberley." Joy pushed her chair back. "My work-in-progress needs some attention, and the brooding duke of something or other—really must give that man a proper title—who's taken on the spirited and frightfully opinionated governess, Miss Olivia Thistledown, for his young daughter needs to get his saus—"

"Does the gentleman have a limp?" Great-Aunt Iris interrupted. She planted her forearms on the table and leaned toward Joy, a look of judgment on her face.

"I'm sorry. What?" Joy asked.

"The chap, Duke What's-His-Face. Does he have a limp?"

"Er…" Joy shot Eliza a glance before quirking an eyebrow at Great-Aunt Iris. "No?"

Great-Aunt Iris sat up straight in her chair. "Good. I've been reading novels by your fellow romance authors, and the number of dukes with limps—especially the brooding ones—is excessive, I'm sure. I'm glad you're not succumbing to such tired tropes."

Eliza choked on a laugh. "You're reading naughty romance novels?"

Great-Aunt Iris's harrumph made neighboring patrons turn their heads. "Of course. I want to see how Joy's work compares to theirs." She patted Joy's cheek. "And I must say, my dear, your books are brilliant. Frightfully detailed." She brushed crumbs from a raspberry scone off her velour tracksuit jacket. "Besides, while the plots are predictable, the details and advice within are descriptive and useful."

Before her great-aunt could elaborate on why the descriptive advice within romance novels had proved so useful, Lucinda approached their table with a good-looking man at her side.

Eliza had never been so happy to see a relative stranger in her life.

E liza stood and shook hands with Lucinda. "Good to see you again."

"Likewise. Seems fate worked in my favor. I bumped into Beckham at the shops"—Lucinda motioned to the tall, handsome man beside her—"and since he was Hunter's mate and business partner, I invited him for a cuppa. They owned CQ Wealth Management together." Lucinda gestured toward Eliza and Joy. "Beckham Quill, meet Eliza Darcy and Joy Bingley."

Eliza introduced her great-aunt then shook Beckham's outstretched hand. "Nice to meet you. I'm so sorry about your friend."

Beckham's smile didn't reach his eyes. "I'm afraid you're one of a select few who are."

Eliza blinked at his bitter tone. It didn't match his smooth, debonair appearance. From his perfectly styled blond hair to his ice-blue eyes to his teeth so white and perfect she suspected they were veneers, Beckham radiated upscale car salesman, the kind who only dealt in Maseratis, Aston Martins, and Bugattis.

Lucinda glanced uneasily between Beckham and Eliza. "Please excuse Beckham. He's had a shock. I was telling him about your poor friend and was about to suggest he help us find Hunter's killer."

Beckham's gaze swept Eliza from head to toe. When he finished his assessment, she felt two inches tall and was tempted to ask if he wanted to toss her into the trash, where he clearly believed she belonged. "And what makes you think *you* can find Hunter's killer?"

Great-Aunt Iris harrumphed. "I say, young man. My great-niece here is plucky and has a snappy brain. She's solved plenty of crimes, and I'll have you know—"

Eliza placed her hand on her great-aunt's shoulder. "I'm not making any promises, but I'll do everything I can to clear Belle of suspicion for a crime she didn't commit."

Beckham snapped his fingers and laughed. "Ah, now I know who you are. You're that American busybody everyone's talking about. Came to England, wormed your way back into the good graces of the most powerful family in the county, and now you stick your nose into everyone else's business. What's wrong? America didn't have enough crimes for you to meddle with over there?"

Great-Aunt Iris's shoulder tensed beneath Eliza's hand. Terrified of the scene her great-aunt would inevitably create, Eliza caught her eye and shook her head. When dealing with hotheads like Beckham, staying cool and collected was the best strategy, even if Eliza's racing pulse disagreed.

"That was rude." Lucinda's West Country accent crept through her scolding tone. "You've hurt her feelings. She might stop—"

"Have I?" Beckham studied Eliza again.

Fighting the urge to slap him or do something equally juvenile like stick her tongue out, Eliza flashed her most dazzling smile. "I'm afraid we Americans are thick-skinned. You'll have to try harder than that."

"Is that so?" Beckham's eyebrows shot up. A flicker of grudging respect sparked in his eyes.

Eliza gestured to the two empty chairs at their table. "Care to join us?"

Lucinda shot Beckham a warning glare before they settled into their seats. She drummed her fingers on the table. "I've been thinking long and hard about Hunter, and it wasn't a pleasant experience, I'm afraid."

"How do you mean?" Joy asked.

"Remember how I'd said we'd fallen apart and only dealt with each other at special functions?"

Eliza nodded.

"Well, I realized it wasn't accidental, not like what happens with some uni mates, right? Sometimes, distance or life changes cause a rift, but the more I thought about it, the more I realized I'd separated myself from him even before leaving uni."

"Why?" Eliza asked.

"I didn't trust him." The hurt in her eyes matched her pained voice. "I feel traitorous even thinking that about a friend, but there it is."

"Do you remember what made you not trust him?" Eliza pressed.

"It's funny what people say when they don't think you're around." Pain glittered in her brown eyes for a microsecond before they once again radiated friendliness. Lucinda jerked her head toward Beckham. "Anyway, Beckham here is one of the few people on the planet who trusted and liked Hunter until the bitter end. Isn't that so?" Lucinda turned toward Beckham, a questioning look on her face.

Beckham fixed his unwavering gaze on Eliza. "Wouldn't you agree, Eliza, that there's a distinction between liking someone and trusting them?"

Eliza clenched her fists under the table and counted to five. Not only was the man's gaze unnerving, but his habit of answering questions with questions was like fingernails on a chalkboard. "You tell me. Is there?"

A small smile tugged at the corners of his lips. "Isn't the only way to like somebody to never trust them at all?"

Great-Aunt Iris clicked her tongue against her teeth. "Oh, poppycock!"

"So, you didn't trust Hunter?" Joy asked.

"However do you think I remained business partners with him for so long?" Beckham replied with yet another question. "Knowing your partner is untrustworthy is half the battle. There's power in knowing the devil you're dealing with, don't you think?"

Eliza gritted her teeth, once again counted to five, and forced her jaw to unclench. "And you didn't trust him because..." She spread her hands, waiting.

"Why on earth would I trust a man who bilked dozens upon dozens if not hundreds of people out of their hard-earned money with his endless Ponzi schemes? Those people might have been complete mugs with no common sense or money sense whatsoever, falling for every cock-and-bull story he spun, but do I look the sort?"

Great-Aunt Iris quivered, her cheeks turning crimson.

Eliza placed a gentle hand on her great-aunt's knee and shook her head slightly. Then she turned back to Beckham. "If you knew he was stealing money from people, why didn't you do anything about it?"

"Ah, how American of you. What should I have done? Horsewhip him and drag him to the town center for everyone to jeer before taking justice into their own hands and hanging him from the nearest tree? Seems Old West, don't you think?"

Eliza wasn't sure she cared two figs what Beckham thought, but she kept her expression neutral. "You could have gone to the police."

"A police force so incompetent that *you* have to step in and solve their crimes?" Beckham asked.

Lucinda placed her hand on his shoulder. "I've never seen you act like this before. What's gotten into you? You're behaving like a bloody plonker." She glanced sheepishly at Great-Aunt Iris. "Sorry, Mrs. Darcy."

Great-Aunt Iris's fierce gaze never wavered from Beckham's face. "I assure you, Miss Fairchild, your language isn't nearly adventurous enough."

Before her great-aunt could add fuel to an already-tense conversation, Eliza cleared her throat. "Were you involved with any of his money schemes?"

"Even if I were, would you expect me to own up to it?" Beckham rose to his feet. "If you want to continue sticking your nose into other people's business, you could try Basil Huxley. But might I offer some unsolicited advice? If you go around kicking at every bee's nest in this case, you'll eventually kick the wrong one and get stung." Without another word and without Lucinda, he left the tearoom.

"Well." Great-Aunt Iris tutted. "I never."

Lucinda clasped Eliza's hand. "Please don't let this upset you. Beckham is under a lot of stress. This won't... You haven't changed your mind, have you? About investigating. Hunter..." Lucinda's throat worked. "He wasn't a good man, but everyone deserves justice, right? You'll stay on?"

"Much to the chagrin of a certain DCI, I never abandon a case I start."

Chapter Eight
Cloudy with a Chance of Toads

The weather has kept us all indoors, providing me an opportunity to observe the Crawfords' behavior when they called to escape the solitude of Berryhill Manor. I couldn't help but keep Lady Dennison's news in my mind as Mr. Crawford regaled us with tales of his travels. When I asked if he'd ever traveled through Northamptonshire, he blushed and made dismissive comments ranging from "nothing but sheep" to "tiresome relations and their expectations." Little Fitz's cries brought our time together to a close, for which I am glad. Miss Crawford seemed to think it odd that a lady of my social standing spends time with her baby instead of handing him off to the nurse. What atrocious rot.
Lizzy Bennet Darcy
Pemberley 1815

A cold wind had whipped up during their time at the Trusty Teapot, and Eliza clutched her coat tightly around her neck, hunkering into it as she helped Great-Aunt Iris, who insisted she didn't need a boost, into the Range Rover. Eliza hauled herself into the passenger seat and thunked her head against the headrest.

Joy mirrored the action on the steering wheel with her forehead as she punctuated each word: "Beckham. Quill. Is. A. Right—"

"Dodgy blighter," Great-Aunt Iris piped up from the backseat. "Absolute rubbish, that one. Hasn't got the manners God gave a goose."

Eliza peered over her shoulder. "You're cheeky today, aren't you?"

"When you reach my age, my dear, you realize there's no need to suffer fools gladly. And I'll tell you, that Beckham Quill—ghastly name, might I add—isn't worth a second of your time."

"Except he could well be our killer," Eliza said. "He didn't answer any questions. Plus he didn't seem overly upset about his friend's death."

"Add the fact that he knew about Hunter's dodgy dealings." Joy winced and flicked a glance in the rearview mirror. "I'm terribly sorry about what he said in there about Hunter's victims. He had no right, and he's dead wrong."

"No matter now. What's done is done."

Eliza wanted to argue, but judging by the hard line of her great-aunt's lips, she wasn't about to win the battle. "Beckham knowing about Hunter's money schemes makes him a prime suspect. I wonder if he ever tried blackmailing his good old pal."

Joy pulled away from the curb and headed back toward Pemberley. "I can't picture Hunter as the sort to let anyone muck about with his plans. Blackmailing him could've meant that person getting permanently sorted, if you catch my drift."

"That's an interesting thought. Beckham could have known that or, at least, thought that. So he has all this juicy information, right, but he figures he can't use it against Hunter without risking his own neck. But that information is a gold mine, and with Hunter dead, Beckham can... What?"

"If he had a part in the money misdealings, he'd get a full cut, right?" Joy asked.

"Unless Basil was Hunter's partner." Eliza frowned out the passenger window, watching the countryside cloaked in dreary fog fly past. "We need to visit him."

"Well, I, for one, am not going with you," Great-Aunt Iris declared.

"I thought you loved adventures and sleuthing. Are you feeling okay?" Eliza asked.

"Pish posh, girl. I haven't been ill a day in my life, and I don't plan to start now."

Eliza decided against reminding her great-aunt of her close brush with influenza the previous fall. "So why don't you want to go with?" Eliza remembered her great-aunt's dislike of the man at the New Year's Eve ball. "Besides the fact that he's a reprobate."

"The man has a ... What do you call it nowadays? A crush. He has a crush on me, and it's scandalous how he flirts. I'm a married woman, you know."

Joy sniggered and was rewarded with a light flick to the head from a knitting needle. "Ow." She whipped her head around and narrowed her eyes at Great-Aunt Iris before turning back to the road. "First of all, how'd you reach me, and secondly, what was that for?"

The Cheshire cat grin on Great-Aunt Iris's lips said it all.

Joy turned into Pemberley's driveway. "Well, if Great-Aunt Iris doesn't want to chat up Mr. Basil Huxley, looks like you're on your own, Eliza."

"What do you have that's so pressing?" Eliza asked.

"Remember What's-His-Duke's sausage? I'm happy to announce that Miss Olivia Thistledown is about to have a renewed appreciation for—"

"You mean to tell me that you're ditching me for some fictional man's..." Eliza waved her hand in the air, trying to conjure the correct word.

"Tally—"

"Great-Aunt Iris." Eliza cringed. "I didn't even know you knew words like that."

Her smile was anything but innocent. "I'm sure I don't understand what you mean, my dear. I was going to say tallyho."

"Yeah, right," Joy mumbled and shot Eliza a look.

Great-Aunt Iris smoothed her hair. "Why, back in my day, girls didn't have their minds in the gutter, I can tell you." The mischievous glint in her great-aunt's eyes contradicted the scolding tone.

"Yes, ma'am." Eliza grinned, and after the SUV lurched to a stop, she hopped out and moved to assist her great-aunt. "So, who's left to go sleuthing with me?"

"The weakest link, of course." Great-Aunt Iris patted her cheek. "But I'm sure Mr. Tilney has other strengths that make it worthwhile to keep him around." She waved away Eliza's offered elbow. "I'm old, but I'm not past it yet. I'm going to find your great-uncle. Time for our afternoon kip."

As Great-Aunt Iris tottered off in her white sneakers, Joy trailing behind and peppering her with questions about what she'd been going to say about her fictional duke, Eliza checked her phone. Three in the afternoon, and with the exhaustion gnawing at her bones, she was tempted to head to her room for a nap too.

She tapped the green phone icon then Heath's name.

After a few rings, his deep voice greeted her. "Hiya, love."

The day's stress melted away, and Eliza sighed.

"You all right?" Concern threaded through his voice.

"I'm fine. Just tired." Eliza filled him in on the day's events.

"Sounds like you and the gang have been busy without me. I'm jealous."

"Are you, though?"

He chuckled. "It's a tough choice between tedious paperwork and your great-aunt's flirtations with the deli bloke."

"Speaking of flirtations—long story—can you meet me at Basil's? Both Great-Aunt Iris and Joy are ditching me for men."

"Let me guess. Joy's is fictional?"

"Well, without Willoughby here for her to boss around, she has to take out her frustrations on her fictional characters instead."

"Poor sod." From Heath's tone, though, he clearly enjoyed the fact that Joy was tormenting the unfortunate Willoughby.

"You don't sound sorry for him. Is this because he tried to hit on me when I first arrived at Pemberley?" She grinned at Heath's low growl. "In all fairness, I never thought I'd see a certain handsome Brit from the plane again."

"Don't remind me how close that prat came to interfering."

"Don't insult my intelligence. Can you imagine me and Willoughby? It's as ridiculous as picturing you and Joy together for two years."

"Touché." Heath chuckled.

"I'll make sure Basil's ready for a visit, grab some curry on my way over, and meet you at your apartment around five."

"Brilliant." From the low rumble in his voice, Eliza knew he wasn't talking about the curry.

Eliza unlocked Heath's Lambton flat and used her hip to nudge open the door. Even with her arms full of curry takeout from their favorite restaurant, she paused to breathe in the familiar scent of sandalwood, cinnamon gum, and Heath. She flipped the light on with her elbow, set the bags on the kitchen counter, gathered plates and utensils, then leaned against the counter and studied Heath's flat.

She'd loved it from the moment she first toured it after Heath moved in following his new job as head of field archaeology for a research company based in nearby Bakewell. And not because they were finally safe from Great-Aunt Iris's knitting needles. Heath's flat was masculine and soothing with its earth-tone colors, mahogany furniture, and leather couches. She was safe there, and every time she crossed the threshold, she couldn't help feeling like she was already wrapped in Heath's embrace.

Muscled arms slipped around her from behind, and Heath pulled her close against his chest, resting his chin on top of her head. "Mmm, smells lovely."

Eliza turned in his arms and squeezed him back. "Me or the curry?"

"Don't make me choose. That's cruel of you." He placed his finger under her chin and tipped her face up for a kiss.

After they both lost the ability to breathe, Heath kissed the tip of her nose. "Jury's in. It's the curry." He dodged her playful swat and dished out the food until two plates were equally heaping with jasmine rice, chicken tikka masala, and samosas.

"What's your take on the case so far?" Heath asked after they'd made small talk over their meal.

Eliza gathered their plates and moved to the kitchen sink. "Nothing too earth-shattering. It's going to be as we expected earlier and all boil down to who suffered the most because of Hunter."

"Talk me through it. I haven't got anything you could use for your infamous murder board." Heath rinsed and dried the plates and utensils Eliza had washed. "Oh, hang on. We'll use the mirror in my bedroom. I've got some dry-erase markers. When are we meeting with Basil?"

"He was put out that we were coming at all, but he agreed on seven. It's good Lucinda is doing some of the groundwork, or we'd have a difficult job getting anybody to talk."

After they tidied the kitchen, Heath gathered the markers and met Eliza in his bedroom. The space was tidy, warm, and masculine.

Eliza sank onto the Oxford-blue comforter and bounced a little. "Great-Aunt Iris would have a conniption that I'm not only in your bedroom but also *on* your bed."

Heath flashed her a cheeky grin. "Oh, I wouldn't be so sure about that."

"What do you mean?"

"New Year's morning, I woke early and was going to sneak out of your room, thinking I could escape being seen by your family, and... Well ..."

Eliza gasped. "You ran into her, didn't you?"

"If you're talking about the white-haired terror who's mad about alien programs on the telly and wields a pair of knitting needles like a samurai, then yes, one and the same."

"And? What happened?"

Heath chuckled. "She looked me up and down, gave a little nod, and walked away. If my hearing's as good as I think it is, she said something like 'About time, young man.' She also mentioned something about a wedding, but by then, she was nattering on to Caesar, so she could have been planning his future."

Eliza's face burned as she collapsed back on Heath's bed, throwing her forearm over her eyes. "So that's why she's been looking at me like I'm her next project. She knows."

"And she's apparently planning our future nuptials." Warm hands pulled her hands from her face, bringing Heath into view. "Would you mind? Future nuptials?"

"Ours or Caesar's?"

Heath dipped his head and captured her lips in a quick heated kiss. "We'd better meet Caesar's intended missus before any ceremony happens." He hauled Eliza to her feet and pressed the markers into her hand. "Right, then, Mrs. Sherlock. You have the floor."

"We have several suspects." She wrote with the red marker as she listed the names. "Harry Foster—"

"That man does make brilliant sausages," Heath said.

Eliza gritted her teeth. "If I hear one more word about Harry Foster and his sausages, I'll... I'll..." At Heath's laugh, she chucked an extra marker at him. "Oh, jog on, as you Brits say. Anyway, he's at the bottom of my list, but he's still on it. Hunter messing with Harry's daughter then stealing money from him gives him clear motive." She jotted those points down then wrote out *Beckham Quill.* "This guy's a real piece of work. Do you know him?"

"Only by reputation. According to the rumor mill, his first investment business went belly-up in London. Some say it was due to unethical practices." Heath shrugged. "Whether any of it's true is hard to tell. I'm surprised that Hunter and Beckham even tried to keep their business going in this tiny village. It wouldn't have surprised me in the least if they'd packed up and left for another unsuspecting community."

"Well, he knew about the Ponzi schemes and kept emphasizing how much he didn't trust Hunter." She wrote under his name and tapped the capped marker against her bottom lip. "Maybe killing Hunter was his way out. Trying to start afresh... again... without his scheming partner. Perhaps Beckham wants to go honest and just couldn't with Hunter tagging along."

"But what would he gain from killing Hunter?" Heath asked.

"Not sure. He's sketchy enough and looked as guilty as sin about something, so on my board he goes." After glaring at the mirror for a moment, she wrote *Hubert and Henrietta Crawford.*

"You think his parents could have killed him?"

Eliza filled him in on the strange meeting she and Uncle Fitzwilliam had had with them two mornings ago. "They seemed more heartbroken over staffing issues and not being able to poach Mrs. B. than they were about their son's death. Besides, as Uncle Fitzwilliam pointed out, the timing is suspicious. They dropped the lawsuit right after Hunter died. Hubert especially seemed furious with his son."

The bedroom fell silent as Eliza made neat bullet points under their names and filled in details.

Heath studied the list and tapped his finger on *seemed mad at son.* "Angry enough that he finally snapped and killed his only child?"

"People have murdered family for less."

She wrote Lucinda Fairchild's name on the board and scrawled *college friend* after it.

"Didn't you say she's been a great help?" Heath asked.

"She's more a character witness, and because she was involved in Hunter's life, she gets a place on my board."

"You don't suspect her?"

"I have no reason to. There's zero motive. Faded friendships aren't usually fodder for murder. And while she was at the party, giving her opportunity, I spoke with most of the staff, regular and hired, and they all recall seeing her throughout the night at various intervals, and she left with the last of the guests. There's no way she could have bludgeoned Hunter over the head and not gotten blood splatter all over her."

Heath checked his watch. "We've got about an hour before we meet Basil. Take a picture so you can transfer this to a proper board when we get to Pemberley, and let's go finish our episode of *Peaky Blinders*."

"Perfect." She snapped photos of the information. "Voilà."

"And something tells me that after our chat with Basil, we'll be adding another name to the list," Heath said, placing his hand on the small of her back as he guided her toward the living room.

B asil Huxley's house was an ostentatious display of wealth, especially for the headmaster of the prestigious boarding school that shared the property. The brick behemoth resembled a gingerbread castle from a child's fairy tale, looking utterly out of place as it jutted up from the manicured lawns and gardens locked in their winter slumber. Unlike Pemberley, which blended seamlessly with the surrounding woods and gardens, Basil's residence seemed determined to crush nature beneath it. No wonder the red ivy wrapping around the building gave the impression it was trying to strangle the life out of it. Two large bronze lions, turning green with age, stood as sentinels on either side of a red-brick pathway that led to a massive oak door.

Eliza studied the sprawling complex of school buildings, which had all been built in the same gingerbread design. "Pretty quiet for a boys' boarding school."

"They're all home for holiday. Unless there are some poor souls left here to celebrate with the headmaster." Heath opened the metal gate leading to the house and gestured for her to go through.

"How sad. Did you go to boarding school?" Eliza asked as she stepped past him.

"Yes. It wasn't so bad. I met a lot of good mates, and since my home life wasn't the happiest, I often dreaded going home for holiday."

Eliza frowned, wishing they weren't approaching Basil's doorstep so quickly. She and Heath had had many talks about their home lives and upbringings, and every time Heath mentioned his childhood, Eliza mourned for the little boy so affected by his parents' narcissism and harsh expectations. After she'd met Heath's parents and two older siblings during Christmas, she'd gotten a better idea of what Heath had endured as a child. And while the day had been pleasant enough, the underlying tension had made her relieved when it ended.

Heath must have sensed her thoughts and clasped her hand gently. "That was a long time ago now, and despite my upbringing and my parents' toxic relationship, I didn't turn out half bad." He grinned at her, but despite his dimples flashing, the laugh lines around his eyes didn't crinkle like they normally did.

She pressed her hand to his cheek. "You turned out pretty amazing, and whether it's because of or despite what Thomas and Veronica Tilney set out to do, I owe them something for at least bringing you into this world."

Heath gave her a quick kiss. "We shouldn't keep Basil waiting."

Eliza grabbed the bottom loop of the gold knocker shaped like a lion's head and let it fall against the door. "I wonder what's in store for us."

Heath didn't have time to answer, as the door swung open, releasing a wave of heat and the smell of dust, mildew, and something odd that reminded her of her high school biology classroom.

Basil stood in the doorway, a red smoking jacket tied tightly around his generous potbelly, black dress pants covering his legs, and red velvet slippers on his feet. "Ah, Miss Darcy and Mr. Tilney, welcome to my humble abode. Please come in."

"Thank you, Mr. Huxley, for agreeing to meet with us," Eliza said as she stepped over the threshold. It took a moment for her eyes to adjust from the waning twilight to the glaring foyer lights, but when she could see properly, she wished she hadn't tried so hard.

At Heath's murmured "What in the bloody hell is all this?" Eliza realized what she was seeing wasn't her imagination. There were, in fact, on every surface of the foyer, at least a dozen realistic-looking frogs. Or toads. She'd never known the difference, and it seemed pointless while surrounded by them, especially since they were all dressed in different outfits representing the world's cultures. Togas, multicolored tunics and matching sombreros, geisha gowns, and cowboy chaps and hats were the beginning of the endless cultural fashion parade. Eliza squinted at one particular frog cowboy. No, her eyesight wasn't failing her. The tiny amphibian was playing a banjo.

"Eliza." Heath touched the back of her hand. "Mr. Huxley asked if you'd like some tea."

"Ah, no, thank you. I'm sorry. I was so intrigued by your... collection. The artist who made these has an uncanny knack for realism." Eliza hoped her smile didn't look like a grimace.

Basil beamed, plucked the monocle from his left eye, polished it, and wedged it back in place. "They are my pride and joy, Miss Darcy."

He gently lifted the largest exhibit and stepped closer. "This here is a cane toad, originally from the Amazon, but I got this little blighter from a dealer in Florida. They're an invasive species there, originally brought in to control pests in sugar cane fields. This little guy had the misfortune of being in the wrong place at the wrong time."

Eliza stared at the poor toad, its webbed feet attached to a bronze pedestal, its waxy body squeezed into surfer board shorts, its tiny webbed fingers clutching a green-and-red-striped surfboard. She stepped back and bumped into Heath's chest. "These are real?"

Basil tilted his head and studied her as if she were the weirdo. "Of course they're real."

Not wanting to alienate the odd little man, Eliza forced another smile. "I'm surprised is all, ah, at the creative use of the clothing and props."

His scowl softened, and he gestured for them to follow him. "Yes, it catches people off guard more often than not, but it gives each of my tiny creatures a personality, don't you think?"

Eliza wasn't sure *what* to think as she followed him into a large room covered in dust, crammed with books, and stuffed with more taxidermized amphibians. She sniffed, and the familiar scent from her advanced biology classroom hit her—formaldehyde. She sneezed.

"Bless you." Basil settled behind a giant desk cluttered with stacks of papers and books, all teetering on the edge of collapse, and gestured for Eliza and Heath to take the chairs facing him.

Eliza sat down carefully, afraid that any sudden movement would bury the man in a paper-and-book avalanche. "Again, thank you for meeting with us about Hunter."

"We understand that you and he were close, and we were hoping you could help shed some light on Hunter so we can find out who killed him," Heath said.

Basil ran a hand over his impressive mustache and studied Eliza with calculating eyes. His left eye appeared slightly magnified behind the monocle, making her feel like an insect pinned under a microscope. "I have a stuffed boa constrictor in my library. Would you care to see it?"

Eliza's skin crawled. "Not a big fan of snakes."

"Then tell me, Miss Darcy," Basil said, leaning forward slightly. "Why do you care about a man who was more serpent than my boa constrictor? Hunter destroyed more lives—human ones, at least—than that snake ever could. He got exactly what he deserved."

Chapter Nine
Ponzis and Pretentious Prats

Darcy has threatened to not be at home the next time the Crawfords call. Not that I blame him in the least. However, they are our neighbors, and as Mr. Crawford has every intention of buying the place and planting roots here, I reminded Darcy we must set the example of kind neighbors. Darcy tires of Mr. Crawford's not-so-subtle comments on Darcy's social status and Pemberley's wealth. Miss Crawford is no better, and I can't help but feel she visits more to evaluate the worth of our belongings than to build an acquaintance. Our neighbors seem more calculating than charming!
Lizzy Bennet Darcy
Pemberley 1815

Eliza blinked at Basil's harsh tone. "I'm sorry, but since Lucinda and Beckham suggested we talk to you, I thought you'd be willing to help us."

Basil grunted. "Those two wouldn't know a frog from a toad. Why you're taking advice from those two absolute muppets is beyond me."

Eliza's cheeks warmed. She didn't know a frog from a toad either and was put out that that piece of knowledge served as Basil's measure of intelligence. But since she needed his help, she took a deep breath and willed her vocal cords to relax so her voice wouldn't sound strained. "Please, Mr. Huxley, any information you can share, even details that seem unimportant, could shed light on this case. My friend Belle is under suspicion, and—"

"Where might I find her so I can shake her hand?" Basil interrupted.

"Excuse me?" Once again, she found herself blinking at the odd monocle-wearing little man.

"Your friend. Where can I find her so I can thank her for ridding the world of the likes of Hunter?" Basil leaned back in his chair, intertwined his fingers, and rested his hands on his potbelly.

"But she didn't do it," Eliza said.

"How d'you know?"

Eliza sputtered. "Because I know she didn't do it."

"None of the evidence points to her?"

"Well ..." Eliza pinched the bridge of her nose. "She didn't do it, and if you're going to sit there and—"

"Mr. Huxley, Lord Darcy also mentioned you'd be a brilliant resource for our situation. He even said he couldn't think of a better chap to help us out." Heath grabbed Eliza's hand and gave it a gentle squeeze.

Basil preened and practically glowed as if God himself had anointed him Eliza's Little Helper. "I always knew Lord Darcy possessed an excellent talent for reading people. Yes, I'd be delighted to give you as much information as I can to help you find Hunter's killer."

Eliza swallowed her snort and plastered a smile on her face. "Thank you. I'll be sure to let my uncle know how *helpful* you were. Beckham was most adamant that we talk to you. Were you and Hunter close?"

"I'm not sure what you mean." Basil smoothed a trembling hand over his bald head.

"Beckham gave the impression that you two were business partners." It wasn't exactly what Beckham had said, but the idea of making Basil squirm didn't hurt Eliza's conscience one bit.

"Ah... I wouldn't say he and I were business partners. We were more..." His hand circled as if he were trying to conjure the right word from the study's ether. "Business acquaintances."

Eliza quirked an eyebrow. "And what does that mean? Were you aware that he was bilking people for thousands upon thousands of dollars?"

"What? He was?" But his surprised anger came a beat too late. "I hadn't a clue." His gaze darted about the room, refusing to land on either her or Heath.

"Surely as his business *acquaintance*, you knew or at least sensed his dodgy dealings," Heath said, carelessly flicking at a dust mote that had landed on his pants. Despite his casual air, Heath's jaw muscle twitched.

Eliza smiled. Pity the fool who let the stoic-looking British gentleman lull them into a false sense of security. Warmth pooled in her core as Heath's jaw muscle ticked again at Basil's stuttered attempts to clear himself of any wrongdoing.

"Now, Mr. Tilney, that's not what I meant."

"What exactly did you mean? Did you or didn't you know about Hunter's Ponzi schemes?" Heath asked.

The phrase made Basil nearly jump from his chair. His face flushed an unhealthy shade of purple, and Eliza feared the man would keel over right then and there. DCI Wentworth would have a field day reminding her what happened when she stuck her nose in police business.

Basil took a few deep breaths, and his face returned to its normal mottled complexion. "I haven't the foggiest what you mean about Ponzi schemes. It's hardly Hunter's fault that those investments didn't deliver the promised returns. It's down to the investor for not doing their homework on those investments, isn't it?"

Oh, yes, blame the investment and the investor, you little toad.

Eliza's hands curled around the chair's arms. "Were the victims of your and Hunter's 'investments' aware they were pouring their hard-earned money and retirement funds into nonexistent entities? Did they know you and Hunter were using Peter to pay Paul? Which works beautifully until Paul wants his promised returns. That's how it works, right? You find new victims to keep up the illusion with the first victims, and things go swimmingly until the original investors want their money back. And because you've used the money to fund your lifestyle"—Eliza flicked a glance at all the stuffed amphibians scattered about the room—"you don't have the money to pay them. I'm sure Hunter's charm and charisma bought you some time. Perhaps he convinced them to keep their money in a little longer to make them even more money, but that can't go on forever. And when they finally demanded their money, that's when the gig was up. Let me know if I got anything wrong."

Basil's face turned purple again, and his tongue darted out to lick his lips. "Now, Miss Darcy, you've got it all wrong—"

"Do I? How?"

He stared at her as if waiting for her to fill in the gaps.

"I'll answer that question for you, shall I?"

He blinked at her, sweat beading on his shiny forehead.

"You and Hunter left a long trail of victims in your wake, and because you chose your targets carefully, you felt secure knowing their shame at being swindled would keep them quiet. You deliberately picked elderly people, already stereotyped as naive about finances, ones whose pride would prevent them from going to the authorities. I'm sure you and Hunter crossed every T and dotted every I so that if someone did come forward, Hunter would appear to be an innocent investment banker, equally surprised and heartbroken that the promised investment didn't perform as the market suggested." She fixed him with a piercing stare. "How close am I?"

He swallowed hard and dabbed his forehead with a handkerchief from his smoking jacket pocket.

"My only question, Mr. Huxley, is how you fit into all this. You're the headmaster of a prestigious boarding school. What on earth were you doing playing at Ponzi schemes with Hunter?"

For a moment, Eliza thought her question might kill Basil outright, and she shot Heath a worried glance. "Mr. Huxley, are you all right?"

When he continued gaping at her, his purple lips a garish contrast to his crimson face, Eliza jumped up, circled his desk, and slapped him on the back. She doubted it would help, but doing something beat doing nothing. The slap freed a breath trapped in Basil's chest, and he wheezed, coughed, and wheezed again.

"Put your head between your knees," Eliza ordered then reconsidered Basil's flexibility. "Actually, rest your forehead on the desk. Yes, like that. Now take several deep breaths and focus on steadying your breathing."

Basil turned his head sideways, pressing his cheek against the desk, and stared at her owlishly, but he followed her instructions. Within moments, his breathing eased, and aside from a few lingering shudders and light coughs, he was as good as new. Well, at least as new as someone like Basil could ever be.

Heath poured a glass of water from a carafe on a nearby cart and placed it in Basil's hand. Basil sipped tentatively then downed the rest in one gulp. He wiped his mouth with the back of his hand and held the glass out to Heath, who refilled it and set it in front of him.

After Basil guzzled the second glass and Eliza was ninety-nine point nine percent certain he wouldn't collapse, she reclaimed her seat and waited for him to break the silence. She'd learned that when dealing with people she wanted answers from, it was best to let them speak first.

Between his furtive glances at her and Heath and the heavy silence making the dusty, dank room feel more oppressive, Eliza was five seconds away from calling it a night.

Basil drummed his fingers on the desk. "You say your friend is innocent of murder?"

"Yes."

He nodded.

"Well?" Eliza prompted when his silence stretched on.

"I want none of this coming back to bite me on the arse." He motioned toward the window, which would have offered a view of the school buildings in daylight. "I've invested far too much of my life, my soul, into this... this bloody soul-destroying job to have Hunter's convenient demise linked to me or this school in any way whatsoever. Do I make myself perfectly clear?"

"You still haven't answered my question," Eliza said, glancing around the dusty, unkempt room. There had to be a reason a headmaster had gotten mixed up in Hunter's Ponzi schemes.

"Some questions never get answered, Miss Darcy, and I do hope you can forgive an old man for wanting to keep certain secrets buried where they bloody well belong. If you want to continue your snooping, I'd start sniffing around the Crawfords." Despite his attempt at lightness, fear flickered in Basil's eyes.

"Why them?" Heath asked.

Basil leaned back and drummed his fingers on his potbelly. "You two are the ones with all the questions. Why don't you ask them yourself? Now, if you'll excuse me, I have important matters of business to attend to."

Clearly dismissed, Eliza and Heath stood, thanked him—for what, Eliza wasn't sure—and left the musty study as quickly as they could.

Once back in the fresh, cool air, Eliza inhaled deeply and exhaled, hoping to expel all the dust motes and old formaldehyde fumes from her lungs. "That was an interesting meeting. What an odd little man with an equally odd collection of stuffed frogs."

Heath shivered. "I'm not keen on frogs, and I couldn't shake the feeling that all those beady little eyes were staring at me."

"I didn't think you were afraid of anything," Eliza teased.

"I'm not *afraid* of frogs. I just don't fancy the little blighters."

"Not even ones dressed up and ready to start a band or take surfing lessons?"

He gave a lopsided grin. "I was struggling to figure out what to get you for your upcoming birthday, but now I know exactly."

Eliza scrunched her nose. "Perhaps I'll get a new boyfriend for my birthday. I'm up for a change of pace anyway."

Heath's eyes glinted, and Eliza's blood ran hot at his smoldering look. He reached out to grab her, but she laughed and jogged down the brick pathway toward Heath's car, which was locked when she tried the handle.

Heath came up behind her and wrapped her in an embrace, his voice a whisper in her hair. "A new boyfriend, eh?"

Goose bumps littered her skin at his husky voice and strong arms encircling her. "I'm afraid I don't associate with riffraff who gift the women they love with taxidermized amphibians."

"Shall I attempt to change your mind? I do have other qualities that recommend me for further boyfriend status."

Eliza's knees went weak. She knew exactly what his other talents were. "I never thought a vast collection of button-up dress shirts counted as a quality, but beggars can't be choosers." At his chuckle, she turned in his embrace, wrapped her arms around his neck, and pulled his head down for a kiss. "I suppose I'll keep you. You're useful, and Great-Aunt Iris does love you so. She'd be heartbroken if you left."

"No, she'd be destitute because she'd need to find another set of ribs to sink her knitting needles into." He kissed the tip of her nose, opened the passenger-side door, and, after shutting it, jogged around the front of the car and slid into the driver's seat. "Was Basil telling the truth?" Heath asked as he pulled away from the ostentatious gingerbread-esque house.

"Yes and no, but which parts were truth or fiction, I've no clue." Eliza clunked her head against the passenger-side window and stared into the darkness. "He knew about Hunter's Ponzi schemes and played a part, but to what extent and why, I don't know."

"Everyone is throwing everyone else under the bus," Heath said as he took a sharp curve. "Lucinda and Beckham told you to have a word with Basil. Basil pointed us back toward Hunter's parents, and I've got a funny feeling they'll point us in yet another direction."

Eliza feared Heath was right. *Poor Belle.* Her heart twisted at the thought of her friend and the thundercloud of suspicion hanging over her. It was only a matter of time before those clouds broke and the storm unleashed itself.

T wenty minutes later, Eliza knocked on the doorjamb of Belle's open bedroom door. "Coming to check in on you. Mind if I join you for a bit?"

Caesar, who had followed her to Belle's room, sat on his haunches and glared into the bedroom, his slitted gaze fixed on Belle. At Belle's returned glare, Caesar blinked at Eliza and sashayed back down the hall. Clearly, absence hadn't made the heart grow fonder for Belle and Caesar.

Belle, sitting up in bed, patted the quilted comforter embroidered with purple and pink hyacinths. "Please. I'm going stir-crazy by myself."

Guilt gnawed at Eliza's conscience for abandoning her friend. She convinced herself that she'd had to, that it was the only way to save her. Eliza settled herself on the bed and studied her friend. Belle's dyed-red hair was pulled back in a ponytail, which only emphasized her drawn face and tired eyes.

She gently squeezed Belle's hand. "How are you feeling?"

A fighting spirit glinted in Belle's eyes. "I'm determined to get back to normal. I'm tired of sitting around like a broken doll."

"Have you had any memories from that night?"

"I still can't remember what happened. Everything after Hunter's and my walk through the garden is a black hole. I don't remember anything until they found me." She gripped Eliza's forearm. "Why can't I remember? What happens if I never get the memory back?"

"Don't overthink it." Eliza patted her friend's hand, which still gripped her arm with viselike strength. "Let it come back naturally. It will. Trying to force the process might do more harm than good."

"But I can't help feeling that I hold the key to what happened. I was there. I must have seen the killer." Belle released her grip on Eliza and pressed her palms against her temples, massaging them roughly. "Think, think, think." With a frustrated curse, Belle huffed and clenched her fists in her lap.

"Look at me." Eliza waited until Belle's eyes met hers. "It will come. I promise. You need to relax and stop overthinking." An idea sparked in her mind. "Returning to the scene might help jog your memory."

"I don't see why it wouldn't." Belle swung her feet over the side of the bed. "Let's go."

Eliza placed a gentle hand on Belle's arm. "Not so fast. It's pitch-dark outside. And it wouldn't help anybody for us to twist our ankles."

"I hate it when you're right." Belle's grin reminded Eliza of her old self.

"I'm never wrong when I'm right." Eliza patted Belle's knee. "I'll let you get some rest, and tomorrow morning, we can go."

At Belle's nod, Eliza left the room, closing the door softly behind her. She turned to walk down the hallway and gasped at Tash's silent figure looming before her.

"Terribly sorry, Miss Eliza, for startling you. That wasn't my intention."

"You missed your calling, Tash. With stealth like that, you'd have been perfect for MI5."

Tash's weathered face lit up, and a rare smile tugged at his lips. "Perhaps, Miss Eliza, I am."

Eliza laughed. "But if you told me, you'd have to kill me, right?"

Tash tapped the side of his nose. "The best-kept secrets, Miss Eliza, are just that. Secrets."

"You know, Tash, it wouldn't surprise me in the least to discover that you and Great-Aunt Iris were working together for the government. Between the two of you and your talent for becoming invisible, you'd make the perfect team."

Tash's eyes twinkled. "That's something to consider, miss. Now, you have an evening visitor. Detective Chief Inspector Wentworth is waiting in the drawing room."

At the mention of the officer's name, dread settled in Eliza's stomach. Not that she didn't enjoy Wentworth's company—most of the time—but his presence that night was unlikely to be social.

Before entering the drawing room, she took a deep breath and braced herself for whatever bad news he'd surely come to deliver. After forcing a smile onto her face, she pushed through the door. "Good evening, Wentworth. What brings you by at this hour?"

Wentworth's haggard face and disheveled hair told the story of a rough day. "I'm afraid I don't have good news, Eliza." He gestured for her to take a seat then settled into his own chair after she'd arranged herself in the embroidered brocade armchair. "We got the tox screens back—"

"That was quick."

"Several people at the lab owe me favors. Let's say I called one in." He scratched at the salt-and-pepper stubble covering his brown cheeks. "The lab found no sign of drugs."

Eliza's instant joy deflated at the serious look in his eyes. "That's great news." She tilted her head and studied him. "Right?"

"And her blood alcohol level wasn't off the charts enough to warrant the supposed amnesia she's having."

Eliza's vision blurred for a few seconds as Wentworth's words hit home. "Supposed? What on earth do you mean with that adjective?"

Wentworth's face was a tight mask, but regret glinted from his eyes. "She wouldn't be the first person to claim amnesia after committing a heinous crime."

"She was as drunk as a skunk. Of course she doesn't remember. She's a notorious lightweight. I remember a time in college when she drank too much—and by too much I mean four drinks instead of three—and wandered off, and when we finally found her, she couldn't remember where she went or who she'd been with. She still has no memory of that event."

"That'll be valuable information for her barrister. Right now, though, I have to work with the facts before me." His throat worked for several moments. "I had my team scour the crime scene again. There's too much evidence to process quickly, so I have nothing to rule Belle out entirely, but the facts prove that she had the mental and physical capability of attacking Hunter. And she had Hunter's blood under her fingernails." He shuffled his feet. "My hands are tied by the powers that be. The commissioner is salivating for an arrest, and as Belle is the most likely suspect with the evidence we have, I'll need to take her in."

"You can't be serious. You have no definitive proof. If she was fending off an attack from Hunter, of course there'd be blood, right?" Her voice pitched up.

"Now, Eliza, you've always struck me as a young woman whose loyalty to her family is one of her greatest strengths, and I assume you feel the same toward your friends. You risked your freedom for me last autumn, so I know how far you'll go to protect people you respect and care about."

Eliza's eyebrows shot up. Wentworth wasn't the type of man to hand out compliments willy-nilly, and he wasn't known to wax poetic about anyone's, especially Eliza's, qualities. "You don't pull off the good-cop routine well, Wentworth."

That earned her a grim smile. "Can't fault a bloke for cushioning the giant fall he's about to take. The only traces we can identify at the crime scene so far—keeping in mind the lab has much more evidence to process—belong to Hunter and Belle. That means no one else was there. She was the last person to see Hunter alive, his blood was literally on her hands, and we now know she was fully capable of delivering a lethal blow. I know how fierce your loyalty runs, so I'm asking you to think logically, not with your heart."

Eliza went numb. She lost track of how long she simply sat there, blinking at Wentworth. "What exactly are you saying? You think Belle purposely took another human's life?"

"With no evidence suggesting anyone else was there, it's the only logical solution at this point. I won't be able to hold off the commissioner for long. I'll do what I can, but I can't promise anything." He rubbed the back of his neck and swore under his breath. "I haven't got a bloody clue what to think. I'm keeping an open mind, though." He stood and rested his large hand on her shoulder. "And I reckon you ought to do the same. I'll be in touch."

After Wentworth left the drawing room, Eliza remained seated for several minutes, staring at the door until her vision blurred. No, there had to be something they were missing. There simply had to be. And come the next morning, she'd begin the hunt anew.

Chapter Ten
Nature Versus Nurture... A Study in Evil

It is a truth universally known that a lady's true colors will soon appear, whether that lady likes it or not. At tea today, Lady Dennison had more news to share. She'd received a letter from a friend who lives near Mansfield Park. Apparently, not everyone approves of the Crawfords, and they had left the estate "rather suddenly" and there had been "some unpleasantness regarding engagements that came to nothing." Lady Dennison's letter was not detailed, but her point was clear: Beware the Crawfords and their charming manners.

Lizzy Bennet Darcy

Pemberley 1815

Usually, Mrs. Bankcroft's raspberry scones with clotted cream could lift Eliza's spirits. But as she brought the last bite to her mouth and chewed thoughtfully, none of the usual rush of dopamine hit.

She scowled at the information she'd transferred from what she and Heath had scribbled down the night before to the old chalkboard in the unused nursery. Memories of solving her first crime at Pemberley flickered through her mind. She had thought then that she would surely fail and that her dead body would soon join the victims. But as the third day of the new year dawned, seven months after her first foray into murder and mayhem, her future wasn't the one at stake. Belle's was. Eliza swallowed hard.

"What's got you in such a state, my girl?" Great-Aunt Iris asked.

Eliza glanced at her great-aunt, who was seated next to Joy. Both sat upright in uncomfortable-looking wooden chairs made for children. How Great-Aunt Iris had lowered herself into one or how Eliza was supposed to get her out of it, she had no clue. "What if I fail?"

"You? Fail?" Great-Aunt Iris tutted and rifled through her large purse then unearthed her knitting needles and a ball of variegated mint-and-lilac-colored yarn.

When she started knitting with gusto without answering the question, Eliza quirked an eyebrow at Joy, who looked heavenward and poured herself another cup of tea.

Accepting the apparent rhetorical question for what it was, Eliza grabbed the piece of chalk she'd set aside earlier when Tash had come in with a morning snack courtesy of Mrs. Bankcroft. "So, ladies, where were we?"

"We were discussing whether Hunter's parents might've done him in," Joy said.

"And what's our consensus?" Eliza asked.

Great-Aunt Iris's knitting needles fell silent, and she stared at the board for several moments, tilting her head as if straining to catch a distant sound. "I remember a young lad from my village. About my age, he was. A right nasty piece of work, or so everyone said. So rotten that even his own mum and dad couldn't stand him. When he grew up—I'd married William by then and moved to Lambton—he terrorized the young girls, interfering with them, if you catch my meaning. The local constabulary couldn't find proper evidence. Didn't have all these fancy forensics and DNA back then. None of the girls would speak up. But everyone knew it was him. This went on for ages, until one of the girls turned up dead. Again, no evidence the police could use, but in the end, it didn't matter. A nearby farmer found the boy's body while working his fields. Story goes his own father killed him. Sacrificed him to save the innocent girls of the village."

Joy gaped. "You're having me on, aren't you?"

Eliza's skin prickled at the deadly serious look in her great-aunt's eyes. "You're not joking."

"No." Great-Aunt Iris's knitting needles resumed their comforting clickety-clacks, filling the nursery once more. "His name was Tommy Macquire, and people always said he was the devil's own spawn." She tutted softly. "Always reckoned they had it backward. Should've been talking about Tommy's dad instead. Never could abide that man. No matter how the village sang his praises, I pitied poor Tommy having a father like that. On the surface, Old Man Macquire was every inch the gentleman, but even after I'd grown up and visited my village as a married woman, he terrified me. Perhaps that's what went wrong with Hunter. Maybe he was born straight from the devil."

"You've been glued to too many of those paranormal shows on the telly. Devil's spawn? That's complete rubbish. People aren't born wicked. Something's got to shape them first, hasn't it?" Joy looked at Eliza, clearly seeking backup. "Am I right?"

Eliza underlined Hubert and Henrietta's names printed on the chalkboard. "Ah, the age-old question. Are we shaped by nature or nurture? Is a 'bad' kid that way because he was born that way or because of his environment? Can a kid born 'good' be twisted by forces beyond his control? You're both right, but we need to decide which factor played the bigger role and whether one of these two"—she tapped the chalk on *Hubert* and *Henrietta*—"decided to take justice into their own hands."

"From what people have told us, Hunter was a thorn in his parents' side," Joy said.

"Yes, but a kid being the reason you can't keep house staff isn't the biggest motive for killing your child," Eliza said.

"It could be for some people," Great-Aunt Iris pointed out.

"Sadly, you're right." After all, people had killed for less throughout history. But since murder had landed in Pemberley's backyard, that grim reality took on a tragic weight that twisted in Eliza's stomach.

Eliza put a star by Hunter's parents' names. "We need more information on these two. Let's invite them here. They seemed too eager to please Uncle Fitzwilliam after dropping the lawsuit, which is suspicious by itself. Besides the cost of a lawsuit, why abandon the case so soon after their son's death?"

"Could've been Hunter's idea, not theirs," Joy said.

Eliza added *Was lawsuit over boundary Hunter's idea or his parents'?* to the board. "If he was in a financial mess because people were calling in their chips in his Ponzi schemes, he'd need the capital to pay them and not have people get suspicious. What better way to do that than bleeding the neighboring estate dry?"

"You're forgetting one thing, my dear," Great-Aunt Iris said. "Lawsuits take an absolute age. If Hunter was behind this lawsuit, he would have known that Fitzwilliam would call in a team of solicitors. Once solicitors get involved, it could drag on for years before reaching any proper conclusion. If he needed quick funds, he would have turned to blackmail instead. Nothing as legitimate as a lawsuit, dodgy or not, that would clog up the courts for donkey's years."

Joy raised her teacup in a toast to Great-Aunt Iris. "If Eliza ever decides to uproot herself again and move back to the States, I vote for you to be our sleuthing team captain."

"Just vote me off the island now. Please. Great-Aunt Iris, you're officially in charge." Eliza joined her great-aunt and cousin, slouching into a matching wooden chair and immediately scowling at the sharp pain in her backside. "How have you two managed to sit in these torture devices for this long?"

"I'm afraid my bum went numb several minutes ago." Joy grinned at Great-Aunt Iris. "How's yours holding up?"

"How's my what?"

"Your bottom?"

Great-Aunt Iris stared at Joy as if she'd sprouted an extra nose. "Ladies do not refer to such things. It's simply not done. Frightfully unladylike."

Eliza swallowed a laugh that would surely have earned her one of Great-Aunt Iris's grand sniffs. Apparently, her great-aunt's rules about ladylike conversation didn't extend to her candid discussions about marital activities with Great-Uncle William.

Joy flashed a cheeky grin. "I've never been accused of being lady-like."

Great-Aunt Iris harrumphed and mumbled something. It sounded suspiciously like "Well, I never," but Eliza had no desire to fan the brewing wildfire between them.

Eliza hopped to her feet. "I promised to take Belle to see the crime scene."

"Are the police finished processing it?" Joy asked.

"No, but we'll stay clear of the taped-off areas. She thinks visiting might jog her memory, and I haven't even been there yet. Another sign that my sleuthing skills are seriously waning. I want to get a feel for the place: the distance from the house, the terrain, all of it. Who wants to come with?"

"As much as I'd love to go off gallivanting in the woods, I promised your great-uncle his usual morning exercise." Great-Aunt Iris waved away Joy and Eliza's offered hands, struggled to her feet, and nearly pranced from the room on squeaking white tennis shoes.

"Please tell me his morning exercise is a walk," Joy said as she and Eliza left the old nursery.

"Never ask a question when you don't want the answer."

"And when do you suppose we'll get to the boundary between Pemberley and Berryhill Manor?" Eliza looked cross-eyed at the tip of her cherry-red nose and scowled.

"I thought as a South Dakota girl, you'd be used to the cold." Joy wrapped her scarf tighter around her neck.

"Give me a dry cold any day. It's this wet cold that gets to me." Eliza shivered and glanced at Belle, who had convinced them both that she was up for a walk in the woods despite her greenish bruises and the scrapes still healing across her face. "How are you holding up? We can turn back if you want."

"No. I'm fine. I want to see it." Determination flickered in Belle's eyes.

"Can't be much farther. I had no idea Pemberley's woods were so big." Eliza gave the police tape on her right a wide berth. She had promised Wentworth so faithfully that she wouldn't even step the tippiest tip of her toe over or under the crime-scene tape. Eliza's anger kindled anew at seeing the distance Belle had run in the dead of night. Sweat beaded between her shoulder blades and dripped down her spine. She arched her back and marched forward with renewed purpose.

After a few more minutes of stumbling over nature's debris, they reached the perimeter of the crime scene. Forensics officers in white suits and booties worked within the inner circle, collecting and tagging evidence. A constable stood guard outside the taped-off area, stamping his booted feet and slapping his gloved hands against his thighs to keep warm.

She smiled when he scowled at her and handed him a thermos of hot chocolate. "You must have drawn the short straw, eh?"

His scowl deepened, but before Eliza could warn him that in weather so cold, his face might freeze like that, he unscrewed the top and took a whiff. His eyes took on a dreamy look, but within seconds, his face hardened again. He cleared his throat with a gruff sound. "Can't be hanging around here, yeah? This isn't some bloody sideshow." His voice carried a distinctive Australian drawl.

"DCI Wentworth told you I was coming, I believe." Eliza noted he didn't attempt to hand her back the thermos and tried her most disarming smile. "Eliza Darcy."

The officer straightened and peered down his nose at her. She hadn't noticed how tall he was or how crooked his nose was, but with him towering over her, his chocolatey-brown eyes studying her face, she had no choice but to take stock of both. The constable resembled an ancient warrior god who'd fallen out of the sky, hitting every obstacle on his way to earth nose first. All he needed was a fur cloak and a leather shield, and he could star in a Viking documentary.

The officer quirked an eyebrow at her. Heat rushed up the back of her neck, and she was thankful her nose and cheeks were already ruby red from the cold. She cut a glance at Joy and Belle.

Joy was sizing up the man in question, and Eliza had no doubt that Joy's next fictional hero in her Regency romance bodice-rippers was going to look exactly like Officer Stick-in-the-Mud. Eliza wasn't mad at that idea. The constable could pull off breeches and a waistcoat. He probably rode a horse very well too.

The old Belle would have fired off a few witty remarks at the officer and flashed him a charming smile, but the current Belle stood frozen, her gaze on something behind the constable.

"Belle?" Eliza asked.

When she didn't respond and kept staring into nothing, Eliza's heart hammered. "Belle?" She shook her friend's shoulder, and when Belle gazed at her with blank eyes, Eliza looked desperately at Joy for help.

The officer stepped forward. "Everything all right here? Your mate looks a bit crook."

"My friend Belle, she's…" Eliza waved her hand in front of Belle's face and got a blink and a scowl in return.

"She needs..." Eliza had no idea what her friend needed and finished with a helpless shrug.

"I need a moment is all. To think." Belle rubbed her temples and closed her eyes.

"Are you sure you're okay?" Eliza asked.

"Eliza..." Belle scowled at her. "If you ask me one more time if I'm okay, I'll go crazy. Just give me a moment." She took a few steps away from the little group and studied the section cordoned off by crime-scene tape.

After giving Belle a side glance, the constable turned his attention to Eliza. "You're tellin' me you're the infamous Miss Eliza Darcy, eh?"

Eliza tried to read the shift in his tone, which was still gravelly and deep but with a playful edge, one that sparked hope he wouldn't march them back to the house with a stern finger and without so much as a by-your-leave. "The one and only, for which I'm sure the world rejoices. And you are?"

"Theo Archibald."

"Well, Constable Archibald, do you mind if Belle takes a moment? I assume she's trying to conjure the events of New Year's Eve." *And I can get a moment to suss out the scene.* She craned her neck to peek around his solid frame, but he stepped directly into her line of sight. *Drat him.*

His gaze flicked to Belle, concern flashing in his eyes. He studied her with the practiced eye of someone who'd seen his fair share of trauma. "Reckon she's right to be out here, yeah?"

"When Belle gets an idea into her head, it would take God himself to change her mind, and even then, he'd have one heck of a time. It was either this or hog-tie her and stuff her in a closet so she couldn't follow Joy and me out here."

The corner of his lips twitched up. "And you're out here... because?"

Eliza crossed her arms and glared up at him. "Because I want to find out who killed the basta—um, Hunter—so I can clear my friend of suspicion." She zeroed in on his twitching lip. "What?"

"Wentworth warned me about you."

Joy snickered. "Good old Wentworth never disappoints, does he?"

Eliza spared her cousin a glance before turning back to Constable Archibald. "First of all, I'd believe everything Wentworth tells you about me since it's probably true. Secondly, what can you tell me about the crime scene that Wentworth refuses to share?"

I f Eliza's frozen face could have smiled, she would have at Constable Theo Archibald's dropped jaw. She rarely got the pleasure of seeing a Viking documentary's leading man looking gobsmacked.

"I'm sorry, Constable Archibald," Joy said, "but my *American* cousin here tends to come off as a bit—"

"If Wentworth got to him first, Constable Archibald already knows all my 'qualities,' I'm sure."

Theo grinned, and if Eliza hadn't already sworn her eternal love and devotion to Heath, she might have been in danger of succumbing to such warfare. "Theo, please. You remind me of my mum."

Joy laughed and nudged Eliza's shoulder.

Eliza couldn't help but wonder what the jail time was for kicking a constable in the shin. "Excuse you?"

His brown eyes twinkled. "My mum. You remind me of her."

"I heard that part."

"She's American, too, and has a right spunk to her. Doesn't think before she speaks," Theo said, a cheeky grin playing on his lips.

Eliza wasn't sure if she should be pleased or offended by his comment, but she decided to hold her judgment—for the moment.

Belle walked back over to them, her shoulders pulled back, her face set with determination. "I remember this place. I remember Hunter trying to kiss me and not taking no for an answer." Belle jutted her chin out. "I slapped him. No... I punched him. Right in the nose. I can still hear the crunch. I ran. I ran as fast as I could. Thank God Pemberley was lit up like a Christmas tree, or I would never have made my way back." Belle shivered.

"Did you hear anything, see anything as you left the scene?" Theo asked.

"I don't think so. Ah, wait. I remember being afraid he was following me because I heard twigs snapping."

Theo slid a glance at Eliza and jerked his head back toward the scene. "Might I have a word?"

Eliza followed Theo to the tape border and crossed her arms over her chest. "Well?"

"I'm only telling you this 'cause DCI Wentworth said I can trust you, and after what you did for him last autumn, I trust you as well." His sharp gaze studied her face. "I can see how much you care for your mate, and I respect that."

"I feel we could have a moment here, Constable Archibald, but our working relationship has already been tainted with the whole 'mother' comment." She grinned up at him.

"Just be grateful I didn't compare you to my sister, eh? Those would be fighting words. Now, then. There was someone else in the woods that night."

"This is the first I'm hearing about it. Did you find new evidence?"

"Nah, and I didn't piece it together until your friend mentioned she thought Hunter was chasing her." He pointed at the center of the taped-off area. "That's where we found Hunter's body. Belle's story about decking him in the nose checks out. The autopsy showed he suffered a broken nose right before death. There were two different blood splatter patterns, yeah? One from the nosebleed after she broke his beak, the other from when someone whacked him over the head with something solid. From where the blood landed, it's clear Hunter never tried to chase Belle. The bloke was dropped right where he stood."

"That makes perfect sense to me, but a good lawyer could spin that evidence so it still points at her. He'd argue that she broke his nose, hit him on the head, and ran off then made up the story about hearing twigs breaking to cover her tracks."

"A barrister can spin a yarn if paid enough, but this here's a fair dinkum breakthrough. I need to ring Wentworth straightaway. Mind if I duck off for a minute?" Theo's gaze fell on Belle, and something flashed in his eyes, catching Eliza's attention.

"Sure."

While Theo made his call, Eliza studied the taped-off area. The crime scene techs were still working, collecting evidence and snapping pictures. The air had grown much colder, and a tiny snowflake drifted down to land on the toe of Eliza's boot. An anvil could have fallen on her toe, and she'd have noticed it as much as she did the snowflake for as numb as her toes were. She tried to curl them in her boots, or at least she thought she did, and kept studying the scene. Small yellow triangles marked various pieces of evidence, and while she couldn't see exactly what they indicated, the rusty color suggested it was blood splatter.

The remote part of the woods struck her as odd. *Why would Hunter bring Belle out here in the first place?* True, it bordered the property line of Berryhill, and from where she stood, she could make out the wooden fence separating the two properties. But Hunter didn't strike her as someone who'd suffer the weather without good reason.

"Wentworth thinks there's something to your mate's story." Theo's voice cut through Eliza's thoughts.

"Do you know anything about the Crawfords?"

"Most folks with half a brain give that whole bloody lot a wide berth." He followed her gaze toward the wooden fence. "What's got you so fascinated with that fence, then?"

The hair on the back of Eliza's neck prickled. "I don't know. I just feel... something. Sounds silly, I know."

"Not at all. It's what we call a copper's instinct."

Eliza glanced back at Belle, worried about her friend's condition. "Never mind. I'll come back after you've cleared the scene."

"You'll never get a wink of sleep if you do that." He jerked his chin toward the fence. "I'll make sure your mates get back to the house so you can investigate your 'feeling.'"

"Don't you have to guard the scene? If I popped up to snoop, someone else might."

"You're not the first. Hubert keeps turning up at the fence, pacing along it. Reckon it's his way of coping with losing his lad. But my replacement's already here, so no worries." He waved at a female constable who'd taken his post. "I'll give her the heads-up that you're cleared to be round here. Real pleasure meeting you, Eliza." His gaze drifted back to Belle. "Maybe we'll bump into each other again, and you can fill me in on what's going on with that fence."

After speaking to the other constable, Theo walked back to Belle and motioned for her to follow him back toward Pemberley. Joy gave Eliza a finger wave and trotted off after the pair.

Eliza waved back, mouthed "Thank you," then slapped her numb, gloved hands against her thighs and wished she'd worn the wool socks Great-Aunt Iris had recommended. But she hadn't listened, so with numb fingers and toes that felt detached from her body, she trudged toward the fence, uncertain what drew her to it.

Chapter Eleven
Eliza Unearths a Dark Hidden Secret

Oh dear. What a day it has been. Little Fitz has wailed from dawn until dusk, and nothing soothes him. Nurse says he is cutting his first tooth. The only one who can calm him is Darcy, so as the sun sets and I write in my journal, my heart sings at the sight of my beloved husband pacing back and forth in the rose garden, his son's tiny head tucked under his chin. Is it possible to fall in love all over again?
Lizzy Bennet Darcy
Pemberley 1815

The first thing that struck Eliza was the remoteness of the area. The weathered gray fence wasn't visible from any of the estate houses or outbuildings, and nothing but dense trees surrounded the property line. Eliza hadn't even known it existed, and in her seven months at Pemberley, she'd barely explored a tenth of the estate's vast expanse. Unlike other grand estates from the height of gentrified glory, Pemberley hadn't been sold off acre by acre until only the house and lawn remained.

Without Hunter's murdered body being discovered there, the fence would have remained a mystery to her for some time until either she stumbled upon it or it surfaced as part of the boundary suit the Crawfords had filed. Her heart thudded. Theo's mention of Hubert visiting the fence and walking along it sent a chill down her spine. The man had shown no outward signs of mourning his son, but perhaps he was a private griever who wanted to be near the last place his son had been alive.

She walked along the fence, paying extra attention to the brown grass at her feet to avoid tripping on a tree root or twisting her ankle in a hidden hole. She smiled ruefully. One thing she missed that she never thought she would: the snow. While England got snow flurries and storms, it never lasted long, and cold, dreary rain often washed away any remaining traces.

She stepped forward and, despite looking for path hazards, stepped into a divot. Her foot slipped sideways, and she hissed in pain. Eliza scowled, squatted, and brushed at the disturbed earth. At first glance, it looked like a wild animal had torn up the area, but closer inspection revealed indentations more reminiscent of a shovel blade than animal claws. She squinted at the gouges in the soil and sat back on her haunches. Her "copper's instinct," as Theo had called it, churned. Someone had tried to dig something up but got interrupted. She didn't know what had spooked them, but Eliza suspected the person's excavation had been cut short by the crime scene a stone's throw away.

She pulled her phone from her back pocket and dialed Wentworth's number.

"Didn't take long for you to put one of my best men under your spell, I see." Wentworth's gruff voice crackled through the phone. "Never took you as a charmer, but here we are."

"Hello to you too." Eliza ignored Wentworth's comments on her obviously disarming ways. "Two things. Belle remembers punching Hunter in the nose. That's probably where the blood on her right hand came from." She waited for a second but only got a gruff grunt. "And second, I think I found something."

"Remember that button you found the first time you played Sherlock Holmes? It was just a—"

"I dig either with you or without you. Which is it?" Eliza clenched her teeth at his growled and vicious swear word. "I'll take that as you'd rather I wait for you?" she asked sweetly.

"Touch anything, and I'll have you nicked for... for..."

"Tampering with evidence?"

"Right, that." The phone went dead.

"Goodbye to you as well." Eliza slipped her phone back into her pocket.

Rather than brave the walk back to Pemberley only to return with Wentworth, Eliza paced along the fence, slapping her hands against her thighs to encourage feeling back into her fingers, and kept well away from the disturbed earth.

Eliza's phone chirped, and she smiled when Heath's text thread popped up.

Heath: *Heard you've made a new friend.*

Eliza: *Joy's got a big mouth.*

Heath: *Apparently, a Viking extra with an Australian accent ran from set and is now pretending to play copper.*

Eliza: *Firstly: Great minds apparently think alike. Secondly, and I repeat: Joy's got a big mouth.*

Heath: *First I had competition with Wentworth and now a Viking god? How shall I ever compete?*

Eliza grinned at his winking-face emoji. *You have a few aces up your sleeve, but I won't stop you from trying to show me how you stack up against them.*

Heath: *Challenge accepted.*

Eliza: *I think I stumbled... literally... onto a clue.*

Heath: *I told you not to have fun without me. Keep me posted. Gotta dash, though. Meeting in five minutes. Love you!*

Eliza: *Love you too! See you tonight for dinner. Great-Aunt Iris recently discovered YouTube videos and has an entire list she wants to show you. Spoiler alert: They're all about aliens.*

Eliza chuckled at Heath's paired horrified-looking emoji and alien emoji then stuffed her phone back in her pocket. Her gaze kept drifting to the disturbed ground. If she started digging solo, Wentworth would confiscate the fake badge he'd given her during their first murder case, and that cheap trinket meant more to her than it probably should.

Shivering, Eliza was contemplating making the trek back to Pemberley when a familiar voice called out to her. "Can't you keep your nose out of police business for once? I leave you unsupervised for a moment, and you go finding more trouble." Wentworth picked his way through the dense, wet underbrush.

"To be fair, I fell into it. I was minding my own business, thank you very much." She decided not to remind him she'd fallen into it because she'd initially been snooping around the crime scene and *not* minding her own business.

Wentworth studied the area she pointed out and crouched beside it. With gloved fingers, he brushed lightly over the surface then fell back onto his backside with a "Blimey." He tore off his gloves, wrestled his cell phone from his jacket pocket, and barked orders at whoever answered on the other end.

"Is it what I think it is?" Eliza asked, hoping whatever someone had tried to unearth—or bury—was treasure or a portal to Narnia. She averted her eyes from the spot, not wanting to see what had made the seasoned detective chief inspector lose his cool and held her hand out to help him off the ground.

Wentworth accepted her hand, nearly pulling her down with his weight, and positioned his body between her and the disturbed earth. "You'd best head back to Pemberley, Eliza."

On a normal day, she would have tried to weasel her way into the situation, but from the sad look in his amber eyes and the droop to his normally rigid shoulders, Eliza knew it wasn't a normal day. Things wouldn't be normal at Pemberley for a long while.

S omehow, discussing a recently discovered dead body on Pemberley's property didn't seem appropriate conversation over tea and raspberry scones with clotted cream. But since Pemberley didn't have a dungeon to fit the dark topic, the drawing room, with its cheery fire crackling against the cold night, would have to do.

Everyone, including Great-Uncle William, sat in silence after Wentworth shared the news. While Eliza had suspected the worst when Wentworth fell on his backside in surprise and horror, hearing that the police had unearthed a body sent her gut swirling and her head spinning. She rested her head on Heath's shoulder, letting his familiar scent of Irish Spring soap ground her. He brought his arm around the back of their shared couch and gently traced circles on her shoulder.

"What else can you tell us?" Uncle Fitzwilliam asked, his cheeks pale.

"Not much, I'm afraid. The body's condition doesn't allow for immediate identification, but the skeleton is small in stature." Wentworth took a sip of brandy from his cut-crystal glass, swirled the rest, and studied the amber liquid. "Can't say for certain, but the poor soul's been in the ground for some time." He shook his head. "The pathologist believes it's a child."

Great-Aunt Iris gasped and looked wildly at Great-Uncle William.

He laid his wrinkled and gnarled hand on her knee. "What is it, love?"

"You don't think it's…" Great-Aunt Iris clutched her hands over her heart. "It can't be, can it?"

"Can't be what?" Great-Uncle William asked.

"Don't you remember, dear? Oh, years ago—twenty? No." She crinkled her nose and shook her head. "It's so hard to keep track of all the years, but there was that dreadful missing-person case involving a Lambton girl. She was the loveliest little girl with a voice of an angel. Most people came to church just to hear her sing in the children's choir. Can't recall her name off the top of my head. She was never found—at least not that I know of."

"Mrs. Darcy, I think you're the brains of the illegal sleuthing operation Eliza's running," Wentworth said. "I've requested all files on missing persons and cold cases from the past thirty years, and I hope something will surface and give us a proper lead."

Joy, who'd been staring into the fire, snapped to attention. "Are you talking about Rosie Harley?"

"That's the one." Great-Aunt Iris shook her head. "She was the loveliest girl Lambton had ever seen. As sweet as anything. An absolute angel. That's what some people chose to believe when she disappeared. They claimed God had taken her straight to Heaven. Bunch of rubbish, that."

Wentworth narrowed his eyes at Joy. "I remember hearing about that case. That was..." He tapped his fingers together. "What? How many years back? You couldn't have been more than a nipper."

"Eighteen years ago. I was eight, and I'll remember that case until the day I die." Joy's voice trembled.

"What happened?" Belle asked from her spot on the floor, wrapped in a blanket and staring into the fire.

"Mum and I were here on a quick holiday. Turned out to be a bloody nightmare." Joy took a swig of her brandy.

"I remember now," Great-Aunt Iris said. "Your mum and I took you to Lambton for the Spooky Spectacular festival. It started as such a jolly day." Her gentle smile faded into a frown. "You had met a playmate."

"Rosie Harley." Joy stared into her glass for several seconds. "After palling around with each other for a few hours, we were 'best mates,' of course, and we'd made plans to meet up the next day, same time, same place. Only she never showed up, did she?"

"Never saw so many people rally round like that. The whole village turned out to search for her," Great-Aunt Iris said.

"Poor girl. Her poor parents," Eliza murmured.

"Her parents never recovered. After two years with no answers, they moved away." Great-Aunt Iris's knitting needles clacked harder than necessary. "People always said it was the father pushing to leave. Rosie's mum wanted to stay put, hoping her little girl would come wandering back. She didn't want her child to come home to an empty house or one filled with strangers."

Eliza wiped at a tear rolling down her cheek. "And nothing was ever found?"

"As far as I know, nothing. Not a hint, not a whisper. It's like she vanished into thin air."

"Until now," Joy whispered.

The room fell silent. Eliza fought the urge to squirm under the heavy quiet and the growing certainty that Hunter's case was somehow connected to the eighteen-year-old missing-person case, which was likely a murder.

After a restless night filled with dreams of a little girl crying in the woods, Eliza woke feeling boneless and exhausted. She trudged to her en-suite bathroom, scowled at her reflection, and made herself at least presentable to the rest of the household.

Before leaving her bedroom, she checked her calendar. Not usually thankful for an open weekend, which didn't help Pemberley's finances, she thanked her lucky stars that no group had booked a tour or getaway the first weekend of the New Year. She wasn't sure how she'd manage to save her friend while entertaining guests. She had a week and a few days before the next scheduled event. By then, she hoped everything would be sorted, and a police presence wouldn't be the daily norm anymore.

Besides, having crime scene tape somewhere on the property, though not visible from the house, left a heavy atmosphere hanging over the place. The publicity and media buzz around the murder on the estate would draw people from all over to gawk at Pemberley, like the last time, but for all the wrong reasons. She'd need to add beefing up security to her growing to-do list.

She drew an *X* through the first, second, and third of January and tapped her pen on the fourth square, wondering what the day would bring. There was only one way to find out.

Within a few moments, she joined her uncle in the breakfast room. Normally one to leap up and seize the day, Uncle Fitzwilliam slumped in his chair, haggard and exhausted. He wasn't sporting his usual attire of a sweater, slacks, and Oxfords. Instead, he wore a baggy sweatshirt she'd never seen before, and his feet were tucked into worn slippers.

Eliza pecked his whiskered cheek and sat beside him. "You look like you slept as well as I did."

Uncle Fitzwilliam poured her a cup of coffee. "I can't recall a night quite as awful as last night." He gave a hollow smile. "And you know I've had some awful nights."

Eliza squeezed his hand. They had shared some of those terrible nights together. "This one's different somehow, though. I couldn't get the image of that little girl—" Her throat burned, and tears stung the backs of her eyes.

"I know." Uncle Fitzwilliam sighed.

Silence filled the room, but Eliza didn't know how to break it. There were no words for the tragic loss of a child, the trauma inflicted on the family, or the injustice served to little Rosie Harley if their assumptions were correct, abandoned to some lonely grave.

The breakfast door opened, and in squeaked Great-Aunt Iris in her white tennis shoes, followed by Caesar. "Ah, I see you two look as rested as I am."

"Must be a running theme around here." Eliza helped settle her into a chair. "You look pale. Are you getting sick?" She placed the back of her hand on her great-aunt's forehead.

Great-Aunt Iris swatted it away. "I haven't been ill a day in my life, might I remind you. No one around here can remember a thing."

Eliza shared looks with her uncle.

"Now, now, Aunt. Eliza's concerned about you. Remember how you nearly succumbed to influen—"

She sniffed. "That was nothing more than a sniffle. And people do not pop their clogs from sniffles, Fitzwilliam."

While her uncle and great-aunt were playing the semantics game on different illnesses and their severity, Eliza piled plates for herself and Great-Aunt Iris from the buffet and sat beside her. With the conversation still in full swing, Eliza broke off a piece of bacon and held it out to Caesar, who paused his assault on a piece of yarn poking out of Great-Aunt Iris's purse long enough to snatch it without any hint of gratitude before returning to maul the baby-blue strand.

"You're welcome," she told her cat pointedly, though he ignored her sarcasm.

When a lull in the aunt–nephew debate finally allowed, Eliza jumped into the conversation. "Does anyone have a brilliant idea of where we go from here?"

"I rang Wentworth this morning, and there's nothing fresh to report on that front. They're still processing the scene, and there's no word yet on gender or how long the body's been buried. That all takes time."

"But we don't *have* time." Eliza's appetite curdled, and she pushed her eggs around the plate. "Does the buried body have any connection to Hunter's death?"

"It does seem suspicious that both crimes happened practically on top of each other," Uncle Fitzwilliam said. "Could be a coincidence, though. That part of Pemberley is secluded, and it's been well over a year since I've walked that boundary line." He furrowed his brow. "If it weren't for that anonymous caller, who knows how long Hunter's body would have gone unnoticed."

"Could they trace the phone call?" Eliza asked.

"I asked Wentworth the same question, and all I got in return was a terse no. I suspect the caller used a burner mobile."

Eliza shivered. "But why call it in anonymously? There are only two reasons someone would do that. Either they committed the crime and wanted the body found for some reason, or they witnessed it but didn't want any part in the investigation, which is suspicious in itself."

"Which means the witness must have been at our New Year's Eve ball," Great-Aunt Iris said. "One doesn't simply wander onto the property and explore. Not on New Year's Eve and not when it's bitterly cold and pitch-black outside."

"When I walked along the fence earlier, I noticed that Berryhill's estate is as wooded as Pemberley," Eliza said. "Whoever killed Hunter or witnessed the attack had to be from either Pemberley or Berryhill Manor. The location is too remote for any passerby to notice. The crime scene sits easily a half mile through thick woods. I seriously doubt the murderer is a stranger."

"Then what are we waiting for?" Great-Aunt Iris pushed back her chair and stood. "Let's be off."

Eliza squinted up at her. "Where exactly?"

"Young people nowadays. Back in my day, we were always game for adventures. We never needed to be asked twice."

"I'm not saying I won't go on an adventure with you, but I'd like to know what it involves."

"Does it matter?" Great-Aunt Iris asked.

"Do I need to pack road-trip snacks?"

"Since you didn't eat breakfast, you might get peckish on the drive to Lambton." Great-Aunt Iris bustled from the room, Caesar trotting at her heels. She paused in the doorway. "I'll rouse Joy from her fictional chaps." Without another word, she swept out of the breakfast room.

Hands on hips, Eliza quirked an eyebrow at her uncle.

He chuckled, set his napkin on the table, and stood. "Don't look at me. She's *your* great-aunt." He patted her shoulder. "Best of luck, and don't forget those snacks."

Eliza sputtered. "Well... What are you going to do while Great-Aunt Iris kidnaps me?"

"I'm going to make some calls." His good humor vanished.

"Take care of Belle while I'm gone? I know the threat of an imminent arrest's been weighing on her. I don't know how much I want her traipsing around Lambton. People might talk. Not that they aren't already."

"Don't worry, my dear. I'll take good care of your friend. And if she's lucky, I'll introduce her to *Fawlty Towers*."

Eliza cringed. "Maybe I will take her into Lambton after all."

"Or perhaps she has better taste in television programs than you do." Uncle Fitzwilliam embraced her in a quick hug and left the breakfast room, his normally broad, stoic shoulders slumped with worry.

Having no clue what to expect or where her great-aunt was taking her or for how long, Eliza grabbed a roll from the table and hurried back to her room to ready herself for whatever adventure lay ahead.

After checking in on Belle and filling her in on her upcoming brain-numbing television experience, Eliza joined Great-Aunt Iris and a confused-looking Joy in the foyer.

"Well, girls, are you ready?" Great-Aunt Iris asked, resplendent in a black dress, pearls, and spotless white tennis shoes.

"Ready for what exactly?" Joy asked, glancing down at her leggings and oversize emerald-green cable-knit sweater. "I've got the sneaking suspicion that either you're overdressed or I'm under-dressed."

Great-Aunt Iris tutted and walked out the door.

"She didn't fill you in either?" Eliza asked Joy as they followed Great-Aunt Iris out of the house, through the courtyard, and to the Range Rover parked in front. Feeling woefully underdressed in boot-cut jeans, a long-sleeved white shirt, and a pink puffer vest, she wondered what they were walking into.

"Now, where would the fun be if life didn't throw you a few surprises, eh?" Great-Aunt Iris waved off all help and hoisted herself into the back seat.

Eliza, for her part, was sick and tired of surprises, but she kept her mouth shut and silently slid into the passenger seat.

Chapter Twelve
When Golden Girls Go Rogue

Why, oh why, did I not tell Hutchinson that I am not at home? Miss Crawford's reason for calling this morning, ostensibly to discuss engaging local servants for Berryhill Manor, quickly devolved into a tedious conversation about matrimony and settlements. She had strong opinions on marrying for security rather than affection, claiming love a myth and unnecessary for a happy union. I attempted to tell her of Darcy's and my happiness due to love and affection, but she laughed and called me "charmingly naive." It is a godsend that little Fitz decided to have another bout of teething.

Lizzy Bennet Darcy
Pemberley 1815

Eliza watched through the passenger window as Joy zipped past all their usual haunts, following Great-Aunt Iris's directions.

"Where are you taking us?" Eliza squinted at a business she'd never seen before. "Are you sure we're not lost?"

"I haven't been lost a day in my life, my girl. I'm always exactly where I intend to be." Great-Aunt Iris tapped the back of Joy's headrest with a knitting needle. "Take the next left. There's a good girl."

"Right you are," Joy murmured and turned as directed.

"Now take a right down this alleyway," Great-Aunt Iris said.

"You having me on?" Joy asked, slowing down and eyeing the garbage cans lining the backs of businesses.

"This is no Bond Street, that's for certain, but it's also not Westminster."

"The Abbey?" Eliza asked.

"No." Great-Aunt Iris raised an eyebrow and sniffed. "I read an article this morning claiming that Westminster has the highest crime rate of all the boroughs." She clutched her purse as if they'd been dropped into the seedy underworld outside Buckingham Palace.

Not bothering to fact-check her great-aunt, Eliza stared at the crumbling brick building Joy had parked beside. "I'm not doubting your navigation skills, Great-Aunt—"

"I've come to an executive decision."

Eliza studied her great-aunt.

Great-Aunt Iris tilted her head and gazed at the back of the building they were apparently about to enter. "How old do I look?"

Eliza would have smiled at the question if her great-aunt's face hadn't shown a seriousness rarely present when she discussed her age. "Since the first moment I met you, I always thought you looked much younger than your peers."

Great-Aunt Iris fixed her with a look. "You didn't answer my question, Eliza. How old do I look?"

Eliza shared panicked looks with Joy. She knew her great-aunt was in her eighties, but since the woman remained mysteriously vague about the digit following eight, Eliza had always respected her evasiveness. It suited them all. In truth, her great-aunt defied her age with boundless energy, robust health, infectious vivacity, and a skin-care routine that Eliza had yet to weasel out of her.

It was never wise to guess a woman's age, especially those in their golden years, but judging from her great-aunt's quivering knitting needles and determined expression, Eliza knew she'd better take a stab at it. "You could easily pass for someone in their seventies." Which was true. Great-Aunt Iris didn't suffer fools gladly—or at all, really—and her bloodhound nose for truth would sniff out a lie from a thousand miles away.

Great-Aunt Iris preened and smiled, though her expression quickly soured as she narrowed her eyes at the back of the building. "Quite right. When we enter, don't refer to me as your great-aunt. Aunt will do perfectly well, Eliza."

Before Eliza could ask for clarification, Great-Aunt Iris opened her door and climbed out. Before shutting it, she pursed her lips and murmured, "I might have you drop it altogether. It's a mouthful, and it does make me sound frightfully old." She slammed the door, walked to the back entrance, swiveled on her white tennis shoes, and gestured for Eliza and Joy to join her.

Moments later, Eliza walked through the back door and blinked as her eyes adjusted to the dim interior. The dingy entrance should have smelled musty, but the tantalizing aroma of tea and delicate pastries teased her nose instead.

"Where are we?" Eliza asked, lightly gripping her great-aunt's arm to keep her from tripping on the threadbare runner as they navigated the poorly lit hallway.

"We are in a place we'll never speak of again in mixed company," Great-Aunt Iris whispered, pausing at a closed door.

Feminine voices drifted through the wood, and the scent of an excellent tea service made Eliza's stomach grumble.

"Now remember, both of you, I am *just* Eliza's aunt. These... These... women..." She gestured toward the door, shook her head, and rapped out the opening beats of "God Save the King," finishing with one hard knock that Eliza assumed served as the exclamation point.

Great-Aunt Iris straightened, pulled her shoulders back, fluffed her cloud of snow-white hair, and motioned for Joy and Eliza to follow suit.

The door opened to reveal a woman with salt-and-pepper hair and flawless skin, who greeted Eliza and Joy with suspicious eyes. As much as Eliza wanted to peer past her, the woman had angled her body to block any curious onlookers. Besides, she stood two inches taller than Eliza, making it impossible to see over the woman's head.

"Regina." Great-Aunt Iris narrowed her eyes and practically glared at the woman.

"Lady Beaumont, if you please." Regina sniffed, turned her eagle-eyed examination to Great-Aunt Iris, and smiled with barely concealed malice. "*Iris*, how absolutely *lovely* to see you."

Eliza opened her mouth, but Great-Aunt Iris stepped firmly on her toe. Eliza swallowed her squeak of surprise.

"It's been a long time. I believe the last time you joined one of our gatherings was last spring. Health problems keeping you from gracing us with your presence?" Regina asked sweetly—far too sweetly.

Eliza's blood boiled as the pressure of Great-Aunt Iris's foot on her toe increased.

"Poor health is something I believe you're the only one suffering from, *Regina*, as I recall a lengthy stay at a..." Great-Aunt Iris placed her finger to her chin as if in deep thought. "Rehabilitation center last winter. Something about—"

"Yes, it was quite the ordeal, but enough about poor health. It dampens the mood, wouldn't you say?" Regina glanced over her shoulder.

"Quite."

Joy jabbed Eliza and grinned. Great-Aunt Iris had put the towering sourpuss in her place.

"Now, Regina, if you would allow us entrance. I'd like to introduce my girls to the group."

Regina gave Eliza and Joy the stink-eye but eventually nodded and moved aside, revealing a sunlit room resplendent with furniture to make any Regency Era aficionado jealous. A beautiful gilded three-tiered cart overflowed with dainty sandwiches and desserts, while seated women in various stages of their golden years wore clothes more fitting for a ballroom than an old building on the seedier end of Lambton.

Regina let them pass through, and Joy leaned over and whispered, "Looks like she's been sucking on lemons all day, the miserable cow."

Eliza grinned in agreement and came to a halt when the pack of ladies rose to their feet and moved toward them, revealing not a coffee table as Eliza had expected but a poker table piled high with chips.

"Blimey, what in the bloody hell is this place?" Joy whispered, her gaze flicking between the demurely dressed women and poker tables strewn with playing cards.

Great-Aunt Iris puffed out her chest and rested her hand on Eliza's forearm. "Golden Gamblers, please meet my niece, Eliza Darcy, and"—she rested her other hand on Joy's arm—"my young relation, Joy Bingley."

The women swarmed the newcomers and peppered them with questions, some directed at Eliza, others at Joy. In the end, three questions mattered most. Yes, Eliza Darcy was Iris Darcy's American *niece*. Yes, Joy Bingley was *that* Joy Bingley, whose book covers showcased half-naked men cradling half-naked and swooning women to their hardened chests. And yes, she'd be chuffed to autograph their physical copies.

While Great-Aunt Iris chatted with the women, who were all friendlier than Lady Beaumont, aka Regina the Sourpuss, Eliza leaned toward Joy and whispered, "It seems we've stumbled upon a secret den of iniquity."

"I wonder what it takes to become a member," Joy said. "This is absolutely brilliant."

A throat cleared behind them. Eliza and Joy whirled around and looked down at a gray-haired woman, easily two inches shorter than Great-Aunt Iris, who beamed up at them and pushed her gold-rimmed glasses back up her nose. "I'm afraid you're ill-qualified to join our group at this time, Miss Bingley." She wagged her finger at Joy like she was scolding a naughty child. "You're far too young, my dear."

Joy stuck out her hand. "Please call me Joy. And you are?"

"Gertrude. Or if you want to be fancy and snobbish like some people"—she shot a glance at Regina, who scowled at every-one—"Lady Townsend." She turned her attention to Eliza and sized her up. "And you must be the famous Eliza Darcy, Iris's niece."

Great-Aunt Iris's sudden insistence on Eliza dropping the "great" made sense. Compared to her great-aunt, most of the women in the room, clearly in their retirement or golden years, looked years if not decades younger. Their fashion choices and obvious surgical en-hancements didn't hurt the situation, and perhaps dropping "great" when discussing her niece helped Great-Aunt Iris seem younger among the group.

"Some would say infamous," Eliza said.

"It's great to finally meet you. She's talked about you for so long I feel like you're my own niece." She gestured toward a grouping of chairs. "Care for some tea? There's plenty to go around, I assure you."

Eliza didn't need to be asked twice. After creating a small pyra-mid of sandwiches and cakes on her china plate, she settled into a chair. "This all looks delicious. I don't know where to start."

Gertrude eyed Eliza's plate, smiled apologetically, leaned for-ward, and nabbed a cucumber rye sandwich right off it.

Eliza gaped at her, torn between astonishment and annoyance at having her favorite type of sandwich thieved from her plate.

"Do forgive me, Eliza—can I call you Eliza?—but that sandwich isn't edible." She dropped the small triangle into an abandoned cup of tea. Bubbles formed as the sandwich sank to the bottom. "You see," she whispered, motioning for Joy and Eliza to lean closer, "Lady Beaumont the Great brings those, and her cook is dreadful, but no one else will work for that woman. Good cucumbers are hard to come by this time of year, and there's only one grocer in the village that stocks decent ones. Why, the other day, one of our ladies saw Regina's cook buying cucumbers from the *other* grocer on the edge of town." She nodded as if that explained everything.

Eliza hadn't realized they had two grocers in Lambton, much less one that sold questionable cucumbers. "Well, thank you." She balanced her plate on her knee and gestured to the room. "What do you ladies have going on here? I was joking earlier with Joy, saying we'd accidentally stumbled upon a den of iniquity."

Gertrude chuckled. "You're not far from the truth, but we're a bunch of old women who still love a few thrills in our lives, and this is one of them. It's a closely guarded secret, though. The past vicars have gone on endlessly about the dangers of gambling. This new one seems less strict, but by now, the fun of meeting secretly once a month is far more entertaining than the actual game." Her eyes twinkled with mischief.

"And I'm too young to join?" Joy gazed around the room. "These women are my sort, I tell you. Are you sure you can't make an exception?"

"Sadly, I cannot. To be part of the group, you must be at least sixty-five."

"Bloody hell," Joy murmured and sipped her tea.

Gertrude laid a warm, papery-skinned hand on Eliza's arm, an understanding glint in her eyes. "I suspect that's why your great-aunt insists on calling you her niece instead of great-niece at our little gathering." Gertrude flicked her gaze toward the towering Regina, Lady Beaumont, who scowled at everyone from the corner of the room. "Your great-aunt and her archnemesis were born on the same day, same year, and Regina lords it over your great-aunt that she looks younger." She dropped her voice to a whisper. "Of course, no one mentions the work Regina's had done or the chemicals she pours into her body to look like she bathes in the fountain of youth every morning. Unlike Regina, your great-aunt doesn't pump her forehead full of Botox. Instead, she plays the semantics game."

"I should give Regina a piece of my mind," Eliza said.

"You could try." Gertrude patted her hand. "That woman has rocks for brains. Wouldn't know what to do with the piece of your mind you give her."

"I don't have many favorite people, Gertrude," Joy said, "but you've slipped into my top ten."

Gertrude beamed at Joy then turned her smile to Eliza. "Do you know why Iris dragged you here?"

Eliza glanced around the room, taking in all the women dressed in their finest, chatting in small clusters. No one had returned to the poker tables, but the presence of chips and cards kept the gathering from feeling like an ordinary tea party. "I have no clue."

Great-Aunt Iris appeared behind them, resting her warm hands on Eliza's shoulders. "Because, my dear, these women are the eyes and ears of this village. If anyone can tell you about Hunter Crawford and poor, poor Rosie Harley, they can."

The room fell silent. Several women's faces paled, leaving only bright spots of crimson on their cheeks.

"I get the sense, Aunt Iris, that you opened Pandora's Box," Eliza whispered.

Great-Aunt Iris huffed. "Some boxes are meant to be opened, wouldn't you say?"

After the hubbub from Great-Aunt Iris's declaration had died down and the ladies had regained their healthy color, Gertrude motioned for everyone to find a seat, which they promptly did.

"Now, now, ladies, this isn't the time to get all missish. You know as well as I do what a proper scoundrel that Hunter was, and I think we've all had granddaughters or great-nieces bothered by him... or... taken advantage of... financially." Gertrude blushed and studied the tips of her chunky heels.

Great-Aunt Iris rested a hand on Gertrude's shoulder. "You're not the only one, Gertie. That, I can promise."

Eliza's heart raced with her anger. *Did Hunter swindle poor Gertrude out of money as well?* From the steely looks around the room, Eliza could tell that Hunter had touched all their lives with his weaselly, wicked ways.

"Like father, like son," one lady at the back of the group added.

"You should have met the grandfather," someone else chimed in. "Why, from what I gather, there wasn't a maid who didn't leave that place with a child and no reference. Some say his wife died of a broken heart. Others say he poisoned her so he could continue his wicked ways."

"The Crawfords have been riddled with scandal for as long as anyone can remember. My great-grandma used to tell stories about the family." A tiny lady with silver hair and sparkling blue eyes grinned mischievously. "Of course, she always thought I was fast asleep during her gossip sessions with her friends, but I was crafty back in those days."

A few women laughed, but the seriousness soon settled over them again like a stifling blanket.

"So, why do you want to know about poor Rosie Harley?" Gertrude asked.

Eliza blinked at all the women staring at her and only snapped out of it when Great-Aunt Iris jabbed a knitting needle into her ribs.

Why the woman had brought knitting supplies to a poker-and-tea party, Eliza had no clue, but she didn't doubt that all occasions, at least in her great-aunt's mind, required them.

"I, ah ..." Eliza had no clue what Wentworth wanted disclosed to the public. He hadn't said not to tell, but she hated starting a firestorm that could potentially hurt the investigation. He'd turn thunderous if she accidentally—or intentionally, in this case—revealed what he needed kept secret. She could, of course, blame it all on Great-Aunt Iris and had no doubt she could hold her own against the detective chief inspector's wrath, but Eliza didn't want to risk burning a bridge unnecessarily.

"Come on, then. Spit it out, my girl," Great-Aunt Iris whispered.

"The little girl's name came up in conjunction with the ... the Crawfords. Since I'm invested in Hunter's murder case, I was simply wondering if there was a connection." Eliza crossed her fingers that the women would accept her half-truth as the whole story.

A few of them exchanged glances, but no one called Eliza out on her semifalsehood.

"I still remember the day Rosie Harley went missing." A lady swathed in pastel pink, her makeup more reminiscent of the fifties than modern application, dabbed at the corner of her eye with an embroidered handkerchief.

"That's right, Gladys." A nearby lady patted her gently on the back. "Rosie was your granddaughter's friend, wasn't she?"

Gladys sniffled. "That day and the days after were the worst of my life. Even losing my beloved George didn't pain me nearly as much as this poor little thing going missing. I've never witnessed such suffering." Tears slid down her cheeks, carving white rivulets through her foundation.

"If you don't want to talk about it, I understand," Eliza said softly.

"No, I do." Gladys took a shuddering breath. "I can still remember it like it happened yesterday. Such a lovely day. Brilliant weather.

A day that spoke of such promise. I remember Rosie making a new friend. I think her name was Joy—" Gladys did a double-take at Joy. "You. You were the new friend."

Joy wiped the tears from her cheeks with trembling hands. "Yes. Yes, I was."

"Oh, you poor dear. I'm sure you and Rosie would have been the best of friends if... if..."

The room grew so heavy with sorrow that Eliza thought she might scream under the weight of it all.

Gladys clenched her pink-skirted thighs until her knuckles went white. "We looked all day and into the next and the next and the next..."

"She was never found?" Eliza asked, though she already knew the answer.

"No," Gladys whispered, her voice cracking.

Some women dabbed at their eyes with their handkerchiefs. Others cried openly, tears carving tracks down their cheeks. A few sat stone-faced, but the pain in their eyes was enough to tear a hole straight through Eliza's heart.

"I'm so sorry," Eliza said. As much as she hated to pry, justice for Rosie Harley came first. If she was going to solve both cases she'd stumbled into, she needed details. A little girl didn't just vanish from a crowded village square. She drew in a deep breath and pressed on. "I hate to ask, but can you tell me anything about her disappearance? Did she wander off? Did someone take her in plain sight? Had she told anyone she was meeting somebody? Was there... Was there any sign of foul play or... violence?"

"No," Gladys said. "There was no sign of foul play or that there'd been a struggle. We always thought someone, someone she trusted, had lured her away, then... then..."

Gertrude broke the silence. "Some say Old Man Tanner did it, but there was no proof whatsoever. The only thing that rumor ever accomplished was sending a man who wasn't quite right in the head to an early grave. Poor soul."

"Everett Tanner?" Great-Aunt Iris's forehead creased.

"Don't you remember?" Gertrude asked. "Worked for—"

"The Crawfords." Great-Aunt Iris clicked her tongue. "Was their gardener. Poor old fool. Always was a bit addled, but he was as harmless as a baby lamb. He'd never have hurt that girl."

"Who would start such a terrible rumor?" Joy asked.

"Henrietta Crawford," Regina said flatly from the back of the group.

Everyone swiveled their necks and gaped at the towering woman behind them. She'd been as silent as a church mouse until that moment, and Eliza had forgotten she was even in the room. But there was no mistaking the real presence of Regina, Lady Beaumont, not with her quivering frame, clenched fists, and crimson cheeks.

"That's quite the statement, Regina." Great-Aunt Iris glared at her. "I'm no great admirer of Henrietta, but that's bold, wouldn't you say?"

Regina returned Great-Aunt Iris's scowl with equal fire. "Henrietta is an absolute viper who, if given half the chance, will strike and pump her victim full of venom. I was there the day she opened her mouth and poured it into those greedy little ears surrounding her—proper toadies, the lot of them. They wanted nothing more than to boast that Henrietta was their bosom friend." She sniffed disdainfully. "What rubbish. That woman wouldn't know genuine affection if it bit her on the backside."

"And you didn't counteract the tittle-tattle when it started pouring through the village?" Gertrude asked, her face twisted with fury. "It didn't merely ruin Everett. Those dreadful gossips nearly destroyed his entire family, hounding his poor wife right out of town. If she hadn't had grown children to flee to, heaven knows what might have become of her."

"And what precisely would you have had me do? You, as well as everyone else in this room, are perfectly aware of the circumstances that required my going into *treatment* that month. If I wished to keep the matter hush-hush and not broadcast to the entire village, I'd have been a complete fool to take on the likes of Henrietta, wouldn't I?" She squared her shoulders defiantly.

"For your own misguided pride, you allowed an innocent man to go to his grave early, victim to village busybodies?" Great-Aunt Iris demanded, her voice trembling with indignation.

"Don't you dare lecture me about misguided pride, Iris Darcy. I know perfectly well that you have chosen silence over justice when it comes to the Crawfords."

Silence smothered the room, and Great-Aunt Iris's cheeks turned crimson.

"Right, then, ladies. That's enough." Gertrude rose, clapped twice smartly, and slid Eliza an apologetic look. "Shall we get on with our game? I fear our time's running short this morning."

After the women dispersed, all shooting Regina withering looks, Gertrude pulled Eliza aside. "I'm sorry to cut our time together short, but I thought it best. Not everyone knows about Hunter's dealings with Iris, and I thought it better to keep it that way." She glanced toward Great-Aunt Iris, who huddled with a few other women, their gray and white heads shaking as they whispered together.

"Understood. Thank you for letting us stay and for allowing me to ask questions. I hope I didn't cause anyone too much pain," Eliza said.

Gertrude squeezed Eliza's hand with surprising strength. "Some questions need asking. And some ghosts of the past shouldn't be laid to rest, no matter how painful for the living."

After saying goodbye and thanking the ladies for their time, Eliza walked back to the Range Rover in silence, followed by Joy and Great-Aunt Iris.

Great-Aunt Iris tutted softly. "I never thought I'd see the day where I was glad I was in Regina's presence."

"For all her seemingly awful qualities, she did provide a vital clue," Eliza said as she climbed into the passenger seat.

"Maybe she feels bad for not sticking up for the Crawfords' gardener when she had a chance," Joy said.

The only response was Great-Aunt Iris snorting from the backseat.

Chapter Thirteen
More Questions Than Eliza Can Shake a Stick At

Lunch was a quiet affair. Eliza had never experienced such a silent meal with the family, and Great-Aunt Iris, who shared tidbits from her day or educated them all on what she'd seen on the telly, didn't even say, "Pass the salt." Even Caesar had gotten the message early on and slunk from the room when no one, not even the white-haired lady who always snuck him food, lavished him with attention.

Eliza wiped her mouth with her napkin and laid it across her plate, hoping Mrs. Bankcroft wouldn't notice she'd hardly eaten a thing. Nothing would get past the lump in her throat, and thoughts of poor Rosie Harley had her stomach tied in knots. From the looks of other people's nearly full plates, including Belle's, she wasn't the only one.

"I take it you found something out in your little jaunt into town?" Uncle Fitzwilliam asked, his voice gentle but his eyes keenly studying Eliza.

Eliza told him everything they'd discovered, leaving out the part about the Golden Gamblers. Though judging by the twinkle in his eyes and the slight twitch of his right eyebrow when he glanced at his aunt, she figured he already knew about the illicit gambling den.

"Lady Beaumont is a proper snake herself, so it's no wonder she can spot one of her own kind." Uncle Fitzwilliam sipped his after-lunch coffee.

"Did you find anything out with the phone calls you were going to make?" Eliza asked.

"Yes, something interesting," Uncle Fitzwilliam said. "Berryhill Manor is mortgaged to the hilt, and the Crawfords are practically drowning in debt."

"I wonder if Hunter had anything to do with that," Belle said, breaking her silence since entering the dining room.

"I'd wager my entire Jimmy Choo collection that Hunter wouldn't have cared two hoots if he'd left his parents utterly skint and begging in the streets," Joy said.

Eliza shuddered. "What a family. Makes the nasty ones in ours look almost angelic."

"It's safe to say that every family has nasty members, secrets, and skeletons that some would do wicked things to keep hidden." Uncle Fitzwilliam pushed his chair back and stood. "I'll be in my study."

After Uncle Fitzwilliam left, Joy soon followed to make a phone call to her agent.

Eliza fiddled with her napkin. "Do you think, Great—"

"Did I not tell you, dear girl, to drop the 'great'? Makes me feel positively ancient."

"Yes, but I thought, since we're not with your Golden Gambler friends, that—"

"Yes, yes, but it's a mouthful, wouldn't you say? And well... Well... " Her eyes shimmered with tears, and Eliza caught a depth of emotion that the lady from the old guard couldn't voice. She placed a warm hand on Eliza's cheek. "You've been living under Pemberley's roof for some time now, and the title 'great' creates distance, doesn't it?" She gave a wobbly smile. "It's not up for discussion, I'm afraid. I've made an executive decision. You must call me 'aunt' from now on. I am unanimous in that."

Eliza smiled at the reference to one of her great-aunt's favorite television characters, Mrs. Slocombe from *Are You Being Served?*, and embraced her.

Great-Aunt Iris wriggled free, patted Eliza's cheek, and headed toward the door, stopping to gently grasp Belle's hand. "And how are you holding up? You look peaked. I can have Mrs. Bankcroft cook you up one of her magical concoctions she makes for me when I'm feeling under the weather. Tastes like dirty feet, but you'll be as right as rain after."

Belle chuckled. "As appetizing as that sounds, I'll have to pass." She took in a shuddering breath. "I'll be okay."

Great-Aunt Iris opened her mouth but was interrupted by Tash entering the room.

"Miss Eliza? DCI Wentworth to see you."

Tash moved aside, revealing a grim-looking Wentworth. Constable Theo Archibald stood stoically behind him. Wentworth's gaze landed on Belle, and his eyes flickered with regret.

Eliza's heart slid to her toes, and from Belle's gasp, she figured her friend had seen the writing on the wall too.

"Belle Knightley, I'm arresting you on suspicion of the murder of Hunter Crawford. You do not have to say anything, but anything you do say may be given in evidence. When..."

As Wentworth finished reading Belle her rights, Eliza's ears filled with buzzing and her peripheral vision grayed. She was only partially aware of Great-Aunt Iris's clammy hand clutched in hers.

Belle rolled her shoulders back, stuck out her chin, and met Wentworth's gaze. A spark of pride ignited in Eliza's chest at her best friend's courage, and a new sense of strength flooded through her. Belle flicked a gaze to Eliza, and it said all Eliza needed to know: She was okay.

"Have you lost the plot?" Great-Aunt Iris asked, her voice vibrating with anger.

Wentworth cast a gentle gaze over the quivering octogenarian and gave the signal for Theo to escort Belle, uncuffed, from the room.

After they were gone, Wentworth dropped his voice. "I'm sorry, Eliza. My hands are tied on this one."

"But... But she didn't do it," Eliza said, hating the weakness in her voice.

"I must follow the evidence. I hope you can see that." He gave her shoulder a reassuring squeeze. "I'll do what I can and make sure she's well taken care of. I won't quit looking for an alternate solution, okay?"

"You mean the truth." Eliza bit her inner cheek to stem the hot tears damming behind her eyes. She would not cry. Of all the men she could trust, Wentworth was at the top of the list, but she couldn't help feeling like the floor was opening up, threatening to swallow her whole.

Great-Aunt Iris sighed as Wentworth left the room. "Poor girl. Of all the people to get trapped in Hunter's web..."

Eliza's heart thudded, and she nearly ran to the door. "We need to get back to work." She glanced back at her great-aunt. "Ready for a gossip session with Monica?"

"What do you think about my visiting the Crawfords? I'm as harmless as a lamb—"

Eliza gaped at her. "You? Harmless? Why, you're the most—"

"Ancient-looking, fluffy-haired old lady outside of the village care home. No, the Crawfords won't suspect me or my motives.

They'll just chalk it up to an elderly woman's penchant for seeking out gossip. We need to get to the bottom of that odd pair."

"What would I do without you?" Eliza asked.

Pink bloomed on Great-Aunt Iris's cheeks, and she preened.

"They were on my list, especially after my visit with Basil, but I think it's far better that you meet up with them. They wouldn't take my visit as mere nosiness."

"There's benefit in being an old bird." A mischievous light glinted in her eyes. "I might even don my tweed just to give me an extra flair of a gossiping country biddy. I'll come back with a full report." She patted Eliza's cheek and waddled from the room in her squeaky white tennis shoes.

Before fetching Joy for a trip into Lambton, Eliza found her uncle in his study and filled him in on Belle's arrest.

Uncle Fitzwilliam's face turned beet red. "Never took Wentworth for a fool, but there's a first time for everything."

Eliza settled a hip against the mahogany desk. "We need to find evidence that someone else was there, that someone else dealt the fatal blow. Great-Aunt Iris is on her way to visit the Crawfords. I'm going to snag Joy and head to the Trusty Teapot for any new information—"

"You mean gossip."

"Which is usually based in some version of truth. There's no smoke without fire."

"As much as I want to disagree with you, I can't. What would you like me to do?"

"How about tackling Basil? He's clearly a toady, and while he was tight-lipped with me, he might open up a little more to you or be so in awe of you that he accidentally says something he didn't intend to."

Uncle Fitzwilliam shivered. "Have an easier job for me?"

"No, I'm afraid we all must suffer the toads."

In ten minutes, Eliza and Joy were headed to Lambton.

"I can't believe Wentworth actually arrested Belle. Maybe the man does have more than just a mean bark," Joy said.

Eliza hung on for dear life as Joy took a curve much too quickly. "We can't solve Hunter's murder if we're both dead."

Joy let up on the accelerator a bit. "Maybe I shouldn't drive angry."

"Then you must be angry all the time when you drive."

Joy slid her a look. "Touché."

Eliza took a sip of her usual Ethiopian spiced tea and sighed. Because of the crush of customers, she hadn't been able to snag her favorite table by the window, leaving her stuck in the farthest corner of the tea shop. "Where did all these people come from?"

Joy blew on her cup of tea. "I have a strange feeling that a murder and all this rehashed gossip about little Rosie Harley are giving the town's gossips an excuse to crawl out of the woodwork."

Eliza shivered. "Revolting, but maybe we'll glean something useful from it."

As if on cue, Monica rushed over to their table. Her face was flushed, and her brown hair, normally tamed back in a ponytail, had various flyaways that stuck out. She crouched next to Eliza. "Haven't got much time today. Everyone and their dogs are here to wallow in the misfortunes of others." She placed her forearms on the table. "Word about Rosie Harley's been spreading like wildfire."

"I figured." Eliza shook her head. The moment Great-Aunt Iris had dropped that bombshell with the Golden Gamblers, Eliza knew it would get around the village. She sent up a little prayer that Wentworth wouldn't trace the rumor back to its source.

"There's more, though," Monica said. She waved Eliza and Joy closer and dropped her voice. "Basil and Beckham were in here a few hours ago, and they had the most dreadful row. Basil got so red in the face I thought he might keel over from a heart attack right here in the tearoom."

Eliza narrowed her eyes and leaned in. "What did they say?"

"Difficult to catch everything. Hard to when people's rows are nothing but vicious whispers." She cocked her head. "I didn't want to be too obvious, but I made sure their teacups stayed topped up, didn't I? The whispers soon turned to shouts, and the manager booted them both out before I or the rest of this lot"—she gestured to the packed tearoom—"could catch any juicy details."

"What *did* you catch?" Eliza asked.

"Not much, but I did latch on to the phrase 'well-buried secrets.'"

"Could you tell which one said what?" Joy asked.

Monica shook her head. "No, I couldn't hover over them, could I? And they were both whispering so fiercely."

Eliza kept her suspicions about the well-buried secret possibly being poor Rosie Harley to herself for the moment. She still wasn't sure what Wentworth wanted kept under wraps, and while she trusted Monica, one careless slip would quickly spread around the village and surrounding area.

"I wish I had more for you, but I've got to dash. Customers are shooting me daggers. I'll keep my eyes and ears open for any gossip." After flashing a quick smile at Eliza and Joy, Monica hurried off to tend to other customers.

Eliza scrunched her forehead. "I need to get all the information in my head on paper. Let's grab our drinks to go, head back to Pemberley, and catch everyone up on what we have so far, which, sadly, isn't as much as I'd like."

Armed with to-go drinks for themselves and the rest of Pemberley's residents, Eliza and Joy left the Trusty Teapot and walked down the sidewalk toward the Range Rover. They passed a Tudor-style real estate building, and catching sight of the business name, Fairchild Real Estate, Eliza stopped in her tracks.

"Sweet ride." Joy pointed at a sleek black Mercedes CLS coupe parked at the curb.

"Wait. This must be Lucinda Fairchild's business. How did I never make that connection? I pass this storefront all the time." Shaking her head, Eliza made a beeline for the door. "Let's see if she's in. She was so helpful when we were making initial headway on the case." Then she paused. "Give me two seconds."

Eliza speed-walked back to the Trusty Teapot, ordered an orange pekoe tea, and within minutes, stood back at Fairchild Real Estate's rustic door. She pushed it open, and bells chimed their entrance.

A middle-aged woman sat behind the reception desk and smiled warmly at them. "May I help you?"

"Yes, I'm Eliza Darcy, and this is my cousin Joy. We're here to see Lucinda if she's available."

"Do you have an appointment with her?" The woman rifled through an appointment calendar.

"No, sorry. We were in the area, and I thought I'd poke my head in and see how she's doing. Nothing urgent," Eliza said.

"Let me check if she can see you." The woman rose from her desk, walked down a short hallway, and knocked on a door. Muted voices drifted down the corridor, and within seconds, Lucinda Fairchild appeared with a welcoming smile.

"Eliza, Joy, what a lovely surprise. I was thinking about you and wondering how our investigation was progressing. Still championing your friend?"

Eliza shifted the four-compartment drink carrier to her left hand and shook Lucinda's hand. "Sadly, yes. I'm afraid things have gotten worse and not better."

"I'm sorry to hear that. There's always hope, though. Justice will prevail in the end. Always does. Just takes some time." Lucinda gestured down the hall. "I see you've got hot drinks to deliver, but I can spare a few minutes."

Eliza and Joy followed her down the short corridor into a sunlit office brimming with old books and potted plants. They settled into matching leather chairs across from Lucinda's desk.

"I didn't mean to interrupt your busy day, but when I spotted your office building, I finally connected that you were the Fairchild who owned this business. I wanted to stop by quickly and thank you for paving the way with Harry and Basil," Eliza said, handing over the to-go cup of orange pekoe tea.

"Cheers." Lucinda inhaled the tea's aroma appreciatively. "You're not interrupting anything except my getting lost in my own thoughts. I've been thinking about Hunter a bit lately. I do have fond memories of him from uni." She folded her hands on her desk. "Death has a funny way of grounding the living, doesn't it? Anyway, did you manage to get what you needed from Basil and Harry? Were my introductions helpful for our little venture in justice?"

Eliza shrugged ruefully. "They were enough to muddy the waters."

"Don't be too hard on yourself. From the local chitter-chatter I hear about your sleuthing skills, you'll get our man soon enough." Lucinda smiled kindly. "And how's Belle holding up under all this?"

Joy snorted. "Funny you should ask. Just this morning—"

Eliza nudged Joy's foot. "She's holding up relatively well. As well as can be expected under the circumstances." The truth of Belle's arrest would soon flood the gossip pipelines, but she wanted to keep it quiet as long as possible.

"It's brilliant that she has a support team like the Darcys. It's not fair, though, that she is in this situation to begin with." Pain tinged her voice. "Imagine the police thinking she murdered Hunter. I hope they'll sort themselves out soon and realize they've lost the plot." Her West Country accent crept through, and she clenched her fists.

"Truth be told, though, I can see why they're having such a time pinning the murder on the right person. Half the townsfolk—nearly all the people in Lambton—are dead chuffed he's dead." She clapped a hand over her mouth and stared at Eliza with wide eyes. "Oh, I'm ever so sorry. I know I shouldn't speak ill of the dead, especially an old mate, but despite Hunter's shortcomings..." Lucinda studied her white knuckles. "Sorry. It's all so much to process, you know?"

"Please don't apologize," Eliza said. "What did you mean by the whole town being glad he's dead?"

Lucinda gestured toward the bay window. Pedestrians milled back and forth, some deep in conversation, others with earbuds in, ignoring their fellow man, still others wandering with tourist-like energy. "I can think of only a few people who weren't touched negatively by his money schemes. I do know the water was heating up around him, and I'd heard rumblings that he was about to pull up shop."

"And Beckham too? They're partners, right?"

"Good question. Like I've said, Hunter and I don't talk much anymore, and Beckham's pretty close-lipped about business, but I get the sense that Beckham is—was—not happy with Hunter."

Eliza recalled her interaction with Beckham at the Trusty Teapot. "Yeah, there didn't seem to be any love lost between them."

Lucinda grimaced. "I think it's worse than that, but I don't have any facts to back up my opinion. All I know is that Hunter was a snake in the grass, and I think everyone was finally sick of it. One person especially, if you can connect Hunter's death with his financial misdealings."

"You were never taken in by him, were you?" Eliza asked.

"No." Lucinda chuckled. "I never needed financial advice and never sought out his 'brilliant' investments." Her gaze flicked to the window, where the luxury car sat parked out front.

Eliza's phone dinged. "Sorry." She swiped at the screen and smiled at Heath's text message.

Heath: *I'll be done at half five. Pemberley or my place?*

Eliza: *Why don't you come to Pemberley? We can discuss the case.*

Heath: *See you in a few hours. Love you!*

Eliza: *Love you too!*

Eliza slipped her phone back in her pocket and stood. "Thank you, Lucinda, for giving us a moment of your time."

"It's my pleasure, and good luck with bringing about proper justice."

"Thank you."

Eliza and Joy left Lucinda's office with lukewarm drinks in tow and headed back to Pemberley.

After dinner, Eliza put the final touches on all the information they'd gathered over the past few days, displaying it on the chalkboard in the old nursery. She dusted off her hands. "Ta-da!"

Great-Aunt Iris tilted her head as she studied the board. "You might want to bump the Crawfords further up on your list. I wouldn't be surprised if they have a giant jumble sale, selling off all their gaudy trinkets to save the estate." After she had everyone's attention, she gestured for Eliza to write on the crime board. "There are only two staff members besides the cook. Henrietta wouldn't be caught dead with such a minimal number."

"Which means that either all the staff have left or they can't afford any more or to replace the ones who've left," Eliza said, jotting down the information on the board. "Notice anything else?"

"I was left unattended for quite a while, and I took a self-guided tour of Berryhill."

"You never cease to amaze me," Joy said, linking her hands behind her head and leaning back against the wall.

"What'd you find?" Heath asked.

"Rooms full of furniture—rather ghastly pieces, might I add—stacked and tagged." Great-Aunt Iris shivered. "What that woman's thinking getting the prices listed on the inventory list, I'll never know."

"And how did you find the inventory list?" Uncle Fitzwilliam asked, his lips twitching with a smile.

"Haven't I taught you anything? You can't find anything if you don't look."

"Did anyone catch you snooping around?" Eliza grinned.

"First of all, I don't snoop. I investigate. Second of all, they did, but I pretended to have a moment of senility and said I got lost while I was looking for the loo."

Heath chuckled. "I'm glad you're on our side."

Great-Aunt Iris preened and blushed. "Go on with you now, young man."

Eliza finalized the notes under the Crawfords' names and pointed the piece of chalk at her uncle. "Find out anything from Mr. Toadman that we didn't already know?" She tapped the piece of chalk on Basil's name and worked her way down the bullet points. "A. He knew about Hunter's Ponzi schemes. B. Admits to being a business acquaintance of Hunter's. C. His snake comment tells me he detested Hunter. D. Had a public fight with Beckham at the Trusty Teapot."

Uncle Fitzwilliam massaged the back of his neck and sighed. "He's certainly worried about his position at the school. Claims his job is on the line if the wrong people get the wrong end of the stick about his dealings with Hunter. Begged me to stay quiet, repeated over and over that more lives were on the line if that 'pesky niece' of mine didn't quit snooping around."

Eliza snorted. "Did you manage to weasel any more information out of him?"

"Unfortunately, no. He got so tightlipped I'd feared he had an episode." Uncle Fitzwilliam's eyes flashed with mischief. "Mentioned Hunter's name just to get him to snap out of whatever stupor he'd fallen into."

"Then why not turn on his mate?" Heath asked. "Now that Hunter's dead, Basil could claim he knew about the schemes and spin whatever sob story he wanted about not wanting to go along with the plan, but Hunter coerced him, blah, blah, blah. There'd be no one to contradict him."

"Unless Beckham is also in on the secret," Eliza said, tapping the chalk on Beckham's name. "He also knew about Hunter's schemes and admits to not trusting Hunter, even though they were friends."

"The skeleton Basil doesn't want dragged out of his closet must be an earthshattering one." Eliza added some bullet points under his name.

"Could his secret involve the school?" Joy asked.

"It could." Eliza recalled Basil's posh digs. "Does a headmaster's salary explain Basil's lavish lifestyle?"

"Probably not, but I can dig deeper into it." Heath pulled his phone from his pocket and typed a note to himself.

"Thanks," Eliza said and wrote *Possible underhanded dealings with his school?* under Basil's name. "If his secret involves his role as headmaster, the question is: 'Would it be enough to destroy him?'"

"And would he kill to keep that secret?" Great-Aunt Iris asked.

"Good point." Eliza added *Would he kill to keep a secret?* as another bullet point. She tapped Hunter, Basil, and Beckham's names. "These three were working together, and one of them ends up dead. We know they ruined lives like Harry"—Eliza pointed at his name—"who hates Hunter for abandoning Paisley and stealing money from him." She tapped the chalk on Paisley's name. "And we know Paisley had a secret she didn't want uncovered enough to live in poverty instead of force paternity on Hunter. What if Hunter had tried again to blackmail her for something? She did say she'd do any-thing for her daughter."

"What about his parents?" Joy asked.

Eliza underlined *Was lawsuit over boundary Hunter's idea or his parents' idea?* under Hubert and Henrietta's names. "I wish we knew the answer to this. Whether it was legit or not, someone must have believed it was. There were shovel marks right where we found the body. Someone felt threatened enough to try removing evidence of their crime."

Eliza wrote *Discovery of Body* and underlined it. Below that, she added: *Who is the victim? Who is the killer? Who buried the body? Why bury it on Pemberley's side of the fence? Who tried to dig up the body? Why?*

"Could whoever was digging have been interrupted when Hunter coaxed Belle near that spot?" Joy asked.

"Maybe, but why dig on such a cold night? The ground must be frozen solid. Besides, it's so isolated that someone could dig during the day without being spotted," Eliza said.

"I'm guessing they either got interrupted or realized halfway through how impossible it would be this time of year. They probably thought they could scatter some leaves over the holes, and no one would notice," Heath said.

"Yeah, until I came along, tripping over it." Eliza reread the ques-tions on the board. "Why, after all these years, try to dig it up?"

"If the lawsuit had reached a head, they would have resurveyed the land. They would have discovered the body, or that's what the original killer thought," Great-Aunt Iris said.

"Hang on a bloody minute," Joy interjected. "That means who-ever killed the poor buried soul not only knew about the lawsuit but had access to the land between the two estates."

"I'm afraid so," Eliza said, jotting the connection on the board. "The question is: 'Did the same person who killed the buried victim also kill Hunter?'"

"And why was Hunter killed near that exact spot? He's far too young to have had anything to do with Rosie Harley's disappearance and death if our assumptions are correct. But I don't think his presence and murder there is coincidental," Heath said.

Eliza studied the board. "I wish Belle could remember more about that night. Why did Hunter take her so far from the property? What did he say to her?"

"There was also another person there, remember," Joy said. "Didn't Constable Archibald say that Belle's recollection indicates a second person? Hunter was killed right where he stood after Belle punched him."

Eliza shivered. "Why didn't the killer go after Belle?"

"Perhaps he didn't think she was a threat, since she was already legging it and didn't see him?" Joy suggested.

"That's a risk most killers won't take," Heath replied.

"There is another possibility," Great-Aunt Iris said quietly. "What if someone killed Hunter to protect her?"

"But who?" Eliza asked. "She doesn't know anybody here except for you guys, and I don't think any of you would kill someone when simply making yourself known and stopping the attack would've worked fine."

"Eliza's right," Heath said. "There is real anger behind this attack. Someone hated Hunter enough to bash his skull in, and nobody besides us knew Belle well enough for some vengeful stranger to kill so brutally."

Eliza turned to the chalkboard and wrote: *Was Hunter killed because he knew about the buried body? Was Hunter killed because someone was protecting Belle? Was Hunter killed because he knew something he shouldn't have?*

Staring back at the questions, Eliza worried she'd never find the answers that would set her friend free.

Chapter Fourteen
A Riddle in Death

I had maintained a neutral position on the Crawfords and the gossip surrounding them. Until today. This morning, he appeared in our garden while I was playing with Adelaide Rose. He wished to discuss some matter regarding the boundary between Berryhill and Pemberley. I informed him that Darcy was from home on estate business. His conversation then became far too familiar, speaking of his admiration for "spirited women," his body language indicating he was speaking of me. When I tried redirecting our conversation, he persisted in making impertinent personal observations. I begin to believe the gossip.
Lizzy Bennet Darcy
Pemberley 1815

A knock sounded on Eliza's bedroom door. She rolled over in bed, grabbed her phone, and glanced at the time—six a.m.

Another knock echoed through the door, that time accompanied by Tash's voice.

"Coming," Eliza said, shoving her feet into slippers and pulling on a robe. She opened the door with a smile on her lips, but her expression crumpled at the look on Tash's face. "What's wrong?"

"Lord Darcy and Detective Chief Inspector Wentworth would like to see you in the study, Miss Eliza."

Dread settled in Eliza's stomach. "I'll be right down."

Eliza got ready as quickly as she could, and within five minutes, she found herself sitting next to Wentworth, facing her uncle across his desk.

She fidgeted with a loose string on her oversize hoodie and couldn't stand the silence filling the room. "If one of you doesn't start talking, I'll be forced to tell a bad joke, and trust me—none of us wants that."

Wentworth pulled a plastic bag containing a sheet of paper from his briefcase. "One of my constables found this near the cordoned-off area. They believe someone delivered it after midnight, since it wasn't there during their perimeter search." He handed it to her. "Have a read."

Eliza scanned the eight-by-ten sheet of paper covered in cut-out magazine letters, and her blood ran cold. Bile churned in her stomach, and goose bumps prickled her skin as she reread the message:

Detective Darcy thinks she's so clever,
But the innocent suffers while the guilty endeavor.
Get the police off Belle's back, or you'll see—
Another body's blood will be on thee.
The friend with torn silver pays for his sins,
While the true monster hides their grin within.

Wentworth slipped the plastic-protected paper from Eliza's numb fingers, and she stared at the ornate carvings on her uncle's desk until her vision blurred.

A warm hand on Eliza's shoulder brought her back to the present. Her uncle's face was haggard and pale, and fear glinted in his eyes.

"I want you off this case. Immediately." Uncle Fitzwilliam's voice cracked.

"I agree," Wentworth said, his hand trembling as he placed the letter back in his briefcase. "The killer knows you're involved and has their eye on you. You need to keep your nose well out of it."

For a moment, the less courageous parts of Eliza wanted to cave to her uncle's and Wentworth's demand, but Belle was currently sitting in a jail cell. She wouldn't stand by and let anyone intimidate her into abandoning her hunt for the truth.

"No."

"I'm sorry, Eliza, but I'm putting my foot down on this one. I must insist that you leave this alone," Uncle Fitzwilliam said, an edge creeping into his voice.

Eliza stood and planted her hands on her hips. "I won't be cowed by anyone, especially an anonymous letter writer...who sucks at writing poetry, no less. I won't let him dictate my actions."

"If I have to lock you in a cell for your own safety, I'll—"

"You'll what, Wentworth? Falsely imprison an innocent person? You've already done that. Besides, I'm sure the press would have a field day hearing how you locked the niece of *Lord Darcy* in a cell to rot."

"Eliza," her uncle chided her.

"I'm sorry, but I certainly won't watch two men I respect cave to this person's demands."

"But your safety comes first. I don't fancy having another dead body on my hands," Wentworth all but growled.

"We're not put on this earth to be safe. We're here to do good, and sometimes, that means doing the hard and dangerous things." Eliza sank back into her chair and rubbed her temples. "I'm not saying I'm not terrified. I'm scared spitless, but I won't quit."

Uncle Fitzwilliam sighed and ran his fingers through his salt-and-pepper hair. "You're stubborn, you know."

"I know. We've had this discussion recently."

Wentworth slumped back, steepled his fingers under his chin, and studied her. "Are all Midwesterners as pigheaded as you?"

"Probably, but I got more than the usual dose."

"Right," Wentworth grumbled. After a few moments, he pulled out his notebook and pen and flipped to a fresh page. "Well, then, what have you got so far?"

Eliza stood and motioned for them to follow her. "It's better if you can see my board. To the old nursery we go."

A few minutes later, all three of them stood before the chalkboard.

"And when were you planning to share this with me?" Wentworth asked, shooting her a stern look.

"After I woke up and had my breakfast this morning, but that little note you brought changed my plans," Eliza said.

Wentworth scratched the stubble on his cheeks and studied the names on the chalkboard. "You've got quite a list here. You favor one over the others?"

"Not at this point. I do believe that Basil, Hunter, and Beckham were working together on Hunter's Ponzi schemes. It's possible that one of them killed Hunter to keep their secret safe or to break free from his control. Basil especially seems desperate to hide something. Maybe Hunter knew about it and threatened to expose him."

"Blackmail, then?" Uncle Fitzwilliam asked.

"That's my suspicion," Eliza said.

"What about Lucinda?" Wentworth asked as he scanned the bulleted list under her name.

"Plenty of people saw her throughout the night." Eliza shrugged. "It's hard to get exact pinpoints because everyone was so busy, but she left with the last of the guests. There's no way she could have come back covered in someone else's blood and no one noticed. Why willingly come back to a party and stay until the end when you've just killed someone when it'd be far easier to slip back into the house after the deed, grab your coat, and leave? Besides, whenever I've sought out her help, she's been obliging."

"And Harry?" her uncle asked. "You think he's a reasonable suspect?"

"Unfortunately, yes. He has plenty of motive."

"What about means and opportunity?" Wentworth asked.

"That's where it gets tricky. He wasn't at the ball, so there's no opportunity, and Hunter wasn't even invited. He was a last-minute plus-one for his parents. Someone could have tipped Harry off about Hunter being there, but then to follow Hunter *and* Belle out to the woods?" Eliza shrugged. "Seems far-fetched."

"Well, someone had to have followed Hunter and Belle," Uncle Fitzwilliam said.

"True, but why? Why would someone follow those two into the woods? If they planned to kill Hunter, why do it with a witness? If they didn't plan to kill Hunter, why follow them only to decide later to kill him? It doesn't make sense," Eliza said.

Wentworth tapped the phrase scrawled on the board. "Did the killer murder Hunter to keep Belle safe? This is an interesting angle."

"That was Aunt Iris's theory," Eliza said.

"Aunt?" Uncle Fitzwilliam smiled.

"She made the royal decree that I'm never to let the word *great* pass my lips again, unless, of course, I'm talking about her personality."

"Surprised it took her this long." Uncle Fitzwilliam's smile faded as he studied the board. "One of these people thinks you're getting too close to the answer and wants you dead, Eliza."

Eliza's mouth went dry. "I know, but I won't quit." Eliza tapped her finger on the Crawfords' names. "I need to know exactly what skeletons are lurking in their closet."

"Right you are, Captain," Uncle Fitzwilliam said. "I'll see what I can do. I'll visit them and do some Aunt Iris–level snooping."

"What about Paisley Foster?" Wentworth asked.

"She's next on my list." Uneasiness settled in Eliza's gut. Time was not on her side, and her shoulders sagged under the weight of it all.

"Wentworth held up a finger. "You're missing someone's name on your board."

"Whose?" Eliza asked, though she suspected his answer.

"Belle's. She's the only one with direct evidence linking her to Hunter's murder."

Eliza frowned at him. "Because I can claim with one hundred percent certainty that she didn't do it, despite what the evidence says. I can't say that about the rest of them." She gestured toward the board. "I'm keeping real options open, not wild, irrational ideas."

"Shots across the bow, Wentworth," Uncle Fitzwilliam said.

"Even the anonymous letter writer and wannabe poet told you you're barking up the wrong tree, Wentworth," Eliza said. "Why don't we join forces, get this case solved, and get my friend out from under suspicion?" She held out her hand.

Wentworth eyed it as if it might jump out and slap him but shook it. "I'm still the boss."

"Of course," Eliza said, crossing her fingers behind her back.

After breakfast and breaking the news about the death threat to Joy and Great-Aunt Iris—and subsequently calming down the octogenarian—Eliza led the troops to the nursery. Silence marched alongside them, and the weight of responsibility pressed down on her. She regretted not calling Heath about the note, but with the hard deadline he was trying to hit at work, she hadn't wanted to distract him. If only she had the strength of his presence, she wouldn't feel like she was suffocating.

Wentworth wasn't even there to help ease the burden. He'd refused breakfast and rushed off, promising to track down information on their two main suspects: Basil Huxley and Beckham Quill. Eliza didn't get the sense that Beckham would play nice with her, but she figured it wouldn't take long for Wentworth to break Beckham's annoying habit of answering questions with questions. A smile played on her lips at the thought of a pale-faced Beckham quaking before Wentworth's formidable presence.

"Eliza!"

She spun around at the sound of Heath's voice and hurried footsteps. The pressure that had been building in her chest lifted, leaving her feeling weightless.

"Heath? What on earth are you doing here? I—"

"Didn't ring me because you thought my job was more important than you? That I wouldn't give a damn if someone made a death threat against you?" His cornflower-blue eyes searched hers.

"I knew you had a deadline, and I didn't want to pressure you or make you feel like you had to leave work."

"Eliza, there's never a time in my life when I won't want to protect and support you. I've sorted things at work. Right now, you're my priority."

Eliza squeezed his hand. "But who called you?" She eyed Great-Aunt Iris, Joy, and Uncle Fitzwilliam, all of whom attempted to look innocent.

"A little bird told me, and that's all you'll get out of me," Heath said.

"Until later," Eliza whispered in his ear before leading the way back to the nursery.

Once everyone had gathered, Eliza recapped her discussion with Wentworth and her uncle. She tapped Beckham's name on their list. "Wentworth is questioning him now. We'll see what he can get out of him. As for the rest of us, we need to divide up the remaining tasks. But before we do, I want everyone to understand that this will likely turn dangerous. A death threat means we're getting close, and I don't want anyone hurt. Whoever we're up against won't take kindly to our digging around."

From the grim yet determined faces surrounding her, Eliza suspected they already knew the risks and would never back down or abandon her.

"Everyone certain?"

They nodded, their expressions mixing resolve with anxiety.

She pointed at Basil's name. "Basil knows something and has a deep secret he wants kept buried. Not even Uncle could get to his secret. I'm deploying my next weapon." She flicked a glance at her great-aunt.

"I know what's rattling about in that snappy brain of yours, my dear girl, and I won't have it." Great-Aunt Iris clutched her purse to her chest. "The way that dreadful man carries on with me is scandalous. I told you that at the ball, didn't I? And here I thought you had a decent memory."

"I'm sorry, but we're in emergency mode now. Do you feel up to the task? You could always take Great-Uncle William with you," Eliza suggested.

"Not if we don't fancy a spot of violence. My William would surely send Basil to meet his maker if he witnessed how frightfully the man speaks to me. And winks." Great-Aunt Iris shuddered. "Winks! The absolute cheek of it. Winking at me like I'm some common tart."

"And you're certain you want to go alone?" Uncle Fitzwilliam asked. "I could accompany you."

"Utter rubbish, my dear boy. You've already tried cracking that odd nut. Besides, having you there would only turn him into a groveling toady. I won't get information that way. Back in my day, I sorted out—"

"Yes, Aunt, but you're past your day now, aren't you? While you might have been able to manage that fifty-odd years ago, you're not quite... not quite..." Uncle Fitzwilliam tugged at his collar.

Everyone gaped at him, stunned that he'd voiced what they all thought but had wisely kept to themselves.

Great-Aunt Iris took slow, measured steps until she stood before her nephew, who towered over her small frame. Her peach skin flushed, and her body trembled with emotion. She placed her weathered hand on his cheek. "We weren't put on this earth to witness evil win in silence, Fitz. I might not be in the prime of health, but I'll fight until the end, whatever that brings. Some battles aren't won with physical strength, my boy."

Uncle Fitzwilliam covered her hand with his. "You never stop amazing me."

"Good," she said with a slight smile. "Someone has to keep you sharp." She turned to face Eliza. "Give me Basil." As if bracing for battle, she sat down, settled her purse on her lap, and fixed her steely gaze on the board.

"I'll handle Hubert," Uncle Fitzwilliam declared. "I'm confident I can coax something out of him. Not so sure about Henrietta, though. Something tells me she's not particularly fond of men."

"I agree, but I'm not the right person for her either. I'm not refined enough," Eliza said, adopting an exaggerated posh accent. "She'll want someone with real influence and stronger family ties."

"Me?" Joy asked hopefully.

"I don't think so." Eliza glanced at her great-aunt. "Feel like questioning two people?"

"I haven't felt better a day in my life," she said.

"That leaves Harry and Paisley." Eliza tapped their names on the board. "Let's speak with them again. Try to dig deeper. Harry has strong motive, but his means and opportunity are shaky."

"And Lucinda?" Heath asked.

Eliza sighed. "I don't see an opportunity or motive. An old friendship that's faded doesn't jump out as a reason to kill."

"But she does have a connection with Paisley," Uncle Fitzwilliam said.

"Yeah, but that happened so long ago. If Lucinda was so angry about what Hunter did to Paisley, why wait until the next time they bumped into each other to do something about it?" Eliza blew out a breath. "Maybe if it were an extortion case. But killing him wouldn't do Paisley any good."

"So who's tackling who?" Joy asked.

"Whom." At Joy's scrunched nose, Eliza grinned. "Never mind. How about you tackle Harry?" Eliza drew a line under his name. "I'll talk to Paisley and take Willow with me. Might help get me in the door and ease the situation. And I'll swing by Lucinda's office on my way out of town and see if I can get any more information about Hunter."

Heath cleared his throat. "Aren't you forgetting somebody?"

"Not in your dreams." Eliza grinned.

"I don't like your smile," Heath said, taking a step back.

"Women in their golden years love you—"

Great-Aunt Iris snorted.

Eliza shot her a side glance. "Correction. *Most* women in their golden years adore you, so how do you feel about visiting certain ladies after work?"

Heath rubbed the back of his neck and sighed. "I'd be delighted, naturally."

Eliza grabbed the piece of notebook paper Joy handed her. "Aunt Iris, what's Gladys's last name? The one whose granddaughter was friends with Rose Harley?"

"Ivanhoe."

Eliza jotted down the names of three Golden Gamblers with short descriptions after each: *Regina, Lady Beaumont, rude and locked in an age-battle with Aunt Iris, tread carefully; Gertrude, Lady Townsend, kind and helpful, won't let Joy join the group until she's sixty-five; Gladys Ivanhoe, granddaughter was friends with Rosie Harley.*

Eliza settled her hands on her hips and studied her crew. "We'll meet again after dinner and trade notes. And be careful. We've stirred the wasp's nest, and I don't want anyone getting stung."

Within thirty minutes, Eliza, with Willow at her side, stood in front of a ramshackle apartment complex. Even with the sunshine glinting off the grimy windows, Eliza shivered and huddled deeper into her winter coat, wondering if the building had ever housed joy within its walls.

Eliza drew her gaze from the dingy gray edifice and smiled at Willow. "Thanks again for smoothing the way."

Willow tucked a piece of brown hair behind her ear. "I know this needs to be done, but I feel like I've betrayed a friend's trust. She didn't seem too keen for visitors, even with my vouching for you."

Unease settled in Eliza's gut. Paisley hadn't asked for Hunter to walk into her life and destroy it any more than Belle had. Guilt pricked her conscience.

A baby's cry echoed from the building, and Eliza shivered. *There's also a child in all this. A child that doesn't deserve to have her life haunted by the actions and death of an odious man.*

She motioned for Willow to follow her, stalked up to the main door, trailed her gloved finger down the list of unit numbers, and pressed the cracked button next to 313.

"Hello?" A woman's voice crackled through the speaker.

"Hiya, Paisley. It's me. Willow. Here with Eliza Darcy. Can we come in?"

Paisley was quiet so long that Eliza figured they'd gotten their answer and turned on her heel to leave.

The lock clicked, and taking that as permission for an interview, Eliza entered the dim foyer littered with packages and trash bags. The smell of rotting vegetables and dirty diapers accosted Eliza's nose, and she held a hand over her nose as she and Willow passed a wall of mailboxes to the stairs.

"I can't believe Harry lets his daughter live in this hovel," Eliza muttered, stepping over a toy car in the middle of the stairs.

Willow grunted. "More like she won't let him interfere in any way. Says she got herself into her own mess and she'll see her way out."

Eliza eyed the graffiti on the walls as they ascended the third set of stairs. *What has Paisley so handcuffed to her fate?*

Willow took the lead, and Eliza followed her down a narrow hallway until they reached unit 313. Eliza held her breath as Willow knocked.

The door creaked open, revealing a tall, curvy, freckled woman with red hair slicked back neatly into a bun.

"Paisley." Willow smiled. "This is Eliza Darcy. Can we come in?"

Paisley's green eyes scanned Eliza, and Eliza fought the urge to squirm under the intense scrutiny. Without a word, Paisley backed away from the door, leaving it wide open. Eliza took that as a sign of permission to enter and followed Willow into the tiny apartment.

Despite its size and sparse furniture, the place was neat and orderly. Two old couches straight out of the fifties filled most of the living room. A scarred coffee table adorned with a vase of fake tulips sat between them. Kids' toys were neatly stacked in cloth totes in the corner.

Willow gestured to the larger of the couches. "Have a seat. Hazel didn't sleep well last night, and I finally got her down for a little nap, so we'll need to talk quietly," she said as she settled onto the smaller one. "I understand from Willow that you want information about Hunter."

"Yes, but I know this must be hard for you, and if you're not comfortable sharing, I understand," Eliza said, holding out her palms.

Paisley's chuckle lacked mirth. "You understand? You understand nothing. Why would someone like you"—she circled her hand in Eliza's direction—"know anything about my situation?" She spread her arms out wide and glanced about the small space.

"Paisley." Willow leaned over and rested her hand on the young woman's arm. "You can trust Eliza. Like I said before, she's only trying to free her friend from a ridiculous murder charge. Hunter was an arse. Of that, there's no doubt. We're not here to sing his praises. We're here to get a better picture of your dealings with him."

"No, I know why the likes of Eliza Darcy is here." She narrowed her eyes at her. "You want to know if I killed him. Isn't that right?"

"Did you?" Eliza asked.

"No, but if I had, I wouldn't have waited four years. I would have done it the second that bastard called me a whore and refused to acknowledge the baby growing inside me as his."

Eliza blinked at the hatred flickering from Paisley's eyes. "I'm sorry that happened. I really am." Questions lined up, ready for her to fire, but the wounded pain radiating off Paisley kept Eliza's tongue in check.

Willow cleared her throat. "I hope you don't mind me asking, but why didn't you claim him as the father? To fight the accusation, Hunter would have needed a paternity test, which would have proved your claim."

Eliza smiled appreciatively at Willow. The young Pemberley employee might find an honorary spot on their sleuthing team yet.

"I... I..." Paisley's gaze flicked back and forth between Eliza and Willow for a few seconds. "I tried. I told him—" Her shoulders stooped. "I told him I'd go public, start the rumor myself, force his hand..."

"And?" Willow gently prodded.

"I'm sorry. I can't." Paisley clapped a hand over her mouth and stifled a sob.

Willow sat next to her and wrapped an arm around her shoulders. "You can't keep letting the past haunt you."

Paisley studied her clenched hands. "What's that saying? Old sins cast long shadows."

"What happened?" Willow asked.

"I'm sorry, Willow, but I can't. Not now. Not ever. I have Hazel to think of." She jutted her chin out, and her piercing gaze met Eliza's. "My daughter comes first all the time, every time. I'm sorry for your friend, but you'll have to help her without me."

Chapter Fifteen
Sleuthing Team, Assemble!

I do wish I had not told Darcy about Mr. Crawford's familiar conversation yesterday. He now threatens to not only be from home whenever they call but to set his dogs on him. While I do not look forward to their visits and will never entertain Mr. Crawford alone, I reminded Darcy that it would not do to be at loggerheads with the Crawfords. It is better to know of one's neighbor's foibles so one does not easily become ensnared in their nets of deception.
Lizzy Bennet Darcy
Pemberley 1815

After dropping Willow off at the Trusty Teapot with a promise to be back as quickly as possible, Eliza parked the Range Rover in front of Lucinda Fairchild's real estate office. Her secretary led her straight to Lucinda's office.

"Ah, Eliza, what a lovely surprise." Lucinda greeted her with a smile and dropped her pen onto her desk. "You're a welcome distraction." She rubbed her temples. "Some clients are more difficult than others, and if I have to give them the dimensions of the master bathroom *one more time*, I'll scream."

Eliza settled into a chair across from Lucinda's desk. "I don't envy you."

"What brings you by, then?" Lucinda asked. "Any news on our case?"

"That's why I'm here. I hate to keep bothering you, but I keep hitting a brick wall."

"Oh, I'd love to help however I can."

"I know talking about Hunter is difficult for you, but the more I know about him—his past, who he was—the better I can understand why someone killed him. You mentioned that your separation happened because you sensed something off about him," Eliza said.

"Yes. Even in our friendship's early days, I knew something wasn't right. That Hunter wasn't like my other uni mates. He always seemed to take pleasure in causing pain or getting others in trouble, even when he'd done the deed himself. I'd chalked it up to him being a bit cheeky or 'lads being lads' and all that, but the longer I was round him, the clearer it became. He was a proper nasty piece of work, and I distanced myself as much as possible without making it obvious I didn't fancy being mates anymore."

"Did anyone else notice this behavior?"

Lucinda tilted her head and thought for a moment. "You know, I'm not sure. My other mates didn't want to hang out with him either, and he was often the odd one out."

"Did you know anything about his parents, Hubert and Henrietta?"

Lucinda's chuckle jarred against the flash of anger in her eyes. "Good old Henrietta and Hubert. I went to Berryhill Manor once on holiday with Hunter, before I started distancing myself from him, and I tried to have as little to do with them as possible. I couldn't put my finger on it until months later, when I began to get the sense of the man Hunter truly was. Then it didn't take me long to figure out why. I can't imagine the Crawfords ever holding their son to account for his behavior, and I'd wager my life savings that they always tried to blame others. Probably easier that way than dealing with the monster they'd created."

"Do you think they knew what Hunter was?" Eliza asked.

"Most likely. I didn't get the sense that they ever loved him. Don't know if they could or even wanted to. And from the way Hunter spoke about his parents, the feeling was mutual."

"I shouldn't feel pity for Hunter, but that's really sad," Eliza said.

"Pity is an odd thing. I'm not sure that even if he'd had brilliant parents, he would have turned out differently."

"The age-old question of nature versus nurture."

"In my opinion, Hunter was a wrong 'un from birth. What are those people called? Psychopaths? Sociopaths? He was definitely a narcissist."

"And that's why you started cutting ties with him after college?" Eliza asked.

"Right. Figured it wouldn't do me any good. I'd seen firsthand what happened to those who chose to stay in his orbit or couldn't escape his presence."

"Do you mind if I ask who?"

"I'd rather not tell their stories on their behalf, but I'm sure you already know one of them, since you've spoken with Harry."

"Paisley?"

"Yeah. Despite the age gap between us, we met through the RSPCA and connected over our love of animals. We formed a deep friendship." She closed her eyes and pinched the bridge of her nose. "Then Hunter got his claws into her. I'd accidentally brought them together when I invited her along to a social do."

"But Paisley and Hunter lived in the Lambton area. They didn't connect then?"

"They knew who each other were, but nothing in the area really brought them together. Until I came along." Lucinda shook her head. "There he was, and no matter what I told Paisley, they took to each other like a house on fire. Soon, she was left with nothing, her life in tatters."

"That must have bothered you."

"You haven't got a clue." Lucinda gazed out the office window and fell silent for several seconds. "If I could go back in time and change things, I would. I'd give all this up just to give Paisley a proper chance at a normal life."

"None of what Hunter did was your fault."

"Knowing that and *knowing* that are two different things, aren't they?" Lucinda's voice cracked. She cleared her throat and took a sip of water. "If I can do anything else to help, please let me know." She shook her head, her eyes glinting with pain. "I couldn't help Paisley, but if I can help Belle, I'll do everything in my power."

"You've already done so much. Without you, I would have had a harder time with Harry, and Basil would never have opened his door to me."

"You'd have been right as rain with Foster, but Basil, that dreadful old toad, would have slammed the door in your face without so much as a by-your-leave."

Eliza grinned. "So, you've seen his collection, then?"

Lucinda rolled her eyes. "Seen it? Everyone unlucky enough to find themselves in Basil's house cannot escape being introduced to each and every one of those ghastly amphibians."

Knowing her great-aunt was enduring that ordeal along with Basil's flirtatious attempts, Eliza shivered. "What do you know about Basil?"

"Besides the fact that he's somehow kept his headmaster position at the boarding school despite everyone seemingly having it in for him?"

"Having it in for him? In what way?" Eliza said.

"Not in the way you're thinking. People talk. They speculate. Some, because of their suspicions or general dislike of the man, have actively tried to get him sacked. He's a proper oddity and fodder for much gossip. How much of it is true, I have no clue."

"Villages have a way of digging up old skeletons from people's closets," Eliza said. "Any skeleton in particular that draws the most talk?"

"Apart from his toads and how people haven't got a clue how he still has a job?" Lucinda shrugged. "Not really."

"Was he close with Hunter?"

"They were definitely up to something together."

"And Beckham?"

"Oh, Beckham has his fingers in every pie around here and gets mixed up in so many schemes that you'll have a devil of a time unraveling it all. I haven't the slightest doubt that those three were up to something dodgy."

Lucinda's phone rang, and when she glanced at the caller ID, she smiled apologetically. "I'm sorry, but I have to take this."

Eliza stood. "No worries. Thank you for your time."

After Eliza picked up Willow from the Trusty Teapot, they headed back to Pemberley.

"Thanks again for your help with Paisley."

"You're welcome, but I'm not sure she'll ever talk to me again," Willow said, her gaze locked on the wintry landscape outside the passenger window.

"She will. She was angry with me. Not you." Eliza fiddled with the heater knob, cranking it higher. "Do you know what she was referring to with the whole old-sins-and-long-shadows thing?"

"I have no clue. She's always kept things close to her chest. Must be pretty painful, though, for her to allow Hunter to destroy her future."

Time for more digging into another innocent person's life all because one man decided to live his as awfully as he could. While Eliza didn't relish the thought of uncovering Paisley's secrets, she couldn't wait to sink her teeth into Basil's and Beckham's. She couldn't shake the feeling that they were involved in Hunter's demise. But how they connected with the buried body on the property line between Pember-ley and Berryhill Manor remained a complete mystery.

Perhaps the two cases weren't connected at all.

Eliza gripped the steering wheel tightly and hoped that her sleuthing crew had gathered information to beef up their murder board.

A few hours later, the whole crew, including Wentworth, assem-bled in the nursery.

"If we're going to meet here so often, it might be worth moving in some proper comfortable furniture," Joy said as she squeezed her-self into a chair made for a five-year-old.

Wentworth eyed the children's-size chairs and leaned against the wall, his arms crossed over his chest. "Right, then. What did every-one find out?"

"I managed to speak with Gertrude but not the others," Heath said.

"What did she say?" Eliza asked.

"She mentioned Everett's wife again and how dreadful it was that Rosie's disappearance tore up so many lives. After the rumors start-ed, Everett's wife, Cynthia, couldn't cope with the pressure and aban-doned her husband. Some claimed she even believed the rumors and left the village to go live with one of her grown children. Not long after that was when Everett took his own life. No one has any clue what happened to Cynthia or the rest of Everett's family. They seem to have dropped off the face of the earth or at least off Lambton's radar, which is probably for the best."

Eliza wrote out Everett Tanner's name and jotted down the in-formation Heath had given her.

"What about you, Wentworth? How'd your chat with Beckham go?" Eliza handed him the chalk.

He motioned for her to keep it. "My handwriting's shoddy at best. Better you write it all down. I had a *lovely* chat with our Beckham. He admitted to being a business partner in Hunter's legal financial dealings but denied knowing anything about the Ponzi schemes."

"Do you believe him?" Heath asked.

"Not bloody likely. He's as smooth as they come, but he'll slip up eventually. I don't have enough information on him to get a search warrant for his finances or his place, but I've got officers on him, watching him like a hawk."

"Well, according to Lucinda, Beckham, Basil, and Hunter were in cahoots. She didn't know about what exactly." Eliza made a new note under Beckham's name. She pointed the piece of chalk at her great-aunt. "What were you able to weasel out of Basil?"

Great-Aunt Iris blushed. "That dreadful man had the cheek to kiss my hand like we were in some ghastly period drama on the telly, but I managed to keep my composure and not give him a proper slap. Wouldn't do to put his back up, would it? I was concerned about finding a natural way to bring up Hunter. As it happens, I needn't have worried. He brought it up himself."

"Really?" Eliza asked.

"He wanted to know if *Lord Darcy* appreciated how he'd helped my niece and Mr. Tilney a few days ago. I fibbed, naturally, and told him we're all delighted with his assistance. I thanked him ever so much and let slip that we're having trouble finding anyone who didn't loathe Hunter. He agreed. Called him a proper snake."

"That's what he told Eliza and me," Heath said.

"Yes, but I got the sense that Basil not only hated Hunter but feared him. He kept glancing at a particular stack of papers on his desk and made sure that when I stood to leave, he covered the ledger book at the top of the pile with his hand. He was trying to look inconspicuous, but I know subterfuge when I see it." A Cheshire-cat grin curled her lips.

"What did you do?" Eliza asked, knowing full well what her great-aunt was capable of.

"I snuck back into his house after he'd gone off to the main school building."

"You what?" Wentworth gaped at her.

"Don't get your knickers in a twist. I didn't have to break anything or pick a lock to get in. I simply forgot my knitting needles, you see, and needed to collect them. I have to finish this blanket for Maggie May down in the village before her little one arrives." Great-Aunt Iris dug a half-done soft-pink blanket from her oversize purse. "See?"

"*Could* you have picked a lock?" Wentworth asked, a look of horror on his face.

Great-Aunt Iris smiled enigmatically. "That's neither here nor there. Just know that I entered that man's residence legally and for a perfectly good reason." She waved the knitting needles about and narrowed her eyes at Wentworth as if daring him to question her.

He held his hands up in surrender. "You didn't nick anything from his residence once you got back inside, did you?"

"You do think me a daft old bird, don't you, Detective Chief Inspector Finn Wentworth?" Great-Aunt Iris asked, indignation ringing in her voice.

Eliza was certain that if her great-aunt had known Wentworth's middle name, she would have used it.

"Not at all, I assure you, ma'am. It's just that I don't need any more headaches—" He tugged at his collar under Great-Aunt Iris's withering stare. "Not that you're a headache, Mrs. Darcy. It's that... I haven't got time to sort out another person's mess."

Uncle Fitzwilliam slapped Wentworth on the back. "Best to stop digging, old chap."

The smile spreading across Great-Aunt Iris's face told Eliza that her great-aunt knew exactly what she was doing to poor Wentworth and was savoring every moment of it.

To save Wentworth, Eliza tapped her piece of chalk on Basil's name. "What did you find out?"

After shooting one last pointed look at Wentworth, Great-Aunt Iris dug a camera out of her purse and handed it to Eliza. "I took pictures of what looks like doctored accounts. The school's accounts."

Wentworth took the camera from Eliza's hands. "Right. I'll have this developed straightaway. What made you think these were dodgy?"

"No one acts guilty around proper account books, do they? I saw how he kept sneaking glances at it. Daft, of course, because he gave up his little secret by acting so suspiciously. If he hadn't kept shooting it all those side glances, I'd never have noticed it. I have no doubt that with your powers of persuasion, you'll crack him open like a nut."

Eliza quirked an eyebrow at her great-aunt.

"What?" she asked. "I heard that on the telly the other night. Thought it fit the situation."

"Maybe this is what had Basil so worried. If these are the cooked account books for the school, it could prove that Basil was embezzling from it and that Hunter knew about it. For the price of his silence, Hunter could have forced or convinced Basil to help find easy victims for his schemes." Eliza wrote *Embezzling from boys' school* under Basil's name and beneath that wrote *Did Hunter use this as blackmail and/or leverage?*

"This gives Basil a motive for wanting Hunter dead. And he was at the New Year's Eve ball. Basil has means, motive, and opportunity," Heath said. "Blackmail's a bloody dangerous game to play, and I'm thinking Hunter found that out the hard way."

"Joy, anything new from Harry?" Eliza asked.

"He admitted that if he'd had the chance, he would've, and he'd like to personally thank the person who rid the world of Hunter," Joy said. "Oh, and he accidentally let it slip that Hunter and Paisley had been in recent communication."

"What?" Eliza said, swiveling her neck so quickly something popped. She winced.

"Yeah, he immediately clammed up the moment he realized what he'd said. Didn't say much after that, but I get the sense that whatever brought Hunter and Paisley back together again was not amicable."

Eliza stabbed Paisley's name with a piece of chalk. "Leverage and blackmail are both solid motives, even more so after my conversation with Paisley." She wrote under Paisley's name: *Hunter was blackmailing her. Back in communication with Hunter.*

After a few seconds of stunned silence, Eliza brushed her hands free of chalk.

"Well? Did she say what he was blackmailing her over?" Wentworth pressed.

Eliza shook her head. "No. She got real tight-lipped. Even when Willow pressed her for answers, Paisley refused to elaborate. Said old sins cast long shadows. Her hatred for Hunter was darn near palpable. He destroyed her life then blackmailed her. She's got every reason to kill him." Eliza crossed her arms and studied the board. "And now that we know she and Hunter were in communication again after four years, perhaps those old scabbed-over wounds opened back up again."

"But she wouldn't have known Hunter would be at the party unless someone at the party let her know," Heath pointed out. "Could be someone sent an innocent text like 'Look who's here.' The Crawfords were at the party early enough that Paisley could have made it in plenty of time."

"And if they were in communication again, she could have texted him and lured him out to the woods," Joy said, her forehead scrunching.

"We said the same thing about Harry." Eliza massaged her temples. "Could they both be in on it?"

Wentworth scribbled in his notebook. "I'll have my lads check on both of them. Find out where they were on New Year's Eve."

Eliza wrote *Has motive and means but lacks opportunity* under Paisley's name. "I don't see her leaving her daughter at home to go on a killing spree or bringing her child to a murder, but if Hunter finally pushed her too far..." Eliza scowled at the chalkboard. "I feel like we're spinning our wheels here. We have people who wanted Hunter dead, but nothing connects nicely except for this guy." Eliza drew an asterisk next to Basil's name. "And how does Basil or any of these other people connect to the body we found? Does that even matter? Are the two cases connected?" She looked hopefully at Wentworth. "Please tell us you've got some news about the body."

"I don't have a concrete answer, but the forensics lab told me the body was that of a young child. Whether or not it's Rosie will come down to dental records, and those hadn't come back as of an hour ago when I last spoke with the lab."

"It's her. It has to be her. Poor, poor Rosie," Joy whispered.

Silence smothered the room, and Eliza clasped Heath's hand. His touch comforted her, and she took a deep breath. "Yes, Joy, I'm afraid our initial suspicions were correct. The dental records might come back showing it's not her, but I think it's safe to assume the body is Rosie's. Is that right, Wentworth, or do you know of any other missing-child cases?"

"No, I know of no other missing-person case involving a child. I've contacted neighboring county constabularies, and they also have no records or cold cases that match the remains we discovered. I don't often assume in my job, but I'm fairly certain we've found Rosie."

"So how does her tragic death connect with Hunter's, if at all?" Eliza asked.

"I don't believe in coincidence," Wentworth said. "The fact that someone buried the body right on the property line speaks volumes." He turned to Uncle Fitzwilliam. "What did you find out from Hubert?"

"Besides that he's a right arse?" Uncle Fitzwilliam's face turned thunderous.

As her uncle normally didn't use slang or vulgar language, Eliza figured Hubert hadn't impressed him. "What happened?"

"He was practically groveling—Lord Darcy this, Lord Darcy that." He jammed his fingers through his salt-and-pepper hair, creating tufts in his normally immaculate style. "Not a word about his son. Can you imagine? Your son is brutally murdered, and you don't mention him once? It's as if the boy never existed. There weren't any pictures of him, at least not in the rooms Hubert paraded me through in an obvious bid for my approval of all his expensive possessions. I hadn't the heart to tell him they were either frightfully gaudy little things or knockoffs of proper designer furniture. Like Aunt Iris pointed out, everything seemed for sale at the right price, but unlike my aunt, I couldn't go off gallivanting on my own so didn't find the rooms stacked with furniture." He gave her a cheeky grin.

"Was Henrietta with him?" Eliza asked.

"No, she was out, but I believe she's having tea here tomorrow with you, Aunt, right?" Uncle Fitzwilliam asked.

"I figured she'd feel more important than she is by being invited to Pemberley for tea," Great-Aunt Iris said. "Those sorts prattle on more than they ought, trying to seem more important or that they know more than they do. Absolute rubbish." She tutted and resumed her knitting.

"If Hubert didn't talk about his son, what did he talk about?" Heath asked.

"The lawsuit over the property line. Hubert claimed it was all a misunderstanding and that after he'd looked into it further, he realized he'd been wrong and dropped it straightaway."

"Or had known that a property dispute would require a fresh survey of the border, and the body would have been discovered," Joy said.

"Which means he knew the body was there. Either because he put it there himself or he knew who did," Eliza said.

"And Hubert doesn't do anything for anybody, so whoever it was—if it wasn't him—would have to be close to him. His son? His wife?" Uncle Fitzwilliam added.

"But then why would he file the lawsuit?" Heath asked.

"I bet it was Hunter who did it for whatever money scheme he was about to cook up. If that's the case, Hubert must have gone into panic mode, and if Hunter refused to drop it, that leaves Hubert with only one option," Eliza said.

"Kill his son to protect his secret?" Joy asked.

"This is all speculation. Unless we can connect Hubert to Rosie Harley from eighteen years ago, we're dealing with coincidence, not nearly enough for a search warrant. We need to dig deeper and cast our nets wider." Wentworth's phone chirped, and he glanced at it. "Right. I've got to run." As he walked out of the nursery, he motioned for Eliza to follow.

She joined him in the hallway. "Yes?"

"You've got multiple suspects on your board, Eliza, but I'm cautioning you. Most of those people have motive but no opportunity. There's no evidence linking them to the crime scene, and people don't appreciate having their quiet lives disrupted by questions from police or... interested parties. You've already ruffled someone's feathers enough that they threatened your life."

"You think one of them did it?" Eliza asked.

"I'm not thinking about anything right now. All I know is there's one person with means, motive, and opportunity plus evidence linking her to the crime. And she's not on your board."

Eliza clenched her hands, wincing as her fingernails bit into her palms. "We'll have to agree to disagree until I'm proven correct. How is Belle? You're taking good care of her?"

Wentworth's gaze gentled, and he clasped her shoulder. "Belle's holding up well. The barrister your uncle hired is doing an excellent job—don't tell anyone I said that—and she told me to tell you not to worry about her."

"I just don't understand why you won't see reason. With multiple people wanting him dead, how can you be so pigheaded about this?"

"Me? It's not about me. It's about the evidence, which directly links her to his murder. What I think and what others think, including the courts, are two different things. Don't mistake me and assume I'm giving up on your friend. I'm trying to prepare you for what's coming if we can't find another viable sus—"

"But what about Basil? He's got all three. What about the Fosters?"

"You're right, and I'll look deeper into all of them. My men are checking on the Fosters right now. I'll let you know as soon as I know anything. But don't get too attached to your theory. That's a copper's number-one mistake. And before you get it into your head that I called you a copper, I didn't. Keep your mind open. I'll keep in touch, yeah?" His amber eyes softened. "And do be careful, Eliza. Don't go off half-cocked in some renewed effort to clear your friend's name. Someone has already threatened you, and I would never forgive myself if anything happened to you. I'm half-tempted to lock you up in a cell next to Belle." He smiled kindly. "Didn't our last brush with murder and mayhem teach you anything? Trust me, please."

Eliza smiled grimly at Wentworth's mention of their past life-and-death ordeal. "I have your solemn promise you won't give up on Belle?"

"I'll do what I can, but I'm hamstrung by legal regulations, and regrettably, the law doesn't always equate to justice. I'll see what I can do about lining up a visit." He walked away with quiet resolve, leaving Eliza alone with her churning thoughts.

Even though she knew her loved ones waited beyond the door, isolation smothered her, and she struggled to breathe.

Chapter Sixteen
A Toad-ally Awful Scene

Looking back at my diary entries, I realize how much the Crawfords have taken up my thoughts. Well, today, I'm happy to report that they have kept their distance for a few days, leaving me energy to plan for Jane and Charles's visit next week. I cannot express how excited I am to see dear Jane, Charles, and my sweet nephew, Thomas. Adelaide Rose has spoken of nothing but her older cousin, and I'm sure they will tear this house to pieces with their exuberant play. I shall make sure I reward Fanny for having to put up with not one but two rambunctious children.

Lizzy Bennet Darcy
Pemberley 1815

Darkness descended on Pemberley, and Eliza sought refuge in her office. Knowing it had been her predecessor's favorite room brought her comfort and inner strength. Elizabeth Bennet Darcy had possessed an uncanny knack for grace under pressure and never let anyone crush her spirit or destroy her dreams.

Her phone pinged, and her heart dropped at Wentworth's text: *Paisley has no alibi. Claims after having a New Year's Eve meal with her dad, she went home with Hazel. My men canvassed the neighbors, and no one saw her go in or out.*

Eliza: *Does that mean Harry has no alibi either?*

Wentworth: *Yes. Claims he was alone all night after Paisley and Hazel left. And before you jump to conclusions, not having an alibi is not a crime. I'll be in touch.*

In other words, the text thread had come to a screeching halt. Eliza pulled her light-pink robe tighter and gazed out the window into the night. It was hard to believe that five nights ago, a man, no matter how destructive he'd been in life, had been murdered. And now her friend's future hung in the balance.

Despite all her and her team's investigating, they hadn't narrowed down the list of suspects. In fact, the recently uncovered information and no alibis for two of the possible suspects piled guilt equally among them all. Eliza scowled into the darkness. She would not sit back and watch the wheels of justice crush her friend.

Eliza shook off the doubt creeping into her mind. The next day, she'd visit Basil. She hoped the man hadn't gallivanted off for a weekend getaway and would be holed up in his house with his stuffed toads. She shivered at the thought of setting foot in that place again, but needs must.

A light tapping on the open office door pulled Eliza from her thoughts. She turned, smiling at Heath.

"Penny for your thoughts?" he asked as he walked over and wrapped her in an embrace.

She burrowed into his chest and sighed. "Not sure they're even worth that much."

"What's wrong?" He held her at arm's length, and his forehead creased with concern.

Eliza told him about the Fosters' lack of alibis. "I can't shake the feeling we're barking up the wrong tree, and Belle's future hangs in the balance."

"What can I do to help? I'll be your weekend warrior." He cupped her chin and traced his thumb along the curve of her cheek.

"Visit Basil with me tomorrow?" Eliza asked.

"The toads again? You drive a hard bargain, love. What's in it for me? I really, really, *really* can't stand the sight of toads," he said, a mischievous glint sparkling in his eyes.

Eliza pulled his head down and whispered into his ear.

His pupils dilated, and his grip on her tightened. "Right, then. That's what I call a proper deal." He dipped his head and brushed a kiss across her lips. "And when do I collect on this arrangement?"

"After our successful mission."

Heath's five o'clock shadow scratched deliciously against her neck, and goose bumps scattered across Eliza's skin.

"You're putting my reward in the hands of Toad Man?" he asked, his eyes glinting with mirth.

Eliza chuckled. "All the more incentive to get the information we need out of him. The sooner we can get a solid lead, the quicker we can free Belle and get out from under the destructive path Hunter left behind him."

Worry replaced the laughter in his eyes, and his jawline tightened. He sat on a chaise longue and pulled her down next to him, tucked her head under his chin, and played his fingers along her back. "Eliza, I know I promised you that I'd never step in your way or stop you from fighting for justice, but I'm…" His fingers paused their journey up and down her spine.

Eliza sat up and studied his chiseled face, which was made more so by the shadows in the dimly lit room playing over his skin. She placed her hand on his cheek, and her heart skipped a beat when he leaned into it. "What is it?"

Heath caught her hand in his and kissed it. "I'm terrified. The note. The evil surrounding Hunter's life and death. And I know you well enough to know you won't quit, not even when it could mean your life."

"What would you have me do?" Eliza asked, her fingers tightening on his. "I can't stand by and watch injustice trample the people I love."

"I know that, and that's one of the reasons I love you." Heath caressed her cheek with his thumb. "But if anything happened to you—" He puffed out an exasperated breath when Eliza jutted her chin. "You've had two close calls before, remember? If anything ever did happen..." His Adam's apple dipped, and his cornflower-blue eyes studied her as if he were trying to memorize her every last feature. "It would devastate everyone who knows and loves you. It would crush me, love."

Eliza blinked back the hot tears damming behind her eyes, wrapped her arms around his neck, and kissed him. Nothing mattered but the feel of his fingers in her hair, the slight pressure bringing her closer to him. She lost herself in Heath's touch until she couldn't breathe.

Breaking away, she held his face in her hands. "I love you more than anything. I never want to do anything that would hurt you. If you really want me to stop..."

"Oh, Eliza, I'm not asking you to stop. Just promise me you'll never try to do it alone." He pressed a kiss to her forehead.

"I promise," Eliza said, grabbing his hand and dragging him to his feet.

Heath was right, and a renewed sense of fear skittered up her spine. But she didn't want to feel fear, not then, not with Heath. She wanted to give herself a few more hours in which the world didn't matter, and the only two people who existed were her and Heath. "Come," Eliza said and guided Heath to her room.

Eight hours later, Eliza rolled over in bed, evading the morning sunlight that streamed through the bedroom window. She spread-eagled on the mattress and stared into the slitted yellow gaze of Caesar, who perched on the pillow beside her. He sniffed at her hairline, licked her forehead, then bounded off the bed and sashayed toward the door, his tail held high. When she didn't move, he meowed and pawed at the door.

"Coming, you big baby," Eliza mumbled. She struggled out of bed and shuffled to the door. "There, my king. Your wish is my command."

Without so much as a thank-you, Caesar scampered out the door and down the hall.

"You could do without a few of Mrs. B.'s meals," she called after him as he disappeared down the steps.

Eliza chuckled and readied herself for the day and the dreaded visit to Basil's. As she squeezed herself into a pair of skinny jeans, she pouted. "Looks like I could do without a few of Mrs. B.'s meals too." She left her room and knocked gently on Heath's door, and when she didn't find him there, she knew exactly where he'd be.

"Thought I'd find my two men down here," Eliza said as she entered the kitchen.

Heath and Caesar both sat on barstools, patiently waiting for whatever Mrs. Bankcroft was in the mood to gift them.

Eliza eyed the caramel rolls, strawberries, and fresh clotted cream with envy. Project Get-Back-Into-Her-Pants was in full swing, and she waved away Heath's offer of a roll. She filled a bowl with strawberries and a slight dab of clotted cream and sat beside Heath.

"Morning, Mrs. B.," Eliza said.

"Morning, lass." The cook narrowed her gaze at the meager portion in Eliza's bowl. "That all you're having for breakfast, then?"

"Yeah, afraid so."

"You'll waste away if you don't put something on those bones." Mrs. Bankcroft moved to the stove, where a skillet sputtered with bacon grease. "Fancy some bacon? Fresh off the griddle?"

"No, thanks," Eliza said and glared at Heath and Caesar, who both volunteered to relieve Mrs. Bankcroft of the first round of bacon.

Mrs. Bankcroft's forehead furrowed. "Are you sure you're feeling all right, lass?"

"Perfectly well, thank you, Mrs. B." Eliza rested her elbows on the counter. "Heath and I have somewhere to be soon, so I'll eat later. Some BLTs for lunch?" There was no way she'd ever convince Mrs. Bankcroft that she didn't need food in her belly.

"You might want to get your strength up for Toad Man." Heath waved a piece of bacon around before popping it into his mouth.

"You're off to see Mr. Huxley, the one with all them frogs?" Mrs. Bankcroft asked, her eyebrows nearly reaching her hairline.

"The one and only," Eliza said. "Why? Do you know him?"

"I know *of* him." Mrs. Bankcroft shuddered. "A school chum of mine married well, and we've kept in touch over the years. Her grandson attends Lambton Prep, and from what she tells me, the boys despise Mr. Huxley. They call him Mr. Toad behind his back, they do. There's rumors, too, that he's into something dodgy. Plenty of money flows into the school, but precious little to show for it lately, if you catch my drift. Parents and donors are demanding an audit, or so my friend says."

"Interesting." Eliza finished her strawberries. "Thanks for breakfast and the intel."

As they left the kitchen, Eliza's phone pinged. She breathed a sigh of relief at Wentworth's text: *I've arranged a quick visit for you and Belle. Be at the station in fifteen.*

Putting their visit with Basil to the side for a moment, Eliza and Heath made it to the police station in record time. Despite the building's cottage feel, the white stone and thatched roof looked ominous in the morning light. Eliza's heart thudded.

Heath laid a warm hand on top of hers. "Want me to come in with you?"

"No." Eliza pulled in a deep breath. "I'll be fine. Why don't you make sure Basil's up for company."

Before she lost her courage, she kissed Heath's cheek, jumped out of his Ford Puma, and took the steps to the two-paneled wooden door two at a time.

Constable Theo Archibald sat behind a large wooden desk, and his face lit up when he saw her. "Good morning, Eliza."

"You riding a desk?" Eliza asked, surprised to see the warrior constable doing desk duty instead of being Wentworth's boots on the ground.

"Nah, Wentworth wanted to make sure you got your visit with Belle and put me in charge." He gestured for her to follow him down a hallway. "Right this way." When they reached the last door on the left, he opened it. "Have a seat. I'll be back shortly."

Eliza spent the next few minutes drumming her fingers nervously on a banged-up old metal table and squirming on the uncomfortable metal chair. Just when she was about to give up and go search for Belle herself, the door opened, and Theo ushered her in.

Eliza jumped to her feet and squeezed Belle in a bear hug. "How are you holding up?"

Belle pulled away from her embrace, a soft smile on her lips. "I'm doing okay." And she looked it. Wentworth had allowed Belle to wear her own clothes, and her red hair was pulled back in a messy bun. And besides a tinge of purple under Belle's eyes, she looked her normal, spunky self.

After they settled in chairs, Eliza reached across the table and clutched Belle's hands. "Are they treating you well? Because if they haven't, Wentworth had better brace himself."

"They've taken good care of me under the circumstances." Belle slid a glance at Theo, who had pulled up a chair and sat in the corner, trying to look inconspicuous. Her cheeks bloomed pink, and she dipped her head when Theo caught her eye.

A matching blush washed over his cheeks. "Belle here is one of our few customers. Let's just say the lads—"

"And the girls," Belle pointed out, smiling.

Theo brushed away her comment. "You've heard Wentworth. We're all his 'men.' Anyway, the constables are doing all they can to make her comfortable. She's probably fair dinkum tired of all the attention."

"Theo's been kind enough to bring some of his books in for me. We found out we shared a love of Victorian ghost and werewolf stories, so I've been devouring those."

The boulder that had sat squarely behind her sternum for days eased up, and Eliza took a deep breath. "Don't get too used to the free books, though. You'll be out of here in no time." Eliza filled Belle in on all they'd found out since Belle's arrest. "And I drew the short straw and am off to see Toad Man... again." She shivered at the thought of all those sightless toads staring at her.

After hugging Belle and thanking Theo for taking good care of her friend, Eliza left the station, feeling lighter than she had for days. Hope was on the horizon. Basil was suspect number one, and she was about to prove it.

"How's Belle?" Heath asked as Eliza slid into the car.

She settled in the passenger seat and grinned at him. "She's doing surprisingly well. Doesn't hurt that she's got the undivided attention of the constables. One in particular." Eliza rubbed her hands and held them in front of the vent. "Ready for our lovely meeting with Basil?"

"He certainly didn't seem excited about our coming over, but he grudgingly agreed." Heath chuckled. "Seems he dislikes us as much as we dislike him."

Ten minutes later, they pulled up in front of Basil's house. In the morning light, it looked even more ridiculous and ostentatious. The school and surrounding grounds, a stone's throw away, clearly needed maintenance. No wonder parents had demanded an audit, and no wonder Basil had been so rattled when Great-Aunt Iris descended upon him.

If Hunter had known about Basil embezzling money from the school and tried to or had used it for blackmail, it was not a stretch to think Basil had snapped and cracked Hunter over the head. *Means, motive, and opportunity.* Maybe that would convince Wentworth and his superiors to get off Belle's case and focus on someone else. But Eliza needed the smoking gun, and the only way to get it was straight from the source: Basil himself.

The only question was how.

Straightening her shoulders, Eliza marched up the sidewalk to the green door with Heath in tow. She lifted the knocker and let it slam against the wood.

Silence followed.

Eliza waited several seconds before trying again.

Once more, only silence answered.

She glanced at Heath.

"Bit odd, that."

Eliza tried the door handle and jumped slightly when it opened.

She stuck her head around the doorframe. "Mr. Huxley? Eliza Darcy and Heath Tilney here. Can we come in?"

The only thing that met her request was the sound of silence and the stares of dozens of stuffed frogs in the foyer.

"Mr. Huxley?"

Heath pushed the door open and stepped inside. "Mr. Huxley?" When no response came, he walked deeper into the foyer.

"He said he'd be home," Eliza said then spotted a stuffed toad on the floor, its tiny surfboard cracked in two. She picked up the surfing toad and placed it back on the shelf. A queasy sensation made her gut churn, and without hesitating, she opened Basil's study door.

The same cluttered mess greeted her, but instead of the usual organized chaos of leaning paper towers and dusty books, everything was scattered across the floor. Desk drawers hung askew from their slots, while others lay splintered on the floor.

"What in the world?" Eliza murmured, nudging a book with her toe. "You just spoke to him. Was he in that much of a rush to grab something and dash before we arrived?"

"I don't think that's it."

Eliza's head snapped up at the grim tone in Heath's voice. He stood on the other side of the desk, staring down at the floor.

"What?" she whispered, her skin prickling with dread.

Heath extended his hand to her. She rounded the desk and came to an abrupt halt.

Basil lay face down on the floor, sprawled unnaturally. The back of his head was matted with blood, and beside him lay a large paperweight smeared with a red substance.

Eliza's stomach lurched, and she pressed a hand over her mouth.

Then her training kicked in. He could still be alive. Heath had spoken to him on the phone ten minutes ago. She crouched down and pressed her fingers to his carotid artery.

Nothing.

She pulled herself to her feet, grasped Heath's hand, and led him out of Basil's study before calling the police.

Even though the sun beat down on those huddled outside Basil's house, its warmth couldn't dispel the chilly January morning or thaw Eliza's frozen soul at the thought of another life lost to murder. Eliza rested her head against Heath's chest as law enforcement officers milled about.

On the far side of the house, where it bordered the boys' school grounds, a strip of crime-scene tape held back dozens of uniformed students. Basil's murder wouldn't stay quiet long, not with all those cell phones and busy fingers flying over screens.

She raised her chin as Wentworth emerged from the house, ducked under the tape, and walked toward her.

"Anything?" she asked.

Wentworth jerked his head toward his car, and Eliza and Heath followed. He stuffed his notebook and pen into his jacket pocket. "Same MO as Hunter's murder. Blunt-force trauma seems to be our killer's weapon of choice, and twice now, the murderer's grabbed something from the crime scene to kill with."

"I take it you got definitive proof from the lab?" Eliza asked.

"Traces of bark were found in the wound. The lab ran DNA testing on the flora and matched it to a tree right where Hunter was killed."

"Was the branch ever found?" Heath asked.

"No. The killer likely took it and dumped it among other fallen branches on their way out of the area."

"If the killer used random things at the crime scene, is it possible he or she never intended to kill in the first place? That both murders happened in the heat of the moment—look around for something, and *wham!* over the head?"

The door of Basil's house opened, and paramedics wheeled out a stretcher with a black body bag.

"Could well be." Wentworth threaded his fingers through his salt-and-pepper hair. "We won't know for certain until we catch them and get them talking."

"The first murder could have been planned, the killer knowing they could pick up a tree limb anywhere in a forest. But this one seems different, doesn't it?" Heath asked. "I mean, what would the killer have done if there was no paperweight? There's nothing else in the room that could serve as a convenient murder weapon."

Someone called for Wentworth, and he jogged away, ducked under the tape, and disappeared inside the house.

Eliza kicked at a pebble. It skittered across the graveled path and pinged against a tree trunk. "Basil's death doesn't clear anything up. And you were right about the killer's intention. If they'd come planning to kill Basil, they'd have brought their own weapon. Using the victim's paperweight suggests a crime of passion."

"Unless they were familiar with Basil's house and knew what they could use." Heath shrugged. "I wonder if those cooked books for the school are gone."

"That's a great point, and I hope Wentworth will share with us later." Eliza nodded toward the house. "He'll be tied up here for a while, I'd guess. Let's head back to Pemberley and revisit our board. We should let everyone know what's happened."

A half hour later, everyone had gathered in the nursery, a tea tray laden with goodies sitting in the middle of their sleuthing circle. Eliza stood beside the chalkboard and finished scrawling the newest note under Basil's name.

Joy helped herself to a raspberry scone and gestured to what Eliza had written. "*Killed with his own paperweight.*" She shivered. "How bloody dreadful. And here we thought he was our number-one suspect."

Eliza wrote, *Was he killed because he knew something he shouldn't have, or was he killed because he was a loose end?*

"By loose end, do you mean he was in on Hunter's murder, and his accomplice wanted to eliminate the only person who knew they'd done him in?" Uncle Fitzwilliam asked.

"It's something to keep in mind." Eliza set the chalk in the trough. "He hated Hunter, and if Hunter was blackmailing him, I can see a man like Basil wanting to rid himself of his problems by any means necessary. If he could carelessly collect once-living animals and proudly display them in those macabre settings..."

"Not everyone who collects taxidermized animals is a murderer," Uncle Fitzwilliam said. "If that were the case, most of the English gentry would be in prison. Plenty of normal people fill their homes with prized taxidermy."

Great-Aunt Iris tutted. "Basil was not a normal individual. He was a weak little man with a weak little mind, and men like him do cowardly things like murder."

"Whether or not he was involved in Hunter's murder, he's now a victim himself," Uncle Fitzwilliam said.

"I wish I knew whether the faked school accounts were taken. That could tell us a bit more about the situation. If the book is missing, it means someone knew about Basil's embezzlement and wanted to hide it," Eliza said.

"But why?" Belle asked.

"Before we answer that question, we need to know if the notebook was taken." Eliza pulled her phone from her back pocket and tapped out a quick text to Wentworth: *Any sign of what Aunt Iris claimed to have seen on her last visit?*

Great-Aunt Iris gathered her knitting, shoved it into her purse, and headed for the door.

"Where are you going?" Eliza asked.

"I need to get dressed for this afternoon."

"What's this afternoon?" Eliza asked, slightly panicked she'd planned something and forgotten it.

"Tea with Mrs. Henrietta Crawford."

"I don't suppose you'd mind my eavesdropping through the peephole from the tunnel, would you?"

"I'd be disappointed if you didn't. Any sleuth worth her salt needs to snoop with aplomb." Great-Aunt Iris winked. "I'll even make sure to have her sit where you can see her clearly." With that, she left the room, her tennis shoes squeaking and a thread of yarn trailing from her purse. The only thing missing was Caesar pawing and batting at his elusive prey.

Eliza's phone chirped. She pulled it from her back pocket again and glanced at the text from Wentworth.

Wentworth: *No.*

"Well, that settles that question," Eliza said, writing, *No sign of cooked books,* under Basil's name.

"That bloody muddles the waters now, doesn't it?" Joy threw her hands into the air.

"That, it does." Eliza brushed her hands together and scanned the board. "One of these people murdered both Hunter and Basil. But who?" She arched her back to alleviate the feeling of dread crawling up her spine.

"Or," Heath said, "Basil could still have killed Hunter and someone else killed Basil."

"You're not helping." Eliza rested her head on his shoulder and glared at the board.

"We're back to square one, aren't we. Who's determined enough to kill to keep their dirty little secret and threatened to kill you?" Uncle Fitzwilliam asked, worry threading through his voice.

"Trust me. I haven't forgotten." Eliza shivered and crossed her arms. "How can we be so close yet have no clue?"

"The killer is apt to make a mistake," Heath said.

Eliza groaned. "But at what cost? When? Who?"

At promptly four p.m., Eliza entered the secret tunnel through the library and made her way down the passage until they reached the peephole overlooking a rarely used sitting room. It wasn't Eliza's favorite, as it still bore Nancy's obnoxious decorating style. She made a mental note to tackle the room after solving the murder case. But judging from Henrietta's cooed oohs and aahs drifting through the peephole, she knew Henrietta hadn't realized she was being wined and dined in the household's least favorite room.

Eliza stepped onto the stool she'd brought for spying and pressed her eye to the hole. Sure enough, her great-aunt had positioned Henrietta perfectly so Eliza could see her face and hear every word.

"What a lovely room, Mrs. Darcy." Henrietta helped herself to several dainty cakes from the elaborate tea tray before her. "The decorations in here remind me of my beloved possessions. Do you know where you acquired these?"

"I'm afraid I don't make the decorative decisions, though I'll pass your compliments on to Lord Darcy." Great-Aunt Iris poured two cups of tea and handed one to Henrietta. "I'm so glad you could make our tea this afternoon, especially with all the kerfuffle over another death in the community."

Eliza smiled at her great-aunt's theatrical shiver.

Henrietta's pout was as fake as her hair color. "Yes, poor, poor Huxley."

"Were you well acquainted with him?"

"Not at all." She pressed a hand to her chest as if the thought pained her. "I only knew him slightly through his small dealings with Hunter." She pulled a handkerchief from her purse and dabbed at her dry eyes. "My poor, poor Hunter."

"I am so sorry for your loss, Mrs. Crawford. I, too, have lost a child, and the pain, even though I lost him so long ago, feels as raw at times."

Even though Eliza could only see the back of her great-aunt, the stoop of her shoulders and the tilt of her head clearly revealed her painful memories of the boy she'd lost so long ago. What a contrast to the shallow, empty mourning of the woman across from her.

"That's why I've invited you, Mrs. Crawford. I wanted to offer my support in your loss. Suffering shouldn't be tucked away in silence, should it?"

"How kind of you, Mrs. Darcy." Henrietta's smile didn't reach her eyes.

"And now with the death of an acquaintance..." Great-Aunt Iris sipped her tea.

"Quite so." Henrietta nearly spat the words. "The police have already been round."

By her tone, Eliza figured Henrietta viewed a visit from the police like a plague of locusts.

"The police?" Great-Aunt Iris asked.

"Yes, yes." Henrietta swatted at the air as if shooing away the thought of law enforcement officers. "Dreadful business. Asking all sorts of questions about Hunter's relationship with Huxley. As if my son would have anything to do with that man beyond what was merely civil."

"I had thought Hunter was an influential donor to Lambton Prep and thus had become a close confidante of Huxley's," Great-Aunt Iris said.

"Certainly not. My Hunter didn't rub shoulders with the likes of Basil Huxley." Henrietta's face turned crimson.

From the vitriol in Henrietta's voice, Eliza had the fleeting idea of pegging her as Basil's murderer.

"Forgive me, Mrs. Crawford," Great-Aunt Iris said. "I didn't mean to cause offence. I simply always thought it splendid of Hunter to throw himself into such a brilliant local institution and financially support the school. I'd assumed he and Basil were both frightfully keen on the boys' education. My mistake."

Henrietta smiled tightly. "No, my apologies, Mrs. Darcy. Everything is at sixes and sevens right now. I misunderstood you. Yes, Hunter enjoyed working with Huxley on raising money and awareness for the school. Beyond that, I'm not sure they had much in common." Henrietta squirmed in her seat, fidgeted with her napkin, then grabbed another sandwich and pastry.

Eliza's heart thudded. Henrietta knew something was going on between Hunter and Basil. *She looks as guilty as sin, but of what, I have no clue.*

"There's no need to apologize," Great-Aunt Iris said. "I'm taking it badly myself. I had a word with Mr. Huxley the day before he died."

"You did?" Henrietta nearly shot out of her chair.

"Yes, I wanted to make a substantial donation, you see."

"I see." Henrietta leaned forward, a greedy glint in her eye.

"When one plans on donating over five hundred thousand pounds, one wants to be assured their money will be put to good use."

"Five hundred thousand pounds?" Henrietta asked, more to herself than Great-Aunt Iris. She blinked several times and snapped out of whatever trance the mention of money had put her in. "How frightfully generous of you, Mrs. Darcy."

"It's nothing. But in the end, I decided to take my money to another local cause. After getting a peek at Mr. Huxley's accounts while his back was turned, I didn't think it wise to entrust my money there."

Henrietta's face drained of color, and two splotches of red bloomed on her pale cheeks.

"Of course, I'm sure you agree with my decision. I think Hunter would have been appalled at the state of the books, wouldn't you say?" Great-Aunt Iris kept talking as if she hadn't noticed her guest's sickly pallor. "Your poor lad probably had a hard time reining in Huxley's excessive spending." She tutted and moved to pour her guest more tea. "I say, Mrs. Crawford, is everything all right? You look peaky."

"I'm fine," Henrietta said, her voice thin and reedy. She cleared her throat and patted her chest. "Simply overcome with emotion at the mention of my boy. That's all."

"Oh, how thoughtless of me," Great-Aunt Iris said. "What a dreadful thing to do."

"No, no, there's no need to apologize." Henrietta stood. "Thank you ever so much for the tea, Mrs. Darcy, but I'm afraid I must dash. Feeling a bit wobbly."

"Of course." Great-Aunt Iris rang the bell. "While we wait for Tash, I did have another question. A silly one, I'm sure, but I was having a chat with the gardener the day I visited Berryhill Manor about a special variety of clematis I've only ever seen on your beautiful estate. He claims that one of your previous gardeners grew that particular variety. I was hoping you could help me."

Henrietta's forehead creased, and she tapped a manicured finger against her bottom lip. "I'm afraid my horticulture knowledge isn't up to par, Mrs. Darcy."

"Oh, more's the pity." Great-Aunt Iris smiled gently. "I'll have to ask around the village to double-check. Maybe someone can recall who your gardener used to be. Or might your current gardener be able to help me? You see, I'm desperate for that clematis variety."

Henrietta's eyebrows shot to her hairline. "Our current gardener couldn't tell the difference between a rose and a carnation if his life depended on it. Decent help is frightfully hard to come by these days."

Great-Aunt Iris sucked in a sharp breath and clutched at her chest. "Oh dear."

Henrietta jumped to her aid and settled the octogenarian back in her chair. "Mrs. Darcy, are you all right?"

Eliza nearly leaped off her stool, but after catching the sly glance her great-aunt sent toward the peephole, she forced herself to take a deep breath.

"Yes, yes, I'm fine." Great-Aunt Iris waved Henrietta away. "Just the mention of a rose—" A small sob escaped her lips, and she pressed her wrinkled hand to her mouth. "I'm so sorry, Mrs. Crawford. I'm so silly. Just a blithering ninnyhammer, really. You see, some friends and I were gossiping a few days ago about the past, just a bunch of old birds nattering on, and one of them brought up the subject of little Rosie Harley." Great-Aunt Iris hung her head and dabbed at the corners of her eyes. "So silly of me to get so emotional over the mention of a flower."

Henrietta's eyes nearly bulged from their sockets, and her skin turned a sickly shade of green. "Rosie Harley?"

"You do remember that dreadful business, then. Yes, that poor little girl. Eighteen years ago it was. Hard to believe so much time has passed." Great-Aunt Iris patted Henrietta's hand. "Oh dear, I seem to have put my foot in it again. My nephew says I should think before I speak, and I often wonder what fun there is in that. But I forget that other people might not take too kindly to my chirping. I'm a blithering fool this afternoon. Forgive me?"

"There's no need to apologize, Mrs. Darcy. That was many years ago now. We should all be satisfied in some way that the man responsible had punishment enough for what he did to that poor young angel."

"Perhaps you're right."

The door opened, and Tash walked through. "Madam?"

"Mrs. Crawford, Tash will see you out. Thank you again for joining me, and I'm so sorry I brought you distress on both counts. My nephew keeps telling me I'm going barmy, and I wonder now if he's right."

With a crimson face and clenched fists, Henrietta smiled tightly, thanked Great-Aunt Iris for a lovely tea, and followed Tash from the room.

Great-Aunt Iris turned around and smiled cheekily at the peephole well concealed in the wallpaper pattern.

Chapter Seventeen

When the Secret Weapon Isn't Great-Aunt Iris

Jane, Charles, and Thomas made it safely this afternoon, and Adelaide Rose and Thomas wasted no time in getting into mischief. Little Fitz is too small to join in the fun, but I have no doubt that within a year or two, he'll be toddling along right beside them. Jane and Charles had happy news: she is with child! Jane wants only a healthy baby, but from how Charles dotes on Adelaide Rose, I'm positive he's hoping for a girl to spoil. In other news, Darcy was speaking about the Crawfords, and Charles did not have joyful tidings. He knows of Mr. Crawford through mutual acquaintances and agrees with Darcy that he should set the dogs upon him.

Lizzy Bennet Darcy

Pemberley 1815

An hour later, the family and Wentworth gathered in the dining room. The only one missing was Belle. Eliza's heart pinched, and she rubbed over the spot. She scowled at her plate of Salisbury steak and potatoes with one stalk of asparagus—just enough greenery to cover the whole eating-vegetables requirement.

Wentworth caught her eye and gave a comforting smile. "Belle said to tell you to quit moping about."

"I'm not moping," Eliza said, swirling her mashed potatoes around with her fork.

"And she also said you'd say that." He sighed. "Please know I'm doing my best under the circumstances and that I'm doing all I can to make her comfortable."

Despite his smile, his drawn and weathered face made Eliza wonder if he'd gotten any sleep. Something was not right in Wentworth's world, and for the first time since meeting him, Eliza wasn't sure she wanted to know what weighed down the detective chief inspector.

"I know." She offered a small smile. "Thank you."

The door opened, and Great-Uncle William shuffled in. Eliza rushed over to him, hooked her arm through his, and led him to a chair next to Great-Aunt Iris.

She kissed his cheek. "I'm so happy you could join us."

Great-Uncle William usually took his meals in their rooms, but he looked chipper and ready to take on the world—well, as much as a ninety-something-year-old could.

He patted her hand with his liver-spotted one. "How else am I to see my lovely wife when she's out and about, solving crimes?" he asked, laughter in his voice.

Eliza chuckled and sat back down between Heath and her great-aunt. "Well, I, for one, don't know what I would do without her. Aunt Iris, you deserve an Oscar for your performance with Henrietta."

"Oh, pish-posh." Great-Aunt Iris fiddled with her silverware. "Like taking sweets from a child."

At the puzzled expressions from those not privy to the acting feat of the century, Eliza filled them in on Great-Aunt Iris's interrogation techniques.

"If we ever have a vacancy in the force, madam, you'll be top of my list," Wentworth said.

Great-Aunt Iris preened and brushed at imaginary lint on her velour tracksuit the color of a creamsicle. "With people of that sort, one simply waves a great deal of money about—even if it's fictitious—and they go brainless. I don't think she realizes everything she gave away in our brief chat."

"Probably not," Wentworth said, stabbing the asparagus spears on his plate with unusual vigor.

"It's clear she knew Hunter and Basil were up to something sketchy, and her reaction when Aunt Iris mentioned she'd seen the books proves she was well aware the nonsense involved money. Dirty money, at that," Eliza said.

"If she knew about the money laundering or even the Ponzi schemes, she could have had something to do with her son's murder and Basil's too," Heath said. "And with her reaction to Rosie Harley's name, not only does she remember the case, but your gossip session with the Golden Gamblers hit the mark: She did start the rumors about Everett Tanner abducting the little girl. She's old enough to have been involved in Rosie's disappearance and murder. Maybe she started the rumors to pin the blame on some poor soul before suspicion could fall on her."

"It wouldn't surprise me if Henrietta kidnapped the girl herself and blamed it on an innocent person for a laugh," Great-Uncle William said, his usual soft, gravelly voice hard.

"So the Golden Gamblers weren't overexaggerating her less-than-stellar qualities?" Eliza asked.

"If anything, they didn't highlight them enough," he said.

"They never... bothered you, did they?" Eliza asked, her fists tightening at the thought of the Crawfords messing with the kindest soul she'd ever met.

"No, they were never interested in making an ally or enemy out of me. I'm the wrong Darcy, you see. As only a guardian to the next heir after the death of Fitz and your father's parents, I was powerless and, in their eyes, useless. The moment they realized I was not an important cog in the Darcy machine, they wrote me off. But I remember my brother having a dashed hard time of it with Hubert's father.

Those Crawfords have always been a nasty lot. Which is why, Iris, I would not have let you be alone in a room with that woman if I'd known."

Great-Aunt Iris cupped her husband's cheek. "Which is why I didn't tell you, my love."

"You putting yourself in danger is—"

"Exactly what needs to be done, and you know me well enough to know that I always do what needs to be done. No matter the cost."

For a moment, Great-Uncle William seemed on the cusp of arguing, but he clasped his wife's hand to his chest and gazed at her with such adoration that Eliza's heart hummed.

Eliza cleared her throat around a sudden lump of emotion. "Well, the Crawfords were always on my list prior to this, but Henrietta has moved up. As for the connection to little Rosie..." She glanced across the table at Wentworth. "Anything?"

Wentworth's shoulders sagged. "Dental records confirmed it's Rosie Harley."

Silence smothered the room until Eliza thought she'd scream from its crushing weight. Her stomach twisted. That poor little girl, torn from the world by someone evil then left alone all those years. She'd still be alone if Hunter hadn't been murdered. There had to be a connection, and Eliza suspected it had something to do with the unpleasant bunch at Berryhill Manor.

"Have you informed the parents?" Great-Aunt Iris asked, her voice carrying the pain of someone who understood losing a child.

Great-Uncle William gently squeezed her hand.

"I have," Wentworth said, staring at his untouched plate.

Eliza shivered.

"Could they give you any fresh details about the day she disappeared?" Joy asked.

"Nothing we hadn't already pulled from the old case file or learned from the ladies' chat with their gambling friends."

"Any evidence pointing to her killer?" Eliza asked.

Wentworth shook his head. "That'll take weeks, months. Because of the body's condition, evidence might be long gone. It's a gamble at this point."

"We're running out of time and options," Eliza said. "Let's focus on Henrietta. I'm certain she started that rumor about Everett. But why? People don't spread rumors for nothing, especially about abducting a child."

"I'm on it," Wentworth said. "The less you Pemberley lot have to do with the Crawfords, like Mr. Darcy says, the better." He smiled grimly at Great-Uncle William, steepled his fingers, and studied Eliza over the tips. "There's something else."

Eliza's stomach dropped at the ominous tone in Wentworth's voice. "Yes?"

"We found another note on Basil's body."

"What?" Eliza asked, nearly launching from her chair. "I didn't see one."

"It was crumpled and shoved into his fist."

"What did it say?" Heath asked, his hand curling protectively around Eliza's.

"Another awful riddle," Wentworth said, digging out his phone. He tapped on his screen a couple of times and cleared his throat. "Ready for this rubbish? 'American meddler, you seek the truth but believe the lies. Your friend struck back but didn't kill, yet she's under suspicion still. Justice demands what was denied. Two have fallen. More will die.'"

"Atrocious bit of poetry," Eliza mumbled despite the sensation of spiders skittering across her skin.

"What does that even mean?" Joy asked, her face drawn and pale.

"It means our killer has a twisted sense of conscience. He doesn't want Belle taking the blame for Hunter's murder," Heath said, squeezing Eliza's hand.

"Then why not own up to it?" Joy asked.

"Nearly all murderers don't want to get caught. Most don't give a toss if others get blamed for their crimes, but this one..." Wentworth's shoulders slumped. "This one is willing to kill multiple times yet somehow considers the police targeting Belle an injustice they can't bear."

"It doesn't make sense," Eliza said, rubbing her temples.

"Not much about this case does." Exhaustion weighed down Wentworth's voice.

"Any more on the Fosters?" Eliza asked.

Wentworth shook his head. "Nothing new to report."

"You think it could be one of them?" Uncle Fitzwilliam asked. "They might have had reason to kill Hunter, but Basil? Besides, they don't know Belle from Adam. Why try to protect her?"

Eliza set her napkin over her half-eaten food. "I have no clue."

"I've put security around your house, Fitzwilliam, and Eliza, you're not going anywhere without one of my men." He held up a finger, cutting off Eliza's protest. "This isn't a suggestion. It's an order. If you can't do this, I'll have you under house arrest."

"He's right, love," Heath said, a flitter of fear in his voice.

Eliza bristled at the restriction, but after seeing the worried, fearful looks around the table, she relented. "I promise."

After Wentworth left, Eliza excused herself and headed for the door.

"Eliza, dear, where are you off to now?" Great-Aunt Iris asked. "Working on our crime board?" She struggled to her feet.

Eliza glanced at Heath, who caught her unspoken message that she needed alone time and smiled at Great-Aunt Iris.

"Actually, Mrs. Darcy, I was hoping you and I could give Joy and Darcy a proper thrashing at whist."

Joy shot Heath a look of shock.

Uncle Fitzwilliam grinned. "Haven't I fleeced you several times in whist, Tilney?"

"There's always hope I'll be the one fleecing you," Heath said. "Besides, I have the secret weapon, and you have ..." He made a swirling motion at Joy. "Her."

Joy reciprocated Heath's devilish grin and sauntered from the room. "I'll get the table set up."

Heath held his arm out to Great-Aunt Iris. "Are you up for the challenge?"

She nearly jumped to her feet. "I've never lost a game of whist in my life, young man. Are you up for the challenge of not being the reason I lose my first?"

Heath smiled gamely. "I'll do my best."

Great-Aunt Iris patted her husband's hand. "Care to watch me teach these young whippersnappers a thing or two, dearest?"

At the old man's boyish grin, Great-Aunt Iris led the small group out of the dining room, toward the drawing room.

Heath was safe from Great-Aunt Iris's wrath. At least he knew how to play the card game. Eliza smiled as she headed toward the old nursery, seeking a quiet place to think. She had to be missing something, a connection she hadn't noticed yet.

After flipping on the nursery's light switch, she stood with her arms crossed and studied the chalkboard. She glared at the alibiless Fosters, who had every reason to kill Hunter but no reason to kill Basil or try to free Belle from suspicion. With a sigh, she wrote, *Started rumor about Everett Tanner—why?* under Henrietta's name and added, *Seemed to know about Hunter and Huxley's money schemes.*

She glanced at Beckham's name. If Henrietta knew about the monetary schemes of her son and Basil, she knew whether Beckham was involved. And since Basil was dead, Beckham was the biggest wild card in the whole case. He was the linchpin for the whole thing, and she had to figure out what his role was. But even if he had motive, he lacked both means and opportunity, since he hadn't been invited to the New Year's Eve party.

But that didn't mean he couldn't have snuck in. Her staff was eagle-eyed. If Beckham had been at the party, surely they would have spotted him. *But why didn't they say anything? Because they were only working off the guest list, and there were over a hundred people on it.* They probably assumed, like she had, that if someone was at Pemberley, they'd been invited in good faith.

More fool me, Eliza thought as she slumped into a child-size chair. *Next time I throw a big shindig, I'm beefing up security.*

Angry with herself for not following up on that lead sooner, she dashed off to find Tash.

She found Tash in the butler's pantry, polishing a set of silver candlesticks, a leather apron over his uniform. As soon as she entered, he stood.

"No, no, have a seat, Tash, please."

When he remained standing, his eyes trained on hers, she sighed. "Please sit. I need to ask you something."

He reluctantly sat down. "What can I do for you, Miss Eliza?"

"Do you recognize this man?" Eliza pulled up a picture of Beckham. It hadn't been hard to find one, and she used the business photo from his and Hunter's wealth management website.

Tash squinted at it, and recognition flashed in his eyes. "Yes, miss, I do. He was at the New Year's Eve party."

"What?" Eliza's heart stuttered. "Are you sure?"

"Quite sure, miss."

"Was he on the guest list?" Eliza asked, hoping she hadn't missed his name when she'd scoured it days ago.

"I have the list in my files." Tash stood and left the room then returned within minutes. "Here you are." He handed it to her.

Eliza scanned the names, her lips moving silently as she read. No Beckham.

There was no doubt about it. She'd screwed up royally. She should have shown her staff pictures of the suspects from the start, but she hadn't and had only her own stupidity to show for it.

"Where did you see him?" Eliza asked.

"I only saw him once all evening. He was in the garden."

"Did you see him talking with anyone?"

"No, miss, he was alone when I spotted him." Tash's kind eyes studied her. "Is something wrong, Miss Eliza?"

Eliza patted his hand. "Nothing I can't handle now. Thank you, Tash. You've been a godsend." She grabbed the list and rushed from the butler's pantry to her uncle's study, where he sat enjoying his pipe.

His welcoming smile faded into a frown. "What is it, Eliza?"

She placed the list on his desk and showed him the picture. "Beckham was here the night of the party. He wasn't on our guest list, so I never thought to check whether he'd attended."

Uncle Fitzwilliam raised an eyebrow.

"I spoke with Tash, who recognized him. Said he spotted him in the garden. Alone." She massaged her temples. "Stupid, stupid, stupid."

"Go easy on yourself, Eliza, dear." Uncle Fitzwilliam stood and pulled her into an embrace. "Sometimes, you can't see the forest for the trees, and this is one of those moments." He held her at arm's length. "Now that we know, I'll have a word with Wentworth. He can take it from here, right?"

"Is Beckham our man?" Eliza asked. "How could he possibly be connected to Rosie?"

"Men like Beckham have a nasty habit of getting tangled up in other people's troubles. Besides, remember—the murder and the discovery of the body could be pure coincidence."

Uncle Fitzwilliam's lackluster tone didn't make Eliza feel any better, and with a sinking feeling in her gut, she went searching for the card-playing crew. But instead of finding all four of them, she found only Heath sitting on a settee, scrolling through social media.

"Where's everyone else?" Eliza asked, settling beside him and curling into his side with her knees pulled up.

"Joy's sulking somewhere, licking her wounds."

"You and Aunt Iris must have won, then, since you're still breathing and in one piece."

Heath chuckled. "I've never been so terrified in my life. Your great-uncle came in clutch, though. Gave me some excellent hand signals on the sly." He pressed a kiss to her temple. "And you? How did your alone time go?"

"Cut short by my own stupidity." She filled him in on the Beckham situation.

"Odd that no one mentioned seeing him."

"That was my first thought, too, but the staff were swamped, and the guest list was massive. Why would they notice one guy they don't even know? Besides, if he only stayed in the garden, he might have barely set foot in the house long enough for anyone to spot him. Tash only caught sight of him once."

"Do you think he's our man?" Heath asked.

"Funny... I asked Uncle the same thing. He's climbed higher on my suspect list since last time. We should go after him again."

"Didn't we relegate Wentworth to that task? Not sure you'll get him to break."

"Which is exactly why I'm not going to try."

"Then who is?"

"Willoughby."

"What? Why him?"

"Because Beckham has no idea Willoughby's connected to us. Most people don't know he's tied to Pemberley at all unless they're family friends. Plus, he looks like a smooth-talking wheeler-dealer with flexible ethics. That's something Beckham will recognize and trust."

"Tell me how you really feel about Willoughby," Heath teased, a grin tugging at the corners of his mouth.

"Oh, you know what I mean. Willoughby isn't that way. Well, maybe a little, but he does have morals. Something Beckham clearly lacks."

"Want me to ring him?"

"Yes. Have him come to Pemberley tomorrow. Sunday's a good day to recuperate, discuss options, and form a new strategy."

Heath slipped from Eliza's embrace, pulled out his phone, and paced the room as he dialed.

As Heath talked quietly with Willoughby, Eliza formed a game plan. With fresh reinforcements and a promising new clue, she hoped they'd soon crack the case wide open.

E liza wasn't surprised that Jack Willoughby had jumped at the chance to join their investigation. What did surprise her was how quickly he'd arranged time off work, packed his bags, and traveled from London to Lambton. And judging by the looks he'd been giving Joy since arriving, Eliza suspected he wasn't just excited about sleuthing.

But Joy was different around him. A glint of determination lit Joy's eyes when she looked at him. Hope ignited in Eliza's chest. Perhaps Joy was ready to embody the courage she wielded ninety-nine percent of the time and apply it to the one area in which she'd been a coward.

Eliza pushed Joy and Willoughby's complicated relationship drama to the back of her mind as everyone settled into the drawing room. Each held a drink, snacks were artfully arranged on the coffee table, and a fire crackled in the fireplace. It would have been perfectly cozy if not for the grim nature of their discussion.

Willoughby crossed his arms and leaned back in a maroon-and-gold brocade chair. "Let me get this straight. You want me to pose as an investor seeking out CQ Wealth Management's services?"

"Precisely." Eliza grabbed a chip from the bowl sitting between her and Heath on the settee and popped it into her mouth.

"I told you he was a quick study," Joy said, her voice dripping with sarcasm.

Heath snorted.

Eliza playfully jabbed him in the ribs with her elbow. "Be nice," she hissed.

All she'd heard about Willoughby for the past eight months was how dense the man was, and honestly, if he couldn't figure out that Joy was head-over-heels in love with him, then Eliza wasn't sure he was a quick learner. But rumor had it that men were notoriously dense when it came to matters of the heart and not so in other aspects of their lives, which Eliza hoped and prayed was the case. Everything was riding on what Willoughby could gather from Beckham.

"And I have to pretend to be some rich, entitled tosser?" Willoughby asked.

"Shouldn't be too much of a stretch," Joy murmured, her fiery gaze studying him.

Eliza was tempted to lock them in a closet until they figured things out. From the glint in Great-Aunt Iris's eyes, Eliza feared she had more devious plans: lock the two in a bedroom with the vicar until they came out married.

Eliza shot Joy a warning glance and turned her attention back to Willoughby. "Exactly. You're a man with too much money to know what to do with. You need to give off a sense of entitlement and arrogance and hint that you may or may not be willing to bend some rules to make yourself even more stinking rich."

"You're missing one important thing, though. I'm not filthy, stinking rich. What do I do when he wants to see my financial portfolio?"

"We're one step ahead of you." Eliza gestured toward her uncle, who was standing by the fireplace. "Uncle knows a guy who knows a guy..." She made a rolling gesture with her hand. "You know how that goes. The 'guys' multiply until you reach the one with the shady skills. Anyway, this tech whiz who apparently owes Uncle a favor cooked up some fake bank accounts and whatever financial documents you need."

"Is it that chap you went to uni with? The dodgy one with the shifty eye?" Great-Aunt Iris asked, her hands clutching a teacup.

"The very one." Uncle Fitzwilliam's smile slipped, and he poked at the fire. "It passed my inspection." He met Willoughby's gaze. "The only way Beckham will know the accounts are fake is if you give it away."

Eliza cocked her head. Her uncle had never spoken with such an underlying edge. Goose bumps prickled her skin. The mission was not one to take lightly. With any misstep on Willoughby's part or if Beckham smelled a rat, they were done for.

"Looks like you lot have planned everything out perfectly," Willoughby said, fiddling with his wineglass.

Eliza leaned over, closing the space between their chairs, and rested her hand on his forearm. "Remember when we first met?"

"Ah yes, the infamous croquet game where I was rudely interrupted by that bloke." He saluted Heath with his wineglass, a grin twitching at the corners of his lips.

"Charlie warned me to be wary of you. Said you were an insufferable twat and that I—"

"I never knew how bloody wise my brother was until this moment," Joy said, shooting a pointed glance at Willoughby.

"Joy, what did I ever do to you?" Willoughby asked, his voice dripping with exasperation.

Joy jumped to her feet and stood over him, her index finger pointing at his heart. "Nothing. You've never done anything to me. And that's the whole point. Are all men this daft when it comes to romance?" Joy caught her bottom lip between her teeth, glanced at the gaping faces around the room, and hurried out.

"I don't..." Willoughby ran his finger under his shirt collar and looked pleadingly at anyone who'd make eye contact with him. His lips moved silently, seeming to replay Joy's words back through his mind. It didn't take long for his face to flush and his eyes to widen. "You mean... Joy... and me..." He gestured toward the door Joy had just left through and to himself, and a boyish grin spread across his lips. "I... Bloody hell. I should..." He pointed toward the door.

Eliza cleared her throat. "Perhaps after this, you can find Joy?"

Willoughby's face paled, and he swallowed hard. "Right. But you were saying earlier about our first meeting?"

Eliza grinned. "Be the arrogant twat Charlie said you would be."

"But... But... Is this how people see me?" Willoughby asked, his eyes fixed on the tips of his stockinged toes.

"Not those who know you well," Heath said.

"But strangers do?" Willoughby pressed.

Everyone exchanged glances, and Eliza imagined them all saying, "Not it!"

Uncle Fitzwilliam walked over to Willoughby and clapped him on the shoulder. "Consider the first impression you give off as an asset, particularly for your task tomorrow."

Willoughby puffed out his chest, and despite the trepidation glimmering in his eyes, confidence flickered across his face. "I won't let you down." His gaze kept traveling to the door, and his feet tapped impatiently. "Do you mind if I dash off? Find Joy?" Without waiting for a response, he bolted from the room, calling out, "Tash! I say, do you know where Joy's got to?"

Great-Aunt Iris set her teacup down with a loud clink, took up her knitting, and sniffed. "Finally. I'm too old to buy green bananas, and I'm far too old to wait for two young people flopping about in love like a pair of wet lettuces."

Eliza chuckled. If only her investigation into Hunter's murder would go as smoothly. From the cement block still lodged firmly in her chest, she feared it wouldn't.

Chapter Eighteen
Willoughby's Tête-à-Tête

My respite from the Crawfords was short-lived, I'm afraid. They called this morning. While Crawford went out with Darcy and Charles to see to a new horse Darcy purchased, Jane and I suffered the insipid conversation of Miss Mary Crawford. I am not sure that woman can speak on topics other than money and social standing, but I tire of it, and I'm afraid my face speaks volumes. Even dear Jane, who hardly finds fault in anyone, was clearly annoyed with the woman and her attempts to hint that perhaps our children should go play in the nursery instead of at our feet.

Lizzy Bennet Darcy
Pemberley 1815

Eliza's leg bounced uncontrollably under the table at the Trusty Teapot. The Monday-morning crowd was sparse, and for once, she wished for the usual packed room. Anything to distract her from what was happening a few blocks down from the teashop. With only a handful of occupied tables besides theirs, where Eliza sat with Joy, Heath, and Great-Aunt Iris, she felt exposed, as if every ear in the place was tuned in to their conversation.

"We should have stayed at Pemberley," Eliza muttered, scowling into her second cup of Ethiopian spiced tea.

"Nonsense," Great-Aunt Iris said. "If we were home, you'd have driven me to distraction. Since I know where the cupboards are and who has keys to them, I would have locked you in one myself."

Eliza gaped at her. "You wouldn't have."

"Yes, she would have, and I'd have helped her." Joy grinned.

"*Et tu*, Joy?" Eliza asked.

"'Fraid so. You're driving me bat-crap crazy."

"And you?" Eliza fixed Heath with a pointed look. "Would you have locked me in the closet?"

Heath grinned. "No—"

"See?" Eliza gestured triumphantly at Heath. "This is what true loyalty looks like. This is what—"

"I would have asked to be locked in with you." Heath waggled his eyebrows playfully.

Great-Aunt Iris beamed at him with pride.

Eliza smacked his chest. "You are incorrigible."

"Spending too much time with Willoughby, I see," Joy teased.

Eliza shot her a sideways glance. They hadn't had a free moment to discuss Joy and Willoughby's breakthrough, but judging from Joy's carefree tone and lighter mood, Eliza assumed they'd chatted and the result wasn't unfavorable.

Keeping her fingers crossed that all the Joy-and-Willoughby drama was finally over, Eliza shifted the conversation to Willoughby's current mission. "How do you think he's doing?"

"He looks every part the arrogant prat. He'll do well," Heath said, stirring a splash of milk into his refreshed teacup.

"And if he doesn't?" Joy asked.

"Then we're back to square one," Eliza said.

"It's got to be him, though, hasn't it?"

"In a perfect world, yes, but you've seen our crime board," Eliza replied. "Everyone on it has a motive to kill Hunter. The only catch is finding a link to Rosie—"

"If there is one," Great-Aunt Iris interrupted.

"Exactly. If there is one, then we have to connect the killer to Basil as well."

"That should narrow down our suspects," Heath said. "Not many people hated Basil. People might have found his toad collection off-putting but not enough to murder him over it. It's got to be someone who wanted both of them dead."

"Have you heard anything from Wentworth?" Great-Aunt Iris asked.

"Besides him giving us the go-ahead to run our little playacting with Beckham? No. Wentworth seemed pretty dejected that he couldn't get Beckham to break," Eliza said. "I was hoping he'd have some lab reports for us. Something to take Belle definitively off the list."

"Lab reports take forever, and unlike us, he's got his hands tied by procedures." Heath rested a comforting hand on Eliza's back.

The teashop doorbells tinkled with a new arrival, and Eliza swiveled in her chair. "It's Lucinda," she hissed. "She can't know what we're up to. What if Willoughby comes in and starts telling us about his meeting with Beckham? He doesn't know Lucinda at all. He'll blow his cover."

"Can't we text him?" Joy asked.

"I don't want to disturb him or the meeting in case he doesn't have his phone on silent," Eliza said.

"I'll wait for him outside," Joy said, scooting her chair back. She scowled at the light snowfall covering everything in a powdered-sugar dusting of white. "There's a bookshop down the street that he has to pass. I'll keep watch for him there."

A few seconds after Joy left the table, Lucinda walked up to the group with a smile. "Good morning. What a pleasant surprise. I came to grab coffee with Beckham, but he's not here yet. Mind if I join you?"

"Please do." Eliza gestured to the chair Joy had vacated.

"Thank you." Lucinda slipped a giant purse to put Great-Aunt Iris's to shame off her shoulder and sat. After giving her order to the waitress, she folded her hands on the table. "I'm glad I ran into you. The whole village is buzzing about Basil's murder. Don't suppose this helps the investigation, does it?"

"More like muddies everything up." Eliza scowled into her teacup.

"I have no doubt that you'll solve this case. From what I've heard about your skills, you'll bring justice to Hunter and catch his and Basil's killer in no time."

The door opened, sending a waft of cold air swirling through the teashop. Eliza shivered, and when she turned to see who'd dropped the temperature a few degrees, she froze.

Beckham strode to the sales counter, placed an order, and scanned the room. His gaze locked on Lucinda, and he made his way to the back of the shop. "Traded my company for others', I see. I told you when you invited me for a cuppa that I'd be slightly late. Had a last-minute meeting. Ran over."

Lucinda huffed. "Not my fault if your meeting ran late. I simply decided to bide my time with friends."

Beckham looked down at Eliza. "Picking up strays, I see, Lucinda. How generous of you."

Eliza had read in a book how a character looked down their nose at others, and while the phrase had always confused her and she ended up going cross-eyed trying to replicate it, Beckham managed it without doing the same.

The effect hit its mark, and Eliza felt like a bug under his shoe. She had the inexplicable urge to kick him in the shin, but a man like him would have a lawyer on retainer and would sue her for the simple inconvenience of a sore shin bone. She tucked her feet under her chair.

Heath straightened his shoulders. "Beckham Quill, isn't it?"

"Do I know you?" Beckham asked, adjusting the leather satchel crossing his torso.

"No, but I've heard some interesting tales about you through Oxford lore. You left quite the legacy."

Beckham's smile was razor thin. "Must have had epic adventures, then, if people are still banging on about them." He turned his attention to Lucinda. "Care to finish your tea with *me*?"

Lucinda's face turned crimson. "I'd be delighted." She smiled apologetically at Eliza. "Sorry about this—" She shot Beckham a side-eye.

"No worries. We'll catch up later?"

Lucinda stood and swung her large purse over her shoulder, nearly clobbering Eliza in the head. "I'm so sorry."

Eliza waved away her apology. "No harm, no foul. With Great-Aunt Iris's large purses occasionally whirling through the air, I've learned to dodge them."

"Lucinda, shall we?"

She smiled tightly and followed Beckham to a table near the front. As soon as they sat down, they put their heads together. From Eliza's angle, she couldn't catch what they were saying.

When her phone buzzed in her back pocket, she dug it out. "It's Joy. She's retrieved the package and is waiting in the Range Rover."

Eliza paid the bill, and as she walked out of the Trusty Teapot, she glanced back at Beckham and Lucinda, who were still sitting with their heads together, whispering.

Shrugging, Eliza left the tea shop and jumped into the SUV, eager to hear about Willoughby's adventures with Beckham.

E veryone gathered in the nursery, settling into tiny chairs or giving up and sitting cross-legged on the floor.

Eliza stood with chalk in hand next to the board and, in a move reminiscent of her teaching days, pointed at Willoughby. "How did things go? Did he take the bait? Were you able to find anything out?"

Willoughby held up a hand. "Steady on. One question at a time. First of all, I channeled my inner prat and pulled it off nicely. I should be worried about how easy it was, but everyone has to have some talent, haven't they?" Without waiting for an answer, he continued, "Beckham took the bait hook, line, and sinker. Wants to take me on as a client. Thinks he can 'work some magic' or some such rot."

"And?" Eliza asked, tapping the space under Beckham's name on the board. "Anything I can put here?"

"You know, when I first met you, you weren't so demanding," Willoughby said, his eyebrow arching.

"When we first met, I didn't have a best friend on the line for a murder she didn't commit," Eliza shot back. She took a deep breath. "Sorry. You're right. I feel like we've never been closer to solving this but at the same time further away from any real answers."

"Not to worry. I was able to weasel some information out of him. While he was poring over my accounts, I started asking questions, hoping he wasn't paying too much attention to why I was asking them. I mentioned how sorry I was about the death of his business partner. His smooth car salesman demeanor cracked for a moment. I'm not even sure he noticed it, but his face went as white as a sheet, and his finger moving around on his laptop's trackpad started to shake. It was all over in a second or two before the suave businessman was as right as rain again."

Eliza jotted down Beckham's reaction under his name. "Would you say the reaction was rooted in fear, anger..."

"Beats me. He didn't look sad or depressed or anything like that, and when he talked about Hunter's death, his voice was tight, like those words were hard for him to get out."

"Guilty conscience?" Heath asked.

"Maybe," Eliza said, adding *Angry, scared?* under Beckham's name.

"If he seemed scared, it could be because he knows who the killer is. After Basil's murder, he might be terrified of being the next victim," Joy added.

"There's more," Willoughby continued. "I made some remark about how he'll be busier than ever, trying to serve all his clients now that he's on his own. I pushed the issue, making it seem like I wasn't sure he could meet my demands."

"Brilliant," Joy said.

Willoughby blushed and found a nail hole in the tiny wooden chair he sat in fascinating.

Great-Aunt Iris's knitting escalated to a fever pitch, and she murmured something about "Another baby blanket to make, I should think."

Eliza bit the inside of her cheek to keep her grin in check.

Willoughby cleared his throat, drawing his attention back to Eliza. "Beckham was quick to assure me that he could handle all existing and new clients, especially clients like me. But he also did something I find odd. He threw his dead partner under the bus."

"What do you mean?" Eliza asked.

"Without any prompting from me or in response to anything I'd said or asked, he essentially insinuated that he was better off without his business partner because—and I quote—'Hunter often made risky business decisions that made our elderly customers nervous.' I kept in character, said that was the way with old people—sorry, Mrs. Darcy—" He smiled apologetically at her. "And that I wasn't averse to risky decisions, since I had enough money to play with."

"D'you think he noticed he'd spoken badly of Hunter?" Heath asked.

"No. Again, he was poring over my accounts, so I don't think he was paying attention to what he was saying." Willoughby ran his index finger over his chin. "I got the impression that Beckham wasn't the least bit sorry his business partner had died."

Eliza jotted that down under Beckham's name. "Anything else?" Willoughby shook his head.

"Where does this leave us?" Eliza asked, gesturing to the board.

"It proves that Beckham had motive, means, and opportunity to do away with Hunter," Joy said. "If what he let slip is true, that Hunter was a dangerous business partner, he got rid of the problem permanently. He also would have had a connection with Basil through Hunter. If Hunter was causing issues for the business and Basil was involved, Beckham could have taken them both out of the equation. Maybe if we take this to Wentworth, he'll see the possibility and let Belle off the hook."

Eliza's blood ran cold. Belle was supposed to fly out in three days. Her vacation, which had started with such high spirits, had spiraled into chaos. And if the police didn't see the light through the circumstantial but damning evidence, Belle wouldn't be able to go home, where her family and business eagerly awaited her return.

"Possible. That's the problem. *Everything's* possible. Without solid evidence, I'm afraid we haven't made much progress." Eliza scowled at the crime board and slammed the chalk into the tray. It shattered on impact.

The nursery door banged open, startling everyone.

Wentworth filled the doorway, his overcoat glistening with rain. The usual hard lines of his face looked sharp enough to cut diamonds, and his amber eyes glittered with barely contained excitement.

Great-Aunt Iris slapped a hand over her chest and shot him a withering look. "Good heavens! Is it your mission in life to give little old ladies heart attacks?"

"Mrs. Darcy, I do apologize." He slipped off his wet overcoat and draped it across a chair. "Though you'll forgive me for saying that after the time I've spent in your company these past months, I've learned there's nothing either little or old about you. You're a dark horse, Mrs. Darcy."

Great-Aunt Iris's knitting needles tumbled from her lap as she gazed up at Wentworth, a blush blooming across her weathered cheeks. Her eyes sparkled, taking decades off her age. "That was rather cheeky of you, young man, but I'll let it slide." She bent to retrieve her needles and pointed one at him like a weapon. "This once."

Wentworth inclined his head and turned his attention to the crime board. "You've been busy, I see."

Eliza tilted her head. "Well, out with it. What did you find?"

Wentworth stepped around her, plucked the largest chalk fragment from the tray, and drew a bold circle around Beckham's name. "Got him."

"What's the evidence?" Eliza asked.

"You name it, it's there. Fingerprints. DNA. You know how these things take time to process, but the reports confirm Beckham was at Basil's murder scene."

"Were Beckham's fingerprints already in the system?" Eliza asked.

"No, which is why it took so bloody long. I had one of my lads nick a cup he'd been drinking from at the Trusty Teapot. Got prints off that, ran them through, and Bob's your uncle." Wentworth placed a chalk dot in the middle of Beckham's name.

"Nothing to tie him to Hunter's murder, though?" Heath asked.

"Afraid not. Getting DNA or any usable trace evidence from Hunter's scene has been a Herculean task."

"And you're certain he killed Basil?" Eliza asked.

"There's enough evidence to arrest him on suspicion of murder."

"Anything on the Rosie Harley connection?" Joy asked.

"Sadly, no." Wentworth scrubbed at his five-o'clock shadow. "With all the lab work and the delicate nature of the case, that'll take weeks, sometimes months. Well, I must be off. I'll keep you posted."

"What does this mean for Belle? Is she still under suspicion?" Eliza asked, crossing her fingers.

Wentworth grimaced and threaded his fingers through his hair. "'Fraid so. With nothing new clearing her from Hunter's murder, she's still the number-one suspect."

"But she couldn't have killed Basil, and Beckham's fingerprints are all over that crime scene. Are you thinking that we have two killers loose?"

"All I know is that Belle remains where she is. I promise I'll do all I can, but without definitive evidence clearing her of Hunter's murder, she's our only viable suspect." He held up a hand, stemming Eliza's retort. "Feelings and emotions don't count in a court of law. You know that. My hands are tied. I can't release her."

"Have you officially charged her?" Uncle Fitzwilliam asked.

"No, but the ninety-six-hour limit the crown prosecutor gave us is quickly approaching."

"Then?" Eliza asked, her voice barely audible.

Wentworth rested a hand on her shoulder. "Let me deal with Beckham first. Chin up."

As he left the room, Eliza's shoulders slumped and worry churned in her stomach.

Needing fresh air, Eliza bundled up and sought solace in the hibernating gardens of Pemberley. Frost-covered plants glistened in the sunlight, and she breathed in deeply, savoring the crisp air before expelling it in a cloud of white.

She should have felt relief. Wentworth had found his man and the evidence to back it up. But Eliza knew from past experiences that evidence could be fabricated. As much as she wanted to believe Beckham guilty of murder, she couldn't make the facts align with what she knew about Beckham and his type.

Footsteps preceded muscular arms wrapping around her. "Thought I'd find you out here." Heath spun her around and tipped up her chin. "What's wrong?"

She played with the zipper on his coat. "I don't think Beckham's our guy."

He entwined his fingers through hers and led her down the hill and toward a large yew maze that was green and vibrant against the flocking of white. "Talk me through it."

"Does Beckham strike you as an idiot?"

"A prat, yes. An idiot, no."

"Exactly. If he did murder Hunter, he'd have to know he'd be on the suspect list, right? Why draw more attention to himself by killing Basil, another known business partner? He doesn't seem the person to make foolish mistakes."

"Do you think he could have been the one to lure Hunter into the woods? And when Hunter brings Belle along, Beckham sees his chance to strike and allows an innocent woman to take the blame?"

"That tracks with what we know of him, but then why the notes suggesting the police nabbed the wrong suspect? Not a chance. He'd have no qualms in watching someone else rot in prison for the rest of their lives for a crime he committed. And don't forget the anonymous phone call. If Beckham did kill Hunter, why call it in? Hunter's body could have gone undiscovered for a very long time. I don't see any reason for Beckham wanting to advertise Hunter's murder."

"Unless Hunter was never his main victim after all. Maybe Basil was the intended target all along, and Hunter was either collateral damage or a smokescreen," Heath said.

"That's a possibility." Eliza trailed her fingers along the yew branches. "All I know is this feels too convenient. I can't picture Beckham leaving his DNA and fingerprints scattered across a crime scene. He's too careful. He'd make sure he left no trace."

"Think he was framed?"

"My gut tells me that Hunter, Basil, and Beckham hurt so many people through their financial crimes that someone out there has developed a Robin Hood complex. What better way to bring justice to the 'poor' than by destroying the 'rich'?"

"And letting one of them take the fall for it." Heath gave a low whistle. "That's why the killer left those notes. Didn't want to see another innocent person become a victim of Hunter and Basil."

"But why not confess and turn themselves in?" Eliza asked.

"Because he isn't finished yet." Heath's fingers tightened on Eliza's.

"That means that if Wentworth is wrong about Beckham being the culprit..."

"He's the next victim," Heath finished.

Eliza dialed Wentworth's number and growled when it went straight to voicemail. "That man never answers his phone." She tapped out a text: *I have an idea. You're not going to like it. Call me ASAP.*

"What about Rosie Harley? If we think the two cases are linked, what did Hunter and now Basil have to do with her death?" Heath asked.

Eliza clutched Heath's arm. "Only a few people on our crime board are old enough to have had anything to do with her disappearance."

"And Basil is one of them."

Eliza texted the sleuthing gang: *Meet Heath and me in the nursery. Fifteen minutes.*

Eliza and Heath found Willoughby in the nursery, his hip cocked to one side, his hand holding his chin as he studied the board.

"I know I'm new to this whole sleuthing business, but aren't you ignoring what's right there on your crime board?"

"What do you see that I don't?" Eliza asked.

"Did Henrietta like Basil?"

"No. In my eavesdropping, I got the distinct impression she loathed the man."

"Then why on earth would she start a rumor about her gardener being involved in the poor girl's disappearance unless either the gardener did it or she knew bloody well who abducted the girl and wanted to draw attention away from the real culprit out of either love or duty?" Willoughby asked.

Eliza gaped at him.

"What? Have I put my foot in it?"

"No, you said what none of us thought of, even though we've been staring at the same crime board for days."

"This brings us back to the Crawfords." Heath tapped his finger on Hubert's name. "Two possibilities. Either Henrietta abducted the girl herself and blamed an easy target, the gardener, to remove suspicion or for laughs, or she was protecting either her son or her husband."

"Only one of them is old enough to have been involved," Eliza said. "The question is: 'Does Henrietta love anyone enough to slander an innocent man?'"

She continued, "Lady Beaumont called Henrietta a snake, and no one jumped to the woman's defense. There's precious little suggesting she and her husband love each other, much less can bear each other's company."

"If she doesn't love him, why protect him if she thought him guilty? It would have been her chance to be rid of him," Heath said.

"Ah, you young people nowadays." The sound of squeaky tennis shoes filled the room, and Great-Aunt Iris along with Joy, Willoughby, and Uncle Fitzwilliam soon stood next to them. "That's where you're forgetting something."

Eliza grinned. "How long have you been standing there?"

"Long enough to know you'd all be lost without me. You're overlooking something often more powerful than love: greed and status.

If there's one thing Henrietta loves more than herself, it's her position as lady of the manor and the prestige she gets from marrying into a prominent family. If her husband had been even rumored to have had anything to do with the crime, she'd have been ruined. She'd never have been able to hold court with her sycophantic followers again. The crown she thinks she's entitled to wear would have been stripped right off her head by the people who'd earlier kissed the ground she walked on."

"I got that impression when they visited the day after we discovered Hunter's body," Eliza said. "I chalked it up to the stress of losing a child, although neither of them seemed too cut up about it. I get the sense that the Crawfords are playing the long game with this crime. I'll double-check with the staff on Crawford's movements the night of the ball. Not sure it'll turn up much, but maybe the Crawfords went unseen for an extended period. Be that as it may, I'm sure Wentworth is about to arrest the wrong man for a murder he didn't commit."

Great-Aunt Iris rubbed her hands together, a mischievous glint in her eyes. "And you have a plan?"

"Of course, and it's an idea that Wentworth will shoot down and yell at me through the phone for, but we have to smoke out the true killer before it's too late."

Chapter Nineteen
Belle Takes One for the Team

With a heart galloping in her chest, Eliza dialed Wentworth's number, praying he'd pick up. He answered on the third ring, and before he could even say hello, Eliza hurriedly told him her wild idea.

A beat of silence followed before Wentworth released a curse word. "You bloody *what*?" Wentworth bellowed. "First, you fight me tooth and nail to get your best friend off the suspect list, and now you ring me up, demanding I officially press charges for a murder you've kept telling me she didn't commit?"

Eliza held her cell away from her ear and smiled sheepishly at her sleuthing gang.

She covered the receiver. "He's taking this well, considering—"

"I heard that, Miss Eliza Darcy, and if you think for one bloody minute... Blasted cat, are you trying to trip me to my death?"

The sounds of strained breathing through the phone shifted to footsteps—loud footsteps, ones that were not coming through the phone anymore but real ones echoing down the hallway, increasing in speed and volume.

"Dear Lord." Eliza stared in horror at the closed nursery door. "What's he doing here?"

"And he sounds terribly upset, my dear." Though Great-Aunt Iris sounded anything but concerned for her great-niece. She practically quivered in her seat.

Eliza put the phone back to her ear. "Wentworth, are you currently stalking down the hallway?" Maybe Tash was out power walking the halls. Even though she'd never seen him do that, she could always hope.

The door flew open, and the hulking figure of a huffing DCI stood in the doorway, Caesar winding himself between Wentworth's legs. He put his phone to his ear and looked directly at Eliza. "Yes." With deliberate movements, he stabbed his phone with his index finger and tucked it into his overcoat pocket.

"How did you... Weren't you..." Eliza sighed. "I thought you'd be in Lambton. Either that, or you broke several speed limits getting back here."

"I hadn't left. I was in your drive, sorting an arrest warrant for Beckham over the phone. Those always take more time than one anticipates," he muttered, his forehead furrowing. "Then much to my surprise, though I haven't a clue why I'm shocked anymore, I get a call from you with an idea so ludicrous..."

"Yes?" Eliza asked sweetly.

Wentworth's gaze swept the others in the room and landed on the chalkboard. "An idea so ludicrous it might work."

"But... I thought..." Eliza pointed at the phone still clutched in her other hand. "I thought you were here to..." She cocked her head. "What exactly was your plan when you came stalking up the staircase, terrorizing my cat, and crashing through the door?"

"Probably to finally arrest you for being a public nuisance." Joy grinned.

"That thought has occurred to me several times before this, so keep that in mind." Wentworth removed his overcoat and let it drop to the floor. The sleeve landed squarely on Caesar's back. "Sorry, Caesar," he muttered when the orange feline fixed him with a slitted-eye glare. He turned his attention back to Eliza. "However, now that you've got my undivided attention, you have two minutes to make your case."

"I don't think—and I'm pretty sure you don't think—that you've got the right killer. I'm convinced Beckham, although he's a horrible human being, is not a murderer. I believe he's the next victim."

"And what makes you believe this?" Wentworth asked.

Eliza and the gang took turns explaining their new theory.

Wentworth scratched at the salt-and-pepper scruff on his face and studied the crime board. "Keep talking."

"Well, that's when I had the idea to smoke out the true killer. He doesn't want an innocent person, aka Belle, to get arrested. So if you officially charge her and make a public spectacle about it, the killer will strike again."

"And whoever this person is will target Beckham?" Wentworth asked.

"That's what my gut says, and it's what the evidence points to. Hunter, Basil, and Beckham were all involved in some shady activities, and there's no honor among thieves."

"So why don't you think Beckham killed the other two?"

"He wouldn't have written those letters trying to save someone other than himself. He's far too much of a narcissist. Beckham isn't stupid enough to leave numerous traces of himself at a crime scene. Besides, he was a frequent visitor to Basil's, so his DNA and fingerprints would be everywhere, including on the paperweight. I was even tempted to pick it up and examine it when Heath and I were talking with Basil."

"But what makes you think he's the intended victim?" Wentworth stabbed his finger on Beckham's name.

"These men destroyed countless lives." She gestured to all the names on the chalkboard. "And this is only a small sampling of people whose lives were ruined by their money-grubbing schemes. This person is trying to rid the world of three horrible people so other innocents don't fall victim to them."

"Hypocritical of them," Joy said. "Using murder to justify ridding the world of evil people."

"You'd be surprised at the mindsets of some vigilantes. They think their sins are absolved if they're committing violence or crimes against the sinful." Wentworth shook his head.

"What's our game plan?" Eliza asked.

"Let me make a call to the crown prosecutor and get her take on this. And don't you think you'll need to talk to Belle about this?"

Eliza's stomach dropped. She was officially the worst friend in the world. "Yes," she whispered, studying the tips of her slippers.

Wentworth reached out his hand. "Your mobile, please."

Eliza handed it to him, and after punching in a number and talking with someone, he handed it back to her, his eyes flickering with understanding.

Eliza left the room and paced the hallway, pressing her phone to her ear.

"Eliza?"

Eliza's stomach slid to her toes at the sound of Belle's voice.

"Belle?"

"What's wrong?" Belle asked, her tone laced with concern.

Guilt swirled in Eliza's gut, and she feared she'd be sick. But time was running out for Belle. With no hope on the horizon for a break-through, the dog-and-pony show of an "official" charge needed to happen. If not, Belle would *officially* be charged with murder, and the wheels of justice would begin squashing her friend under its relent-less speed. Clutching a hand to her stomach, she cleared her throat. "Remember all the times I've had a stupid idea, and you've gone along with them every single time?"

"Haven't lived to regret any of them. Why? What did you do now?"

Eliza squeezed her eyes shut at the forced levity in Belle's voice. "I, uh, am asking that Wentworth officially charge you for Hunter's murder."

Belle was silent so long that Eliza squinted at her phone screen in case the call had gotten disconnected or Belle had hung up on her. But no, the call was still active.

"Belle, say something, please. You can say no. I'll find another way to get you out. Yeah, scratch my stupid idea. One of the worst, actually. Forget I said anything."

"Yes."

"Really?"

"Yes," Belle said, her voice unwavering. "I trust you. You've never let me down before."

Eliza squirmed under her friend's faith in her. "Are you sure? Like a hundred percent sure? Wentworth's getting the crown prosecutor in on it. The charge will be just for show. Not official. We need to smoke out the—"

"Eliza, this isn't only something I have to do. It's something I want to do. You've worked tirelessly, trying to clear my name, and if all I have to do is sit in one of Wentworth's VIP cells, reading Theo's books he's lending me, I'll be fine."

"Have I told you recently how awesome you are?"

"No, but you can make that up to me once I'm out of here," Belle said with a laugh.

Wentworth stepped out into the hall and gestured for Eliza's phone, and she handed it to him, mouthing, "She said yes."

Wentworth scrunched his nose and shook his head. "Belle, I see you're as crazy as your friend... Yes, I see that now. I spoke with the crown prosecutor. She's a go for it... Yes, purely for show." Wentworth studied Eliza. "Yeah, it's crazy enough it might work... Good lass... Anything you want me to take you while we wait out the rest of this carefully orchestrated farce?... Got it. Cheers." Wentworth hung up and handed Eliza her phone. "Remind me to take vacation the next time your friend comes for a visit. I'm not sure I can handle two American women as tenacious as you two."

"I'll take that as a compliment," Eliza said, stuffing her phone back into her pocket, and walked back toward the nursery.

Wentworth followed and gently caught her arm before she could open the door, turning her toward him. With a serious gaze, he studied her, killing the moment of levity. "This could get messy."

"I know."

"And dangerous."

"I know," Eliza said. "What about Beckham?"

"I've got officers watching his flat right now. He hasn't left it, and no one's been round to see him. He's safe for now."

"Does he know he could be the next victim?"

"No, but I'll have to sort that ASAP."

"You can't go up to his flat and tell him. The killer could be watching his place. He'll get suspicious," Eliza said.

"This isn't my first rodeo."

After they entered the nursery, Wentworth picked up his coat from the floor and brushed off the cat hair. He pointed at Eliza. "You stay put. Do not leave this property."

Before Eliza could retort, Wentworth stalked from the room.

"Well... Well... I..."

Great-Aunt Iris chuckled. "He's learned the art of saying something he knows you won't like then legging it before you can get a word in edgewise. Clever chap."

Eliza snorted and crossed her arms. "Where does that leave us?"

Uncle Fitzwilliam clasped her shoulder. "It leaves us with the short end of the stick, I'm afraid. We must be patient and wait."

"How well do you know me?"

"Well enough to know that you'll disregard everything you're told and go put yourself in a heap of trouble because you've got sleuthing ants in your pants."

The death threats came flooding back, clear in their promises. Eliza swallowed. "I have no intention of leaving Pemberley."

Heath sauntered over to her, grinned cheekily, and touched the back of his hand to her forehead. "Are you feeling all right?"

Eliza playfully swatted at him. "I'm not that bad."

Great-Aunt Iris snorted, gathered her knitting, and struggled to her feet, waving away the men who rushed to help her. "I don't know about all of you, but I'm going to bide my time elsewhere. If you need me, I'll be with William... having a kip." She nearly skipped from the room in her squeaky white tennis shoes.

"And I'm going to wash my ears out with acid," Uncle Fitzwilliam said with a shudder. "If you need me, Eliza, I'll be in my study. I want to do some more digging on the disappearance of Rosie." He pressed a kiss to her temple. "And you will stay put?"

"I promise," Eliza said.

After he left, Joy and Willoughby shared knowing looks.

"I, uh, I'll go play some billiards," Willoughby said, his gaze darting about the room.

"And I'll pop up to my room and work on my story," Joy said a little too brightly. "My hunky hero is begging for some one-on-one time with the lustful lass who fell into his lap. Literally."

Once they'd gone, turning the same way down the hall, Eliza cocked her head and circled a finger at the door. "Isn't the billiard room in the opposite direction from Joy's room?"

"Sure is," Heath said, wrapping his arms around her.

"Do you think they—"

"I couldn't give a toss about Joy and Willoughby," he said, his pupils dilating as he gazed at her. "I'd rather spend the time on more pleasurable activities. It's stopped raining. Fancy a walk in the garden?" His fingers played along the inside of her wrist, creating a fire in her belly. "And just so you know, I plan on getting us properly lost and stealing a few kisses here and there."

She couldn't do anything on the case for the moment anyway. The wrong move could possibly ruin the ruse Wentworth and Belle were about to put on. Knowing that her best friend was in good hands, Eliza let Heath out the door, and for the next hour, she lost herself in his comforting presence.

A fter Heath and Eliza had returned from their garden adventure, he retreated to her office to make calls and catch up on work while she made her way through staff that had worked the New Year's Eve ball, asking them about the Crawfords' presence. After thirty minutes and the same answer—everyone remembered seeing them in the ballroom, but none could pinpoint how long they'd stayed, as they'd been rushing around all evening—Eliza went in search of Willow and Tash.

She found them in the butler's pantry, preparing the plateware and silverware for the evening's dinner. From the silver fish forks and knives, she knew a fish dish was on the menu. Eliza shivered. She still hadn't gotten used to how Mrs. Bankcroft served the poor creatures: with their heads still on.

"Glad I caught you two." Eliza gestured for Tash to sit back down and sat at the table with them. "Can you give me an idea of the Crawfords' movements the night of the party? They were the couple wearing matching plaid outfits."

Willow scrunched her nose. "Yeah, I noticed them off and on. Pretty hard to miss."

"You didn't notice their absence for longer than ordinary?" Eliza asked.

"I was right busy that night. Near wore a hole in my shoes." Willow pursed her lips and tapped her finger on her bottom lip. "There was a moment when I only saw Mrs. Crawford for a while."

"Do you know how much time went by?"

"Sorry, no."

Eliza looked at Tash. "Did you notice anything?"

"Sorry, Miss Eliza. Except for seeing Mr. Quill in the garden, I didn't see anything untoward that evening. Granted, I wasn't looking for anything suspicious either."

"Sorry I wasn't much help with the Crawfords, but... " A blush blossomed on Willow's cheeks. "Can I speak to you? In private?"

Tash stood. "I'll start sorting the dining room."

After he left, Willow scooted closer to Eliza and dropped her voice. "Paisley called me this morning. I meant to come find you, but..."

"No worries. What'd she say? If you're willing to tell me, of course."

"She's in a right panic. Doesn't know what to do. Said she couldn't trust anyone, and she's right." Willow scrubbed her face. "Here I am squealing to you."

"You don't have to. I completely understa—"

"Hunter went to Paisley just after Christmas, demanding that she embezzle money from her father's business. Said if she didn't, he'd reveal her secret to the world."

"But how would she do that?"

"She's the bookkeeper and handles the business side for him." Willow's face crumpled, and she swiped at a tear running down her cheek. "You should have heard her, Eliza. I've never heard her like that. She's terrified the police will find out about Hunter's request and suspect her of killing him."

"Do you think she did?" Eliza asked, studying Willow's blanched face.

After a too-long beat of silence, Willow shook her head. "No."

"And the secret? Did she tell you what it was?"

"No. I didn't even ask."

"Thank you for telling me all this. I'll do what I can to keep Paisley's business a secret, but I can't promise anything, especially if she… Well, you know." Eliza rested a hand on Willow's shoulder. "If you can remember anything else, even if it doesn't seem important, please let me know." Eliza scootched her chair back, the legs squeaking on the tile floor.

"Wait." Willow wiped her cheeks, jumped to her feet, hurried over to a counter, and rummaged through a drawer. She grabbed a white slip of paper and handed it to Eliza. "One of the staff cleaned the cloak room this morning and found a cloak ticket."

Eliza turned the ticket over and smoothed her finger over the number twenty-five. She quirked an eyebrow at Willow. "I don't understand."

Willow gave an exasperated sigh. "When guests arrive, they hand their coat to the cloak attendant, who redistributes coats at the end of the evening, and—"

"I understand how that all works, Willow," Eliza said with a smile. "I just don't get why you're showing this to me."

"This ticket is the one the coat owner gets," Willow said, taking the ticket from Eliza and waving it about.

"And he or she probably dropped it by accident."

Willow sighed. "Then how did they get their coat back? There's no record that whoever had number twenty-five retrieved it at the end of the night, but there were no coats left behind either."

"Maybe they grabbed it without informing the attendant."

"At the end of the night? No, there was a steady stream of people in line, handing the attendant their ticket. It would have been impossible for someone to just grab their coat," Willow said, handing the ticket back.

"Maybe the person left the party early and when the attendant wasn't there. Figured they'd just grab it and leave, dropping their ticket in the process." Eliza played her thumb over the slip of paper.

"Well, I thought it weird enough to let you know about it." Her forehead furrowed. "There's also something odd about the end of the party, but I can't put my finger on it. With everything going on with Paisley... " She sighed and shook her head. "Oh well, mustn't have been that important."

Eliza tucked the ticket into her pocket. "I'm glad you brought this up." She smiled again. "You never know. Even the smallest clue can break a case wide open. If that elusive thought comes to you, let me know."

Thirty minutes later and after adding what she'd just learned and taping the cloak ticket to the board, Eliza joined everyone in the dining room and enjoyed a lovely feast of fish without their heads and savory clam chowder. After everyone had eaten their fill and exchanged pleasantries, a heavy silence settled over the table.

The restless feeling under Eliza's skin intensified as she turned to her uncle. "Did you discover anything else about Rosie's disappearance? Any initial suspects?"

"A few gossip columns hinted at suspected people using initials—one being E. T., which would be Everett Tanner. There was a B. H., likely Basil Huxley, and several other initials that didn't match anyone on your crime board," Uncle Fitzwilliam said.

"Anything more in the gossip columns about Everett Tanner?" Heath asked.

"Once the scandal heated up, he became the talk of the town. The accusations in those articles were ill-informed at best and disgusting at worst. Even after the poor man took his own life, these viper-tongued gossips wouldn't leave him be."

Eliza fiddled with the cloth napkin on her plate. "So, where does this leave us?"

"I know I'm new to this whole sleuthing business, but is it possible that despite the lack of motive connecting Hunter and Beckham to Rosie, both murders and the planned third stem from revenge over poor Everett Tanner's tragic death?" Willoughby asked.

"Keep this up, my boy, and you'll be an official member of our little group." Great-Aunt Iris studied him over the rim of her after-dinner coffee. "I'm beginning to see what Joy sees in you."

Willoughby's chiseled face turned bright red, transforming him from his usual suave charmer into a nervous schoolboy. "Right. Thank you?"

"I wouldn't take what Mrs. Darcy says lightly, mate. She hasn't even granted me the title of official member yet. Keeps calling me the 'weakest link,' doesn't she?" Heath's eyes sparkled as a cheeky grin played on his lips.

Great-Aunt Iris sucked in a breath and set her coffee cup down with a sharp clink. "Well, I never—" She snapped her mouth shut, crimson flooding her cheeks. She shot Eliza a sideways glance. "Have you been telling tales out of school, you cheeky thing?"

Eliza smiled sheepishly. "I may or may not have accidentally let slip that you called him that."

"I see where your loyalties lie, my dear." Great-Aunt Iris's lips twitched before she chuckled. "Exactly where they ought to be." She turned to Heath. "Can you ever forgive a foolish old woman?"

"Already done, Mrs. Darcy." Heath smiled warmly at her.

"Back to what Willoughby said," Joy interjected. "We've never approached the case from this angle before. What changes if we do?"

"Let's find out." Eliza stood.

Five minutes later, they gathered around the crime board, and Eliza filled them in on what Willow had told her.

Eliza tapped her finger on Everett's name. "No one on this board has a direct connection to Everett Tanner except for Henrietta, and she started the rumor anyway. She clearly wanted to throw him under the bus. Why would she change her mind years later and want to avenge his death, especially when she essentially caused it?"

"Does anyone know anything about Everett's children?" Heath asked, pointing at the bullet points under Everett's name. "Just because no one in Lambton has seen or heard from his family doesn't mean they don't exist, right?"

"No, but that's easy enough to sort out," Uncle Fitzwilliam said. "I'll check the registers office and see what I can dig up about Everett."

After he left the nursery, Eliza frowned at the chalkboard. "I should have followed this thread to the bitter end earlier, but we didn't."

Eliza put a star by Hunter's, Basil's, and Beckham's names. "Where do these three men fit into all this? Why them specifically? Did they have some connection to Everett? They're far too young to have been involved in Rosie's disappearance, so what ties them together?"

"Could Hunter be the connecting point?" Heath asked. "After all, the case started with his murder. Without his death, we would never have found Rosie's body. Now we have another death on our hands and one more coming if you're right."

"Do we all agree that Rosie's case connects to the current murders?" Great-Aunt Iris asked. "Because if so, only two people could be our suspects: Hubert and Henrietta. They had the means and opportunity. They were here the night of the party, and with the place crawling with people, they thought they could slip out unnoticed. They also had motive. With the lawsuit looming, they knew the body would be discovered, which is why one or both of them tried to dig it up. But they got interrupted or realized digging through the frost line wasn't as easy as they'd thought."

"And they never got a chance to come back and finish the job because their son was killed in almost the same spot," Eliza said. "I bet that's why Constable Archibald spotted Hubert walking along the fence line. He wasn't mourning his son's death. He was checking to make sure the grave hadn't been disturbed."

"Right, but there was something he didn't count on," Heath said, a smile tugging at his lips.

"And what's that?" Eliza asked, raising one eyebrow.

"Your odd little habit of falling onto or into clues."

Eliza grinned. "We're all burdened with a superpower."

"Even with the trifecta of means, motive, and opportunity, I still don't think they killed their son," Joy said. "Even if they did, why at the spot they've been trying to hide for nearly twenty years? That's absolute rubbish. If they had killed him that night, they would have tried to move the body as far away from that spot as possible, and they wouldn't have done it with a witness present. They might have had a 'reason' in their twisted little minds to kill their son, but Belle's presence throws a spanner in the works."

"Joy's right." Eliza planted her hands on her hips and cocked her head at the board. "And I don't see either of them making an anonymous phone call or alerting the police that they have the wrong killer. I see them gleefully celebrating, knowing they got away with it."

Great-Aunt Iris pointed one of her knitting needles at the chalkboard. "If the Crawfords didn't do it and Beckham is the next victim, who is our killer?"

"I have no clue." Eliza fought the panic surging through her and squinted at her crime board. Harry and Paisley's names taunted her. They had no alibis and plenty of motive, especially because Paisley had been backed into a corner. Panicked people often did irrational things. It was also possible that she'd pegged Beckham wrong as the next victim rather than the murderer. Perhaps he was simply an inept criminal with a heart of gold.

Uncle Fitzwilliam entered the nursery with a smile. "Bingo," he said and wrote on the chalkboard, *Everett—Cynthia Tanner: Josiah, Henry, Catherine, and Cecelia.*

"That was quick," Eliza said.

"I didn't have time to dig into their lives," Uncle Fitzwilliam said.

"We can do that—" Eliza winced. From the droop of their shoulders to the purple smudges under their eyes, she knew everyone needed a good night's sleep. "In the morning. Let's all get some rest, and we'll meet up again tomorrow."

After sharing a few quiet moments and a few kisses with Heath before he left for the night, Eliza trudged to her room, shut the door, and crawled into bed, hoping the morning would bring answers to put the whole case to rest.

Dawn broke with a barrage of knocks on Eliza's bedroom door. She sat up, startling Caesar. He glared at her.

"Don't blame me, Mr. Sleepyhead. I'm not the one walking around at"—she squinted at the time on her phone—"six a.m., pounding on people's doors."

The knocks came again, followed by Uncle Fitzwilliam's voice. "Eliza?"

She shot out of bed, slipped her robe over her pajamas, and opened her door to find a haggard-looking uncle wrapped in his robe, his hair standing on end. "What's wrong?"

"Wentworth's here. Says it's urgent."

Eliza didn't bother making herself look the slightest bit presentable and hurried after her uncle to his study.

Wentworth's back was to them, his hands clasped behind him as he stared out the window into the predawn darkness. From the slump of his normally broad shoulders, Eliza could tell the news he carried wasn't good.

Eliza cleared her throat, and Wentworth whirled around. His eyelids drooped over his bloodshot eyes, and more salt-and-pepper whiskers covered his brown cheeks than usual. His wrinkled clothes and loosened tie told Eliza he hadn't slept in his bed—or at all.

"Is it Belle?" she asked.

"No," Wentworth said, his voice barely above a whisper in the morning stillness.

"How is she?"

"She's a trouper. I'll give her that. She told me to tell you to quit worrying about her. Said she'll be fine. She's moved on from werewolf lore to Joy's novels." Wentworth gave a slight shudder.

Eliza's shoulders sagged with relief, and the tight knot in her stomach finally loosened. "You look like you've had a long night," she said, guiding Wentworth toward a leather chair. "Should I ring for tea or coffee?"

Wentworth waved her off. "No, thanks. I can't stay long." He sighed as he settled into the chair and rubbed the back of his neck.

"What's wrong?" Eliza asked, taking the leather chair beside him.

"Beckham is our murderer, not the next victim."

"What?" Eliza nearly shot from her seat.

"What did you discover?" Uncle Fitzwilliam leaned back and steepled his fingers.

"It's a long story—"

"I love long stories," Eliza said, leaning forward with her elbows on her knees. "Spill."

"We've been watching Beckham since yesterday afternoon, right after we 'officially' charged Belle. Everything seemed normal. He stayed in his flat. No one came or went. Then Beckham slipped out around two a.m., creeping about like he was hiding something. He was sneaking toward his car when a figure dressed all in black came after him."

"Who?" Eliza asked, perched on the edge of her seat.

"Not sure. The black-clad figure ran after him, and Beckham legged it. I called for backup, and the black-clad figure sprinted off in the opposite direction. I lost track of him, and by the time I tried following the path I thought Beckham had taken, there was no trace of him." Wentworth's eyes gleamed a little, and from his briefcase, he unearthed a ledger encased in an evidence bag. "Except for this, found in the satchel he'd dropped. He must have been scared witless not to bother turning around to grab it or come back looking for it."

"He had the ledger?" Eliza asked, blinking at the bagged evidence.

"Yes, and his fingerprints are all over it," Wentworth said.

"Well, they would be if he, Basil, and Hunter were in cahoots over monetary shenanigans," Uncle Fitzwilliam said.

Eliza stood and paced in front of her chair. "Taking evidence from the crime scene is practically a confession. A mistake I don't see him making. He doesn't strike me as the kind of man who'd make dumb errors like that."

Wentworth scratched at his facial stubble. "It's often the most brilliant people who are the stupidest criminals. They think they're cleverer than the police and make daft or arrogant mistakes."

"Have you located Beckham or the mystery person?" Uncle Fitzwilliam asked.

"No." Wentworth furrowed his brow. "Not a peep and no sightings of a mysterious figure clad in black."

Eliza continued pacing. "So, what now?"

"We're turning over every rock in this county. I've sent Beckham's information to the neighboring counties, so plenty of eyes are looking for him. Once we find him, I'll nick him for suspicion of Basil's murder, and that'll be the end of it."

"But you can't connect him to Hunter's murder, and what about the connection to the Rosie Harley case?" Eliza asked.

Wentworth's eyes flashed with anger. "I don't know what to tell you. I can only work with the evidence in front of me. I haven't got the luxury of using my imagination to spin stories that fit whatever narrative I think happened."

"But—"

"I don't know what to think. All I know is I'd be failing in my duty as a police officer if I didn't arrest Beckham on suspicion of murder."

Eliza opened her mouth to argue but snapped it shut.

"I'm sorry," Wentworth said, his voice tired and worn thin. "All I know is that I've got enough evidence to arrest him on suspicion of Basil's murder. I went along with your theory for a while. It clearly didn't pan out the way you expected. The rest of the pieces will fall into place once I have that man in my interview room."

"What does this mean for Belle?"

He sighed and rubbed his temples. "She's still in custody. The crown prosecutor wants an official charge today. No exceptions."

Eliza flung out her arms. "I don't understand. How can none of this make sense?" She held up her index finger. "First, there's no way Beckham would try to protect Belle." She held up another finger. "Second, he wouldn't have had anything to do with Rosie Harley's death, and I'm certain those two cases are connected. There's far too much coincidence to ignore." Eliza crossed her arms and tapped her toe impatiently.

"Those are things I plan on finding out once he's in my interview room," Wentworth said, glancing at his watch. "I've got to go, but I'll be in touch. I'm keeping a PC on patrol around the property until we get Beckham in custody. He knows you've been poking about in all this business, and he doesn't strike me as a bloke who easily accepts defeat."

Phantom insects crawled across Eliza's shoulders, and she shivered. No, Beckham wasn't the one she had to fear. It was a nameless, faceless vigilante killer.

Chapter Twenty
Not Everything Yellow Is Cheery

It seems that the Crawfords' pride is more than their sense. Miss Craw-
ford had the audacity to visit this morning while Jane and I were play-
ing in the garden with the children. I will not waste ink in describing
her outward display of annoyance at children being anywhere outside
the confines of the nursery. It is clear she strives to save her and her
brother's name with the story she wove Jane and me about how a
"strumpet" had misled Henry and that the young woman tricked her
poor, helpless brother. If it had not been for Jane's steadying presence, I
do believe I would have set Miss Crawford on her ear.
Lizzy Bennet Darcy
Pemberley 1815

Eliza scowled at the door Wentworth had slammed shut and planted her hands on her hips. "What in the world was that about? How can he possibly think Beckham's the murderer?"

Uncle Fitzwilliam sagged in his chair. "He's not wrong, you know. Looking strictly at the facts, it's reasonable to assume Beckham is the culprit."

"Facts shmacts. I don't like it one bit." Eliza moved toward the study door. "Wentworth's as tenacious as a bulldog. Once he sinks his teeth into something, he won't let go."

Uncle Fitzwilliam arched his right eyebrow, and his lips twitched. "Something you two have in common."

Eliza scowled. "I don't like it when you're right, you know. How's your search on Everett's family tree coming along?"

"Is that a hint for me to restart my investigation?" Uncle Fitzwilliam's eyes twinkled.

"Yes, please. I'll look into it, too, once I get the facts on these crimes straight. It might not lead anywhere, but at least we'll know we did our due diligence, especially since I should have done it right after talking with the Golden Gamblers." While she knew she needed to pull every thread, she doubted that particular string would unravel the whole case. Eliza scrunched her nose. *Probably knot everything up in a tangled mess.*

"You can't blame yourself for mistakes or things you should have done but didn't. That's a brilliant way to drive yourself mad." He settled deeper in his chair and cocked his head when she didn't move. "What is it?"

Eliza gazed out the window. Pink and orange streaks stretched along the horizon, promising a sunrise. The ambient light reflected off frost that had covered every tree, plant, and blade of grass, and the winter wonderland beckoned to her, urging her to lose herself on a walk through Pemberley's sleeping gardens.

"I need to go for a walk. Clear my head."

Uncle Fitzwilliam's shoulders tensed, and he flicked a glance at the window.

"Don't worry. If I do go for a walk, I'll be sure not to go alone."

His shoulders relaxed slightly, but the vertical line between his eyebrows remained firmly etched in his skin. "I need your word on that."

Eliza held up three fingers. "Scout's honor."

"You were an actual Girl Scout?"

"Yes."

"For how long?"

"For as long as it took me to realize I hated every minute of it and I preferred eating the cookies to selling them."

Uncle Fitzwilliam chuckled, stood, and dropped a kiss on the top of her head. "With the chaos that often surrounds you, my dear, it's no wonder your father's got more gray hair than I have." He squeezed her hand. "I'll be in my study."

After getting dressed in leggings and an oversize cream knit sweater, Eliza made a quick detour to the nursery and snapped a few pictures of the crime board. She headed to the kitchen, offered Mrs. Bankcroft a cheery good morning, poured herself an early cup of coffee, and headed to her office.

Her phone pinged with a notification from her scheduling app. Growling at the interruption, she set her phone to vibrate, then she grabbed a few pages of copy paper and rewrote the facts from the chalkboard. Ten minutes later, she sat back, interlocked her fingers behind her head, and gazed out her office window, which faced a now-hibernating rose garden all flecked with frost and sparkling in the morning light. Past the rose garden, over a hundred yards away, the woods began—the ones where Hunter had attempted to assault her friend then lost his life and where someone had buried an innocent life. She shivered and wondered if she'd ever be able to see those woods the same way again.

Right outside the window, Blue Star juniper bushes quivered in the cold wind, and the red berries of the holly bushes glistened against the waxy dark-green leaves flocked with frost.

Eliza wrestled the shawl she kept on the back of her office chair over her shoulders and ran through the facts in her mind. They were nothing but a jumbled mess. She fisted her hair and tugged hard.

"Think, Eliza. Think," she whispered. "Forget everything but the basic facts. Hunter died on New Year's Eve. Why?"

A knock sounded on her door, and Great-Aunt Iris's voice echoed through the heavy oak.

Eliza opened the door and gaped at the tea tray her great-aunt held.

"Here. Let me take this. Why on earth are you walking around carrying that? Where's Tash?"

"I didn't want to disturb him, and I'm perfectly capable of carrying my own tea tray, thank you very much." Great-Aunt Iris handed it over and marched into Eliza's office. She was dressed in her usual tracksuit, that time one in a lovely shade of mint, and her ever-present purse large enough to carry Caesar if the octogenarian could have lifted him in it. Instead, Caesar was up to his old tricks, batting at the loose thread dangling from the depths of the bag. "Fitzwilliam said I could find you here."

"I thought everyone was still sleeping." Eliza set down the tray, moved a wooden chair closer to her desk, and offered her great-aunt the comfortable office chair.

"I'm not here to take your chair, girl. I'm here to make sure you're okay." She settled into the wooden chair and placed her purse on the floor. Caesar immediately pounced on it, rolling himself in the wool.

Eliza sank into her chair. "I'm going crazy."

"Have you met your family? That's already in your cards." Great-Aunt Iris tutted. "Some are barmier than others, so you'd better face the facts now."

"Whether I'm crazy or not, this case doesn't make sense. We all got lost in the difficulty, when I have a strange feeling it's been simple from the beginning."

Great-Aunt Iris poured two cups of tea and handed one to Eliza. "Walk me through it. What's on your mind?"

Eliza took a sip of the bracing brew and sighed. "What's the most basic fact in this whole mess?"

Great-Aunt Iris fell silent for a moment. "Hunter took Belle from the party and headed to the woods with her, and someone killed him."

"Exactly. But why? And there are two whys here. Why did he take her into the woods in the first place? Did he plan to walk back to Berryhill with her?"

"If he came with his parents, he couldn't have taken the car. Too many questions to answer if he'd been caught."

Bile roiled in Eliza's gut at the thought of Hunter going through with whatever awful plan he'd cooked up for her friend, and she took several deep breaths to settle her stomach. "Secondly, why did someone choose to kill him in the woods, someone who didn't bring their own weapon but grabbed a random tree branch to bash his head in?"

"And why let Belle live?" Great-Aunt Iris added. "She wouldn't have been able to hide, and according to her memory, which that dishy constable corroborates, she heard footsteps that couldn't have been Hunter's."

"This means the killer didn't plan to murder Hunter, that this person was likely watching out for Belle, as you mentioned several days ago, making sure she stayed safe." Eliza circled the clue *Was he killed because someone was protecting Belle?* she'd rewritten on printer paper.

"Which means this person knew Hunter well enough to recognize his bad intentions. Otherwise, only a complete nutter would leave a party to go traipsing through the woods."

"But they went with the idea of protecting Belle, not necessarily killing Hunter, or they would've brought a weapon," Eliza said.

"If we follow this line of thinking, who at the party knew Hunter well enough to realize Belle might be in danger and cared enough about her to brave the chilly night and risk a confrontation?"

A panicked meow came from under Great-Aunt Iris's chair, and she glanced down. "Caesar, now look what you've gone and done, you daft pussycat, you."

Caesar, rolled from head to tail in green-and-lilac wool, yowled and glared at her as if it were Great-Aunt Iris's fault he'd gotten tangled up.

She tutted, untangled the cat from a literal cat's cradle, and grabbed her purse with too much enthusiasm, swinging it overly high and nearly clipping Eliza's head.

"Oh, sorry, dear. Sometimes, I don't know my own strength. Why, the other day..."

A buzzing sound filled Eliza's ears.

The same motion from the previous day flashed through her mind—the same size purse, one large enough to rival Great-Aunt Iris's.

Eliza squeezed her eyes shut, revisiting every moment from the Trusty Teapot. She remembered the odd tension between Lucinda and Beckham, her oversize purse pressed against his open satchel, which was already stuffed with ledgers and notebooks, at their shared table. The purse was large enough to hold a ledger. *She could have slipped it in, and it's quite possible he wouldn't have noticed it among his own things.*

Eliza's eyes flew open, and she gasped. Her great-aunt's lips kept moving, but she heard nothing. Her blood turned to ice, and goose bumps prickled her skin.

"Eliza?" Through a thick fog, someone called her name.

He was a proper nasty piece of work.

Nausea churned in Eliza's stomach, and she breathed carefully through her nose to keep from losing her breakfast.

"Eliza?" A knitting needle accompanied the voice.

She winced and rubbed her ribs.

"Talk to me, girl," Great-Aunt Iris demanded.

"Oh God. I know who did it. Or I think I do." Eliza groaned and dropped her forehead onto her desk. "I've been so, so stupid. So incredibly stupid."

"Who?"

"You agreed that the killer had to know Hunter's vicious character, right? They'd watched him destroy several women, maybe even a close friend." The words *If I could go back in time and change things, I would. I'd give all this up just to give Paisley a chance at a normal life* echoed through Eliza's mind. "So when they saw Hunter leave with Belle, they wanted to stop him or at least try. Which means they were a guest at the party."

Great-Aunt Iris tilted her head and studied Eliza carefully. "Yes, and if that's true, there's only one person from our suspect list who fits. But it doesn't add up, does it? What's Lucinda's connection to Basil? Or Beckham? And what about Rosie?"

"I don't know, and I'm afraid we all lost the plot, as you like to say, once the clues started piling up." Eliza groaned and rubbed her neck. "Forget about the why for now. What's the how? How could she possibly bludgeon someone over the head and come back to a packed party and no one notice blood splatter?"

Great-Aunt Iris gasped. "Willoughby. I knew he'd come in handy eventually. The color of Lucinda's dress. It was maroon." She tutted when Eliza tilted her head in confusion. "Maroon. Blood wouldn't have been as noticeable, and she could have slipped into any of the bathrooms and washed up before returning to the party."

Eliza shook her head. "It's possible, but it still doesn't make any sense. Could a four-year-old event cause someone to suddenly snap and commit murder?"

"It's not an old wound anymore, though, is it? Hunter came back into Paisley's life, threatening her. That might have been enough to push Lucinda over the edge."

"And how does Rosie's case connect to all this?" Eliza asked.

"Quite well, my dear, especially if we focus on the second victim in Rosie's case. Everett. He and his entire family were destroyed by those vicious rumors. His wife left him, he took his own life, and the Tanners vanished from Lambton until…"

Eliza snapped her fingers. "Until… Until…" Words spoken by or about Lucinda swirled through her mind, and she pictured the chocolate-box cottage where they'd first met and the fact that Joy had been unsuccessful in tracking down the owner. "One finally moved back."

Eliza called Wentworth and frowned when it went to voicemail. She hung up and fired off a quick text asking him to dig into the ownership of Lucinda Fairchild's cottage. She added a *please* in all caps and threw in a praying-hands emoji to cover all her bases.

Eliza was ninety-nine point nine percent certain that the woman living in that pretty English cottage was connected to Everett Tanner somehow. She'd mentioned a beloved nan, tried to mask her accent, one that could reveal her home county, and was the perfect age to be Everett's granddaughter. Hatred had flashed through her eyes at any mention of the Crawfords.

A knock preceded her office door swinging open, and Willow hurried in. "I remember."

Eliza cocked her head.

"The weird thing? That night, all the guests were lined up, waiting for their coats. There was a woman who didn't have a coat. Left without one. But why wouldn't she have a coat on a freezing-cold night? That's odd, right?"

"Did you recognize her?"

"No."

Eliza pulled up the browser on her phone, found Lucinda's real estate website, and scrolled until she found a headshot of Lucinda. She showed Willow the photo.

Willow's eyes widened. "That's her."

Eliza tapped her phone against her palm. "Let's say the ticket is hers. That means she came with a coat and left without one because..."

"She wore it when she bludgeoned Hunter over the head," Great-Aunt Iris said.

Eliza's blood ran cold, and goose bumps exploded on her arms. "Then where's the coat? The police didn't find it, and they searched nearly every inch of the woods."

"Could it be in the house?" Willow asked. "This place is big enough to hide an elephant. A coat would be no issue. She could have even thought she'd come back for it under the pretense of a visit."

Great-Aunt Iris hoisted herself out of her chair, smoothed down her velour jacket, and headed toward the door. "Why are you two standing there gaping at each other like dying fish? We have a coat to find."

Eliza and Willow started to follow her when Uncle Fitzwilliam hurried in, moving past Great-Aunt Iris and waving a piece of paper.

"Eliza, you'll never guess what I've discovered. Lucinda—"

"Fairchild is Everett Tanner's granddaughter," Eliza said, glancing at the family tree her uncle had sketched out. She folded it and tucked it into her leggings pocket.

Uncle Fitzwilliam gaped at her—a rather unlordly expression—snapped his mouth shut, then opened it again. "Good Lord. How on earth...? Blimey."

Great-Aunt Iris gently placed a hand on her nephew's cheek and tutted softly. "Your niece has a snappy brain, Fitzwilliam, and I do wonder why you still doubt that." She beamed at Eliza. "Shall we start hunting?"

At her uncle's quirked eyebrow, Eliza filled him in on the recent turn of events.

"Blimey." Uncle Fitzwilliam massaged the back of his neck. "Never would have thought." He offered his crooked arm. "Shall we?"

"Yes, give me two seconds. Can you gather the troops in the nursery? I want to update everyone and divvy up the hunting grounds for that coat, and I want to text Heath to see if he can video call during our little assembly as he gets ready for work."

After receiving a *Brilliant, can't wait* from Heath, Eliza took her uncle's arm. As they walked toward the gathering, her phone vibrated. She checked the screen. "It's Wentworth. Perfect timing."

Uncle Fitzwilliam jerked his chin toward the staircase. "I'll help Aunt Iris round up the troops and bring them up to speed on our discovery about Lucinda. Take your time."

"Thanks." Eliza answered the call as she headed back toward her office. "Do you know who—"

"Blimey, hello to you too," Wentworth's gruff voice cut through the phone. "And yes, I bloody well do. Had one of my boys dig into it. The cottage belonged to a Cynthia Cunningham and—"

"Cynthia? Are you certain?"

Papers rustled during the brief pause. "Yes, Cynthia—"

"Tanner."

"How in the bloody hell did you know that?"

On a normal day, Eliza might have grinned at the slight crack in his voice, but the air seemed to thicken around her, making it difficult to breathe.

"Eliza?" Wentworth's voice snapped like a whip.

Clutching the phone tighter, she drew in a deep breath. "Because I finally figured out how stupid I've been this whole time. Lucinda is Everett Tanner's granddaughter."

Choice expletives sailed through the speaker, and Eliza cringed as each one hit her ears. She held her phone away until the tirade ended. "First off, you're a right menace. You know that, yeah?"

"So I've been told by multiple people." Eliza pulled the Tanner family tree from her pocket and smoothed it across her desk.

"And secondly, how long were you planning to keep quiet about figuring out Lucinda's connection to Everett Tanner? I could have you up for impeding an investigation, you know." His words carried a legit threat but no heat or weight. Instead, exhaustion crept into his gruff voice.

"Uncle and I worked it out right before you called." She traced her finger down the family tree sketched on the paper. "Cynthia Cunningham married Everett Tanner. Since he was the gardener for the Crawfords, they must have lived on the estate but kept the cottage in her name, leaving it empty. None of their children wanted it, though. They all left the area long before Rosie Harley went missing, including Cynthia and Everett's daughter, Cecelia, who"—Eliza squinted at her uncle's handwriting—"married a Thomas Fairchild. Locals had no clue where she'd gone or who she'd married. When you put two and two together, there's only one solution: Lucinda is Everett Tanner's granddaughter. She came back to the village without anyone knowing. No one realized she was connected to Lambton, much less the Tanners. That's why we didn't make the connection."

"And this is exactly why I tell you to keep your nose out of police business, Eliza. If Lucinda's behind it all, she also knows how much you've been mucking about in all this."

Icy fingers skittered along Eliza's spine, and Wentworth's voice sounded like it was coming through a long tunnel.

"Any word on Beckham's whereabouts?" Eliza's pulse quickened.

"No. No one's seen hide or hair of him. Why all these questions? Are you planning something foolish? I'll have the officer stationed at Pemberley arrest you right now, and I'll lock you up for your own—what is it, Archibald?"

Eliza winced at a particularly vulgar swear word.

"I have to dash, Eliza. Apparently, there's a domestic violence scene at Berryhill Manor. Don't—and I repeat, do *not*—do anything daft. You hear me?"

"Loud and cl—"

Wentworth hung up.

Eliza glared at the phone. "Serve you right if I do go off and do something stupid," she muttered and slipped it into her pocket.

A soft knock echoed through her office door.

"Come in," she called.

The door opened, and Lucinda Fairchild rushed inside, her pristine dark-brown hair frazzled and wild. Her brown eyes were enormous in her pale face, and her chest heaved as if she'd sprinted a mile. "Thank God you're here. We've got a situation."

L ucinda shut and locked the door behind her, slipped off a jacket more for spring than winter, and draped it over her arm. Eliza breathed deeply through her nose to calm her racing thoughts. No sense alerting Lucinda to the fact that Eliza knew exactly who she was and feared the woman had taken justice into her own hands.

Eliza gestured toward the chaise longue. "Is everything all right? You look..." *Panicked.*

Lucinda ignored the offered seat and rushed to Eliza, clasping her hands in her cold, clammy ones. "It's Beckham."

Eliza's throat tightened, and she forced her body to relax. "What about him? I haven't seen him since yesterday at the Trusty Teapot."

"He's gone. Vanished." Lucinda released Eliza's hands and paced, her fingers clutched so tightly that her knuckles turned white.

"I'm sorry to hear that. I'm not sure how I can help, though," Eliza said. *Play dumb, Eliza. Play dumb!* "Have you been to the police?" Her skin crawled as the petite woman paced frantically, wearing a hole in the aged Oriental carpet.

Figuring out what Lucinda knew and what she didn't would require careful navigation.

Lucinda's laugh was harsh. "The police?" She nearly spat the words. "No, we—you and I—need to find him before they do. If we don't, our plan is ruined, you see?"

Eliza's skin crawled again, but she feigned nonchalance. "Plan? What plan?"

Lucinda spun around, her eyes glinting with something that made Eliza's toes curl in her slippers. Madness, lunacy—whatever it was, the Lucinda Fairchild standing before her was not the woman Eliza had come to know. Her heart hammered against her ribs, stealing her breath.

"How can you not remember?" Lucinda gave a little chuckle. "It was New Year's Day. You came to my cottage. Asked for my help. Remember?"

All the times Lucinda had used "we" or "our" during the investigation flickered through Eliza's mind. Her throat tightened as she carefully chose her words. One wrong response, one misplaced word could shatter whatever delusion was keeping Lucinda from turning violent. Buying herself a few extra seconds to think, she led Lucinda to the chaise and encouraged her to sit then settled in a chair opposite.

"Yes, but I don't remember any plan we made. You simply—"

"I gave you names. Contacts. Set the investigation on the right path, didn't I? Basil would never have agreed to meet with you without me."

"Well, I—"

"And Beckham? I introduced him to you at the teashop, remember? He was rude to you, too, the absolute tosser."

"Yes, and that was all so helpful and..."

Lucinda's eyes closed, and her twisted facial features softened. "I'm so glad you think so." She pressed a hand to her chest and offered a crooked smile. "I've been content to work in the background, let your obvious talents shine, but it's the eleventh hour. We must find Beckham before the police do."

Eliza's skin prickled with unease. "Why?"

"Because justice won't be served." Lucinda clasped her hands beneath her chin as she leaned closer to Eliza. "If you don't help me, if you don't go along with the plan, everything will be ruined, and... and..." She reached across the short distance between them and clawed harmlessly at Eliza's arm. Her eyes, wide and wild, searched Eliza's face. "Please," she whispered. "We must bring justice to all who've suffered. Don't you see that? I thought you understood. That's why I..." Her gaze darted wildly about the room before locking onto Eliza again. "That's why I did what I did. Helped you. Gave you clues. Told the police how inept they are."

Desperation clung to Lucinda like cloying perfume, and Eliza struggled to breathe. Her pulse pounded in her ears, and cold sweat broke out across her skin. Eliza's phone, stashed away in her pocket, taunted her, but she feared any sudden movement would escalate the situation. No, she had to drag this out until she bought herself enough time or until someone in the nursery grew impatient enough or worried enough to come find her.

Icy fingers of dread slithered down her spine.

If anyone came looking for her, they'd be in danger too. Eliza had no idea what weapons Lucinda might be carrying. If she was the murderer, her pattern had been using whatever she found at each scene, but she had lost all control. Some twisted sense of justice was driving her every move.

Buy time, Eliza. That's all you need to do. Buy time.

"I see that, Lucinda, and you're right. I'm sorry if I seemed out of sorts. I was startled to see anyone outside the family here. Wentworth posted an officer and everything."

A smile flickered across Lucinda's lips, and her eyes sparkled with the glee of a five-year-old on Christmas morning. "See? This is exactly why our partnership has so many benefits." Lucinda rummaged around in her spring jacket and pulled out a bright-yellow device that resembled a handgun.

Eliza's skin felt too tight on her body, and the room went gray at the edges. All she could see was the canary-yellow police-issue Taser normally attached to Derbyshire Constabulary utility belts.

"I know what you're thinking. But I couldn't have the police interrupt us, now, could I?" Lucinda's West Country accent slipped through as she set the stun gun in her lap. "No one will bother us now."

"How—" Eliza's voice squeaked. She swallowed hard against the lump in her throat. "How'd you take it from him?"

"Her. She looked the nosy sort too. Took her out with a blow to the head." Lucinda held her hands out to Eliza as if soothing a spooked animal. "Don't worry yourself, though. I checked her pulse. She's innocent enough, even if she is part of *them*."

Eliza's mouth went dry, and queasiness sloshed in her gut. *Keep playing her game. Keep playing her game.* "So, where do we go from here?"

"I thought you'd never ask. I have an idea where Beckham might be hiding, but I'll need your help to take him out and dispose of his body."

Bile snaked up Eliza's throat. She fought for composure and rested her hand over the pocket where her phone was. "Of course. You'll have to forgive me, but I don't remember Beckham being part of our plan."

"Oh, you daft thing. However can you forget?"

"Stress has this effect on me."

"Course it does. It's my fault. I put too much burden on you, and that's not what good partners do. I should have done more, been there for you when you needed me. But I failed. Just like I've failed my other friends."

Despite the fear slithering down her spine, Eliza's heart twinged at the pain in Lucinda's voice. Terrified of making one wrong move, Eliza took a deep breath and leaned forward, patting Lucinda's hand. "No, you've been such a great help. I couldn't have gotten as far as I did without you. You've been invaluable." Eliza smiled sheepishly. "I'm sorry I've failed you."

"No, we must think more positively. We still have a chance to bring justice for the innocent. For girls like Paisley, for your friend Belle, for all those whose lives are ruined by people in power, those who think they're better than everyone else. You see, it's our job to ensure the innocent are never hurt again."

Eliza's phone vibrated in her pocket, and she prayed that Lucinda didn't hear it. She shivered and pulled the blanket resting over the back of her chair into her lap to help muffle the sound, and leaning forward, she pressed her forearm down on the blanket.

Relief flooded through her when Lucinda didn't seem to notice. Now, if only the person who'd called would get suspicious that Eliza hadn't returned the call and come looking for her.

"I admire your sense of justice. Can I ask, though..." An oily sensation sloshed in Eliza's gut. Her next question could either break open a treasure trove of information or doom her to whatever the occasional flicker of crazy in Lucinda's eyes unleashed. "Do you mind sharing why? We've never really sat down and talked about it, and I feel I could help you more if I understood. Be the partner you need me to be."

Lucinda cocked her head and studied her for what felt like hours. The ticking grandfather clock in the corner filled the room until Eliza thought she'd scream from the deafening sounds.

"There have been very few people in my life I could trust, Eliza. Until now." Lucinda gave her a quivering smile. "And I have no doubt that after you hear everything, you'll resume your quest for justice."

Eliza forced a smile she didn't feel and crossed her fingers. "I promise to do all I can to make everything right again."

Chapter Twenty-One
Old Sins Cast Long Shadows

I fear Darcy will suffer an apoplexy. Not even my normal means of... distracting him... which normally work like a charm, have assuaged his worry over the Crawfords. Darcy had no interest in assisting the sibling duo in gaining back their respectability in the neighborhood. And to this, Crawford has fabricated a land dispute, claiming that Pemberley is encroaching on Berryhill Manor land. No matter my assurances that it will come to nothing, Darcy worries that the precedent set now will impact generations after us who will call this lovely estate home. I do hope, for once, that my dear Darcy is incorrect.
Lizzy Bennet Darcy
Pemberley 1815

"My grandfather was Everett Tanner," Lucinda whispered and stared at her hands, which still clutched the weapon.

Eliza feigned surprise. "I'm so sorry about what happened to him. So tragic."

Lucinda's gaze met Eliza's, and Eliza sucked in a breath at the pain and torment shimmering in her eyes.

"The Crawfords, they, they..." She pinched the bridge of her nose. "After what that devil did to that poor little girl, the Crawfords killed my grandfather," Lucinda whispered, her eyes bright with tears.

Eliza's blood ran cold. "Hubert?"

"Yes. After I found out what he'd done, how he'd coaxed her from the festival then..." A sob exploded from Lucinda's chest, and she cradled her arms around it as if trying to hold herself together. "Can you imagine? How frightened she must have been when..." She bit her lip, and tears streamed down her cheeks.

Sweat beaded on Eliza's clammy skin as she fought to keep her stomach contents where they belonged. Not long ago, she'd sat in Pemberley's drawing room with a child abductor and murderer. "I know how Henrietta's lies led to your grandfather taking his own life, Lucinda, and I'm so sorry." Those were the truest words Eliza had spoken since Lucinda barged into her office.

Lucinda's chest heaved, and a great sob wracked her body.

"That must have pained you, hearing the truth of your grandfather's death," Eliza said.

"It shattered my world," Lucinda whispered. "You want to know how I found out? I overheard Hunter and Beckham talking about it at a uni party. They laughed." She clasped her free hand over her mouth, stifling a sob. "Didn't take long for me to piece together the rest. Basil was a blackmailer who already knew—or ferreted out—the secrets of the elite and powerful so he could hoard the truth and keep men under his thumb. Hunter and Beckham had somehow sniffed out Basil's dark secret."

"Basil knew the whole time what had happened?" Eliza asked, icy fingers slithering over her skin. The man had once called Hunter a snake, but he should have looked in the mirror first. That also must have been the secret he was so terrified would come out, and he was right: it would have ruined him. Anger that Basil had escaped true justice burned like acid in Eliza's gut.

"He knew about it from the beginning. He knew what happened to poor little Rosie, and instead of going to the police, he... he... let Hubert get away with murder all for a price, which led to my grandfather taking his..." Lucinda's throat worked. "And my nan?" Her voice broke. "It destroyed her. Destroyed my family."

Lucinda's hand clutching the Taser shook with such force that Eliza feared the woman would accidentally fire it.

"Is that why Hunter had to be punished? Was it because he knew the real story behind Rosie's abduction and murder and, like Basil and his father, kept it a secret? Or were you simply protecting Belle from the likes of Beckham?" Eliza shook her head and made what she hoped was a sympathetic sound. "And of course, Hunter had threatened Paisley again, hadn't he?"

Lucinda's face reddened, and her tongue flicked across her lips. "It all happened so fast." She held out her free hand as if pleading for Eliza to understand. "I saw Hunter lead Belle away. It all came crashing back. Paisley's pain, her fear…" Her breathing hitched. "The cloak attendant was missing. I grabbed my coat, and I… followed them. I had to make sure she was safe. From *him*." Lucinda ran her fingers along the bright-yellow Taser, her gaze locked on Eliza's. "I couldn't abandon her. You see that, don't you?"

Eliza swallowed and nodded. "I'm glad you were there for my friend when I couldn't be."

Lucinda preened. "I knew you'd approve."

"What happened that you had to take drastic measures, though?"

"Fate, Eliza. That's what happened." Lucinda's eyes glittered with madness, and she played with the weapon, tossing it carelessly from one hand to the other. "The stars aligned, and I took it as my sign."

"What stars? What sign?" Eliza struggled to get her words past her windpipe.

"Hunter was nearing the spot where poor little Rosie Harley was buried."

Eliza's head jerked as if Lucinda had slapped her. "How did you know where she was buried?"

The smile that crept along Lucinda's face made Eliza's skin crawl. "Please don't judge me, Eliza. I don't know if I could bear it if you did, but blackmail can go both ways. Once I knew what Hubert had done and Basil had covered up, I made sure I milked Basil for all he knew, including the burial spot."

"But... But... how did he know?"

"Caught Hubert in the process of getting rid of... the evidence."

"How awful. And you've been carrying this burden this whole time?" Guilt at stringing along Lucinda, a woman clearly unhinged and tormented by past ghosts, ate at Eliza's conscience, but two men were dead, another's life was at risk, and her best friend was still firmly under the unwavering eye of the Derbyshire Constabulary.

Lucinda clutched at her chest. "As they neared the spot, I heard him laughing. Laughing! Can you imagine? Nearing a spot where you know a little girl is buried due to your father's evil actions, and you laugh? That's when I knew. A man like that, who knew the truth, had kept it hidden to probably use later for his own advancement, should not be allowed to live." Lucinda's eyes gleamed. "As I followed them, I picked up a branch I thought would do the trick."

Eliza's phone vibrated again, sending jolts of panic through her. She leaned harder on the blanket, forced herself to nod, to put an understanding lilt to her voice. "I would probably have done the same in your shoes. What happened next?"

"Hunter and your friend—" She cocked her head. "How is she, by the way?"

Eliza blinked at the sudden change in topic, which only reminded her of the knife edge she was balancing on with the partially unhinged woman sitting across from her, discussing murder as if they were discussing the weather.

"She's fine. Thank you for asking." Eliza gestured for her to continue. "You were saying?"

"Oh yes. Hunter and Belle stopped some yards away from where I knew Rosie was resting. That's when he tried to kiss Belle. I was about to step in, but your friend's a fighter. She punched him then ran off."

"And that's when you saw your opportunity. Brilliant." Eliza nearly choked on the compliment.

Lucinda beamed with pride. "I knew you'd approve once you finally found out the truth. We're the same, you and I. Seekers of justice."

Eliza's stomach twisted, but she gave what she hoped was a supportive smile.

"I had finally found a way to fix all the horrible things done to me, my family, and that poor little girl at the hands of evil people." Her eyebrows dipped together as she studied Eliza. "I'm not a murderer. I'm an executioner. And I saw my opportunity, a gift of the gods. Get rid of Hunter, who only hurt people and was threatening to do it again. I realized a little too late that Hunter's body was not as close to Rosie's burial spot as I'd initially thought."

"And Basil?" Eliza asked.

Lucinda shrugged. "If it weren't for that little toad concealing the crime, my grandfather would have lived. He was the one man who could have brought light to the horrible crime against Rosie."

"Then you decided to pin it all on Beckham, the other person who knew the truth and remained silent?"

Lucinda beamed at her. "I knew you'd understand."

"And the anonymous phone call was another brilliant move, by the way. Pure genius."

"Oh yes. For my plan to work, Hunter's body needed to be discovered." She pursed her lips. "There were only two spanners in the works. Belle. I'd never intended for her to take the fall, so when the police moved in, I had to do something drastic."

"The notes."

"Exactly."

"And the second?" Eliza asked, although she already knew the answer.

"The blood. I didn't think I'd get much blood on me, but I was wrong. I did my best to clean up, and thankfully, my coat covered most of my dress, but the maroon color all but made whatever blood was on the material disappear." She pouted. "I suppose I'll have to get rid of the dress now."

Eliza swallowed against the rising bile in her throat. "And the coat?"

"Stashed it in a cupboard in one of the rooms I stumbled into. If you don't mind, could I grab it later?"

"U-Um... sure," Eliza stammered.

Footsteps sounded outside the door, and within seconds, the doorknob twisted.

"Eliza?" Heath's voice echoed through the heavy oak door, and the knob twisted violently in its housing. "Eliza, love? You all right? Say something." Heath's panicked voice, chorused with the voices of her family, echoed through the door.

Lucinda jumped to her feet, placing herself between Eliza and the door. She clutched the yellow Taser, pointing it in intervals at the door and at Eliza. "They're going to ruin everything, Eliza. Everything. Do something."

Icy fingers crept along Eliza's skin, and she shuddered, her gaze flicking between the door and the weapon.

A barrage of knocks thundered through the room.

Eliza's heart stumbled and raced. Adrenaline surged through her as she got to her feet, straightened her shoulders, and drew herself to full height. "I'm okay. I'm having a chat with Lucinda," she called out, never breaking eye contact with her.

Her uncle shouted for Tash, who no doubt had the key to the office.

Lucinda motioned for Eliza to open the window. "Let's go. We need to find Beckham before the police can stop us."

Eliza remained rooted to her spot, her skin slick with sweat and nausea churning in her stomach.

Lucinda narrowed her gaze at Eliza. "I've got the door covered. You get the window."

Eliza slowly shook her head. "I'm sorry, Lucinda. I can't do that."

"What? You... You ..." Realization dawned on Lucinda's face, and her features twisted. "Betrayed me."

More raised voices came from the hallway. Help was coming, but between Eliza and safety stood a madwoman aiming a Taser directly at her heart.

"Eliza, love," Heath's voice came through the door again. "Wentworth's on his way with a whole bloody cavalry of officers. But in the meantime..." His voice trailing off said everything. Eliza was on her own.

The pounding and mention of approaching police had rattled Lucinda, and her nervous gaze darted between Eliza and the door.

Now or never. Lucinda no longer held power or control. A wave of calm washed over Eliza, smoothing her frayed nerves.

Keeping her gaze locked on Lucinda's wild eyes, Eliza stepped toward her. When Lucinda took a hesitant step back, Eliza pressed forward until only a few feet separated them.

Footsteps thundered down the hall, and moments later, the sound of a key sliding into the lock clicked loudly in the quiet room.

"She's got a Taser!" Eliza cried as the door swung open.

Lucinda spun around and aimed the Taser.

Eliza launched herself at Lucinda and tackled her to the floor. The Taser fell from Lucinda's hand, and Eliza kicked it across the room.

Heath, Uncle Fitzwilliam, and Willoughby burst into the room. Her uncle rushed to the curtains and yanked the tie-back cord from its mooring. Heath and Willoughby raced to Eliza, who was struggling to overpower Lucinda in her adrenaline-fueled fight. Heath's panicked gaze swept over Eliza's face for a moment before he turned his attention to the writhing Lucinda.

Willoughby gently pulled Eliza away from the raging figure as Heath pressed his knee into the small of Lucinda's back, pinning her arms behind her and holding them steady for Uncle Fitzwilliam to secure the curtain cord around her wrists.

Lucinda eventually stopped moving and pinned Eliza with a teary gaze. "I thought you understood. You said... You said we were a team. How am I going to bring justice now?" Sobs wracked her body.

Eliza looked away from the pitiful spectacle and collapsed into her uncle's chest the moment he dropped to his knees beside her.

The rapid tap-tap-tap of Uncle William's cane announced his arrival before he appeared in the doorway, slightly winded. "Do forgive me. I came as quickly as I could manage." His weathered hands gripped his cane tighter as he took in the scene: Lucinda sobbing, Heath and Willoughby standing guard over her, a weeping Eliza in her uncle's arms, Joy on the phone, speaking to a police officer, and Great-Aunt Iris standing over Eliza with her wrinkled hand gently resting on Eliza's head.

"Iris?" His gravelly voice cracked, and his cane tip-tapped faster as he made his way to his wife. "Iris, my dear, are you all right?" With one arm, he tenderly drew her to his chest and kissed her forehead. "And Eliza?" His worried gaze searched Eliza's face. "Did she—did she hurt you, my dear?"

Eliza wiped her tears and gently squeezed her great-uncle's hand. "I'm fine, Uncle William. I am."

His shoulders sagged with obvious relief. "I'm not sure what we would have done if anything had happened to you."

Great-Aunt Iris cupped her hand behind his neck and brought his face down for a quick kiss. "We're all right, William. Just a spot of excitement. That's all."

"A spot of excitement, dear?" Uncle William's bushy gray eyebrows rose. "There's a woman trussed up on the floor."

Eliza had lost count of how many times Wentworth had paced the width of the drawing room.

Exhaustion gnawed at her body, leaving her feeling boneless. Five hours had passed since officers escorted Lucinda from Pemberley and only ten minutes since Wentworth had crashed her family's debrief.

Despite the drawing room's crackling fire, the green-and-ivory damask curtains pulled back to reveal a stunning sunset over Pemberley, and a tea tray laden with steaming tea and delicate pastries, the normally cheerful room couldn't compete with the relentless thud of Wentworth's shoes as he marched back and forth.

Whenever Eliza opened her mouth to speak, Wentworth skewered her with a glare and resumed his pacing, clutching his hands behind his back, his umber face as hard as flint.

If anyone else had been in the room, she would have given a confused shrug, perhaps even an eye roll if she'd been brave enough. But she was alone. What had started as a family debrief about Lucinda's attack had morphed into an interrogation of one: Eliza Darcy.

She didn't doubt that Great-Aunt Iris, Joy, and Belle were jostling for space outside, pressing their ears against the heavy oak door. Great-Uncle William was probably there too. He had refused to leave his wife's side, even when his pallor turned ashen and everyone, including Eliza, had urged him to return to the suite he shared with his beloved wife. But no one could convince him otherwise, and Eliza figured it was the same Darcy stubbornness that ran in her blood.

As for the rest of the gang, Heath was probably standing sentinel, his arms crossed, daring anyone who didn't belong to enter. From the moment the police had dragged a pleading Lucinda from Pemberley, Heath hadn't let Eliza out of his sight. Uncle Fitzwilliam was undoubtedly on the other side of the doorframe, matching Heath's stance, his body coiled and ready to spring into action. Willoughby would be lurking in the hallway as well, eager to resume what had promised to be an interesting debrief.

Eliza sighed. Enough was enough. She'd already been held hostage once that day, and she wasn't in the mood to placate Wentworth's storming. "Look, Wentworth, I know you're angry with me, and you—"

"Angry?" Wentworth spun sharply on his heel, stalked over to her, and stopped inches away.

Eliza blinked up at him, her retort dying on her lips at the raw pain and worry in his eyes.

Wentworth sighed, ran his fingers through his hair, and sank beside her. He folded his hands and rested them on his knees, his gaze fixed on the red-and-orange flames dancing in the hearth. "When Fitzwilliam rang me... Told me that you were locked in a room with Lucinda... I—" His deep, gruff voice cracked, and his throat worked. Without breaking his concentration on the fire, he unclasped his fists and kneaded his thighs. "Bloody hell, Eliza. I can't do my job properly if I'm worried about you."

Realization hit her like a sledgehammer, and tears stung her eyes. She blinked them away. She was tired of crying and had done more than she cared to admit in the aftermath of Lucinda's attack. Emotion clogged her throat as she rested her hand on one of Wentworth's. "I'm sorry."

Wentworth stared at her hand for several seconds before placing his on top. "I don't suppose you'll promise to keep your nose out of police business from here on out?" he asked, his voice carrying a thread of hope.

"I could lie to you if that would make you feel better," Eliza said, nudging his shoulder with hers.

"What would make me feel better is if you stayed out of these situations altogether." Wentworth grunted. "You know what I was thinking about while I was trying to get the domestic disturbance with the Crawfords under control? You—and that you were in danger not more than a mile away, and I couldn't get to you fast enough."

Eliza tucked one leg up on the couch and faced him. "I won't make promises I can't keep, but I promise you that I'll fight for those I love, no matter the cost. That's nonnegotiable. It's who I am. I can promise a few things, though."

"Surprise me."

"One..." She held up a finger. "I promise to never go off half-cocked—which I didn't, by the way. Lucinda found me. Two..." She held up another finger. "I promise to always keep you in the loop on any information I find, even if it'll earn me a scolding or a sermon. And three—"

The door burst open. Great-Aunt Iris, Joy, and Belle filed in, followed by Heath, Uncle Fitzwilliam, and Willoughby, with Great-Uncle William bringing up the rear, his cane tapping rhythmically on the floor.

"She won't solve any crime unless we're involved," Great-Aunt Iris announced regally as she sailed into the room, her narrowed gaze locked on Wentworth.

"I thought your list of promises was supposed to make me feel better," Wentworth said, scrubbing at the stubble on his cheeks.

Eliza chuckled and patted the seat next to her for Heath to join her. After he settled in and draped his arm across the back of the sofa, she leaned into him, resting her head on his shoulder. "Think of it this way: Teamwork makes the dream work, right?"

"That or a bloody nightmare," Wentworth grumbled, getting to his feet.

Belle filled Wentworth's vacated spot and squeezed Eliza's hand, gratitude shimmering in her eyes. Great-Aunt Iris eased herself onto a small couch and patted the seat beside her, beckoning her husband of sixty-plus years to join her. Joy and Willoughby sat hip to hip on a small brocade love seat, while Uncle Fitzwilliam perched on an ottoman next to Eliza.

"Have a seat, Wentworth," Uncle Fitzwilliam said, gesturing to a high-back leather chair, the only one left in their intimate circle.

Wentworth nearly collapsed into it and fixed his gaze on the crackling fire.

After a few moments of silence, Great-Aunt Iris aimed a knitting needle at Wentworth. "Well, are you going to spill the beans, or do we have to torture it out of you?"

Wentworth slid her a glance, his lips twitching. "If MI5 ever has an opening, you should apply. You'd be a shoo-in."

She sniffed and narrowed her gaze at him.

"Right, then. What can you tell us?" Joy asked, moving to the tea trolley and heaping goodies onto a china plate.

"Much of it, you already know," Wentworth said. "Lucinda is Everett Tanner's granddaughter, and when she discovered the tragic story behind her grandfather's death, she... well..."

"She went barmy," Great-Aunt Iris said.

Eliza's heart pinched. Despite all the destruction Lucinda had caused, the woman's pain had been nearly palpable. She shivered at the memory of those wild eyes, ones haunted by a tragic past. "Yes and no," Eliza said quietly.

"What d'you mean? She's mental," Heath said, the muscle in his jaw feathering. "She could have killed you. A Taser that close to you, aimed at your heart? She could have—" He stared into the flames. The muscles in his arm resting over her shoulder tensed.

Eliza cupped his cheek, willing him to look at her. "She could have. But she didn't. Besides, I'm a grown—"

"Ass woman who can take care of herself, right?" Heath asked, the smile lines around his piercing cornflower-blue eyes crinkling.

Eliza smoothed her thumb back and forth over his five-o'clock-shadowed cheek, savoring the rough texture against her skin. "I know I can take care of myself, but do you know what gives me the most courage of all? Knowing you're beside me or not far behind, fighting for me even when you're not there."

"Blimey," Joy said, "that's absolutely brilliant. Can I steal that? I'll give you credit, of course, but that's... Bloody hell, I'd better write that down before I forget it." She pulled her phone from her pocket, and her fingers flew across the screen.

Everyone stared at her, and she raised her head. "What?"

Great-Aunt Iris *tsk*ed. "Eliza, what were you saying about Lucinda not being barmy before we were interrupted?"

"I think from the beginning, after she overheard Hunter and Beckham laughing about the tragic situation and Basil's hold over Hubert, Lucinda wanted to see justice done. She just didn't know how. Her move back to Lambton was the first step, but then she stalled. She's not your typical cold-blooded murderer, and I think her grip on reality was fairly strong in the beginning. Cracks probably started at Hunter's fresh assault against Paisley, then it wasn't until she saw Hunter take you into the woods, Belle, that her tenuous hold on reality snapped." Eliza's skin crawled at the memory of her interview with a killer. "Her desperation to avenge the innocent, people whom the Crawfords, Basil, and Beckham had duped, swindled, or destroyed, trumped any sense of justice. She wanted revenge."

A heavy silence settled over the group, broken only by the fire's popping embers. Outside, the wind had picked up, and tiny ice pellets from a fresh sleet storm pelted the grid-paned windows. Eliza shivered.

Heath pulled her closer and traced figure eights on her upper arm.

She breathed in his scent, one of cinnamon and Irish Spring soap, and her body relaxed.

Wentworth moved to the sideboard, where amber liquids filled crystal decanters, poured brandy into two glasses, handed her one, and settled back into his chair. "Have a drink. It'll help with the shock."

Eliza took a sip and grimaced. She'd never learn to appreciate the taste, but its burning sensation warmed her from the inside out as it traveled down and settled in her stomach.

"What about the Crawfords?" Willoughby asked.

"Those two vipers?" Wentworth shook his head. "They're a match made in hell."

"You're being frightfully stingy with the details, Wentworth," Great-Aunt Iris said, her eyes never leaving her knitting. "Do get on with it. Remember, I'm far too old to buy wine that needs aging, and I haven't got time to waste waiting for you to spill all the juicy bits."

"You're not old, my dearest." Great-Uncle William smoothed his gnarled thumb over the back of his wife's wrinkled and age-spotted hand. "You're as spirited as the first day I met you." He patted his heart, and his smile tugged at his lips. "Puts my old ticker through its paces at times."

Great-Aunt Iris tutted, blushed, and smiled at him, making the eighty-something-year-old woman look like a young girl again.

For a moment, Eliza's breath caught in her throat. *This. This is what I want.* She squeezed Heath's hand, and he gazed down at her, squeezing her hand in response.

Even Wentworth wasn't unaffected, and after watching the elderly couple for a few moments with a small smile on his lips, he cleared his throat. "Right, then. Turns out old Hubert fancied a divorce, and Henrietta wasn't having any of it. Had the poor bloke cornered with a shotgun pointed straight at his chest."

Eliza shivered. "As much as that should surprise me, it doesn't. She'd lose her status as lady of the manor—or whatever she thinks she is—and that would've destroyed her reputation in the community."

"What reputation?" Great-Aunt Iris murmured with a sniff.

"Well, a divorce wouldn't have helped matters. That's certain. But what do you think she did in response to his demands for a divorce, besides pointing a deadly weapon at him?" Wentworth asked.

"Threatened to expose what he'd done to Rosie Harley all those years ago," Heath answered, his fingers stalling their featherlight curlicues on Eliza's arm.

"Bob's your uncle," Wentworth said.

"You mean he had no idea she knew about the evil he'd committed?" Eliza asked, leaning forward and resting her elbows on her knees.

"Not a clue," Wentworth said. "She'd put two and two together almost immediately. Apparently, this wasn't the first time he'd assaulted young girls." Wentworth gripped his glass so hard it shook. "The night after Rosie went missing, Henrietta woke up in the middle of the night as he was sneaking off. She followed him and watched as he buried that poor slip of a girl."

Eliza's palms stung. She winced, opened her hands, and stared at the crescent shapes embedded in her flesh. "What dreadful, dreadful people," she whispered.

"And she never breathed a word to anyone?" Willoughby gave a low whistle.

"Henrietta watched her husband bury that little girl's body and said nothing. Instead, she started spreading gossip about Everett Tanner to save her skin and reputation in the community. Wouldn't do her any favors to be tied to a child killer." Wentworth's voice was gruff and raw.

"I take it she flipped on her husband?" Belle asked.

"Didn't take her long, and she sang like a canary once I'd had a proper chat with her." Wentworth sipped his brandy. "She's looking at accessory after the fact, obstruction of justice, and filing false police reports. That woman destroyed an innocent man's life to protect her social standing, and Hubert never even knew she was covering for him."

"And Hubert?" Uncle Fitzwilliam asked. "Without evidence linking him directly to the crime, won't it be difficult to prosecute?"

"Crawford's facing a laundry list of charges: murder in the first degree, kidnapping a minor, sexual assault if there's any forensics to back up that assumption, concealment of a body, and obstruction of justice. Between the blackmail ledger we found in Basil's study and his wife's eyewitness testimony about his burying Rosie's body, we've got him dead to rights." Wentworth grinned ruthlessly. "Besides, I haven't the slightest doubt that a few hours of interrogation will make him sing like his missus."

"What about Beckham?" Joy asked, settling deeper into the loveseat beside Willoughby. "Last we heard, he'd gone missing, and Lucinda was desperate to find him."

Wentworth swirled the brandy in his glass, a smile playing on his face. "Found him cowering in an abandoned cottage about three miles from here. Poor blighter was scared witless, convinced Lucinda was trying to kill him. Claims he figured out what she was up to after he found the ledger she'd planted in his satchel at the Trusty Teapot. Clever enough to run but not clever enough to come to us."

"What will happen to him?" Belle asked.

"He'll face charges for obstruction of justice and possibly being an accessory after the fact to Basil's blackmail schemes but nothing like what he would have faced if Lucinda's scheme had succeeded."

Wentworth's expression darkened. "She wanted him to spend the rest of his natural life behind bars for murders he didn't commit."

"Speaking of that frightful woman," Great-Aunt Iris said, "what's her official prognosis? Besides being barmy?"

Wentworth ticked off the charges on his fingers. "She's been charged with two counts of murder in the first degree, assault with a deadly weapon, breaking and entering, assault on a police officer... The list goes on, doesn't it? She'll be evaluated for mental competency, but regardless, she's looking at life behind bars."

"How is Constable Langley doing?" Eliza asked. "Last I heard, she was recovering in the hospital."

"Her physical prognosis is good," Wentworth said. "It's more the mental side of things now. She's blaming herself for letting Lucinda give her a proper wallop over the head. Every copper does it. Never easy to be caught off guard like that."

Uncle Fitzwilliam cleared his throat. "And what of Everett's name? Will it finally be cleared?"

"Already sorted. Once we have a word with Rosie's family about the true facts behind their daughter's abduction and death, the constabulary will issue a public statement. It's nearly twenty years too late, but his name will be restored."

Joy perked up. "Oh! What about the property dispute? Any clarity on that mess?"

"Not sure," Uncle Fitzwilliam said. "It couldn't have been Hubert who manufactured it, as we discussed, as that would have drawn attention to a crime he desperately wanted hidden. Henrietta wouldn't have dared expose the secret either. If I were a gambling man, I'd wager it was Hunter's way of either trying to make some quick money—rather foolish approach—or simply tormenting his father, making the old man's life utterly miserable. Did either of the Crawfords shed any light on that business, Wentworth?"

"Afraid not, but I'm leaning toward the latter. Hunter, according to the financial records we've got, wouldn't have thrown good money after bad on a lengthy lawsuit involving solicitors. I'd say he found little ways—or big ones, in this case—to make sure his dad couldn't rest easy with his past sins."

Belle leaned forward, dropping her voice to barely above a whisper. "Would... Would Hunter have assaulted me that night? If Lucinda hadn't stepped in?"

Chapter Twenty-Two
True Justice Is Served

One cannot choose one's neighbors, can they? As I pen this, Darcy is pacing behind me, his hair standing in tufts (which is quite adorable), and muttering something about moving Pemberley if he could. While I understand his sentiments about Mr. Henry Crawford putting down permanent roots at Berryhill Manor, I would not wish to move Pemberley elsewhere. It is the beauty of the land, the sereneness of the stream that borders it, and the vast wooded wilderness embracing Pemberley that create the haven I love. Despite one… if not two… odious neighbors, I wouldn't wish to be anywhere but my precious Pemberley. Before I call for Betty to help me dress and do my hair, I believe I will remind my husband of what makes us stronger than our enemies: him and me and our love.

Lizzy Bennet Darcy

Pemberley 1815

The room fell silent. Even with all the dust settled and Belle safe beside her on the couch, Eliza's stomach still churned. She clasped Belle's clammy hand and squeezed tightly.

Wentworth studied Belle's face with gentle concern. "It's quite possible that Lucinda may have saved you. Even if her methods were wrong."

"Do you remember anything else from that night?" Eliza asked. "Anything that might explain why he took you into the woods?"

"I remember him saying he had something to show me. Asked if I was into true crime or something like that." Belle shook her head.

"Beyond that, I can't piece together that night. Maybe it's better that way."

Great-Aunt Iris set down her knitting with unusual force. "Hunter was a terrible wastrel and a menace to all he came into contact with. I don't condone murder, mind you, and Lucinda went about things in a particularly ghastly way, but at least some good came from that woman's madness."

"Hear! Hear!" Willoughby raised his teacup in a toast. "To justice, however long delayed. And to the oddest bunch of misfit sleuths I've ever laid eyes on."

Great-Aunt Iris reached across the space between the couches and jabbed him in the ribs with her knitting needle.

Air whooshed from Willoughby's lungs. "Blimey! What was that for, Mrs. Darcy?" He pouted, his chiseled features taking on a boyish look.

"Calling my niece a misfit, for one," Great-Aunt Iris said, her lips twitching with amusement.

"And number two?" Willoughby asked, leaning closer to Joy to escape the octogenarian's quivering needle.

"Not including yourself among us misfits." She creaked to her feet, steadied herself on the armrest, and batted away Willoughby's attempts to help her before standing directly in front of him. "You had some brilliant ideas, and now that you've come to your senses with Joy, you're not as hopeless as I'd always thought."

Willoughby blinked up at her, his eyes wide. "Right, well... Thank you?"

"If you two hadn't sorted yourselves out in your own time, I was fully prepared to lock you in a room and not let you out until you'd come to your senses."

Willoughby's cheeks flamed, and his Adam's apple bobbed.

Joy clasped his hand and winked at Great-Aunt Iris. "You know, Aunt Iris, I truly believe this world would be a better place if you were running the show."

Great-Aunt Iris tutted, walked over to Eliza, and rested her warm hand on her cheek. A seriousness Eliza rarely witnessed in her great-aunt's eyes replaced the previous mirth. "You were brilliant today."

Eliza leaned into her touch. "Have you changed your mind, then, about ringing in New Year's Eve?"

"Well, this one was more excitement than I bargained for."

"Are you complaining?" Joy teased.

"Good Lord, no," Great-Aunt Iris replied with a mischievous twinkle. "At my age, I haven't got time for boring holidays."

Great-Uncle William struggled from his chair, hobbled over to his wife, and placed a trembling hand on her shoulder. "Shall we, my dear? We've had enough excitement for one day."

"The day's not over yet, William." Great-Aunt Iris cupped his cheek, her eyes glistening, then crooked her arm through his.

Arm in arm, they hobbled from the drawing room, Great-Aunt Iris calling out a cheerful good night to everyone over her shoulder.

Uncle Fitzwilliam grinned ruefully and ran his fingers through his salt-and-pepper hair. "Perhaps Pemberley has now seen enough violence and secrets. After this rough start, maybe the new year will bring some peace and quiet."

Joy snorted. "Have you met Pemberley's inhabitants? I'm sure Aunt Iris will commit a crime herself to have something to solve."

"Don't go conjuring my worst nightmare, Joy." Wentworth drained his brandy and set the glass aside. "Right, then. I should be off. Still have paperwork to finish and criminals to process." He paused at the door. "Eliza, try to stay out of trouble for at least a week, yeah?"

"I'll do my best," she replied with a tired smile.

"That's what I'm afraid of," Wentworth muttered, though his eyes held warmth. He jerked his head toward the door. "A word?"

Eliza followed him from the drawing room. "Yes?"

He studied the tips of his shoes for a few seconds before meeting her gaze. "I'm proud of you. What you did today. How you handled Lucinda."

Warmth spread through Eliza's chest. "Really? That means a lot. Usually, you're—"

"Here." He dug around in his pocket and handed her a folded piece of paper.

Eliza took it, unfolded it, and burst out laughing. "You can't be serious."

"Dead serious," Wentworth said, tapping his index finger on the black-and-white logo of a woman performing a roundhouse kick in the corner of the gift certificate. "If you're going to keep poking your nose into police business, I'm requiring you to take self-defense classes. I want proof you've completed their most rigorous course. No certificate, no sleuthing. Deal?" He stuck out his hand.

Eliza shook it. "You got a deal, partner."

"We're not partners," Wentworth said through gritted teeth.

Eliza wiggled the certificate in his face. "Ah, but after this? Seems you're suggesting we could be a team."

Wentworth growled.

"But I was going to buy myself one of those handy-dandy stun guns off the black market. Easier that way."

Wentworth massaged the back of his neck and hissed out a breath. "Don't tell me those things, Eliza. I'd have you nicked the moment I spotted you with one of those."

"How about pepper spray?" Eliza asked, her facial muscles aching from holding back her grin.

Wentworth narrowed his eyes at her. "Any chance of you buggering off back to the States?"

"And leave you without a partner? Never." Eliza managed a second's worth of seriousness before bursting into laughter. "I'm joking, Wentworth. Not about staying—you're stuck with me. But about the illegal weapons." She rose onto her toes and pressed a kiss to his stubbly cheek.

Wentworth placed a hand over the spot and blinked at her. "What was that for?"

"Thank you." She waved the certificate. "Thank you for caring enough about me to keep me safe when I go off trying to save the world one injustice at a time. And"—she leaned in as if sharing confidential information—"not arresting me and throwing me behind bars when you had every reason to."

Wentworth chuckled. "I can't make any promises that I won't." With one last smile, he bid her good night and left.

Eliza clutched the gift certificate to her chest, a soft smile forming on her lips. *The big old teddy bear is finally coming around.*

S he slipped back into the drawing room, pausing in the doorway to take in the scene before her. The fire had died down to glowing embers, casting warm amber light across the faces of the people she loved. Uncle Fitzwilliam had settled in his favorite leather chair, a cup of tea balanced on his knee, his expression peaceful as he watched the flames dance.

Joy rested her head against Willoughby's shoulder, his arm encircling her waist while his other hand gently swirled the amber liquid in his glass.

Belle and Heath sat on the sofa, their heads bent in quiet conversation. Heath's protective instincts were clearly still on high alert as he kept one eye on Belle and one on the door.

The afternoon's terror felt like a distant nightmare compared to the scene of domestic tranquility. These people—her people—represented everything worth protecting.

"Well, well, look what the cat's dragged in," Joy said with a grin, raising her head from Willoughby's shoulder. "Thought Wentworth might've had you arrested after all."

"Just a friendly chat," Eliza replied, settling into the space Heath made for her on the sofa. "Though he did give me homework." She waved the self-defense certificate with a rueful smile.

"Brilliant," Heath said, pulling her close. "I was going to suggest the same thing myself, but I figured you couldn't say no to him. Especially if you want to keep on sleuthing."

"I resent that accurate observation," Eliza said, earning chuckles from around the room.

Uncle Fitzwilliam checked his watch and rose from his chair with a sigh. "Well, I'll call it a day." He gently cupped Eliza's face. "I know I've said it before, but I'm extraordinarily proud of you. You've become everything your parents hoped you would be and more than this old place deserves." His eyes were suspiciously bright. "Sleep well, all of you. Tomorrow, we start fresh."

After Uncle Fitzwilliam's footsteps faded down the hallway, comfortable silence settled over the remaining group. The sleet had stopped, and pale moonlight filtered through the windows, casting silver patterns across the Oriental rugs.

Joy cleared her throat dramatically, straightening in Willoughby's arms. "Right, then. Since we're all here and awake and not being threatened by deranged murderers, Willoughby and I have something to tell you."

Willoughby's cheeks reddened slightly, and a lopsided smile lit up his face. "We've decided to... er... give it a go."

"How romantic," Belle teased. "Did he propose, Joy, or are you still waiting for him to get his act together?"

Willoughby promptly choked on his brandy, coughing and sputtering as the liquid went down wrong.

Joy thumped him on the back with considerable force.

"Bloody hell, Belle," Willoughby wheezed between coughs. "Give a chap some warning before dropping something like that."

"Oh, don't be such a drama queen," Joy said cheerfully, continuing to pat his back. "Besides, you'll reach that conclusion in a few weeks, anyway, once you realize how brilliant I am." She winked at the others. "Might as well plant the seed now."

Willoughby gaped at her. "Bloody hell, woman, you're terrifying. And spot on, which makes it worse."

Heath walked to the sideboard, poured three glasses of sherry, handed one each to Belle and Eliza, and settled back in his spot before raising his glass in a toast. "To Joy and Willoughby, for finally sorting themselves out."

As they drank to the new couple, Uncle Fitzwilliam's words echoed in Eliza's mind. *Tomorrow, we start fresh.* That night, though, was for celebrating the good that had emerged from such a dark day.

Belle shifted beside her, and Eliza turned to find her friend watching her. "What's wrong?" Belle asked.

"I'm so sorry," Eliza said quietly, the words she'd been holding back all day finally spilling out. "If I hadn't invited you here, if I'd paid more attention at the party, if I'd trusted my instincts about Hunter—"

"Stop right there." Belle held up a hand. "First of all, you did nothing wrong. Second, you saved me today by figuring out who the real killer was. And third, Hunter's to blame. No one else." Her voice softened. "Bad things happen sometimes, Eliza, but that doesn't make them your fault." She patted Eliza's knee and smiled. "Besides, tomorrow, I'm going to wake up in a glorious mansion and have breakfast with my best friend. That's not nothing, Eliza. That's everything." She leaned in closer. "Then I'm going to have lunch at the Foxed Hound with that delicious constable, Theo."

"But..." Eliza's eyebrows dipped. "You leave in only a few days, and—"

"Long-distance relationships have been known to succeed. Besides, this gives me a reason to come back more often."

Eliza theatrically placed her hand over her heart. "And your best friend isn't a good-enough reason?"

Belle chuckled. "You don't have that sexy Australian accent, though. And *that* matters." She winked. "A lot."

After a few more minutes of friendly banter, Joy and Willoughby wandered off, leaving Eliza, Belle, and Heath alone by the dying fire. Belle excused herself soon after, claiming exhaustion but shooting Eliza a meaningful look.

Heath shifted to face Eliza, his blue eyes serious in the firelight. "How are you doing, love? And don't tell me you're fine. I can see those wheels turning in that mind of yours."

Eliza leaned into his touch as his fingers traced along her cheek. "I keep thinking about what could have happened. What if you and Uncle hadn't shown up when you did? What if Lucinda had been more unstable? What if—"

"You can't live in the what-ifs, Eliza," Heath interrupted gently. "Trust me. I've been doing it all day." His thumb brushed across her lips. "What matters is that you're here, in my arms, safe and sound and absolutely brilliant."

"Brilliant?" she murmured against his thumb.

"Brilliant," he confirmed, leaning closer. "The way you kept your head when faced with a killer. The way you protected Belle and fought for what's right." He rested his forehead against hers. "The way you make me want to be better than I ever thought I could be."

His kiss was a searing promise, and Eliza melted into him. There, in Heath's arms, in the room that had sheltered generations of her family, she was exactly where she belonged.

As they broke apart, Eliza looked around the drawing room one more time. It had witnessed generations upon generations of Darcys weather storms and survive. Eliza couldn't help but wonder if her sixth great-grandparents had sat in that very room, discussing the Crawfords, their lives, their children, their love, their hopes and dreams, the lasting legacy of the Darcy line, and if Pemberley would last the test of time.

It had.

And Eliza had no intention of letting that family legacy down.

She was, after all, Mistress of Pemberley and had the stubborn Darcy blood flowing through her veins. Eliza waited for the next adventure, whatever that might be.

Acknowledgments

Writing a book may look like a solitary endeavor, but no story comes to life without the support, encouragement, and hard work of so many wonderful people.

First, to my husband: Thank you for your love, your patience, and your unwavering belief in me. Thank you for supporting my dreams, cheering me on through every high and low, and reminding me to keep going even on the hard days. I am endlessly grateful to have you by my side.

To my publisher: Thank you for believing in this story and in me. Your support and encouragement in my work have meant more than I can say. Thank you for helping make these dreams feel possible.

To my editors: Thank you for your insight, care, and incredible talent. Your thoughtful guidance and sharp eyes helped shape this book into something stronger, brighter, and more polished. Thank you for making my writing shine.

And finally, to my readers: Thank you from the bottom of my heart. The fact that you continue to return for each new story means everything to me. I truly could not do this without you, and I am so grateful for your support, enthusiasm, and love for these books.

This story is for all of you.

About the Author

Jessica Berg, a child of the Dakotas and the prairie, grew up amongst hard-working men and women and learned at an early age to "put some effort into it." Following that wise adage, she has put effort into teaching high school English for over a decade, being a mother to four children (she finds herself surprised at this number, too), basking in the love of her husband of more than fifteen years and losing herself in the imaginary worlds she creates.

Read more at https://www.jessicabergbooks.com.

About the Publisher

Dear Reader,

We hope you enjoyed this book. Please consider leaving a review on your favorite book site.

Visit our site to find more quality books!

Read more at https://RedAdeptPublishing.com.